BERKLEY UK

THE FARM

Emily McKay loves to read, shop and geek out about movies. When she's not writing, she reads online gossip and bakes luscious desserts. She pretends that her weekly yoga practice balances out both of those things. She lives in central Texas with her family and her crazy pets. She also co-writes young adult as Ivy Adams.

The Farm

EMILY McKAY

PENGUIN BOOKS

Published by the Penguin Group
Penguin Books Ltd, 80 Strand, London WC2R 0RL, England
Penguin Group (USA) Inc., 375 Hudson Street, New York, New York 10014, USA
Penguin Group (Canada), 90 Eglinton Avenue East, Suite 700, Toronto, Ontario, Canada M4P 2Y3
(a division of Pearson Penguin Canada Inc.)
Penguin Ireland, 25 St Stephen's Green, Dublin 2, Ireland (a division of Penguin Books Ltd)
Penguin Group (Australia), 707 Collins Street, Melbourne, Victoria 3008, Australia
(a division of Pearson Australia Group Pty Ltd)
Penguin Books India Pvt Ltd, 11 Community Centre, Panchsheel Park, New Delhi – 110 017, India
Penguin Group (NZ), 67 Apollo Drive, Rosedale, Auckland 0632, New Zealand
(a division of Pearson New Zealand Ltd)
Penguin Books (South Africa) (Pty) Ltd, Block D, Rosebank Office Park,
181 Jan Smuts Avenue, Parktown North, Gauteng 2193, South Africa

Penguin Books Ltd, Registered Offices: 80 Strand, London WC2R 0RL, England

www.penguin.com

First published in the United States of America by The Berkley Publishing Group,
an imprint of Penguin Group (USA) Inc. 2012
Published in Great Britain by Berkley UK 2013
001

Printed in England by Clays Ltd, St Ives plc

ISBN: 978–0–718–19742–1

www.greenpenguin.co.uk

ALWAYS LEARNING PEARSON

For Abby and Austin, the young adults in my life.
I love being your aunt. Thanks for making it so much fun!

And, as always, for Greg, Adi, and Henry.

ACKNOWLEDGMENTS

It would be impossible to acknowledge everyone who helps make a story idea into the book it becomes, but since this is my first time writing acknowledgments, I'm going to try.

First off, thank you to my agent, the fabulous and wise Jessica Faust. Thank you for reading about six completely different drafts of this story. Thank you for refusing to send it out before it was ready and thank you for continuing to believe I had the talent to tell this story. Without you this book would never have been possible. Working with you is so much fun. I can't imagine a better agent or friend.

Thank you to Donald Maass. Your Writing the Breakout Novel intensive workshop transformed me as a writer and renewed my faith in my own talent. Thanks to Lorin for organizing the workshop, and to all the great writers I met there: Lisa, Jocelyn, Maggie, Erin, Jo, and all the rest.

Thank you to all my fabulous writing friends. Robyn DeHart, if it wasn't for you, I'd have given up writing years ago and would probably now be working at the Gap. Tracy Deebs, without your brainstorming, Mel never would have gotten out of the van and this book would have no climax. Shellee Roberts, without you, there would be no chemistry between Carter and Lily (thank you!). Sherry Thomas, just hanging out with you reminds me to ratchet up the conflict. Penny, thanks for making sure I got Mel right. And, last, but certainly not least, thanks to Skyler White, Karen Mac-

Inerney, and Jax Garren. Without your fine-tuning, this book would have been a white-hot mess.

Thank you to all the talented people at Berkley who helped turn this manuscript into an actual book. I was awed by your work at every step of the way. Michelle Vega, your editorial insight was outstanding. I can't thank you enough for loving Lily and Mel like I do and helping me to tell their story. Thank you, Pam Barricklow, for your fine attention to detail and for finding the perfect copy editor for *The Farm*. Thank you, Sheila Moody, for being that copy editor. Rosanne Romanello, I know your part in this process is just beginning, but I already love you for all you've done. And, finally, thank you to the art department for gracing me with the most beautiful cover I've ever seen!

CHAPTER ONE

LILY

Some days, you just want to let the bad guys win. My mom, the pro bono lawyer, used to say that to me sometimes, back in the Before. That's how you know you're doing the right thing—it's so hard you want to give up.

I really hoped she was right, because today was one of those days. Of course, my mom lived in a world where the monsters were greed, ambition, and questionable ethics. That all ended when the Ticks swarmed across the Southwest, eating every human in their path. My sister, Mel, and I live in a whole different world and the monsters here are less . . . metaphorical. And even if I sometimes wanted to give up, I knew I wouldn't, because my twin, Mel, depended on me.

Praying for the patience to deal with her, I said, "We've been over this. You can't come with me today." I reached for her hand, but she snatched it away. Okay, not a day for touching.

She stood so close to me, I couldn't shut the door to the storage closet where we'd lived for the past six months. "Stay here."

Mel didn't back up. She stood there, clenching her Slinky, shifting it from one hand to the other and back again, so it made that irritating *sllluuunk* sound. She never went anywhere without the damn thing, but she only jiggled it like this when she was nervous.

Since we'd arrived on the Farm, Mel had followed me everywhere. Mel hadn't always been like this. Yeah, she had all the normal autism spectrum stuff: delayed speech, social impairment, and self-stimulating behaviors. But after years of therapy she'd functioned pretty highly. The stress of living on the Farm had changed all that.

In the past six months, we hadn't been apart even for a few minutes. But for what I had to do today, she had to stay behind in our room. She and I lived in an eight-by-twelve storage closet, tucked in the corner of one of the lab rooms in the science building. Every time I tried to leave, Mel was right on my heels. *Lily's little lamb,* Mom had always called her.

I pulled my cell phone out of my back pocket. There was never a signal, but I plugged it in every night and kept it charged because it was the only way to know what time it was without listening for the chimes. Three fifty-two. I had five, six minutes tops to get down to Stoner Joe's if I wanted to talk to him alone.

Extending a single finger like a hook, I waved it past Mel's face. "Look at me, Mel."

Mel kept her gaze locked on the shelf beside the door where our backpacks sat, crammed full of the food and clothes we'd need if we did escape from the Farm. The pink pack sat on top of a stack of chemistry textbooks. Everything we needed was ready to go at a moment's notice, everything except the stuff we didn't have yet. Things that I could live without, but Mel couldn't. And if I didn't leave the room now to go trade for them, we'd have to wait one more week and then it might be too late.

I tried again, waving my hooked finger in front of her eyes like the occupational therapist had taught me do so many years ago. "Look at me, Mel."

Mel twitched, shifting her gaze from the backpacks to a box of lab supplies wedged onto the shelf of microscopes.

I knew it bugged her, having all this crap in our room, but it was important. If a Collab happened to come by for an inspection, I wanted our room messy enough that he'd give up in disgust rather than search all our belongings.

Again I waved my hand. "Look at me, Mel."

Mom would have told me to be patient. But Mom wasn't here and I was out of time. I reached out and gave her fingers a quick rap. "Damn it, Mel. This is important. Red rover."

Mel's gaze snapped to mine.

Guess I should have led with that. The phrase "Red rover, red rover" was our code for the plan to escape the Farm and cross the Red River. That was one of the benefits of having a sister who spoke almost entirely in nursery rhymes. Most of the time, I hated that living on the Farm had made her regress to how she'd been as a child, but at least it meant we could discuss our escape plans anywhere and no one would know what "red rover" meant.

"When I leave, I want you to wedge the chair under the knob. That way you'll be safe." I swallowed, praying I wasn't about to make a promise I couldn't keep. "I won't be gone long."

Mel just stood there mumbling her senseless distress.

"When I come back, I'll tap out 'Mary Had a Little Lamb' on the door. Don't open the door until then."

Mel's gaze had shifted again. Maybe I should have kept trying, but if she didn't know the plan now, we were probably screwed anyway. Even though I didn't really expect an answer, I asked one last time, "Do you understand?"

Mel bobbed her head, but I knew it wasn't really an agreement. "Red rover, red rover, let Lil-lee come over."

"Yes," I muttered. "That's the idea."

I patted the pocket of my hoodie to make sure the slim box of pills was tucked inside. Then I let myself out the door. This time, Mel didn't follow. A second later, I heard the sound of the chair being scraped across the floor and wedged under the knob.

Okay, step one: leave Mel safely hidden while I go out to trade. Check.

Step two: walk across campus, keep my head down, blend. As long as I didn't give any of the Collabs a reason to stop me, no one would know what I had in my pocket. Not that Collabs needed an excuse to harass a Green. The Collabs were all guys who'd been high school bullies back in the Before. Surprise, surprise: all the jerks who picked on geeks like me were also willing to betray their own species by collaborating with the Dean. On the bright side, Collabs weren't known for their keen intelligence and observational skills, so hopefully none of them would notice when I *didn't* line up in front of the dining hall with the rest of the Greens, but instead went into Stoner Joe's to trade.

The room Mel and I lived in was on the seventh floor, and walking down six flights of stairs gave me plenty of time to think about what I was about to do.

This time of day, all the Greens with the A schedule would be in the dining hall eating. All the Greens with the B schedule—like Mel and I—would be lining up for third meal. I should be able to talk to Joe alone. If someone was there, well, then I'd just hang out until everyone else left. I wouldn't think about Mel by herself in our room. I wouldn't think about the clock ticking away the remaining minutes of mealtime. If Mel and I had to miss third meal, it wasn't *that* big a deal. Technically, Greens could miss one meal a week.

And I certainly wouldn't think about the contents of my pocket.

About those pills that would get me sent to the Dean's office. That was a trip you didn't come back from. Some people just disappeared up there, but if the Dean wanted to make an example of you, you were dragged out at dusk and tied to stakes just beyond the electric fences that surrounded the Farm. The screams seemed to echo for days afterward.

The Dean liked to remind us that those fences were there to keep the Ticks out as much as to keep us in.

As I left the building, the bitter February wind bit through the fleece of my jacket. I glanced around for any Collabs who might be nearby. Their bright blue uniforms made them easy to spot. They would have looked so cheerful if it hadn't been for the tranq guns slung over their shoulders. A couple of them loitered over by the admin building.

Back in the Before, the Farm had been a prestigious private liberal arts college. For more than a hundred years, the college had sat nestled against the banks of the Red River, just south of the Texas-Oklahoma border, home to pampered students. The admin building dominated the east side of the campus. Whatever its purpose had been back in the Before, now . . . now, it just creeped me out. The real monster might be on the other side of the fence, but sometimes, horrible noises came from the admin building and the shadows at the windows seemed to move with inhuman speed.

At the opposite end of campus was the dining hall, with its sleek modern architecture and massive, floor-to-ceiling windows. Between the two buildings stretched the open green space of the quad, a smattering of dorms and academic buildings lining the quad's edges. Our science building was one of them.

Four times a day, all the Greens shuffled out from their various hiding places and ambled over to the dining hall, where we were scanned, prodded, and fed. Yeah, we were treated like cows, except cows lived in the blissful oblivion of *not* knowing their future. We Greens couldn't escape the reminders of what was to come. Not when Collabs took weekly "donations" at the mobile blood bank. Calling it that was their way of making it seem voluntary. It wasn't. And every time we donated blood, they tested it to see how "clean" it was, whether or not it would make good food for the Ticks or if it had too many of the hormones the Ticks seemed to crave. On the Farm, we weren't raising food; we were the food.

When I was kid, my dad used to love showing me these cheesy sci-fi movies—my cultural education, he called it. His favorite was *Soylent Green*, this one where everyone finds out the perfect food is made out of people. For weeks after, we ran around yelling, "Soylent Green is people!" I thought it was so funny. It wasn't funny anymore.

Still, donating wasn't so bad, once you got used to feeling weak all the time. It kept us docile. It allowed us to pretend there wasn't something much worse waiting for us when we turned eighteen.

I tried not to think of that as I made my way across campus. If you wanted to go anywhere on campus without attracting attention, just before or just after meals was the time to do it.

As always, Breeders lounged around the edges of the quad, smugly serene, some of them displaying bellies already round and fertile. They didn't have to worry about eighteenth birthdays. Of course, the ones who were pregnant had other things to worry about.

The Greens all kept their heads down, shuffling across the quad like cattle, and I moved quickly to join them. There was safety in numbers—or the illusion of it—and a little extra warmth, too.

Normally I kept my head down, too, and stayed as close to the center of the pack as possible. However, I was distracted, running through the plan in my mind, and when I glanced up, I was at the edge of the crowd with a clear view between one of the dorms and the education building. Most days, we all did everything we could to avoid looking out beyond the fences. Now I wished like hell I'd been paying better attention, because when I looked up, I saw four Greens tethered to a streetlight on the other side of the fence. They were still alive. They'd been tranqed, but I could see the terror trying to fight through the haze.

This wasn't the first time the Dean had ordered Greens staked out at dusk as punishment. But I'd never seen them. Not like that. Even though there must have been fifty feet between me and those Greens, I felt like I was standing face-to-face with them.

And I remembered all too vividly the incident that had gotten them there. It was yesterday at second meal. The three guys had ganged up on the girl. I remembered her panicked cries. "I'm not a breeder!" she kept saying. She hadn't done anything except try to defend herself. But she was out there, chained to the light post just like the guys were.

She looked *so* young. So vulnerable. She had long dark hair, just like Mel and I. All doped up like she was, her expression was distant and dreamy, like Mel's was sometimes. That could *be* Mel out there. If I wasn't with her, all the time, that *would* be Mel out there.

In that moment, my pace slowed. The crowd flowed past me like the water of the nearby Red River rushing around a rock. The stream of people jostled against me before someone bumped into me hard enough that I broke free of my imagination and stumbled forward a step or two before tumbling down on one knee.

The packet of pills fell out of my pocket as I landed. The pain ricocheting up my leg was nothing compared to my panic as the blue plastic box tumbled to the ground. It landed beside my hand, but before I could grab it, a flip-flop-clad foot kicked it beyond my reach. I saw it disappear into the scuffle of feet. The most valuable thing we owned: gone.

I scrambled rabbitlike after the blue box, launching myself forward to catch it before someone else kicked it beyond my reach. When I saw it a few feet way, I threw myself toward it, but a hand reached down and snatched it off the ground mere seconds before I could grab it.

My heart leapt into my throat, panic making me breathless, even as I felt someone helping me to my feet.

"These must be yours."

I didn't even glance at the guy holding the pills out to me. I wrenched them from his hand, quickly flipping the box over to make sure it was unharmed, even though it had only been out of my possession for a minute. "Thanks," I muttered, hoping he would just walk away.

"Must be pretty important to you," he said, even as I saw him turning to walk away out of the corner of my eye. "You should keep track of your stuff."

I shoved my hand deep into my pocket, still clenching the pills. Relief made me light-headed. Or maybe the Collab who had taken my weekly donation had just taken too much off the top. They did that sometimes, if your blood was particularly "clean" that day. Lately they'd been doing it more often. My head spun when I jerked it up to look for the guy who'd handed the pills back to me. He was impossible to miss, the gray of his hoodie standing out in a sea of scarlet sweatshirts. Among the thousands of Greens making their way to third meal, only a few weren't wearing the colors of the college that the Farm had once been. Mindlessly my eyes followed his progress toward the dining hall.

Why had he handed the pills back to me? Had he not recognized them? Maybe a guy wouldn't have. Thank God.

I clenched my hand around the rigid plastic tightly enough for the edges to bite into the skin of my palm. But I had it. Thank God, I still had the box. When I looked again, the guy in the gray sweatshirt was gone, disappeared into the crowd of Greens.

CHAPTER TWO

LILY

Stoner Joe's had once been a college convenience store tucked into the basement of the dining hall. I'd known Joe since we were both kids and I could trust him. He was a good guy, even if Greens, Collabs, and Breeders all shopped in his store. It was like accorded neutral territory. The Collabs could have shut the place down, but for whatever reason, they let us have it. Left us this one small seed of independence. Maybe they knew we'd be happy with it. Maybe it was just too much trouble to squash every bit of spirit.

The wind picked up as I headed down the steps into the shelter of the alcove and let myself into the store, which was unusually dark for this time of day. Before I had a chance to wonder where Joe was, I felt something cold and sharp press against the side of my neck.

"Holy crap!" I gasped.

The hand holding the blade to my throat slackened and then fell away from my skin altogether. "Lily?"

"Yeah!" I said, accusation in my voice. "What the hell, Joe?" I didn't want to piss him off, but . . . "Seriously. What the hell?"

"Sorry. I've been, like, way tense lately."

My eyes had begun to adjust to the dim lighting and I could

see his sheepish smile. "Obviously. What's with the new security measures?"

I eyed the knife in his hand. It had a long stainless steel handle and a flat face that ended in a sharp, angled blade. If I had to guess, I'd say Joe had repurposed a spatula from the kitchen that shared his building.

"Dark times, Lil. Dark times." Joe nodded gravely, and as he spoke, his voice fell back into its normal cadence, like there was a silent *dude* at the end of every sentence. He extended his hand and clasped mine briefly before giving me a little fist bump. "What can I get you today?"

I didn't ask what he meant by dark times. I didn't like the idea that things might be even worse than I knew. Just one more reason Mel and I had to get out of the Farm.

"I'm here to trade," I said.

"Whatcha need, whatcha got?" he asked, crossing to the counter that bisected the room. He set the shiv down and propped his hands on the scuffed glass top. I couldn't tear my gaze from the weapon. It seemed so out of character. He must have noticed, because he surreptitiously nudged it to the edge of the counter, slipping it between two cardboard displays that had once held packs of gum but now contained old music CDs.

I pushed the shiv from my mind and mustered my courage.

This was it. Moment of truth and all that. Just as I had carefully planned, Joe and I were alone. But I choked. My laundry list of must-haves for the trip north suddenly seemed so . . . risky.

"I, um . . ." I let my words trail off as I shoved my hand in my pocket, relaxing infinitesimally as my fingers brushed plastic. The pills were still there. Still risky, still highly illegal, but still mine.

"What's up, Lil?"

"I'll look around," I muttered, not quite meeting Joe's gaze. "See what I can find."

I didn't linger by the shelves of grooming supplies. Mel and I managed to stay basically clean. It was mostly Breeders who bothered to trade for crap like that. Joe would have thought it strange if I'd looked there.

Listlessly I ran my forefinger down a stack of meticulously folded sweatshirts. Most were red and gold with the stylized kangaroo on the front, but a few sported the gray and blue of the Dallas Cowboys. I poked through them a bit, as if one of them would magically transform into the bulky winter coat I so desperately needed.

The food and snack shelf was looking a little bare. They fed us four mandatory meals a day. You might expect that given how overfed we were, no one would bother to trade for food. But Joe had told me once that the opposite was true. He did most of his business in food. That and the pharmaceuticals that had given him his start back in high school, back long before we were moved to the Farm for our "protection."

The food Joe sold wasn't so much about quantity. It was about selection. Freedom of choice. And, of course, nostalgia.

My fingers hovered a few inches above a can wrapped in dull silver paper.

Joe shuffled beside me, such the attentive shopkeep since the store was empty except for me. "Is today the day you're finally going to buy those peas?"

I jerked my hand back to my pocket and looked up. "No."

"Come on," he coaxed. "You look at them every time you come in. Man, you must love peas."

I'd never known that I loved them, until I couldn't have them anymore.

"You should buy them," he said softly. "I'll give you a good deal, since you're my friend. It'll be like a"—he hesitated—"a present."

He'd probably been about to say *a birthday present*. Or maybe that catch in his voice had been something else. Maybe he didn't know how close Mel and I were to our eighteenth. To our doomsday.

I stuck my hand into my jeans pocket and fingered the tiny pebbles I always kept there. I blurted out, "I need a coat."

"I just got in a couple of new hoodies the other day." Joe rounded the shelf to a haphazard stack of clothes I hadn't noticed.

I stopped him before he could pull any out. "No, I need a coat. Like the biggest, thickest coat you can get." He just stared blankly at me, like he couldn't understand why I'd be so desperate to trade for something like that. Here in Texas, even north Texas, there were only a few days a year when it got cold enough to need a big heavy coat. "It's for Mel," I explained.

"Oh, right." He nodded sagely. "She has that thing about the cold."

That thing was an unwillingness—or perhaps an inability—to tell others when she was cold. Me, I bitch endlessly when I'm cold. I break out my scarf when it's sixty-five degrees. Mel, on the other hand, once stood out in the snow until she was hypothermic.

I still remember sitting by the door in our bedroom, my ear pressed to the crack in the door as I listened to our parents argue about it, because Dad had been in charge and he hadn't noticed how cold she was. *She's not a normal child,* our mother had said. *You can't trust her to take care of herself. You have to watch her all the time. When are you going to accept that?*

Two weeks later, Dad had left and we were on our own, just the three of us. And now it was just Mel and me.

There were so many things I had to leave to chance. Mel

getting cold wasn't one of them. She wasn't normal. Dad may never have accepted that, but I had. If I could have only one thing, it would be a coat.

"I saw Tad Jackson with a pretty big coat the other day," Joe said. "Looked like the kind of thing one of the maintenance workers would have used. He had gloves, too."

"Perfect." I hadn't dared hope for gloves. We had neoprene gloves from the lab and I'd been hoping they'd be warm enough. "Any chance you can get a second pair of gloves?"

"It might take a coupla days, but I'll see what I can do. It won't be cheap, though."

"It's not all I need." I sucked in a breath. I rushed through the next bit. "I need sleeping bags. Two if you can find them." Joe's eyebrows shot up, but I kept talking. Hell, go big or go home, right? "And a lighter."

I think I expected him to argue then. I'd known all along that he would probably figure out what was up—after all, Joe wasn't an idiot—and I'd already decided playing dumb was the best defense. I'd expected him to warn me off, to remind me what had happened to all the kids who had tried and failed, but instead, he just studied me.

"It's because your eighteenth birthday is coming up, isn't it?"

"I . . ." My voice quavered and I cleared my throat. "I don't know what you're talking about."

He frowned. "You're not going to just, you know, wait it out? See what happens after you turn eighteen?"

"It can't be anything good," I argued.

We'd been brought to the Farm because the Ticks seemed to prefer the blood of teenagers. Something about the mix of hormones was what the newscasters had said in the Before. Our parents had been reassured that we'd be free to leave once the government got the Ticks under control. We'd been told that sometime after we turned eighteen, our hormones would even out and we'd be sent home.

"You don't think people go home?" Joe asked, but I could tell by his tone of voice that he didn't really believe it, either.

"Haven't you noticed? Once a Green's testing rate goes up, they're allotted a larger ration of food. If they were just sending Greens home, they wouldn't care how well fed we were." I leaned closer and dropped my voice. "They're fattening people up before they send them to be slaughtered."

"Yeah, but if you get caught . . ."

I thought of the girl who was tethered to the post outside the fence right now. Sometime tonight, the Ticks would come for her. They'd rip her heart from her chest and drink her blood straight from her aorta. That would happen to us, too, if we got sent to the Dean's office.

I could feel my lower lip start to tremble so I clenched my jaw and swallowed. "Yeah. I know. But I can't wait around to be slaughtered, either. We have to at least try."

"You don't have to do this." His tone was serious. "You could get pregnant. That would protect you."

"Yeah. For nine months. After that, who knows what happens. And have you thought about those babies? What happens to them?"

"I don't . . . I don't know." Joe's skin suddenly looked a sickly green in the dim light of the store.

"Exactly. No one knows. And like I said, who knows what's going to happen to the Breeders once their babies are born anyway?" The scorn in my voice barely concealed the fear beneath it.

Yeah, I acted all self-righteous about the Collabs and Breeders. The Collabs worked for the Dean to keep the rest of us in line. They were bad enough. The Breeders, girls who got pregnant on purpose just because the Ticks didn't like the taste of all those pregnancy hormones? Even the idea was repulsive.

But who knows, if it had been just me, I might have ditched the last shreds of my morality and bred like a freakin' bunny. But that wouldn't protect Mel. "Besides, Mel couldn't . . . She doesn't like it when *I* touch her. She couldn't be a Breeder."

Joe's gaze was suddenly glued to an empty spot on the counter. "Yeah, I guess not," he said in a limp voice. He looked like he couldn't decide if he wanted to throw up or burst into tears.

He'd always been such a genuinely nice guy—sensitive, too—and I could tell the thought of what happened to Breeders really bugged him.

"Hey, don't worry about Mel and me." My need to reassure him surprised me. "I've got it figured out."

His gaze shot to mine. Hopeful, almost. "You do?"

"Yeah, I—" I stopped just short of telling him that Mel had figured out how to get off the Farm. "We're going to be okay."

I hoped to God I was telling him the truth. I knew our plan wasn't foolproof, but I hoped it was good enough.

Months ago, Mel had noticed that the Collabs turned off part of the fence every night. They couldn't keep the fence along the river electrified because at night the nutria scurried up the cliff from the river. They'd gnaw on the fences, shorting out the whole system and making the entire Farm reek of seared animal flesh. Which meant the stretch of chain link on the north side of campus was the only weakness in the Farm's security.

If we could make it through and if we could swim across the Red River, we'd be in Oklahoma. It was a lot of ifs.

And I had no idea what we'd find there, but we would head north. Uncle Rodney lived over in Arkansas near the Ozark

Mountains. He was a crazy survivalist type. I figured a guy like that was either one of the first to go or the last to fall. For all I knew, things would be just as bad there as things were in Texas, but at least we'd be moving toward Canada, in the direction of freedom. One of the last reports I remember from the Before was the stunning news that Canada was shutting down the border. Terrified that the plague affecting so many Americans would spread to their own population, the Canadian government had set up roadblocks and was stationing military all along the border. What had previously been the world's longest undefended border was now a no-man's-land.

Canada was our best hope. And if we were going that far, in the winter, Mel needed that warm coat. And whatever else we could find.

I looked Joe square in the eyes and all but begged him to help. "What do you say? Can you do it?"

He studied my face. "Yeah, you and Mel were always so smart. If anyone could get off the Farm it would be you." He nodded slowly, like he'd reached some sort of decision. "You don't have enough credits for all that stuff. You know that, right?"

I started pulling things from my bag to trade. "Two bottles of shampoo, both of them mostly full. A bottle of conditioner."

He looked unimpressed.

I moved on to the things I'd been hoarding for months. "Two toothbrushes and a tube of toothpaste. New in their packages."

He considered and I could see in his frown that he wanted it to be enough, even though we both knew it wasn't. He blew out a breath. "Those will cover the coat and gloves."

"What about the sleeping bags? And the lighter?" I asked, because maybe it would be safer, for all of us, if I didn't have to show him that last thing I had to trade.

Joe just shook his head. “If it was stuff I just had in the store, maybe. But I’ll have to go looking for what you need. Ask around. Attract attention. That’s a lot of risk.”

“But you could do it?”

“Yeah. Sure. Anything for a price, right? I know a guy in Baker Hall whose ‘roommate’”—Joe made air quotes to indicate that by “roommate” he really meant the college student who had lived in the dorm room back in the Before—“was into camping and stuff like that. I could get all kinds of things from him.”

“So you could get the sleeping bags and the lighter?” I pressed. “If I had the right thing to trade? If I had something really valuable?”

“Sure, man. I can get anything.”

I reached into my pocket then and pulled out the plastic box of pills. I had three prized possessions. The first was a pair of gardening shears I found in an unlocked maintenance closet seven weeks ago. The second was a single capsule of Valium. In the Before, I used to carry a couple with me all the time, just in case Mel freaked out completely. I had one pill left. The third was the contents of this box.

Hand trembling, I set the pills on the counter. My fingers seemed to clench of their own accord and I had to force myself to release the box and nudge it across the counter toward Joe. When he just stared blankly at it, I reached over and flicked it open. The box fanned open to reveal three separate compartments, each containing a foil packet of twenty-one tiny pink pills and seven white ones.

Joe frowned as he stared at it. “Dude.” He drew the word out and then looked up at me. “Is that what I think it is?”

“Yes.”

“I thought they were all gone.”

"These were overlooked."

When the Collabs had first been recruited out of the ranks of Greens, their first task had been to destroy all forms of birth control.

"Whoa." His gaze darted to mine, suddenly far more serious than he normally was. "Does anyone else know you have these?"

I thought of the guy out on the quad who hadn't just seen them, but had held them in his hand. I imagined I could still feel the heat of his palm on the plastic. "No," I lied.

"Don't let anyone else see them." He reached out a hand, a sort of reverence on his face. But instead of touching the pills, like I expected, he shoved them across the counter toward me. "Put them away. If someone came in now . . ."

As if I needed to be told that.

I shoved the pills deep into my pocket. Even though I felt better having them so close, I still felt jumpy, too aware of them now, and I found myself looking over my shoulder at the door to Joe's even though I would have heard it open. "But they'll be enough? For the things I need?"

Joe sort of shook his head. "Man, I don't know." He ran a hand through his long, stringy hair.

"But they're valuable, right?"

That was what I was banking on. When the Collabs first searched campus, they ignored all kinds of crazy stuff in the science building, but they confiscated all the birth control pills. Maybe they were just too stupid to know what words like "pyrophoric" meant. Or maybe progesterone was more dangerous.

"Sure. But I'm not sure they're worth the trouble. This kind of thing . . . Man, it's—"

Then he broke off abruptly, as if he'd either just thought of something or maybe decided not to tell me something.

"It's what?"

"Nothing."

"What?" I pressed. "You were about to say something. It's what?"

He leaned forward across the counter, dropping his voice. "It's the kind of thing people would trade."

"Yeah," I said, feeling stupid. "That's why I'm here, right?"

"Sure. Yeah." He answered quickly, though I could tell that wasn't what he'd meant. "Right."

That was classic CYA if I'd ever seen it. "No," I said, puzzling it through. "You didn't mean trade with you. So trade with who? The Collabs?" I kept my eyes glued to his face, but the flicker of acknowledgment didn't come quickly enough. "With the Dean's office?" I asked, not believing for a second that might actually be who he meant. But there it was in his eyes. That subconscious you-nailed-it look.

"They do that?" I had heard rumors, very vague rumors, of that sort of thing.

Joe said nothing, his expression tight and unnaturally still like he'd given away far too much already.

I didn't think I was going to get any more from him, but I asked anyway. "But no one in the Dean's office would need these." I tapped the top of the box. "These have no value to them. Why would they . . ." That's when it hit me. "They wouldn't want the pills. They'd want info about who had them. They'd reward someone willing to betray other Greens." Disgust settled low in my belly. "Who would do that?" Before Joe could even open his mouth, I snapped, "Okay, I know. That sounded stupid."

"Not stupid," Joe said. "Just naive. You and Mel, you've been, like, completely isolated. You don't know how bad it is. And something like this? This could buy someone a trip off the Farm."

"Seriously?" And for that flicker of a second, I considered it. Could I somehow buy Mel's freedom by turning myself in? It sounded so easy. I'd be completely absolved of the responsibility of taking care of her. It was a nice fantasy, even if it wasn't a solution.

Because, of course, I wouldn't trust Mel's safety with anyone else, least of all the Dean. He was worse than the Collabs.

"Will you get me the stuff I need?" I asked, because I couldn't think any more about the politics on the Farm or the many ways people could betray one another.

"Yeah. Sure. I can get it," he said, only a trace of stoner dude left in his voice.

Joe's sudden new gravity only ratcheted up my tension. I patted the box in my pocket. The pills rested right on top of that sick feeling of dread that knotted in my belly.

"How much for the shiv?" I asked abruptly.

Joe looked from the lump in my pocket back up to my eyes. Then he gave a sad little half smile as he pulled it from behind the CDs and slid it across the counter. "I'll throw it in for free. Try to lie low for a couple of days, okay?"

"Mel and I always do." I wrapped my hand around the handle of the shiv and the cool metal against my palm made me tremble.

He nodded. "Come back in two days. I'll have your stuff then." He looked at my pocket again. As I walked toward the door, he added, "And be careful. You and Mel are more memorable than you think. Two girls living alone in one of the academic buildings. A lot of people know where to find you."

Once I was outside of Stoner Joe's, I climbed a few steps until I was able to peek over the wall of the alcove. I could hear Greens around the corner. They wouldn't notice me, huddled in the shadows.

I pulled the pills from my pocket, slipped my hand under my sweatshirt, and wedged the packet into my bra. Then I slipped the handle on the shiv through one of my belt loops. I turned the sharp edge away so it didn't rub against my stomach before tugging the waistband of my sweatshirt low on my hips to hide the weapon.

I was trembling before I even made it up the stairs and out of the alcove. The wind had died down and for the first time in weeks, the sun peeked through the clouds, but its warmth didn't seep through the fleece of my hoodie. Or past the frigid blanket of fear that had surrounded me.

The quad was mostly empty now, with only a few Greens scuttling between buildings. I felt as vulnerable as they looked, the hairs on the back of my neck prickling with that being-watched feeling.

I glanced over my shoulder back at Joe's, wondering if he'd followed me out. He hadn't, but I *was* being watched. A guy in a gray sweatshirt stood at the top stairs of the dining hall. With the sun at his back as he looked out across the quad, I couldn't distinguish any of his features. Then he stilled, his gaze aimed toward me, and I was sure he was the guy who'd picked up the pills earlier.

I shivered in the sun and picked up my pace, praying that Mel and I weren't in serious trouble. Most Greens stuck to the dormitories. It wasn't a rule or anything, just common sense. Greens were like those penguins you saw on nature shows, huddled on the packed ice, waiting for the ones on the edges to get knocked into the water and picked off by the elephant seals. Greens did everything together. Only a few had squatted other places. If Joe was right and these pills in my pocket were enough to buy someone's freedom, then our little closet in the science building wasn't safe anymore. The guy in the gray sweatshirt could easily find us. Thank God our bags were packed and by the door. Mel and I could evacuate as soon as I got back to the room. I didn't know yet where we would go. All I knew was I wanted to still be alive in two days so that I could keep that appointment with Joe.

CHAPTER THREE

MEL

Most days Lily is the steady drumbeat. The rhythm of my heart. The repeating melody of the music in my head. But not today.

Today she is a cacophony of dissonant notes. Just wrong. A jumbled mess. Can't listen.

She's out of rhythm. Trying to rush. Tempo's all wrong. There's no music in her today, only words. Talk, talk, talk, talk.

That's Lily. Never has a thought she doesn't say aloud. Makes her feel like the smart one. The normal one.

As if I count less because I don't jabber. Because I listen to the music instead of talking over it.

I know I'm a burden. How twitchy it makes her, being the rhythm. Being the steady one. Twitchy and nervous. A rat-a-tat-tat.

But we're not ready. If we go now, we'll be caught. Caught like Trickster's bunnies. She thinks I don't know what happens to those rabbits snared out by the fence. But I know. Their music is so loud sometimes I can't think. I block out their noise when I can.

I know we're not ready. Can't make Lily hear it. All she hears is the clock. Tick tock, tick tock, tick tock. She doesn't listen. All she does is talk.

Talk, talk. Talk, talk. Tick tock, tick tock. Talk, talk. Talk, talk.

I try to listen for the both of us, but I can't hear over all her noise. I hold on to Slink and try to block out the noise, but even

Slink doesn't help. Freedom sounds like Paganini, but the pianist is sitting on his hands. The orchestra is too tinny and too loud by itself. Lily never understands that all the instruments have to play together to make music. Otherwise it's just noise, noise, noise.

By myself, I tap my head against the wall. Alone should be a blessing, but I'm haunted by the plan. My plan, Lily's plan, the plan. It's not about what's missing, it's what's out of rhythm.

I try to make the pianist play, try to hear why our plan won't work, but the white noise of the room is in my ears, blocking out the music. All these things Lily has cluttered our room with.

Everything has its own pitch if you listen for it. Most people don't. Lily doesn't listen for the rustling of a box of neoprene gloves or the steady hum of the eighteen microscopes. The high-pitched glassy squeal of the beakers and petri dishes. All of this stuff makes too much noise. I can't hear the music. If I could, I'd know what's missing.

So I sort the things. Everything comes off the shelves. The big black book screamed beside the pink backpack. It slides into silence when I move it beside the twenty-four-roll box of paper towels. The pink backpack, so jittery, quiets once I empty it and place it beside the quilt. I do this, making sense of the chaos. If I can just isolate the melody—hear our escape plan—I'll know what's wrong.

If I can't make the piano play, the rhapsody won't work. Lily might blame herself, but it'll be both of us who die.

Time is not on our side. Tick tock. Tick tock. Tick tock.

Tick. Tick. Tick.

CHAPTER FOUR

LILY

I don't go anywhere these days without an escape route, but today was the first day I felt like I needed it. Today's plan: get back to Mel, grab the bags, and . . . wait? I didn't know yet if the guy in the gray sweatshirt had reported us. So did we leave the safety of the science building on the chance that he had or did we wait and see? Hiding in the dorms was out of the question. We might head over to the gymnasium on the north side of campus and hide there until morning, but there were some jocks who hadn't become Collabs and they lived in the gym. I shuddered to think what it would take to convince them to let us stay there overnight. So far on the Farm, I hadn't traded *that*. But as I walked up the six flights of stairs to the science lab, I knew that I would if I had to.

But if we made it through the night, then what? If the guy in gray reported us to the Collabs, we wouldn't be safe anywhere on campus. We sure couldn't head down to the dining hall for meals. The Collabs would grab us when they scanned our chips on the way in.

We had only one thing in our favor: everything we needed was packed and waiting beside the door. We could be out of the building in minutes. I didn't yet know if we needed to run, but if the Collabs showed up, I wanted to be ready to.

When I got back to the room, I had to tap out "Mary Had a Little Lamb" five times before she'd open the door. Already nervous, my anxiety shot up with each rap of my knuckles. By the time the door swung open, I was frantic. And then I saw what Mel had done while I was gone.

My eyes scanned from shelf to shelf. At first, I didn't even understand. Everything looked different. Things weren't where they were supposed to be. My emergency backpack wasn't by the door, nor was Mel's pink bag. She loved that bag, partly because it was actually hers. She'd brought it with her when she'd come to the Farm. She'd carried it for three years and another just like it for five years before that. It was bright pink, with cheerful flowers in sherbety colors. Right now it was packed with emergency provisions for Mel. Extra clothes. Half of what little food we had. And of course the tiny stuffed flying squirrel Mel had carried with her since she was five. My bag was gone.

Everything else—the carefully distributed chaos of all the lab equipment—was . . . organized. My heart rate jumped. Every item in the room had been rearranged by color. Suddenly I couldn't breathe. Every lungful was a struggle.

Mel stood in the center of the room, the ladder-back chair clenched in her hands. She gnawed on her lip as she rocked.

Heart pounding, I looked from her to the contents of the shelves, as panic crawled up out of my stomach. I raced to one of the shelves, a blazing burst of pink and red across the top of the room. The pink backpack was just beyond my reach. I jumped up, trying to snag the strap and pull it down. Once, twice. I caught it on the fourth jump and it tumbled off the shelf, pulling a cross-sectioned model of a human heart with it. It crashed to the floor, snapping off the stand and breaking open the heart itself to reveal the interior of the chambers. I felt it like a crack to my own heart, a painful slash across my chest that cut off my air. The backpack was empty, its weight almost nothing.

I ripped open the zipper as my gaze searched the shelves. There was a neatly folded pair of bikini underwear on the green shelf. I grabbed them and crammed them inside. Our obscenely cheerful pink quilt was on the top shelf, too. Snagging it sent a model kidney tumbling to the ground. The dull gray neoprene gloves were on the bottom shelf. I dropped to my knees and with shaking hands shoved pair after pair into the bag. Too many. I stood, leaving the overstuffed bag on the floor, and kept looking. I found the hollowed-out *CRC Handbook of Chemistry and Physics.* Its thick spine and worn blue cover made it easy to find, but the gardening shears I kept hidden inside were gone. After that, I ran through the list of other things that had been in the backpack, pulling them off the shelves with one hand and clutching them to my chest with the other. First aid kits—white shelf. Spare socks—black, blue, white, yellow shelves. Bags of corn chips—orange shelf. The map—

Oh, God. The map.

Everything tumbled from my arms to land at my feet. Where would she have put it? White? No. A glance told me the white shelf was nearly empty. And it hadn't been white anyway, had it? The cover had a picture of a road snaking up the side of a mountain. What sound would the map have made for her? The quiet brown for the mountain? Or the thrumming of the blacktop road? Or whistling wind in the blue sky? Or . . . there'd been a car, hadn't there? What color had the car been? Loud red, like classic rock? Or sunshine yellow, like Vivaldi?

But my mind was racing too fast, spinning out of control, and I couldn't remember. Couldn't think. Couldn't plan.

Shit.

The pink backpack tipped forward, spilling stuff all over the floor.

I bit back a scream of frustration, tried to hide my reaction from Mel. But there she was, blissfully humming Rachmaninoff. Like she thought this was romantic or something.

Dad used to call her a musical savant. *Can't you see what an amazing gift it is?* he'd say. *She's an indigo child.*

That crap used to drive Mom crazy. I'd never quite been sure how I felt about it. Now I knew. At this particular moment, when she'd wrecked all our plans, her autism was *not* an amazing gift. It was a curse. My curse.

"Lil-lee," Mel said, in the odd singsongy way she had. "Lil-lee? Lil-lee?"

I swallowed my tears along with my scream and made myself look at her. She held her Slinky cupped in her hands and silent. Like she knew I was one *sllluuunk* away from tearing the thing from her and tossing it out the window. The muscles in my arms clenched and I fought the impulse to sweep everything off the shelves. To throw things and destroy. To stomp on beakers and crush things with rocks.

Instead, I forced a deep breath, then I took her hand lightly in mine. "Listen, Mel. I'm going out again." She tried to jerk away. "Just for a minute. I'll be right outside. You don't even have to lock the door."

She frowned and bobbed her head some more. "Tick tock. Tick tock."

"No," I assured her. "I won't be gone long."

I didn't wait for her to answer. She wouldn't. And even if she did, she wouldn't understand. Plus, I didn't want her to know how badly I'd screwed up. I couldn't even blame her. This was just what she did. I knew this about her and I should have planned for it.

I palmed a geode from the brown shelf on my way out the door. I rounded the rows of waist-high lab counters with their black fire slate tops and crossed to the corner farthest away from the closet. Beside the door leading out into the hall, I dropped to my knees. With seven rows of lab tables between us, she couldn't see me. Not that she would look. Nothing I did really mattered to her. It was all noise in the background.

Hands trembling, I whipped the hoodie off and let it fall to the floor. Then I lifted the rock above my head and slammed it down onto the floor. The sound was muffled a bit by the thick fleece. *If only I'd brought the travel backpack with me when I'd gone out.* I pounded the floor again. *If only I'd been more careful with the pills.* I brought the rock down again. *If only I'd seen the Green who handed me the pills.* Again. *If only* . . . Again. *If only* . . .

So many *if onlys* made my arms ache. All that was left of my frustration was the burn of tears pressing against the backs of my eyes.

I let the rock fall onto the sweatshirt one final time. My body crumpled over it. I pressed my forehead to the rough outer shell of the geode, my chest heaving with regrets.

God, I wanted to be strong enough to do this all on my own. To take this latest disaster in stride, but—

There was a noise in the hall, so soft I barely heard it over my ragged breathing, but I stilled instantly. I crouched there on the floor, bent over the rock, holding my breath as I listened. And tried to remember what exactly that sound was.

Something I knew well, even though I hadn't heard it in months. A sort of mechanical swoosh, as unfamiliar to me now as the turning of a key in a car ignition or the chime over the door at the yogurt shop where I had worked after school.

I sucked in a breath. Elevator doors. I'd heard elevator doors opening. Someone had come up to the seventh floor. Someone not afraid of getting stuck in an elevator if one of the blackouts rolled across campus. Or someone too lazy to walk up the stairs, which described pretty much all the Collabs.

I thought instantly of the guy in the gray sweatshirt. *No.*

Had he really been that fast? I'd been counting on it taking longer for him to find a Collab and cut some kind of deal.

I rocked forward onto the balls of my feet and stood, hardly daring to breathe. The door leading out into the hall was open. I crept one step and then another until I was tucked behind the open door. I couldn't see much through the crack between the door and jamb, so I squeezed my eyes shut, listening, as I considered my options.

Even if there was just one Collab out there, we were screwed. Before Mel had reorganized the closet, I'd known exactly where the CRC handbook was, and with it, my only weapon: the gardening shears. But now?

My breath caught in my chest as the realization hit me. I had the shiv. Not for the first time I wondered: would I really kill someone if I had to? In the Before, I didn't even like to kill bugs. And I'd puked the time our old Siamese cat, Trickster, had left a dead bunny on our porch. How could I kill a person? Could I do it to protect Mel? I drew in a shuddering breath, my heart thudding so loudly, I was sure he'd hear it.

Why not? Why not at least *try* to take out the Collab? If there was only one, then I had a shot. It was sure as hell better than waiting for him to go get reinforcements.

I could hear footsteps in the hall. Coming closer. Was it one guy or two?

I stood there for a torturous minute, listening to his steady footsteps. Each pause of his stride, punctuated by the sound of a knob turning and a door sliding open and shutting with an ominous click. Only one guy, I was almost certain. But these weren't the sounds of casual exploring. This was a methodical search. He was looking for us.

And he would find me. Soon.

I'd carelessly left the door to this classroom open. It was a miracle he hadn't noticed it already.

Wedged between the door and the wall, heart pounding, eyes squeezed shut, I reached down and slid the shiv free of my belt loop, my palm damp against the metal handle. Through the gap between the door and the doorjamb, I saw a flash of gray pass. Not the blue of a Collab's uniform but the heathered gray of a sweatshirt. I pushed aside the doubt that flickered through me. Then he was there, striding past me into the classroom. He paused for only a moment before heading around the rows of lab desks toward the storage closet.

I launched myself at him before he could get too far into the room. Leaping onto his back, I slung one arm around his neck. He gave an oomph of surprise and stumbled back. I brought the shiv up to his neck, but hesitated. That moment of doubt cost me.

His hands reached up to claw at my arms. The shiv slipped and clattered to the ground at his feet. Panicked, I used my free hand to leverage the other arm, squeezing tight against his windpipe. For a second, I seemed to have the advantage. I didn't have to kill him. I only needed him to pass out. Just long enough to get Mel out of the storage closet.

Then he reeled with a grunt and slammed my back against the

wall. The air rushed out of my lungs and I swear I actually felt my bones shudder. Damn, he was big. Not just taller than me, but stronger.

He stumbled forward, reaching his arms over his head to wrench at my hair and tug at my shirt. Blunt fingernails raked against my neck, burning a trail of scratches across my skin. He ran forward a few steps and then back again, slamming me into the wall once more. This time I felt something hard dig into my spine. Maybe a light switch or the fire alarm.

I yelped as agony seared through my back. My grip loosened, but only for a second. He may have been a Green, but he wasn't weak or anemic. Maybe his blood wasn't "clean" enough and they hadn't been taking as much from him. Nor was he fat and lazy the way so many of the Collabs were. I couldn't afford to let him go. He was knocking the crap out of me now. I'd never be able to defend myself face-to-face.

I tried to remember anything from the self-defense class Mom had dragged me to when I was thirteen. Bits of it flashed through my mind along with things I'd figured out through trial and error here at the Farm. The eyes. I knew I could hurt him if I could just reach his eyes. But my grip on his throat was slipping already. Not daring to let go, I tightened my legs around his hips, clinging to him with every ounce of strength I still had. My only hope was to weaken him before he crushed my spine completely.

He staggered forward again and I could hear him gasping for breath, my arm strangling the sounds in his throat before they could escape. He was trying to talk. But I still didn't let go. He staggered back a step, but he was weakening and this felt more like a pat on the back than the assault his previous body slams had been.

A second later, he teetered forward and fell to his knees, his forehead missing the corner of one of the lab desks by mere inches as he did a face plant on linoleum.

Slowly I pulled my arms out from under his heavy weight and pushed myself up. My legs still gripped his waist. I sat there a moment, sucking air into my lungs, straddling his back, too worn out to move, trying to think. His hood was still up. All I could see of him were his hands, which were large and strong. And, probably, had bits of my skin under the nails.

I shuddered at the thought. Clearly, back in the Before, I'd watched too many of those forensic shows on TV, if that was the one thing that went through my mind.

Had I killed him?

I pushed myself off his back, then struggled to flip him over. It was easier than I would have thought, given how much bigger he was. I leaned down and pressed my ear to his chest. I felt it rise and fall beneath my face even before I heard the strong, steady rhythm of his heart.

Relief poured through me. Not just because I was still alive, but because he was, too. I felt my throat close and tears burn my still-tender eyes. I didn't want to be a murderer.

Before my tears could fall, I scrambled back. I didn't want to die, either. I didn't know why he'd come looking for us instead of going straight to the Collabs, but I wasn't going to stay around to find out. I had to get Mel out of there. Fast.

And yet, for some reason, I hesitated as I saw his face for the first time. There was something familiar about him. It was like I should know him, but just . . . didn't. Most of his face was obscured by the beginnings of a beard, too long to be mere stubble, like he hadn't shaved in weeks. Most of the guys on the Farm didn't bother to shave. Still, not many guys our age could grow anything like a beard. Some of the Collabs were older, but he obviously wasn't one of them or he would have been wearing the blue uniform. I studied his features, looking for some hint as to why he seemed so familiar. His nose had a funny little bump in it, like it had been broken.

I pushed back his hoodie to reveal dirty blond hair. A single lock of hair flopped back into place to drape across his forehead. Recognition rocked me back on my heels.

He must have moved the second I took my eyes off him. He sprang up, flinging me flat onto my back, covering my body with his own. My head banged against the floor, and I squeezed my eyes shut against the pain. The impact knocked the breath out of me.

There was nothing groggy or slow about his movements. Obviously he'd only pretended to pass out. I'd fallen for one of the oldest tricks in the book. And as if that weren't bad enough, I felt the cool edge of my shiv press into the skin at my throat.

Damn it!

Could I make any more mistakes today? How had I been so careless as to let him get my weapon? My shiv!

I swallowed hard against my frustration, bumping my chin up a notch to relieve the pressure against the blade.

Slowly I opened my eyes to stare up into familiar blue ones.

I forced a smile. "Hey, Carter. Long time no see."

CHAPTER FIVE

LILY

Carter and I had gone to school together back in the Before. Despite what teen novels everywhere would have you believe, sitting beside a hot guy in ninth-grade biology is not the basis for eternal love—at least, not the requited kind. And, yeah, I admit it, in my more romantic moments, I imagined that I alone saw through his tough, bad-boy exterior to the wounded soul inside. Carter had been the kind of guy who ran hot and cold. One day he'd be all charming smiles, the next brooding glares. Some days he'd flirt with me; others he'd ignore me completely. What can I say, that charming, bad-boy thing he had going was like catnip to a geeky girl like me. And, yeah, my predictability disgusted even me. I'd spent the first two periods of every day reminding myself not to be an idiot—because a guy like Carter didn't even exist in the same social universe as I did—and I'd show up to class ready to banish my crush forever, only to have him flash me one of those crooked smiles that made me melt inside.

Then one day, he'd pushed his parents too far by driving his dad's Lamborghini to school. I still remembered when the police had come to arrest Carter. I'd been standing outside of English, books clutched to my chest, when they marched him down the hall, his hands cuffed behind his back and an I-don't-give-a-crap grin on his face. He'd flicked his shaggy blond hair out of his eyes with a shake of his head. When he met my gaze, he winked at me.

I hadn't seen him since then.

Now, he levered himself off of me and sat back on his heels.

My heart pounded inside my chest as I waited to see what he would do. Carter Olson—who I hadn't seen in years—was alive. He was here at the Farm. And he'd just tackled me. Oh, and I'd tried to kill him.

A second later, I pushed all those emotions aside with more determination than I'd ever managed in the Before. I wasn't that fifteen-year-old girl anymore and I had bigger problems than a hopeless crush.

Carter had seen the pills. He'd followed me back from the quad. He'd disarmed me and winded me. He had every advantage. If he wanted to destroy me, there were about a dozen different ways he could do it.

But instead he held out a hand to help me sit up.

"Hey, Lil," he said.

I blew out a breath. If he was going to kill me or even take me to the Dean's office, would he be offering me a hand up and using that nickname I'd disliked even back then?

I took the hand he was still holding out and let him help me into a sitting position, aches already cramping the muscles of my back. Cringing, I scooched away from him, giving an experimental little twist. A little gasp of pain escaped.

"You alright?"

"I'll live," I quipped, but then cringed a little inside and sent up a silent prayer, *I hope.*

"Sorry about that." He gave a little nod to indicate the brawl. Then he reached out a hand and ran his thumb along the spot on my neck where he'd held the shiv against my skin.

He hadn't broken the skin, but the scratch he'd left burned like hell. Still, there was something disconcerting about his touch and I twitched back from him, not liking the way his gaze went from my neck back to my eyes.

"Hey, nice apology." I aimed for sarcasm, but didn't quite hit it, since I was still winded. "Considering you just beat the crap out of me and all."

"Hey, you're the one who jumped me," he said. He scooted back to lean against the nearest lab table, stretching a leg out between us.

Good point.

"And you're the one still holding the weapon," I countered.

He looked down as if surprised to see the shiv still in his hand. With a shrug, he reached up and set it onto one of the lab tables, then casually draped his arm across his raised knee. "Feel better now?"

Not by a long shot. On the bright side, Carter was definitely the Green from the quad who'd picked up the pills. The fact that he was here now meant he wasn't off turning me in to the Dean's office. Also, a moment ago, I'd been at his mercy. He could have killed me and he hadn't.

On the not-so-bright side, I still didn't know why he'd followed me. Had he recognized the pills? Did he know what they were?

I wrapped my arms around my knees, hoping to hide the trembling in my muscles. My tears were still crawling up my throat and the only way I could keep them down was by talking. Like if I stopped to think about things too long, something inside of me would crack open and the jagged pieces would shred me from the inside out.

So I just kept talking. Like this was all perfectly normal. Like

I hadn't tried to kill him a few minutes ago. "You could have, you know, said hello or something. I didn't know it was you."

"Hey, when you attacked me, I didn't know it was you, either." He stood slowly, smiling as if completely unperturbed by my belligerence. He ran a hand pointedly across his windpipe, which looked red. Then he held out a hand to help me stand. "Besides, I couldn't exactly talk. You were choking me, after all."

Hmm. 'Nother good point.

I gave him a suspicious once-over, but I couldn't ignore his hand, so I took it and let him help me to my feet, even though I dropped it just as quickly.

The way he ran his hand over his throat drew my attention to his jawline. It was too scruffy and unkempt to be a full beard. Still, on Carter, it looked less ridiculous than it would have on a lot of other guys.

When I'd known him back in the Before, Carter had been maybe three or four inches taller than I was. Sometime in the past year or so, he'd shot up a good half foot. Now he towered over me. He used to have a sort of whippetlike leanness to him. That was gone.

Because we gave donations every week, none of us Greens looked really healthy. We ate a lot, but we never seemed to be fed. Not Carter. Whatever he'd been doing, he'd put on muscles that even the benign, genderless hoodie couldn't hide.

Of course, whatever he'd been doing since the Before, he hadn't been doing it here. Not on this Farm. If he'd been here, I would have known about it.

"What are you doing here?" I asked. "Why were you following me?"

"I just got here two days ago. When I saw you on the quad earlier, I knew I had to talk to you."

"Why?" I pressed.

"What do you mean *why*?" He looked at me like I was crazy and brushed at the lock of hair that had once again tumbled into his eyes. "Because you're the first person I've seen here that I knew in the Before. I didn't know for sure if anyone I knew was still—" He broke off sharply as his gaze shifted away from mine. I saw him swallow and got the feeling maybe he was doing that talking-to-keep-from-blubbering thing, too. I looked away until he spoke again. "I was glad to see you." He gave a little chuckle. Like maybe he was embarrassed. "Really glad."

"So why not talk to me then?" I had no way of knowing if his story was true.

"What? Out on the quad?" he asked, mockery in his tone. "You wanted me to just stop and chat with you there? In front of the Collabs? I haven't been here long, but even I know better than that."

"So instead, you just followed me back here to beat the hell out of me?"

Okay, I knew, this was irrational. *I* had attacked *him*. But I was trembling inside and right now my tough attitude was all that was holding me together.

He hesitated, smiling just a little. "Actually, beating the hell out of you was plan C."

I sucked in my breath at his smile, faint though it was. People didn't smile much on the Farm—not Greens anyway—and I'd completely forgotten that warm fluttering feeling a smile could give you.

I shoved the feeling aside. If Greens didn't smile, it was because we didn't have the energy for that kind of crap. We sure as hell didn't have the energy for warm fluttery feelings, either.

"So what were plans A and B? Stalk me for a while and scare me to death?"

"I'd already noticed that Greens don't loiter much on the quad. I was afraid stopping to talk to you out in the open would attract attention. So plan A was to follow you into the dining hall and talk to you there, but you disappeared in the crowd. So I went back out to look for you. When I saw you come into this building, I followed. Some guy I saw on the first floor told me a couple of girls lived on one of the upper floors, so I came up, hoping it was you."

"Hmm." I mulled it over.

Yeah, it made sense, and yet I hadn't kept us alive on the Farm this long by blindly trusting everyone we'd known in the Before.

"Jesus, Lily, you always so suspicious?"

I studied him through narrowed eyes as I stepped over to the desk where he'd placed the shiv. I made a show of picking it up and sliding it back into my belt loop. "Yeah. Lately I am."

"Lately?" He raised an eyebrow. "Only lately?"

Let's see, I'd been hiding a weapon, I'd negotiated the trade of a Class A controlled substance, and I'd bought a homemade shiv from the one guy on campus I hoped I could trust. All while planning a prison break. Any one of those things could get me sent to the Dean's office. So, yeah, lately I was even more suspicious than normal.

Which was why I wasn't about to say any of that aloud. Instead I stated the obvious, speaking slowly, as if he were a total moron.

"Yes, Carter. Lately, vampire monsters have swept across the country, killing everything in their path. We were brought here for our own protection, but we haven't heard anything from outside the Farm in months. So it's feeling more and more like we're just being raised as food. Like veal. And where the hell have you been for the past six months that it hasn't made you paranoid, too?"

I was surprised at how bitter my words sounded. Not that the whole being-raised-as-food thing wouldn't make anyone bitter.

"Hey, Lily, I'm—" Carter reached out a hand toward me.

"Look, I don't have time for this crap. Why did you come find me?" I dodged out of his reach and bent down to pick up the sweatshirt I'd dropped on the floor.

He shoved his hands into his pockets. "Like I said, you're the first person I've seen here that I knew in the Before. As far as I know, you're the only person I know here on this Farm."

A flood of questions rose up inside of me as the implication of his words registered. He'd been on the outside. He'd seen what was beyond the fences. He knew what was out there. I opened my mouth to let out that flood of questions, but felt my throat close over them.

He'd also been glad to see me. Me, even though we hadn't really been friends. I thought about what he hadn't said. The way he'd cut himself off earlier before finishing his sentence.

All my questions sort of hung there in my mind. I could have asked if he'd been to our hometown. If he'd seen my mother. I could have asked, but I didn't. I was too afraid that I knew the answer, and I wasn't ready to hear it aloud.

"Where were you before now?" I asked, my fear making me sound angry. I wasn't brave enough to ask about my family, but if he'd been somewhere else—*anywhere* else—then he might be able to tell me what awaited Mel and me once we got out. I hadn't been beyond the electrified fence surrounding the Farm in over six months. Sometimes I'd go up to the roof of the science building and stare out into the town beyond the fence, looking for signs of life. Signs of anything outside. For miles around, there was nothing but empty buildings, deserted cars, and the path of destruction left by the Ticks.

Maybe this was what every town looked like now. But I had to believe that somewhere out there, civilization chugged on. Truckloads of food arrived every week. That food came from somewhere, right? I never saw anything during the day.

At night sometimes, you could hear the Ticks out there, howling in an obscene cacophony. Like someone was skinning a dozen puppies alive. But we never saw or heard humans from beyond the fence.

"Have you been out there?" I asked softly, wanting to hide how anxious I was for any shred of information about the outside world. "What's it like? Are the Ticks everywhere? Have they killed . . . everyone?"

I'd mindlessly walked closer to him. He searched my face, and there was something unsettling about the intensity with which he looked at me. His eyes seemed to scour my face, taking in every detail, as though he had been desperate to find me. Like I was somehow important to him. I shivered and stepped back.

Jeez, he must have been alone a long time if he was this glad to see me.

He glanced out the window again. "I don't want to talk about what's happened out there."

He sounded so damn vulnerable, part of me just wanted to let it go, but I couldn't. I'd never be able to trust him unless I knew more about where he'd come from and how he'd gotten here. Even though I'd known him in the Before, I couldn't afford to just trust anyone these days. And maybe there was some tiny part of me that still *hoped*.

I was about to risk Mel's life with this crazy escape plan, and I owed it to her to find out everything I could about the outside.

"Please," I begged. "Can't you tell me anything about what's out there? I know nothing about what's going on beyond that fence. When our parents sent all of us here, they were told it was temporary—just for our protection. Just until they could find a way to kill the Ticks. And when they couldn't find a way to kill them, they said that as we got older, our blood would be less appealing to the Ticks and that they could set us free, but I don't think that's what's happening. It's been months since we've seen or heard anything from the outside other than food deliveries. Are there still any humans out there at all? Did you see any sign that the police or the army was fighting back? Is there any place that's safe?"

He sent me a suspicious look. "Why do you want to know all this stuff about what's outside the Farm? There's no way out of here."

Crap. Had I tipped my hand? These all seemed like normal questions to me. Things anyone would want to know. But had he guessed that I actually needed the information?

"Because you just showed up here," I improvised. "Out of nowhere. And I have no idea where you've been or what you've been doing." I let my hand drop to the handle of the shiv. "And unless you can give me a pretty good reason why you showed up now, I think you better leave."

He stared at me for an instant and I got the impression he was trying to decide just how much to tell me. Finally he turned away, stalked over to the windows on the far side of the room, and stared out for a long moment.

I'd just started to wonder if he was going to answer at all when he spoke.

"When I left Richardson High, my parents sent me to this

military school, way out in south Texas. The guy who ran it had some pretty unique military experience."

"You mean he's, like, a Green Beret or something?"

"Yeah, something like that." He spoke in a flat voice, the way people do when they're trying to sound bored but aren't doing it very well. "When everything collapsed, we hunkered down and held out. No one was much interested in some boys' school. So we hung on until . . ."

He let the words trail off like he didn't want to say anything else.

"Until?" I prodded.

"Until we didn't."

The stark simplicity of the statement chilled my blood. He turned back to face me, all traces of his smile gone. Somehow, he looked both less and more like the boy I'd known.

"And now you're here?"

"And now I'm here."

"All of you?" I asked, but he just stared blankly at me, so I added, "All of you from the school are here?"

He looked out the window again. "By the time they were done with us, there weren't enough of us left for the word 'all' to apply."

"Oh." Hell, what else could I say? "I'm sorry." It seemed inadequate, but I said it anyway. "But I don't see what that has to do with me."

"Don't you? You're the first friend I've seen in months. Since being sent off to that hellhole." His voice was edged with frustration, so I decided not to point out that "friend" wasn't the word I would have used to describe us. "Could you just—I don't know—take pity on me or something?"

I could have told him to go find someone else he'd known

in the Before. Sure, out of the thousands of Greens on the Farm, most were strangers, but there were a couple hundred Richardson High alums scattered around. Last I'd heard, there was a group living over in Baker Hall. A few had even become Collabs.

In the end, it was his vulnerability that made me cave. Carter had been a bit of a badass in school. Hell, he'd stolen a car and been sent off to military school. The fact that he was acting all emo now was what wore me down. Because if one of the toughest guys I knew was asking for help, then how could I turn him away?

"Crap," I muttered. This was just the last thing I needed.

He must have realized how close I was to giving in, because he took a step forward and said, "At least let me stay here for a couple of days. You and Mel can show me around."

I studied him, still trying to pinpoint the source of my anxiety. "How did you know Mel was with me?"

"Why wouldn't she be?"

I didn't like that he'd been following me, even if it had been only for a few minutes. Even if it was only because I was the first person he knew from Richardson High. On the other hand, at least I no longer had to worry about some faceless Green selling us out to the Collabs.

"Where have you been sleeping until now?"

"I haven't been. I spent most of the last two nights sitting in the hall in one of the dorms. I slept about thirty minutes the first night. Someone stole my backpack, so I've stayed awake since then."

"You haven't slept?" He *did* look tired, but he hadn't slept at *all*?

"Military school," he said simply. "We learned survivalist stuff like that."

I had the feeling I was going to regret this, but I couldn't just kick him out. I mean, besides the fact that I couldn't *actually* kick him out. Our little tussle had proven that.

"Look, I can't make you leave, even if I wanted to."

He held up his hands in a gesture of surrender. "Hey, I'm not going to force my way in here. I don't have anywhere else to go, but if you want me to leave, I'll leave."

"Okay, leave," I said, trying to be strong enough to send him away. And partly just to see if he would go, because I didn't like being backed into a corner.

"I—" He blinked, looking surprised. "Okay. I'll go." He glanced around the room, like he was looking for anything he might have left behind. I looked, too, for a second, before remembering that he didn't have anything. Everything he owned had already been stolen. He gave his shoulder a little shrug and then headed for the door. "Guess I'll see you around."

I gritted my teeth, shaking my head at my own idiocy. "Look, there are plenty of empty classrooms. I'll loan you a blanket." I knew I'd regret that later, but I couldn't just boot him out entirely. Not when he looked so lost all of a sudden. Not when it was Carter. Maybe he and I hadn't really been friends, but he'd always been so nice to Mel. I had a natural soft spot when it came to people who were nice to Mel. The least I could do was loan him a blanket and let him stay nearby. I'd slept on these floors myself and I knew how hard they were. "I probably even have an extra bag you can use. There's an office two floors down with a wooden chair in it; you can carry it up to wedge under the knob. It's enough to keep people out."

"So I can stay?"

"Just try to stay out of our way. Mel doesn't like strangers and I don't want her to get upset."

"I'm not a stranger," he pointed out. "I know her."

Back in the Before, Mel had been . . . not normal—never that—but her ASD symptoms weren't so severe. She'd been mainstreamed into some classes at school. She's talked, socialized, joked. Yeah, her jokes were usually stiff misfires, but I'd gotten them.

I missed that Mel, almost as much as I missed the person I'd been in the Before. I missed my sister. I missed having someone to talk to.

"Fine. You can walk down to fourth meal with us. I'll see how it goes. But if she can't take it, you leave, okay?"

"Okay."

"There's something you should know, though. Since coming to the Farm, she's been . . . different."

He frowned. "How?"

I could see his curiosity. "When you knew her, she had her ASD symptoms almost under control. I mean, yeah, she was Mel, but she was . . ." I cringed. Why did this seem so awkward? So I just blurted it out. "When we were kids, she did this thing where she only talked in nursery rhymes. Her therapist thought she did it because she was just repeating everything I said. Or maybe because they're so rhythmic and she loves music. But she grew out of it and by the time you knew her in high school—"

Carter reached out like he was going to grab my hand, but then he didn't.

I looked up at him.

"Hey," he said. "You know I'm okay with Mel. I'm not going to do anything to upset her."

"I know." Strangely, I did know that. He kindness toward Mel was one of the reasons it had been so easy to crush on him. Even when he was a jerk to me, I knew he was a nice guy underneath.

"I just thought I'd tell you. That way you won't be surprised. Because she's not like she used to be."

Not that any of us were.

Carter nodded, like he got it. I didn't bother to tell him that he probably wouldn't have to *do* anything. Mel was already freaked out. Between me being gone earlier and my long absence now, who knew what kind of shape she'd be in?

"Go down and get one of those chairs I mentioned. I'll leave the blanket here." I patted my hand on top of the nearest lab table. "For now, stay across the hall. I'll come wake you when it's time for fourth meal."

"Thanks." A slow smile teased his lips. "Then I'll see you at dinner."

I crossed to the door to the storage closet, but glanced back over my shoulder. He was watching me, hands shoved deep into his pockets, looking almost smug.

"And try to find a razor and shave."

He raised an eyebrow. "You don't like the beard?"

"It makes you look too old. You don't want to give any of the Collabs a reason to give you a hard time." Or maybe I just wanted him to look more like I remembered him looking in the Before. Though why that should matter, I didn't know. He wasn't that person anymore. None of us were. "You should try a little harder to blend."

I shook my head, thinking of all the things he didn't know about surviving on the Farm. I had a lot to teach him and not much time to do it.

Plus, I had a lot more questions I wanted answers to. Like how had he escaped from the Ticks attacking his school? From what I'd seen on the news before Mel and I had been shipped off to the Farm, the Ticks were insentient monsters. Yeah, they'd been human once, but exposure to the Tick virus had destroyed their ability to reason and to control themselves. If they'd attacked Carter's military school, they would have eaten everything in their path. Ticks didn't take prisoners and ship them off to Farms. There was something Carter wasn't telling me. Were there adult Collabs on the outside who rounded up kids and forced them to come in?

I needed to know everything that had happened to Carter between the moment his school had been attacked and now. If his story didn't make sense, then I'd worry about whether or not I could trust him. For now, I had to work under the assumption that he was the same basically good guy who'd always been nice to Mel.

That guy may not have been on our side, but he sure as hell wouldn't be on the side of the Collabs and the Dean.

Of course, if he could explain how he'd gotten caught and ended up here, then I had to figure out where he'd gone wrong.

He'd been on the outside and now he was trapped again. I needed to learn from his mistakes. I couldn't let the same thing happen to us.

CHAPTER SIX

CARTER

Carter breathed out a sigh as he watched Lily shut the door behind her with a resounding click. From where he stood in the science lab, he couldn't tell if the room she'd disappeared into was an office or what. He walked close enough to the door to hear the unmistakable murmur of voices, which meant Mel was in there with her.

He'd found them. Lily was alive.

After years of thinking about her and months of praying she was safe, after all the crazy stuff he'd been through trying to track her down, he'd actually found her. She was alive—breathing and unhurt—not forty feet away from him.

He nearly laughed out loud as relief flooded him. Hell, he'd practically wrestled with her. A second later his laughter died out as reality set in. Yeah, she and Mel were alive, but earning her trust was not going to be as easy as he'd hoped. The fact that they lived in this building, isolated from most of the other Greens, said a lot. They obviously kept to themselves. He couldn't slowly ingratiate himself into their circle of friends—not that that tactic was possible now that she'd tackled him and he'd had to fight her off. That had not exactly set the tone for the kind of friendly trust building he'd wanted for their reintroduction.

To make matters worse, he'd seen that plastic case she'd

accidentally dropped in the quad. If that blue case was what he thought it was, then she was either very smart or very stupid. Either way, carrying that crap around could get a girl killed. What the hell was she thinking?

Of course he couldn't ask her that. For now, he was stuck playing dumb and vulnerable.

He could tell she hadn't bought his story about how things had gone down at the military school. He had hoped to have a few days to work himself into her good graces before telling her the whole truth. He hadn't counted on her being so tough. So suspicious. But he kind of admired her for it, even if it made his job harder.

He was going to have to handle the next few days very carefully. If she knew why he was really here and what he really wanted from her . . . if she knew he was playing her, she'd probably slit his throat in the night. For the first time in his life, his motives were selfless and noble—he was trying to save the world, for cripe's sake—but since saving the world involved manipulating Lily, he didn't think it would win him any points with her.

For now, he was just happy he'd found her. After months of searching for her, he'd found her. She and Mel were in the next room. They were both alive and safe. And now that he was here, he could protect them.

Still, lurking outside her door like some sort of pervert probably wasn't the best way to convince her to trust him. So he left the lab room. Out in the hall, he considered his options. Leaving her alone wasn't one of them. It had taken him too damn long to find her. He wasn't going to risk losing her again.

Tonight while they were asleep, he'd find the fuse box and get the elevator shut down so no one could sneak up on them. Then he'd have to rig an alarm on the doors to the stairwells. That should be easy enough.

Later, he might figure out a way to rig her door so he'd hear it if she tried to sneak out, but for now, he'd settle for simple line-of-sight surveillance from the room directly across the hall.

It was a lecture hall, with maybe fifty seats mounted to the floor, set up stadium-style behind rows of narrow desks. With the door to his room open, he sat, back propped against the lectern, arms clenched around his knees, and drew in a series of long breaths, until his heart rate slowed.

Sebastian may have been full of crap about a lot of things, but when it came to taking the edge off an adrenaline rush, the guy knew what he was talking about. Of course, Sebastian would have told him to twist his body into some crazy full-on yoga pose to meditate. Carter, however, wasn't quite ready to risk taking his eyes off the door to Lily's room.

He'd try quieting his mind and being receptive to the universe and all those other Jedi mind tricks some other day. Someday when he hadn't just had his ass handed to him. By a girl.

He'd have thought that the eighteen months of combat training he'd had in military school might have given him an edge, but no, he'd had to resort to playing dead like a frickin' possum. Ah, Sebastian would be so proud.

Though, in Carter's defense, she'd been trying to kill him and he'd been doing his damnedest not to actually hurt her, because if he was right and Lily Price really was the key to defeating the Ticks, he sure as hell didn't want to be the one to accidentally kill the savior of all humanity.

When he felt sure he could talk without Sebastian reading his emotions in his voice, Carter pulled up the right leg of his jeans to where he had a cell phone case strapped to the ankle of his boot. All the cell towers had been knocked out when the Ticks first took over, but his satellite phone still worked. Thank God he hadn't broken it in the fight. Or worse, lost it. The last thing he needed was for her to know he had it. She was smart enough that his phone would have raised a major flag for her.

He had a tiny mirror in his survival kit strapped to his other leg. He set it up on the ground beside the lectern, angled just slightly. Then he retreated to a corner of the room, sitting on the floor with his back against the far wall. If the door to Lily's room opened, he'd see it in the mirror.

He scrubbed a hand down his face. Jesus, he was tired. He hadn't lied to Lily about how little sleep he'd gotten in the past few days. He'd only lied about why.

There was only one number programmed into the sat phone and it didn't take him long to pull it up and dial it. The phone was clunkier than the old iPhone he'd had in the Before, but he'd been using it so long it was second nature by now. Sebastian answered on the first ring.

"You found them."

"Didn't you tell me not to call until I had?"

If Carter hadn't been calling with such good news, Sebastian probably wouldn't have put up with the attitude. Today, he just asked, "What's their status?"

Grumpy. Pissed off. Suspicious. Bruised, if his own status was anything to go by. "Fine," he said aloud.

"Were you right about her?" There was a tension in Sebastian's voice that Carter had never heard before.

If he'd thought—even for an instant—that Sebastian might be capable of emotion, Carter would have called it excitement.

Carter rubbed a hand down his face and considered the question. Was she the one? It had been a long time since he'd last seen her in person. There'd been a chance—a damn good one—that his memory had played tricks on him. That maybe there was nothing special about Lily at all.

He let himself think about her now, not the girl he'd known back in the Before, but the girl she was now. Suspicious. Wary. Tough as hell. But she'd always had a sort of leery reserve to her. Yet even in their brief conversation, even bracing himself against it, he'd felt the pull of her personality. Felt the sway she had over his emotions. He thought of the desire he'd had to comfort her. The way he'd constantly wanted to touch her. The way he'd actually offered to leave if she asked him to.

What had *that* been about? And what the *hell* would he have done if she hadn't told him he could stay?

He guessed he would have left. He'd have set up surveillance outside her building and prayed like hell he didn't lose her. But the very fact that he'd *offered* was proof enough. She made him feel things no one ever had. In short, she made him feel things that *she* felt.

If anything, his memory had diminished the effect she had on him. If she could control his emotions without even trying to, then, yeah, she was the *abductura* Sebastian was looking for.

Once she learned how to control her power, she would be able to control the emotions of everyone around her. She was the one person who could turn the tide in the war against the Ticks.

Finally, Carter said aloud, "Yes. We were right."

"Excellent."

"Look, I have them under surveillance. I don't want to leave, but I need a few things." He rattled them off quickly. "I'm up on the seventh floor of the Walker building. A couple floors down, there should be some wooden chairs in one of the offices. Can you have someone bring one up, leave it in the stairwell? Also some sort of motion-activated camera that I can link into my phone, so I'll know if they try to leave. And see if you can find me a razor and some shaving cream."

"Certainly," Sebastian said, his accent even more droll than usual. "Do you need anything else? Fresh towels? Maybe some hot cocoa from room service?"

Carter pretended not to hear the sarcasm. There'd been few enough times when Carter actually had something Sebastian needed. "Yeah. See if you can find some bubble gum."

"And why would I do that?"

"Because Mel likes it." Back in school, she'd had special permission to chew gum in class because it was quieter than her Slinky. It had always seemed a little unfair that she could chew gum *and* blow the curve on every math test. "If I'm going to worm my way into their life, I need every advantage I can find."

"You told me you were their friend."

"I said I knew them. And if you've anyone else who can give you that, then you're welcome to cut me off and do this without me."

He could practically hear Sebastian grinding his long incisors in annoyance. A second later, he ended the call and slid the phone back into the case on his leg. Sebastian would text him when things were in place. He was clearly too annoyed to bother calling Carter.

Alone with his thoughts, he was suddenly exhausted. And achy.

Not wanting to get too comfortable and risk falling asleep, he pulled his hoodie off and then a moment later also took off the plain white T-shirt he wore beneath it. It was cool enough in the room to help keep him awake.

He just hoped that Lily didn't try to sneak out on him. He wasn't a hundred percent sure he'd win round two.

When he'd known her in the Before, Lily had had a natural suspicious prickliness to her. What she'd been through since then had only reinforced those qualities. He was going to have to work hard to win her over. She wouldn't easily trust him. That was okay. He had all the time in the world.

CHAPTER SEVEN

LILY

Mel was waiting at the door of the storage closet, peering wordlessly through the opening. I wasn't sure how long she'd been there and how much she'd seen.

She stepped aside to let me enter and I pushed open the door, scanning the tiny space. Well, at least she hadn't done any more damage while I'd been trying to kill Carter.

Mel stood there, staring at me. For once, I could offer her absolutely no reassurances. I didn't even have the energy to be sorry.

All I could do was gently shut the door and wedge the chair under the knob, giving us a shred of security. Then, leaning against the bare patch of wall beside the door, I sank to the floor. Pulling my legs to my chest, I wrapped my arms around them and dropped my forehead to my knees.

Adrenaline pumped through my veins and now that I wasn't using all my strength to defend myself, my muscles started trembling. My skin had gone icy cold and my hands shook so hard I almost had trouble holding on to my legs. I wished, desperately, that I hadn't taken my hoodie off and left it out in the science lab. Or that I had a blanket. Something reassuring and cuddly to cling to.

Mel and I had three blankets, stolen from the dorms in the

early days. One was a fuzzy blue polyester job. The other, a thick brown wool. The third, an obscenely cheerful pink quilt. Not the kind someone's grandmother had lovingly made, but the bed-in-a-bag kind. Of course, Mel had stripped our mattress and neatly folded the blankets so the rounded edges showed.

I didn't have the energy to bring Carter the blanket I'd promised him. I was cold and shaky. I could have used a blanket myself. Mel just stood there facing the shelves, positioning and repositioning the items with meticulous care.

So I just rested my head, closed my eyes, and waited to warm up on my own. A different kind of sister would guess how freaked out I was right now. She would wrap a blanket around my shoulders and stroke my hair. Maybe even put her arm around me while I cried. But instead of that nurturing sister I fantasized about, I had Mel. When I opened my eyes, I saw that she'd put her Slinky on the floor beside me.

I swallowed back my tears and smiled at her. "Thanks."

* *

By the time fourth meal rolled around, I'd located and repacked almost everything we needed in our backpacks. I wasn't going to take any more chances. Our bags were once again stuffed and ready to go at a moment's notice. And we wouldn't be leaving the room without them. I started with the easy stuff. Our spare socks and underwear, for example, were all small when folded, so they were in the front, at the beginning of each color row. It had been a trick convincing Mel to let me pack them, but after about twenty renditions of "Red rover, red rover," the underwear and the socks went into the backpacks.

The twelve bags of corn chips were the sole items on the shelf of orange things. The first aid kits should have been simple. The white plastic boxes sat side by side on the top shelf. They were empty. By the time I'd collected all of the Band-Aids and ointments, all the rolls of Ace bandages and tiny packets of aspirin, it was almost time to go to fourth meal.

I'd seen no sign at all of the map. It could be anywhere, tucked into a textbook or filed away with old tests. I tried not to panic. I had only vague ideas about what we were going to do on the outside. Find a car—there were certainly enough of them abandoned around town. Head north—the Tick outbreak had started in the Southwest, so I figured they were strongest there. If the Canadians had succeeded in securing their borders, maybe we could find sanctuary from the Ticks there.

I'd spent a lot of time staring at that map, trying to figure out where to go after we got off the Farm. Maybe I remembered the roads well enough to get us there. All the warm socks and antiseptic moist towelettes in the world wouldn't help us if we couldn't find our way out of Oklahoma.

I'd just finished flipping through my twelfth copy of *Elements of Geology* when I noticed Mel standing by the door. When I looked up, she said, "Jack Sprat could eat no fat and his wife could eat no lean."

"Okay." I set the book aside and pushed myself to my feet. I handed her the pink backpack and swung the green one over my shoulder.

We left the room, but Mel stopped at the door across the hall, which Carter had left open a crack.

"Jack Sprat could eat no fat and his wife could eat no lean."

I gritted my teeth.

"Jack Sprat—"

"Okay, okay. I get it. How did you even know he was there?"

She didn't answer. I hadn't expected her to, but when the only person you ever talked to was autistic, you asked a lot of rhetorical questions.

I gave the door a cursory knock as I pushed it open.

"I thought I told you to put a chair—" I broke off abruptly when I spotted Carter.

He was standing with his back to the door. He'd been in the process of pulling on a T-shirt, so his arms were stretched over his head and I could see the muscles of his back. He paused for a second in midmotion when he heard me speak.

Then he jerked the shirt the rest of the way down. "Hey, come on in. Is it time for dinner already?"

"Fourth meal," I corrected automatically. "No one calls it dinner anymore."

But my words sort of echoed unheard in my ears, because my brain was still stuck on the image of his bare back. On the scars.

The skin of his upper back and shoulders was riddled with them, six or seven on each side. All about the size of a nickel and various shades of red and pink, as though some had been healing for months and others were mere days old.

My hand went to my own neck, to a spot not far from my spine where the Ticks had implanted my chip when I'd first arrived at the Farm.

"Thanks for letting me stay," Carter said.

His voice was overly loud, like he was determined to snag my attention from the bizarre scars.

I looked from his shoulder to his face, my eyebrows jacked up in obvious question.

His only response was to reach for the hoodie he'd draped over one of the lab tables. I noticed a mirror sitting on the floor, pointed in the direction of the door. I was about to ask about it when he picked it up and slid it into the pocket of his hoodie.

"Were you watching our door?" I asked.

"Yeah," he admitted with a sheepish grin. "Good thing, too, since you were about to leave without me."

"No, I wasn't," I lied.

"So how's Melanie doing?"

I could take a hint as well as the next girl, so I let him distract me.

"In general? Like, how's your family, I haven't seen you in a while?"

He chuckled, pulling the hoodie over his simple gray T-shirt and then giving the hem a little tug. "Actually I meant, how is she now? You said before if she couldn't handle it, you'd make me leave."

"She's fine," I said tightly. Then I admitted, "Actually, she pretty much insisted we invite you."

"I'll have to thank her."

I hesitated for a moment, then nodded toward the door. "She's waiting out in the hall."

He followed me out the door and we found her standing a few feet away staring down the hall as she bobbed slightly on her toes. She tapped her ring fingers against her thumbs.

It was one of her self-stimulating behaviors. Watching Mel now—trying to see her through the eyes of a stranger—I was more aware than ever of our similarities and our differences. I could do a fair job imitating her unique behaviors, enough so that I could pass for her if I needed to. But she'd never pass for me.

As Carter walked up to her in the hall, I felt that familiar protectiveness well up inside of me. She watched him in that odd, crowlike way she had, head tilted to the side, as if she was looking at him through only one eye and then, only half interested.

Carter just nodded a little and said, "Hey, Mel, you still have your Slinky?"

She'd been wearing it on her wrist like a bracelet. Now, she slipped it off and clutched it in front of her in both hands, thumbs threaded through the center. She held it up to show him and then shifted her hands up and down so it seesawed from one hand to the other.

Carter laughed. "Yeah. I thought so."

Mel's gaze jerked to mine for only an instant. "Red rover, red rover, let Carter come over?"

I knew exactly what she was asking and it made my heart pound. "No," I told her firmly, praying she'd let it drop. "Jack Sprat, remember, Mel?"

"Red rover?" she repeated.

I searched my brain for another nursery rhyme about food. "Hot cross buns. One a penny, two a penny," I said, improvising. "Don't you want a hot cross bun?"

Actually, the idea made even my mouth water a little. Hot food of any kind was pretty rare on the Farm.

"Red rover," she repeated firmly and this time I didn't argue, because she started walking toward the stairs and that was something.

When we reached the stairs, Mel hung back a couple of steps, just like I'd trained her to do, while I opened the fire door, paused, and listened carefully. The stairwell was one of those completely open jobs. If you stood at the top and looked over the railing, you could see down all seven floors, all the way to the basement. I reached into my jeans pocket and pulled out one of the pebbles I kept there, then tossed it down the center shaft of the stairwell. The stone pinged off the railing several times. The clicks and clanks of its trip down echoed up to us and then there was silence. No scuffling of feet or heads peeking out to look up.

"Okay, come on," I said.

Mel shuffled forward. Carter followed at the rear, looking at me with eyebrows raised as if impressed. "Neat trick. You ever hear anything?"

"Once or twice." I kept my voice pitched low. "There are a couple of other staircases in the building we could take. I don't like the idea of being trapped in such a confined space."

It was a risk we took being on the seventh floor. There were a lot of steps between us and freedom. There was always the potential of being trapped in the building, but I figured it was worth it if it meant we could sleep at night without fear of someone breaking into our room. Besides, six flights of stairs wasn't the only thing between us and freedom.

Tromping down the steps behind Mel, I slipped my hand into my pocket and rubbed one of the pebbles between my thumb and forefinger. These tiny stones gave me the illusion of control. It wasn't real, but I clung to it nevertheless. Was that brave or just stupid?

"So, why don't you call it dinner anymore?" Carter asked from behind me.

I shrugged. "I don't know. It just doesn't seem like dinner anymore. Breakfast, lunch, dinner: those words imply the food is different. Like breakfast should be bacon and pancakes. Or eggs. Lunch should be big turkey sandwiches with lettuce and tomatoes, maybe a bowl of soup on the side." My mouth started watering just thinking about it. I nearly made a slurpy sound, then felt my cheeks burn with embarrassment.

"So what would it be?" Carter asked.

"What?" I asked in surprise.

"What kind of soup? If you could have any kind, what would it be?" There was a playful quality to his voice that made me feel . . . I don't know. Grumpy, maybe.

Ignoring his question, I said, "We call it first meal, second meal, third meal, and fourth meal because we don't have any choice about what they feed us and when we eat." *Whether or not we're eating, or being the food.* I didn't say that part aloud. "I don't want to forget that we're prisoners here."

Mel played with her Slinky behind me. I could hear the *sllluuunk, sllluuunk* noise it made when she was nervous.

He held out his hands in a gesture of innocence. "I'm not saying you should forget you're a prisoner. But remembering what you love about life from the Before, that's not a bad thing."

"Great," I chirped. "Then after fourth meal, why don't we sit around the campfire, sing 'Kumbaya,' and braid each other's hair?"

"Hope is a powerful thing."

I snorted with disgust. "Sure. And if this was the movie of the week, then we'd be in great shape. But since—"

"Po—" Mel said abruptly, then struggled to get out the next syllable. "—tato."

Carter and I both wheeled around to look at her. She was standing a few steps below us, not watching us, but staring at the single incandescent bulb in a wire cage that lit the stairwell.

"What?" I asked, more out of surprise than curiosity. I had heard the word, I just couldn't fathom that it had come from her mouth.

Carter's mouth curved into a grin—as though Mel's response had won the argument for him. "So Mel wants potato soup. Me, I'd kill for a cup of gumbo." He nodded, and with the faintest touch to Mel's elbow, he got her walking again and they headed down the stairs. "What kind of chips would you have with that sandwich?"

"Mel's not allowed to have chips!" I called indignantly from the landing, shock still gluing my feet in place. It was a particularly stupid comment to make—because, God, we practically lived on chips at the Farm. So I had to justify it by adding, "She was on a special gluten-free, preservative-free diet. She's not going to know what kind—"

"N-n-not corn chips." Mel forced out the words.

And Carter, damn him, chuckled, glancing over his shoulder. "You coming?"

But I wasn't. I felt trapped there on the stairs, watching them. Carter had launched into a description of what he'd eat—the grilled tuna salad panini his nanny used to make him, dripping with cheddar cheese, crisp dill pickle on the side—as he and Mel hit the next landing and continued on down.

And I still just stood there, feeling . . . God, I didn't know what. Mel had spoken. For the first time in months, Mel had spoken sensible words. As part of a conversation. Without a nursery rhyme in sight. She'd actually responded to a question. Not once, but twice.

I felt my knees wobble beneath me and I sank to the landing. All this time, I'd assumed it was the trauma of living on the Farm that had made her retreat to those early childhood behaviors. But maybe it wasn't the Farm. Maybe it was me.

CHAPTER EIGHT

LILY

An icy wind swept across the quad and by the time we made it to the crush of people around the steps of the dining hall, I was glad for the protection the extra people provided. The doors to the dining hall weren't open yet, but even though it was a few minutes until eight thirty, the mass of Greens edged closer to the doors.

Mel stood close to my side. My little lamb. She had spoken to Carter, but she was still my responsibility. I looked behind me for Carter and felt a trickle of annoyance when I didn't see him immediately. I glanced around and caught a glimpse of him squatting at the edge of the crowd, messing with his boot. There was something furtive about his posture. More annoyed than concerned, I was about to go rein him back in when I heard Mel squawking.

I spun back around to see her cringing away from a group of guys. They probably hadn't meant her any harm, but she was in their way and rather than skirt around her, their group had oozed forward to encompass her. Flinching like an animal being prodded from multiple angles, she seemed panic-stricken, ready to either flee or collapse in on herself.

Carter could fend for himself. I bolted toward Mel, elbowing the guy nearest her. "Hey, give us a little room."

The guy spun on me. He wasn't particularly big, but his expression flashed from disinterested to belligerent the second I touched him. He puffed out his chest. "You wanna eat, wait in line like everyone else."

His buddies had noticed. Noble pack animals that they were, they moved to his side. Sure, I got it. You needed someone at your back. The problem was, when they closed ranks around him, they cut me off from Mel.

"I am in line." I tried for steady and logical, but I could feel Mel's panic. "I'm with her."

One of the pack animals looked back at Mel. "What? You're with that freak?"

I saw what he was going to do as soon as he reached for Mel's arm. I yelled, "Don't touch her!"

Either he didn't hear me or he thought I was making an empty threat.

The second he grabbed her arm, Mel lashed out. Even if her life depended on it, Mel couldn't have launched a purposeful attack, but her panicked flailing did as much damage. She elbowed him in the solar plexus, knocking the wind out of him with a humph. He doubled over and her thrashing fist caught his face in an awkward uppercut.

Two of the other guys launched themselves toward her. Some part of my rational brain knew they were just trying to help their buddy. But the part of my brain that protected Mel, the stressed-out part that had been responsible for her for months, the part that would do anything to keep her safe, didn't care that they were just helping a friend. I thought about the Greens outside the fence. That girl who would die tonight and who'd done less than this. I threw myself into the fray, trying to reach Mel before the Collabs showed up.

My backpack was heavy with gear and I swung it around to

clear a path. I caught one of the guys in his middle and he bent over, clutching his stomach. I ducked under the arm of another guy. I didn't see what Mel did next, but her attacker crumpled to the ground.

Off to the left of us, a scuffle broke out amid rumblings of *hey, watch it*s and *back off, buddy*s. By the time I'd dodged around another guy, I heard the sickening crunch of punches being thrown from several directions. Fights were breaking out all around. It was as if this one scuffle between Mel and the jerk who'd grabbed her arm was a pebble dropped into a pool of water. Her fear, panic, and anger spread through the crowd like ripples from that tiny pebble. Except instead of dissipating them, distance magnified the waves.

I stumbled up a step, looking for Mel. But the crowd seemed to have expanded. There was a wall of fighting, grunting kids between us. As if that wasn't bad enough, someone bumped into her and the Slinky went flying out of her hands. I was too far away. Her face was bone white, her eyes darting wildly.

I had no idea how this fight had broken out so quickly. We Greens were normally so passive. But the rage that simmered beneath our still surfaces suddenly boiled. Instead of gently gurgling, it spewed out of everyone. We'd turned on ourselves.

Guys were fighting on either side of Mel. She opened and closed her mouth in a silent scream. Then it hit me. She was calling my name. She just couldn't get the words out past her terror. I ducked low to avoid being hit and crawled along the ground amid the kicking feet and stomping boots. Someone's foot caught me in the ribs. And I saw the gray metal Slinky roll away. I scrambled after it, snatching it off the ground an instant before it got crushed under a boot. I struggled to my feet, shoving people aside as I did.

I scanned the area for Mel and finally found her, maybe five feet away. She was recoiling from the fight around her and every step she made took her farther away from me. Between us was a massive guy pounding the crap out of someone much smaller. As I watched, he grabbed the kid by the front of his shirt and picked him up, raising him so high his legs dangled feet above the ground. I knew instantly the bully was going to throw the kid. Right onto Mel. She was too terrified to move. Even though the kid was small, she'd crumple beneath his weight.

It all flashed through my mind, but I couldn't do anything to stop it. I was still too far away. I *had* to protect her, but I'd never get there in time.

Then, as if out of nowhere, someone launched himself at the bully. It was another smaller kid. Maybe one of the victim's friends, I don't know. I didn't even see what he'd done at first, but the big bully howled in pain, then crumpled and—as fast as he'd appeared—the second kid vanished back into the crowd. He left the bright red handle of a screwdriver sticking out of the bully's back.

The kid he'd been about to throw at Mel scuttled away. The bully reached a fumbling hand around to his back, trying to reach the handle.

"Help me!" he cried. "Get it out!"

"Don't touch it!" I yelled. "It'll gush. Leave it there."

I didn't wait around to see if anyone followed my directions, but threw myself past him to get to Mel.

I reached out and grabbed her hand, pulling her close. It was the only time she let me touch her, when she was more afraid of being too far away than she was of being too close. The instant my hand touched hers, relief coursed through me. For once, she looked me right in the eye and her hand even tightened a little, before she grabbed the Slinky from me and clutched it in both hands. I watched the panic fade from her eyes as she regained control of herself. Maybe I couldn't protect her from everything, but as long as we were together, I would try.

The stabbing had been like a bucket of icy water splashed over the crowd. The people nearest all backed away, their horror visible on their faces. The bully was still screaming for help. An instant later Collabs rushed in. They appeared everywhere at once. On the edges of the crowd, I could see them tranqing the few people who were still brawling. A pair of Collabs with a med kit shoved their way through the crowd to the wounded guy.

He saw them coming and tried to bolt, ruthlessly shoving people out of the way, but his wound slowed him down. A second later, one of the Collabs aimed his tranq rifle at the guy and fired. He screamed out one last plea for help and then crumpled to the ground.

For a moment, I watched as they laid him out and popped open the med kit. I could hear the *sllluuunk, sllluuunk, sllluuunk* of Mel reassuring herself her Slinky was okay.

One of the Collabs got out bandages. We didn't stay around to see what happened. I pulled Mel away when the other reached for the screwdriver. I guided Mel through the crowd, trying to squelch the sickening feeling in my gut.

Those Collabs were only stabilizing the guy. They were most likely patching him up so they could tether him with the others outside the fence tonight. They weren't trying to save his life. They just didn't want to waste the blood.

I felt revulsion rise up in my gut, but I swallowed back my vomit. How could they stand to do it? How could they live with betraying the rest of us day after day?

I glanced around, looking for Carter, but he was nowhere to be seen. For a second, my brain raced. Mel was still nervous. We'd lost Carter. Someone had been stabbed and Collabs were tranqing Greens.

I blew out a long breath.

Okay. Yes, this was bad. But Mel and I had made it out. Surely Carter would, too. He'd avoid the worst of the fight and find us later. I didn't let myself consider the possibility that he'd get taken in by the Collabs. He was smarter than that.

I raised my hand and waved a hooked finger in front of Mel's face. "Look at me, Mel." She just whimpered. I waved the finger again, narrowing my own attention down to just her. Like she was the only person in the world. "Look at me."

Her eyes found mine but she wasn't really looking at me. *Slllluuunk.*

"It's okay," I said. "Everything is going to be okay."

Somehow saying the words aloud, I could almost believe it was true. "It'll be okay," I said again. "Everything is okay, Mel."

Her eyes finally focused on mine. *Slllluuunk.* The panic on her face faded to just a frown. "Little Bo Peep lost her sheep."

Okay. That was a new one. Usually I was Mary.

"No, we're together, Mel. I didn't lose you."

She jerked her hand out of mine, a sure sign she was frustrated. "Little Bo Peep lost her sheep."

"I didn't lose anything. I— Oh, you mean Carter?"

Her head bobbed in a nod. "She doesn't know where to find him."

Relief bubbled up in a giggle. Carter was the least likely sheep in the world. I gave Mel a quick hug, even though I knew she'd hate it.

"Carter can take care of himself," I assured her. "Plus, he knows where to find us back at the science lab. He'll be just fine."

Slllluuuuuunk.

That one seemed extra long and I wondered if Mel was reassuring herself or me.

Moments later, the Collabs had suppressed the fight and hauled away the troublemakers. The doors to the dining hall opened and the crowd started filing in.

Even though things had calmed down, I kept close to Mel and looked around for Carter as the Collab scanned the chip in my neck and ushered me through the turnstile. Mel came in right after and together we headed for the food line, where more Collabs were handing out trays of junk food. I still didn't see Carter, but I buried my fears deep. He'd show up back at the science building.

The dining hall was packed. Since I'd dragged Mel down the stairs and out of the way, we were some of the last people to make it in to the cafeteria. I figured Carter had gotten in with the first group and been shuttled back out before we even got our food. Unless there was something else keeping him away. Had I been right to suspect him?

I didn't let myself worry until Mel and I made it back to the science lab and he still hadn't shown up. It was nearly curfew already. Five hours ago, he'd all but begged for a place to stay for the night. I didn't want to think about who—or what—might have kept him from making it back to safety.

Carter may not seem like a very likely sheep, but I'd definitely lost him.

* *

The first curfew bell rang at ten thirty and others would follow ten minutes apart until just before curfew when three chimes would ring every minute for the ten minutes before the final long series of bells. Mel and I never needed all those warning bells. We were always back in the storage closet long before curfew, the chair wedged under the doorknob. Not tonight.

Tonight, an hour from curfew, I sat out in the classroom, perched on one of the lab desks, legs dangling off the side, the shiv resting across my knees. Waiting for Carter. Wondering if we should leave now and find some other place to spend the night.

I figured I'd give him ten more minutes and then we were going. If he hadn't made it back by then, either he'd been taken in by the Collabs or he'd turned us in to the Dean. Only one thing had kept us here this long: the possibility that he'd betrayed us just didn't make any sense. If he had seen the pills, he would have found out where we lived and then the second I'd left him alone, he would have snuck off to find a Collab. He wouldn't have waited all afternoon and then done it now. Something must have happened to him. Or was I only telling myself that because I wanted to believe there was someone here on the Farm I could really trust?

Mel sat cross-legged on the floor at the front of the room, where floor-to-ceiling whiteboards covered the entire wall. A pack of dry-erase markers sat open on the floor beside her Slinky while she drew long rows of dots on the board. She didn't draw the measures or the ledger lines or even the stems. Just the note heads. Her scribbling wouldn't make sense to anyone but her, but I had no doubt in her mind it was exquisite. She hummed along softly as she drew. It might have been Beethoven. Or perhaps Chopin. Sometimes I got them confused even though they sounded nothing alike.

Then, over Mel's humming, I heard a sound from the hall.

"Shh," I whispered, but she'd stopped humming and had her head cocked to the side, listening, too. Listening to the tentative shuffling of footsteps.

Carter had made it back.

I hopped off the lab table and dashed for the door, but I stopped before opening it. I thought about the little mirror I'd seen Carter using. If Mel and I were going to make it through the next few days while we ironed out our plans, I'd need to get one like it. For now, I just held my breath and waited to see who it was. It didn't sound like Carter.

Then a voice called out. "Lily?"

I jerked to a stop, my heart in my throat. It wasn't Carter. It was Joe.

I cracked open the door and peered out. He'd stopped a couple of yards down the hall, in a shadowed spot where the lightbulb had flickered out a few months ago. His hair was pulled back in a scraggly ponytail, and he wore a gimme cap. Through the shadows, I thought I saw a backpack on his shoulder.

"Joe? What are you doing here?" I'd never seen Joe outside of his shop, not even for meals. I had no idea where he lived, but it had always seemed like he was immune to the rules the rest of us had to follow.

"Hey, Lily. Can I, you know, come in?"

"Sure," I said automatically as I stepped clear of the door for him to pass. "Yeah."

He hurried forward, casting furtive looks back over his shoulder and hugging the wall as he did so. I followed him into the room. The second I was inside, he sent one last look down the hall and then closed the door behind me.

Joe looked from me to Mel as he slung a backpack off his shoulder and let it drop. Then he sank to the ground beside it.

I wanted to ask if he'd seen Carter, but the fact that Joe had come here meant we had bigger problems.

Joe let his head fall back against the wall and breathed out again, eyes closed, as though the walk from his shop to here had been long and hard.

"I brought your stuff." He gave the bag a nudge of his knee without opening his eyes.

"O-okay," I said. I picked up a backpack and carried it to the nearest lab table. It was heavier than it looked. Mel stood slowly and walked over as I unzipped it.

I pulled out one item after another. A lightweight down coat was shoved on top. Beneath it, a mess kit in a mesh bag, with a little skillet, plate, cup, and silverware. I'd had one like it for camping trips back when I was in Girl Scouts. Beneath that were gloves. At the bottom of the pack, I could see a tightly coiled sleeping bag. Just like I'd asked for. Probably only one, but it was more than I'd dare hope for. I'd needed the coat. Everything else was just gravy.

I looked up to find Mel hovering nearby. She wasn't looking at Joe or me, or at the bag, for that matter. She'd set her Slinky on the counter beside the bag and her hands were fluttering, birdlike, above the slate countertop. Like nervous finches who couldn't decide where to land, maybe because their brains were no bigger than a pea or maybe because they'd seen a cat slinking across the ground.

I shoved the things back into the bag and tugged on the zipper. "What's up, Joe?"

Joe's eyes flickered open. "Lily. You and Mel gotta leave. Right now."

"What?"

"If you're going to get off the Farm, you need to leave tonight."

"What?" I asked again stupidly. Yes, something was obviously up. But where was this coming from? I dropped to my knees beside him. "What's going on? What's wrong?"

He nodded toward the backpack. "That's what you asked for, right?"

"More or less, but—"

"Then you can leave tonight." He clutched my hand. "You can leave right now."

"I—" I looked from him to the bag and back again. "Joe, I'm not going anywhere until you explain what's going on. Are you hurt?"

He drew in a raspy breath and shook his head. "Doesn't matter. What matters is you and Mel getting out. You have a plan, right? A good plan?"

I ignored his question and asked my own again. "Are you hurt?"

"It's nothing." But he winced as he took a step forward and held his hand protectively across his middle.

I crossed to him and gingerly raised the ragged hem of his hoodie to reveal his stomach. His skin was bright red and blotchy. Like someone had pounded his kidneys. The left side of his rib cage was already starting to bruise.

He grabbed my hand and clenched it tight. "You're not going to let this go, are you?"

"No, I'm not going to let this go. It looks like someone beat the crap out of you. Who did this to you?" I ran a finger lightly across his ribs and he winced.

"Who do you think?"

"Collabs." I muttered the word like a curse.

I went to my backpack and pulled out our precious first aid kit and brought it back to his side.

"A couple of them came in during third meal, not long after you left. I heard them talking."

"But you must hear them talking all the time." I flipped open the kit and looked inside. "They wouldn't beat you up over that."

"Yeah. It wasn't them. It was the other guy." He broke off and held his breath as he shifted into a different position. "There's no time for this. We need to get you and Mel out of here."

I nearly groaned in frustration. "Joe, I'm not going anywhere until I understand what's going on." My fingers hesitated over a pack of ibuprofen. Then I noticed Joe's shallow, labored breathing. I ripped the foil pack open and dumped the pills into my hand before I could change my mind. "Start at the beginning. Tell me everything."

I didn't think I could bear it if this was all because he was trying to help Mel and me.

"That's just it. There's not time to tell you everything. If you're going to get out of here, you need to go tonight."

"Tonight? We can't go at night. That's when the Ticks will be out. If we're going, we're leaving early in the morning, when they should be asleep."

He shook his head even though it seemed to hurt. "No. If you leave tonight, you should be safe. The Ticks just . . . they would have just . . ."

Joe stumbled over his words. My stomach gave a queasy twist as I realized what he was saying. There had been Greens staked out at dusk tonight. The Greens I'd seen on the south side of campus. The Ticks would have already killed them. So any Ticks around the Farm would be full and maybe even sleepy, since the Greens had been tranqed.

Joe must have seen the understanding in my eyes, because he pushed on. "If you're going, you need to go tonight. Those Collabs I heard talking, they all work over in the admin building. They know things."

"What kind of things?" I shoved aside the thought of the

Greens. They were already dead and I had to focus on keeping Mel safe.

"Some new guy arrived at the Dean's office a couple of days ago. Some guy who's even more powerful than the Dean. Some real badass."

"Two days ago?" I interrupted him to ask. That was when Carter would have arrived. It was like a nickel slot going off in my head. *Ding, ding, ding, ding.* "Did he bring Greens with him?"

"I think so. Maybe, I don't know. The thing is, he's beefing up the security system."

"Beefing it up?" I asked in disbelief. "How could security be any stronger than it is now?"

"I don't know. Do I look like I know about all that military crap?"

"No." But Carter did.

This badass that Joe was talking about, Carter must have come with him. So, Carter was a Collab. Or worse.

But Carter had had us completely at his mercy. If he was going to bring us to the Dean, he would have done it then. So where was he?

Joe was still talking and I forced my attention back to his words.

"Mostly I hear the Collabs complain about it. But they said this guy Sebastian has been traveling across the country. He's been to other Farms. He figures out how people are getting out. He fixes the problems. And then no one gets out."

I pulled an Ace bandage from the med kit, my mind racing, trying to make sense of Joe's words. But the pieces weren't fitting together right. Mel had come to stand beside me and I heard the *sllluuunk* of her Slinky.

"I don't understand," I protested, opening the package that held the bandage. I had no idea if wrapping his ribs in bandages would help, but I'd seen people do it in movies. Medical knowledge via TV was probably worse than WebMD, but it was the best I had. "How do these Collabs know what he does in other places?"

I looked up at Joe. He blinked. "Yeah. I mean, that's what I thought, too. They're just talking, right? Just bullshit. But then this other guy comes in."

"Hold up your shirt, okay?" I wrapped the bandage around his chest once, only to have it sag. I considered it for a second, then said, "Exhale."

He blew out a slow breath that ended in a hiss.

I tightened the bandage and asked, "This other guy, was that the guy who hit you?"

"Yeah. Their . . . um, what do you call it?"

"Their superior? Like their captain?"

"Yeah. He comes in." Joe winced again as I tightened the bandage. "He noticed that I was listening. He gave them a hard time. Said they could get kicked out of the Collab program for talking about stuff like that in front of Greens. He sent them back to admin and once they left, he did this to me."

Joe brought his hand to his face and brushed his thumb across the scratch on his cheek. "So I figure, he must not have wanted me to know about it. The guy was serious. Said if I told anyone what I'd heard, he'd flag my chip. Up my testing rate."

"Oh." I swallowed. "I didn't even know you had a chip."

"Everyone has a chip. Mine just says that my blood's no good. It says not to take any donations."

"Oh." I sank back onto my heels, wondering what my chip said.

A faster testing rate meant more donations. Mel and I had been donating a lot lately.

I didn't want to think about that, so I asked, "So why are you telling me this now?"

Joe looked me in the eye and for the first time since he'd walked in the room, I felt my doubts slip away. Like he was being completely and totally honest. "Because, Lily, you're the smartest person I know. If you think you've figured a way out, then you probably have."

I studied him a moment before glancing over at Mel. She bobbed her head in a way that anyone else might take as random movement, but that I knew was nodding. Increasing his testing rate would essentially be the same death sentence Mel and I were trying to avoid. The Collabs would just take donations for a while, but one of these days, they'd test his blood and decide his hormones were within the right range. Then they'd take him off the Farm. If I was just paranoid, he'd go free. If I was right, he'd be slaughtered and fed to the Ticks. If he'd come here to tell me this instead of keeping it to himself, it could only mean one thing.

"You want to come with us," I guessed.

But Joe shook his head. "I want you to bring someone else, too."

"Someone else?" My voice rose with my surprise. Even though there wasn't anyone nearby to overhear me, I dropped back to my knees and leaned closer. Almost whispering. "Who would you want me to get out?"

His gaze shifted away from mine. Though I'd have sworn I'd never seen Joe express any emotion as personal as embarrassment, he blushed. "McKenna."

"McKenna Wells? From school?"

The pink of Joe's embarrassment darkened to red anger. "She's not—"

"If I could get off the Farm, why on earth would I bring her with us? Why would you ask me to?"

"She's a friend," Joe said flatly.

"McKenna isn't a friend to anyone but herself." She was the kind of person who used others to get what she wanted. That had been true long before we came to the Farm. McKenna had gone to school with Joe and me in the Before. She'd been head cheerleader and resident mean girl at Richardson High. I wasn't surprised when she was the first person I knew to get pregnant on the Farm. And she was one of the girls who really flaunted it.

"What'd she do? Trade sex for the promise that you could get her out? 'Cause I don't think you cut a very good deal."

Joe didn't say anything. He just let me talk and pace. Mel watched my progress as I moved around the room. Her eyes never left me and I could tell by the way she twisted her hands that I was freaking her out.

"I thought you were smarter than that, Joe." Mel and I didn't really have enough food saved up for an extra person, but if helping us had gotten him in trouble in the first place, then I had to offer. "Look, I can get you out. Maybe. But not—"

"I'm not leaving without McKenna. And if it's her or me, then bring her."

"Don't be an idiot. Whatever she said—"

"She's pregnant," Joe interrupted.

"Well, duh. She's been showing off that belly of hers for months. She's so proud that all those pregnancy hormones make her unappetizing to Ticks. Like it's some kind of honor—"

"It might be mine."

"Oh." I snapped my mouth shut.

Suddenly my mind raced back to the moment in the store today when I made that comment about what would happen to the babies once the first Breeders started giving birth.

Yeah, I'd thought about it, but I hadn't *really* thought about it. Not in terms of an actual baby. The progeny of someone I knew. I figured the babies were going to be raised to be more Greens, but I didn't know if they would stay with their Breeder moms or not. For all I knew, they'd be raised in cages like veal. And that wasn't even the worst thing that could happen. My stomach gave a sick little flip. This was why the Breeders disgusted me so much. Sure, they'd bought themselves a few more months of life, but at what cost?

No wonder Joe had gone white and acted so strange this afternoon when I'd made the comment.

"I can't leave her." His words poured out. "You think this is the first time someone has offered to take me with them? It isn't. But I can't just walk away from her and the baby. I never really thought anyone would make it out. But if anyone can, it's you and Mel. And if those Collabs were right and this is our last chance to get out, then we need to go now."

I just stared at him for a long moment, my mind spinning as I ticked through all the people I was now responsible for. First Mel. Then Carter. Now Joe and McKenna Wells. If we did make it out, it would be like a damn parade.

I glanced over at Mel, hoping for a second opinion on the matter. But she kept seesawing her Slinky and didn't look any more enthusiastic about it than I felt. She said nothing, but started humming faintly, just so I could barely hear it. Maybe I was wrong, but to me, it sounded like the theme to *Jeopardy*. Very helpful.

"It's probably not yours," I said. Most of the Breeders slept with a lot of guys, trying to get pregnant; mostly with Collabs, but some slept with Greens, too.

"But it might be."

There wasn't hope in his voice. More like a flat resignation.

Which was probably about how I sounded when I finally said, "Okay. You can come. Both of you. I'm not dragging McKenna's ass halfway across the country by myself."

CHAPTER NINE

MEL

Carter always brings Dubble Bubble, which is pink without being noisy, and tastes like math.

Lily's music is more melodious when he's near. It always has been. Not that she'd notice. Silly Lily.

At first I think Carter was what was missing, that having him here will make the plan work. Maybe he can play the piano solo that makes the song so memorable, but then we lost him. The crowd was so loud. A riot of random noise that became a riot of fear I couldn't control. Then Carter was gone and the music unraveled. The melody exploding like champagne flutes in high C.

The clock is ticking now, faster than the metronome.

Joe, who came and dropped his bombshell. He's both more and less than what he seems. Playing one song, singing another, with the drumbeat out of time.

What wasn't right before is worse now. Even if I could have gotten Rachmaninoff to play, this is too soon. It would be wrong even if it wasn't for Joe.

Now we're stuck with Joe and his Bombshell.

Joe leaves and Lily packs, packs, packs. Waiting for him to come back. Waiting for Carter. Going to meet Joe. And her.

I try to tell Lily how wrong it all is. How the plan doesn't sing. The best I can do is Yankee Doodle Dandy. Which doesn't help.

And might not even have been Benedict Arnold's war. Math and bubbles were always my strong suit, not history, traitors, and macaroni.

Not that it matters. Lily isn't listening. Silly Lily. Or silly Mel, since I'm the one trying to make her understand. When the bags are packed and Carter's still gone, I'm the one who asks.

Red rover, red rover, let Lily come over.

CHAPTER TEN

LILY

The three chimes echoed through the frosty night air announcing that final curfew was ten minutes off. Joe and McKenna were nowhere to be seen. Mel and I had waited as long as we could. The plan had been to meet them beside the north wall of the gymnasium where we now sat. When Joe had left to go collect McKenna, he'd sworn he only needed twenty minutes to get her and meet us there. Then we would all leave together. That had been thirty minutes ago.

The thought sent a bead of sweat trickling down my spine, despite the icy wind that beat against the thin denim of my jacket, straight through my many layers of clothes. Mel's humming didn't help. It was some relentlessly cheerful tune I didn't have room in my brain to try to place.

I'd given her the Valium right before leaving the room. Was that why she seemed so upbeat? The good news: she calmly followed me without complaint. The bad news: the song was grating my already frayed nerves.

The second set of chimes followed thirty seconds after the first. Joe and McKenna weren't going to show. Less than an hour ago, Joe had been desperate to get off the Farm, but now, nothing. Something must have happened to them. I'd already given up Carter for lost.

I stood, pulling Mel to her feet. "We gotta go."

For once, Mel seemed to understand exactly what I was saying. She stuck close to my side, not pulling away when I wrapped a hand around her biceps. Not even stumbling as we ducked out of the shadow of the gymnasium and crossed a bare, moonlit swath of grass toward the nine-foot-high chain-link fence that surrounded the football field, cutting it off from the rest of the Farm. There was another fence on the other side of the football field. We'd deal with that one when we got to it.

I hated how screwed up our plan had gotten. In a perfect world, we would have left the Farm just before dawn, when the fence was still off but the Ticks were already back at their nests for the day. I didn't know where they went when the sun was up, but I knew they were nocturnal and we never saw or heard them then. Leaving at dawn would give us all day to find a working car.

This new plan scared me. Leaving at night was dangerous. Getting to a car would be harder. Even though I'd spotted several in the deserted side streets near campus, I just assumed if there were cars near the Farm, there would also be ones on the other side of the river. Could I get one started? Maybe. Showing me how to hot-wire a car had been my crazy uncle Rodney's idea of great postgame Thanksgiving Day fun, much to my mother's dismay. But that had been several years ago. Sure, I'd looked it up in the Farm's library last month to review, but watching, reading, and doing were very different things. When the time came, would I remember how?

Pushing that concern aside, I focused on keeping Mel moving, hugging the fence until we'd reached a sprawling oak. The fence came within three or four feet of the trunk and the night was bright enough that the tree's massive limbs offered some shadowy protection where they dipped close to the razor-wire-topped fence.

The stench of rotting garbage filled the air this close to the stadium. The Collabs dumped trash in the football stadium and the air seemed thick with the scent of their lazy neglect. But at least it overpowered the scent of death from the corpses left tethered beyond the Farm's southern fence.

The lights on this end of campus had burned out long ago and the plump moon cast inky shadows across the weed-choked landscape. Something scuttled through the grass along the fence. Probably a rat. A shudder ran up my spine, but I shoved aside my revulsion.

I looked at Mel. "What do you say, Mel? Time to go?"

She didn't look me in the eye, but muttered, "Red rover, red rover. Red rover, red rover."

"Okay." I squeezed her hand, suppressing my alarm at how icy her fingers felt. A norther was coming through. Like our timing wasn't bad enough as it was. "Red rover."

Yeah, we had the gloves and coat now, but I didn't want her wearing them during our escape. They were both packed in the bottom of Mel's pink bag. Maybe I was being paranoid, but it seemed too early for her to wear them anyway. Like maybe they would jinx us.

Mel's mouth twisted into something that looked almost like a smile.

I tugged my collar up against the cold and then blew quickly on my fingers to warm them. Warning chimes rang in the distance, but I ignored them. I'd lost track of how many had rung. And it didn't matter anyway. It was too late to turn back now. After flexing them a few times, I pulled my prized gardening shears out of my pocket. I just hoped I could use them to cut a hole in the chain-link fence big enough for Mel and me to slip through.

I hoped a lot of things. If we did get out, I prayed we wouldn't run into any Ticks. We didn't have much to fight them off with if we did. A few weeks ago, I'd thought about making modified Molotov cocktails to bring with us. After six months surrounded by chemistry textbooks and flammable chemicals, figuring out how to do it with what I had on hand was easy. I'd chickened out because I didn't want Mel around anything that could blow up or burn her chemically.

Our mom used to have a saying: don't give anything to Mel you wouldn't hand to a toddler. So I'd scrapped the cocktails. Which left us defenseless, except for the gardening shears and the shiv. I tried to ignore the fact that both could kill Mel just as easily as they could a Tick.

We crouched low in the shadows and I got to work.

Most of the Farm was surrounded by two rows of twelve-foot-tall chain-link fences topped with razor wire. Here on the north side of campus, the abandoned football stadium overlooked the swollen Red River. There was an extra row of fencing between the stadium and the rest of campus. Beyond that, on the other side of the stadium, was the fence that was turned off each night. I started running through all those ifs in my head again. If we could get through this fence and the next. If we could swim across the river. If we could find a car. If we could make it to Uncle Rodney's. If, if, if, if.

I clamped the blades of the pruning shears around one of the links and squeezed the handles, using all my strength to cut through the ifs. Finally I felt it yield to pressure then snap. One down.

Beside me, Mel rocked forward and back on her toes. "Red rover, red rover. Red rover, red rover."

"Yeah, Mel," I muttered, moving on to the next link. "Soon."

By the time the long series of chimes signaled curfew, my arms were burning from exertion and sweat dripped down my temple, but I'd cut through a column of links about two feet tall. I wrapped my hands around the bottom corner, ignored the protests of my trembling muscles, and pulled upward, curling the edges of the fence apart.

As I stood back to survey my progress, I heard laughter coming from the other side of the athletic hall. *Shit.*

A beam from a flashlight moved across the ground. A Collab. And he was coming this way.

How long ago had the last bell chimed? I couldn't remember. I'd been concentrating too hard on cutting through the fence. I shot one last glance at the chain link. The gap wasn't big enough to fit through. And if the Collab saw it, we'd be totally screwed. I shoved the fence back in place as best I could, then I grabbed Mel's hand and pulled her away from the hole in the fence.

I tucked the pruning shears in my back waistband and tugged my jacket over them. We'd only made it a few steps when the Collab called out.

"Hey, you there!"

I ignored him, keeping my shoulders hunched as I shifted course and headed for the relative safety of the quad. Maybe I could claim I hadn't heard the curfew chimes.

A hand grabbed my shoulder and whipped me around.

The Collab shone a flashlight in my eyes, making it impossible to see his features. Not that it mattered. One Collab was as bad as the next.

"We're going to our dorm right now," I said, hating the tremor in my voice. I shouldered in front of Mel and prayed the Collab wouldn't notice anything strange about her.

"It's after curfew," the Collab said. He ran the beam of his flashlight down the length of my body. He chuckled. "You two could be in serious trouble."

"We're just running a little late," I said, taking a step back. Mel stepped with me.

The Collab moved his light onto her, the beam traveling up the length of her body to her face. Then he barked with laughter. "Cool. Twins."

His laughter made my stomach lurch with revulsion. Like most Collabs, he was soft around the middle from too much food and not enough exercise. Still, he was bigger than me. I took another step backward, but this time, Mel didn't move. A glance behind me told me we'd been backed up against the side wall of the gymnasium.

"You know," the Collab was saying, "I could bring you up to the Dean's office." Instead of threatening, his voice held a nasty undercurrent of suggestion. What a skeeze. "But I bet we can work something out."

He swung his tranq gun off his shoulder. He held it one-handed, his stance lazily aggressive as he pressed the barrel to my neck then nudged it downward to part the zipper of my jacket. He flashed another stomach-churning smile. "I have always wondered about twins."

In any sane world, a guy like this—all sweat and blubber—wouldn't have a shot with one girl, let alone two. But it seemed unwise to point this out.

He looked at Mel and his expression soured. "What's wrong with her? She doesn't look like a Breeder."

Before he could look at her too long, I knocked the barrel away from my chest. "Get away from me."

Clearly the Collab wasn't used to people talking back to him.

"Isn't it bad enough you betrayed humanity by collaborating to feed us to the Ticks?" I stepped forward, not out of bravery, but so he wouldn't have the room to raise his tranq rifle again. Surprise was the only advantage I had. The words poured out of me in a flood of uncorked resentment. "The rest of us Greens have no rights. But we have to put up with this crap, too?"

I got right in his face. He stumbled back a step. By now, adrenaline was pumping through my veins like battery acid. Fueled by six months of fear and one hell of a bad day, I reached up and shoved his shoulder, praying he wouldn't notice that I was reaching for the pruning shears with my other hand.

But before I could grab them, the Collab overcame his shock.

He was in better shape than I would have thought, because he moved fast, grabbing my wrist and giving it a sharp twist. It felt like he was going to wrench my arm right out of my shoulder. I dropped to my knees with a yelp of pain but he kept twisting, pushing me face-first into the ground. He rammed his knee in between my shoulder blades. The sharp tip of the garden shears dug into my back. He was practically sitting on them. How could he not feel them beneath his leg?

I bucked against him, kicking with my legs. He raised up to flip me over. I let him, hoping I could get an arm back to the shears, but he was back down on me in an instant, his knees pinning my shoulders to the ground.

The Collab tilted his crotch forward so it was right in my face. He laughed. "I do like this."

This close, his body odor clogged my nose, closing off my throat. I turned my head and saw Mel standing just a few feet away. Anyone else would have run for it. Not Mel. She was still staring up at the night sky, her gaze blank and out of focus, her head tilted just so, as if straining to hear the upper register of some distant tune. Why the hell had I given her that Valium?

Beyond the heavy thrust of my thundering heart, I could faintly hear the song she was humming. And I finally placed it. Beethoven's Ninth Symphony. She'd finally reached the "Ode to Joy" part at the end. What a great time for her sense of humor to pop up.

Again I tried to kick up, but my legs didn't come anywhere near close to his back. With his knees on my shoulders and his legs on either side of my chest, both my arms were pinned. My left arm was almost beneath me. I could almost reach the gardening shears, but I needed more room to move. I bucked again, but the guy was like an anvil planted on my chest.

I thought of how Carter and I had fought just that afternoon. Carter was bigger than this guy. Stronger. He must have been taking it easy on me this afternoon. He'd been holding back, trying to keep me safe. This guy didn't care if he hurt me. Maybe he'd even relish it. Suddenly panic flooded me. I was in serious trouble unless I could get my hand on those gardening shears.

His grimy fingers were mere inches from my eyes. His fingers were chubby. His nails rimmed with dirt or grease. He was stronger. He was armed. And—Christ—he was reaching for his belt buckle.

I blinked, trying to force down my fear so I could think.

He'd have to lift his hips off me to get his pants down—again, I had to choke back my fear. If I could get to the shears, I'd have to stab the Collab. If he didn't make too much noise, I could steal his tranq rifle and shoot him. If he was out long enough for me to finish the work on the fence then maybe we had a chance. My list of ifs just got considerably longer.

I fumbled at my back, feeling for the pruning shears. My palms were sweaty and slipped on the handle, but I finally gripped them tightly as he yanked on his zipper.

"Let her go!" a voice called out.

I felt a flood of relief. Carter. Thank God.

The Collab and I both froze. The harsh beam from a flashlight cut across the darkness. For an instant it shone straight into my eyes, then it jerked away, bobbing up and down as he jogged toward us.

My attacker left his belt buckle dangling as he reached for his rifle. With the light slashing across my face, I could see nothing, only hear the steady thud-thud of Carter's footfalls as he ran toward us. The Collab started to stand and I scrambled out from beneath him. He grabbed a hunk of my hair before I could get away.

"Oh. It's you." The Collab holding me let go of his rifle.

"Yeah. It's me," Carter said.

I waited for him to attack the Collab, but he didn't make a move and didn't even look in my direction.

Fear trickled down my spine. How the hell would this Collab know him? And why wasn't Carter helping me? Was Carter a Collab?

Then the flashlight scanned my face. I pinched my eyes shut, willing them to adapt quickly to the dark. The afterimage of the Maglite bulb flashed on my retinas. When I opened my eyes, the first thing I saw was the glossy black boots of a collaborator.

Yep. Carter was a Collab.

CHAPTER ELEVEN

LILY

"What's going on here?" Carter asked.

My brain struggled to make the puzzle pieces fit. Again I wondered, if he was a Collab, why hadn't he brought me in when he'd had the chance earlier?

Unlike this first Collab's, Carter's uniform was pressed and clean. His boots were polished to gleaming. I still couldn't see his face, but his blond hair shone in the moonlight. From this angle he looked as crisply sinister as the Hitler Youth I'd seen pictures of in my history book.

Beside this guy, my original attacker looked scruffy and slovenly. A junkyard dog compared to a trained Rottweiler.

Scruffy floundered for a minute, before protesting, "I was just having a little fun."

"Is she a Breeder?"

Scruffy stood up, keeping his fist clenched in my hair so he pulled me to my knees. "What does it matter? They were out after curfew."

"It matters. Let her go." Carter the Nazi sounded like he was used to barking orders and having them followed. When Scruffy didn't jump to obey, Carter swung the tranq gun off his shoulder in a gesture that was both casual and threatening at the same time. "If she didn't volunteer to be a Breeder, you can't touch her. That's the law."

Scruffy's hold on my hair tightened. I could have fought against it, but I held still, conserving my energy, trying to fight off the residual panic from Scruffy's first attack.

"Whatever," Scruffy slurred before he shoved me away, sending me sprawling on the ground before Carter's gleaming black boots. "Nobody pays attention to that kind of thing."

"They do now. Get back to your duty station."

"What are you gonna do with them? 'Cause there's two, ya know. We could both—"

"I'm taking them to the Dean's office." Nazi Carter shifted his tranq rifle so it pointed right at Scruffy's chest. "It wouldn't be out of my way to bring you along."

Scruffy stumbled back, bringing up both of his hands in a sign of submission. "N-no way, man. The Dean's office?" His voice cracked on the words. "I was just having a little fun. They were only out after curfew."

"Which is almost as serious as being away from your duty post."

Scruffy turned and ran before I even had a chance to scramble to my feet.

"Get up," Carter ordered with a gesture of his rifle.

"I am."

Carter watched Scruffy retreating. I'd just straightened up and was rolling my shoulder with a wince as Scruffy rounded the corner of the gymnasium and disappeared from sight. I opened my mouth, but before I could demand some answers from Carter, he pulled me into his arms. He just squeezed me—really tight—for a second. I could feel his face in my hair and thought I heard him mutter a curse. And then he let me go, taking a big step back. His expression was blank and distant.

What the hell?

Shaking off my confusion, I reached for Mel's hand. She clutched it so tight I expected my bones to crack. "You should have run," I whispered, but she ducked her head and shook it, her fingers slipping through her hair, making her look even more like a wild animal.

"Red rover, red rover. Red rover, red rover. Red rover, red rover."

"I know," I said, trying to soothe her. I had the crazy urge to pull her to me and stroke her hair. To just hold her tight. But I knew she'd hate all that touching. I needed it more than she did.

"Is she okay?" Carter asked. "She seems a little out of it."

"She'll be fine. I gave her a Valium before we left the room. I didn't want her to freak out."

He raised his eyebrows, looking impressed.

I didn't wait for him to comment, but asked, "What's going on? Where did you get—"

"Come on," Carter urged. "Let's get out of here before even more Collabs show up."

He grabbed my elbow and started walking, leading me—and Mel along with me—back toward the shadows of the gymnasium. I automatically fell into step beside him, staggering to keep up with his brisk pace. But it felt good to move. Adrenaline was pumping through my veins and it was either move or curl into a trembling fetal ball.

"What's going on? Have you become a Collab? Is that where you were all evening?" The stream of questions came pouring out. "When you disappeared at fourth meal and then didn't show up back at the science building, I was sure you'd been taken to the Dean's office."

Carter turned to face me, giving his head a little shake to flip his long bangs out of his eyes. Standing out on the open lawn, in the light of the nearly full moon, I could see him almost as clearly as if we were back in the fluorescent lights of the science lab. He'd followed my advice and shaven, so that those long scraggly bangs were the only remnant of the Carter I thought I knew.

"You and Mel are out after curfew. We gotta get you back to safety before someone with a few more brains than that Collab comes along and asks questions."

I glanced around. Damn it, he was right. Anyone could see us here. We couldn't just stand around. All we had going for us was that everyone avoided this side of campus because of the stench from garbage in the stadium.

Still, every step we took away from the hole in the fence was a step away from freedom. I could have told Carter about the escape plan. Hell, an hour ago, I'd desperately wanted him to show up so I *could* tell him. But everything was different now. It wasn't just the outfit, either. Or the fact that the other Collab had known him and deferred to him. It was something about the way he held himself. Like he was *used* to wearing the outfit. Like it *fit* him.

Now I didn't dare tell him anything. Not until I knew what he was up to. Until I knew if the supposed badass Sebastian had brought him here as a Green or as a Collab. So I let him lead us away from our one escape route. Until I knew if I could trust him, I didn't want him anywhere near it.

I comforted myself with one thought. Even if Carter had run off and joined the Collabs in the past couple of hours, I still didn't think he was going to turn us in. Not really. Not after he'd just saved us from Scruffy. And hugged me—whatever that had been about.

Worst-case scenario, he'd walk us back to the science building, we'd pretend to hunker down for the night, and Mel and I would try again in a few hours. Yeah, it wasn't plan A, but it was a hell of a lot better than the plan where I had to stab a Collab with gardening shears.

Still, I couldn't help myself from asking, "Where—"

But he cut me off. "I'll tell you everything, but let's get to safety first."

Knowing he was right, I nodded. Mel and I fell into step beside him, even though it took us far from where we needed to be.

After a few minutes, we reached the corner of the gymnasium and Carter stopped. He peered around the edge, scanning the straightaway that led to the quad. A few steps farther and we'd be in plain sight of any Collabs patrolling the quad. During the day, the quad was sanctuary. Teeming with Greens, it was the one place you'd never get caught alone by a Collab. But I'd never been out into the quad at night. I tried to step around the corner, too, but Carter planted a palm against my forehead and pushed me back, like I was pesky sibling he was nudging out of the way.

When he stepped back into the shadows, his expression was grim. He took Mel's hand in both of his. I was shocked she didn't pull away. "When I say the word, Mel, we're going to walk across the path as fast as we can. Do you think you can do that?"

She tugged at her hair, cocking her head back toward the football stadium. "Red rover, red rover."

He followed her gaze and for a second my heart leapt into my throat, thinking he might know exactly what we'd been planning to do.

"No," he merely said. "No red rover. Jack be nimble, Jack be quick. Got it, Mel?"

The nursery rhyme trick was our own special way of communicating. I felt a stab of betrayal when Mel dropped her hand to her side and nodded. "Jack be nimble, Jack be quick."

He stuck his head around the corner again. Apparently satisfied with whatever he saw, he said, "Okay, let's go."

We moved quickly across the open pathway, not toward the quad, but around the fountain toward the music hall maybe fifty feet away. The moonlight cast the landscape in a silvery glow. Our progress felt slow and endless, and by the time we reached the music hall, my heart was pounding, but I wasn't sure why. Was it the last of the fear from Scruffy's attack, or was it because I knew we couldn't keep wandering around campus forever? We were getting farther and farther away from escape, but we weren't moving in the direction of the science building, either. So where was he taking us? Could I trust him or not? My gut said yes, but the truth was, my gut was tired and underfed and not in any shape to make a decision. I desperately wanted to ask Mel what she thought. To get a second opinion. Mel was right beside me, walking so close I could feel her through my jacket even though she wasn't touching me. Maybe the fact that she was blindly following him meant he really was the good guy I wanted him to be. Or maybe it meant she thought it was all a fun game.

Once we were back in the shadows, we slowed down, but Carter kept moving along the north side of the buildings. Carter had slung the strap of his tranq gun across his chest, so the gun crossed his back. Its inky barrel occasionally gleamed in the shadows like a water moccasin slipping through the water.

I tried to imagine how he could have gotten the gun. And the uniform. I pictured him knocking out some Collab and stealing the guy's uniform. But this uniform fit Carter and no Collab I'd ever seen kept his boots this newly issued shiny.

It was silly, all these bizarre scenarios I'd come up with to explain where he'd gotten the Collab gear. Part of me knew the simplest explanation was the most likely. Chances were, if he looked like a Collab and acted like a Collab, then he was a Collab.

I just didn't want him to be a Collab. I wanted him to be a guy I could trust. A partner I could rely on. Because I was friggin' tired of being the one responsible for everything.

Every step took us farther from the possibility of freedom. Closer to the Dean's office. I couldn't put it off any longer. I needed answers.

I cast a sidelong glance at Mel. Her steps had slowed just as mine had. If it was just me out here with Carter, maybe I could afford to have blind faith in him. But I couldn't risk Mel.

I grabbed Carter's arm and pulled him to a stop. "We're not going anywhere else until you answer some questions."

Carter's eyes scanned the area, like he was looking for potential danger. Or maybe just avoiding my gaze. Finally he gave a terse little nod. "Okay. But if I say the word we've got to keep moving again."

I didn't bother to point out that if *I* said the word, Mel and I were bailing.

"Where have you been since fourth meal? What happened to you? Why are you in a Collab uniform?"

He hitched his thumb under the strap of his tranq rifle. "It's complicated."

"Then simplify it." I looked him up and down, taking in his newly shaven jaw and the crisp perfection of his uniform. "Start with why you're dressed like a Collab."

"Things are not what they seem. I need you to trust—"

Wrong answer.

"Come on, Mel. We're leaving."

"Lily, I know you're trying to escape."

"Well, that's a great leap of intellect. Two girls out after curfew. However did you deduce that?"

"Damn it, Lily, we don't have time for jokes. Just this once could you try not to be such a smart-ass?"

"Okay, fine. Just this once, why don't you try being honest with me?"

"You want honesty?" He bit out the words. "I'm trying to save your ass here and I'd appreciate it if you didn't make this any damn harder than it has to be."

I threw up my hands in a WTF gesture. "Wait a second. You're mad at me? Why are you mad?"

"Oh, come on, Lily. I thought you were the smart one. You just damn near got yourself raped and killed. If I'm mad, it's because you're taking reckless risks with your life."

"Reckless? Carter, in case you haven't noticed, this is a Farm. Our lives are at risk every single day. And those days are numbered. I don't know exactly what's going to happen when Mel and I turn eighteen, and I'm not going to wait around to find out, either. In my head, the risks we're taking are anything but reckless."

For a second he just stared at me. "But you've got a few months, right? Before your birthday." Suddenly he didn't sound angry anymore. He sounded puzzled.

"No. Our birthday is in four days."

"What? That's not right."

"You think I don't know when my birthday is?"

"Your birthday is in June."

"Um. No."

"When we were together in math, Mel said she was a Gemini."

"Yeah, that's because she's a twin. Plus, this is Mel. She doesn't care about astrology. Why does this matter anyway?"

Carter muttered a cursed and scrubbed a hand down his face. "It doesn't. I just can't believe I was almost too late."

"Almost too late for what?"

"To save your ass, that's what."

"Hey, I was doing just fine saving our asses before you came along." I moved toward Mel, ready to grab her arm and get going, but Carter stopped me.

"You weren't going to make it. Your plan was flawed."

"You don't know shit about our plan."

"You didn't even make it off campus. When I found you, that Collab—"

"Yeah, well, I had a plan for dealing with him, too."

Carter cocked an eyebrow. "What were you going to do, stab him with your gardening shears and then steal his tranq gun?"

I gritted my teeth. "How did you—"

"Know about the gardening shears? When I found you with that Collab, your shirt had pulled up in back. I saw them tucked into the waistband of your jeans. So I deduced that your plan might have involved using them against that guy." Carter stepped closer to me and, beside me, I felt Mel tense. "But even if you had dealt with that Collab, you still wouldn't have made it off the Farm."

"You don't know that."

"I do know that. I know that you'd planned to cross through the football stadium to the north side of campus. That you'd figured out that the electrical fence is down on that side because of its proximity to the river."

Dread knotted my stomach. The only person I'd told the

plan to was Joe. I'd told him all the details before he went to get McKenna. If Carter knew it now, he must have heard it from Joe. If Carter had been just another Green and he'd heard about the plan, then he and Joe would have both been here and we'd all be escaping together. Since that wasn't how it was going down, I could think of only one other explanation. Joe had been taken to the Dean's office. Worst-case scenario, he had already been taken off the Farm and fed to the Ticks. My friend could be dead already. Because he'd tried to help me and because he'd had faith that my plan could get him off the Farm.

Nausea rolled through my belly and I wanted to curl up into a ball and cry.

"I don't—" I said weakly.

"There are fail-safe measures in the security system you couldn't possibly know about. And if you—"

His words snapped me out of my momentary stupor, and the more practical part of my brain kicked in. If I was right about Joe being caught and interrogated, that meant Carter really was a Collab.

"Oh, but you *do* know about them. Because you're a Collab. Not just a Collab, but someone with enough seniority to have all this secret information about the security system. Someone the other Collabs know and respect."

"I'm not a Collab," he said in a low hiss. "If you don't believe me about the security system, ask Mel. I bet she knows there was a problem with your plan."

I glanced over at Mel. "Red rover?" I asked, suddenly uncertain.

She gave a quick shake of her head and then started humming Rachmaninoff again.

Damn it. If there was a problem with the plan, then why hadn't she said so? Why couldn't she have—just this once—broken free of those crazy knots that kept her tied up inside of herself and just spoken to me? She could tell Carter she liked potato soup, but she couldn't freakin' tell me we were about to walk into a death trap?

My mind spun as I tried to come up with an alternative plan. "Look," I began, talking more to Mel than to Carter, "if Joe has been caught, that's all the more reason to move quickly. Even if we tried to make it back to the science lab and regroup, we're never going to have a better shot to get out. If we're going to go at all, we need to go tonight."

But it was Carter who answered. "If you try to make it out tonight—"

"I know, I know," I snapped. "We'll get caught." I waved a hand dismissively. "If you're so worried about these fail-safe measures, then tell us what they are."

"I can't do that." Carter reached for me and even though his touch on my arm was light, it felt like a shackle. "Sebastian knows I'm out here looking for you. If someone else catches you, you'll be completely screwed. But if you come back to the Dean's office with me and—"

"No way!" I jerked my arm free. "Are you crazy?"

I couldn't believe I'd tried to help him. That I'd actually worried about him. And what did he mean *back to the Dean's office*? Was that where he'd been since we'd lost him before fourth meal? And if he'd been in the Dean's office, was he the guy who'd beat up Joe?

"Lily, you have to trust me. I can protect you, but first I have to take you to the Dean's office."

I stumbled back a step, pulling Mel up with me. "Screw you, Carter." I pointed an accusing finger at him, my voice rising louder than it should. "I'm not letting you take Mel to the Dean's office."

"Lil, I have to—"

He reached out a hand, but I danced out of his grasp.

"You want to take me to the Dean's office, you're going to have to tranq me first."

Then, clenching Mel's hand in mine, I turned and walked into the darkness. Carter might be a Collab, but one thing I knew about him for sure—he would never shoot someone in the back.

But then he did.

CHAPTER TWELVE

CARTER

"You tranqed her?" Sebastian asked.

Sebastian wasn't one to let his emotions show but there was no hiding the surprise when he stared at Lily's prone body draped over the sofa.

"I didn't have much choice," Carter muttered.

Carter backtracked to the office door. Mel hadn't followed him in. She stood in the hallway of the admin building just down the hall from the office Sebastian had appropriated when they'd first arrived, where any Collab wandering by could see her. She stared at him warily, clutching her Slinky. After he'd tranqed Lily, he'd had to dig around in her bag to find it.

Great. *Now* she was freaking out. He'd friggin' shot her sister in the back and she'd been okay with it. But now that she was thirty feet from safety, she freaked out. Brilliant. Perfect time for the Valium to start wearing off.

Sebastian, who had followed him out into the hall, studied Mel. "Let me see if I understand this properly. You didn't shoot the autistic girl. You shot the normal one?"

"Yes, I shot Lily."

"The one you claimed had a crush on you in the Before?"

"Yes." He tried to lure Mel into the office. "I have gum."

Her fingers stilled and she cocked her head to one side. "Dubble Bubble?"

He turned back to Sebastian. "Is it Dubble Bubble?"

Sebastian looked bored. "How should I know? It's green."

Carter and Mel exchanged a look. He gave her a hey-I-did-what-I-could shrug. "It's probably spearmint or something."

She considered for a moment and then—finally—walked down the hall to the office door. She gave Sebastian a wide berth, nearly flattening herself against the doorway to ooze past him.

Carter glanced at the vampire, trying to see him through Mel's eyes. Clearly she sensed something off about him, though he easily passed as human. Yeah, the guy was ridiculously good-looking. Standing next to Sebastian, Carter always felt like a Neanderthal.

But Sebastian's unnatural good looks were the only indication that he was something other than human. In the months that Carter had been traveling with Sebastian, no one they'd met had pegged him as a vampire. Certainly not at first glance.

On the other hand, Mel looked leery, but not afraid. So maybe this was just normal Mel stuff.

"So," Sebastian continued in the same mocking tone, "you were able to lure one sister here with a Slinky and the promise of gum, but you couldn't get the other sister to come with you at all? And the one you thought liked you, even. How embarrassing. Gum's on the desk, by the way."

Carter hated like hell that he'd tranqed her *for her own good.* Yes, it was true, but it didn't sit well with him. It reminded him all too much of the times his father had meted out harsh punishments for *his* own good.

"I wouldn't have had to tranq her if you hadn't called me on the Bat phone right before fourth. Things were going great until then."

"If I hadn't called you back to the admin building, you would not have known they were planning an escape."

"She would have told me eventually," Carter insisted. If only he'd had a few days with her instead of a few hours.

"Or they would have tried to escape tonight on their own and they'd be dead now. We should be thankful Joe came to us with the information about their plans."

"Right. Thankful that friggin' Joe Mateo was willing to stab them in the back to save his own ass. Thank the Lord for that."

"Yes, you made your feelings about Joe quite clear when you beat him senseless before sending him back for more information. But what I want to know is why you couldn't convince your Lily to come with you using simple logic. Why did you have to complicate things by using the tranq gun?"

"Yes," came a voice from the doorway. "I'm most interested in that as well."

Sebastian and Carter both swung around toward the voice.

The Dean stood in the doorway. Though the man was neither tall nor physically powerful, only a fool would mistake him for weak. This wasn't a world in which weak people held power.

He wasn't an idiot, either. Which he proved by saying to Sebastian, "Of the nearly five thousand Greens on this Farm, why do you want this one so badly?"

Sebastian's gaze became deadly cold. "What business is it of yours how I choose my Greens?"

"Everything that happens on this campus is my business." The Dean's smile was greasy with false congeniality.

The Dean barely spared a glance for Carter. Instantly adopting the persona of a vassal, Carter tucked his hands behind his back and ducked his head, trying to look meek and intimidated. This wasn't the first Farm he'd been on with Sebastian. The routine was always the same. Sebastian was the front man. He cut the deal with the Dean. Carter's job was to blend with the Greens, find people who might be useful on the outside, and get them out without attracting attention.

But it was different this time. Lily and Mel were important, and if the Dean decided to make this an issue, Carter wouldn't back down. He glanced at Mel and Lily. Lily still lay sprawled on the sofa. Mel sat beside her, watching her intently.

The Dean barely glanced at them, but he studied Sebastian as he said, "If this Green is particularly valuable, then perhaps I'm unwilling to part with her."

Sebastian cut a deadly look at the Dean. "I trust you are not thinking of reneging on our bargain."

"No, of course not," the Dean reassured him. "However . . ."

"Our deal was I solve your bookkeeping problem and in exchange you pay me with four Greens of my choosing." He leaned back against the desk and stretched his legs out in front of him. Casually, he picked up something off the desk and began toying with it. His Confederate-era "Arkansas toothpick"—a nine-inch-long, wickedly sharp blade, which was no less deadly for being a century and a half old. "I trust you are not backing out now."

The Dean's gaze hardened just a little. "Are you threatening me?"

"Not at all," Sebastian said smoothly. He didn't unsheathe the dagger, but slapped the leather scabbard against his palm. "I'm merely reminding you that your computer records do not reflect well on you right now. If Roberto were to pay you a visit—as he will eventually—he'd discover that the number of residents on record greatly exceeds the number of warm, red-blooded bodies. That is a very real problem for you. One that I have promised to fix for the right price."

Carter could feel Mel tensing. He had hoped that she wouldn't pick up on the subtle undercurrent in the room. She started rocking in her seat, tapping her ring finger against her thumb the way she had out by the fence.

He had to get her out of here, but as long as the Dean thought he was a vassal, he couldn't suggest it himself and Sebastian couldn't suggest it, either, without revealing how badly they needed Mel and Lily.

Unfortunately, the Dean turned toward the sofa to look at the girls. As he looked from Mel to Lily, greed lit his eyes. The question was, did he want them only as bargaining chips, or did he know why they were important?

Sebastian slammed his knife down on the desk, leather slapping against wood with a resounding smack. "I tire of your games. We have an agreement. You will not renege."

The Dean leaned over and ran a hand down Mel's hair, then moved to tip her chin up so he could look at her better. She flinched away from his touch, retreating into the corner of the sofa. With a calculating gaze, he turned his attention to Lily, rubbing a strand of her hair between his thumb and forefinger. "I would never dream of reneging on our bargain, but I must make an amendment to our original agreement. You can have any four Greens on campus. Except these two."

It was all Carter could do not to launch himself at the Dean. Sebastian did it before Carter had a chance. In one wickedly fast movement, he sprang at the Dean, slamming his body into the other man's. The force of the impact drove them both into the wall with a crack that splintered the paneling.

Carter half expected to see Sebastian step back and the Dean's dead body crumple to the ground, his neck cleanly broken.

Instead, a strangled wheezing sound emerged from beneath Sebastian. Sebastian leaned back, keeping his forearm pressed to the Dean's neck. The Dean's face was starting to turn red. More wheezing gurgled up from his throat. Slowly, a smile split his face. He was laughing.

Sebastian must have realized it at the same moment Carter did, because he instantly increased the pressure of his arm. "These are the girls I have chosen. I suggest you not get in my way when I leave with them."

"This is . . . a most interesting . . . development."

"No," Sebastian growled. "This isn't interesting at all. The only thing interesting is why I haven't killed you yet. Do not forget you are little more than kine to me. It is only by my grace that you live at all."

Carter tensed, ready to get the girls out of the room in a hurry if he needed to. He was amazed that the Dean would antagonize a vampire at all. Sebastian—like, from what Carter knew, all vampires—was a mercurial, temperamental creature. When vampires lost their temper or got caught up in their bloodlust, there was no reasoning with them. Carter didn't want Mel or Lily anywhere near Sebastian if that happened.

The Dean's mouth twisted into something that might have been a grimace or a smile. "You don't dare kill me. Not here. Then Roberto would know what you've been up to."

"Do you honestly think I fear him?"

"I think you're a sneaky bastard and you don't want him to know what you're doing here. If you're here looking for an *abductura*—"

The Dean's voice cracked as Sebastian increased the pressure on his throat.

Carter's heart slammed against his rib cage. If the Dean truly suspected them, then Sebastian would have to kill him. But the Dean was right. Roberto couldn't know they were here.

Carter moved on instinct, bolting across the room to pull Sebastian off the Dean—not that he'd likely succeed, but he had to do something. However, before he reached them, Sebastian stepped back, releasing the Dean, so the other man crumpled against the wall. Then Sebastian threw back his head and laughed.

"You think either of these girls is an *abductura*?" His laugh deepened to a full belly cackle, a sound as unnatural as a lion purring while pouncing on an antelope. "Look at them."

The Dean must not have recovered fast enough for Sebastian. He grabbed the Dean's arm and spun him to face the girls on the sofa.

"Look at them." Derision coated Sebastian's voice like honey. Contempt for humanity came naturally for the vampire. "Do either of these puny teenage girls look capable of controlling all of humanity?"

Sebastian still held the Dean's arm and the Dean squirmed against the obvious pain. "I—"

"This one is autistic. She can barely communicate." As if to prove his point, Sebastian released the Dean, prowled across the room, and grabbed Mel's chin. He stared at her, his eyes coldly devouring her features.

Only once had Sebastian looked at Carter like that. Right after they'd all escaped the Tick attack on the school. When Sebastian was trying to judge whether or not Carter was serious about taking the remaining boys and starting a rebellion. That assessing gaze had lasted ten seconds, maybe less. But Carter still remembered what it felt like to be caught in the sights of humanity's only natural predator. To know a monster was deciding if you were more useful alive or as food.

Carter couldn't believe that Mel didn't flinch away from Sebastian's gaze. He had. Hell, it had been all he could do not to puke all over the floor.

But Mel stared at Sebastian in that unblinking, crowlike way she had. Sebastian must have been as disconcerted by her behavior as Carter was, because he jerked his hand away from her and straightened. For a single second, his expression looked stricken.

But when he turned back to the Dean, his mask of contempt was back in place. "What do you think? Honestly? She doesn't even have the sense to fear a vampire. And yet you think she's an *abductura*."

The Dean's face reddened. "The other one—"

"They're identical twins." Sebastian laughed. "You Deans have the most vivid imaginations."

The Dean stepped away from the spot where he'd been squashed against the wall and tugged on the hem of his jacket to straighten it. "If she's not an *abductura*, then let me keep her."

"No," Carter and Sebastian both snapped at once.

Sebastian glared at Carter. *Shut the hell up,* the look seemed to say.

"We've already invested two days in these girls." Sebastian gestured at Carter as if he were annoyed. "This is what we do at Farms. While I do my job, my vassal blends in with the Greens. He seduces a girl and convinces her she's in love. Then it is easy to talk her into coming with us."

"Either you think I'm an idiot or else you're the most sentimental vampire in the world."

"Not at all," Sebastian said smoothly. "You merely do not understand what it means to be a vampire. The Greens I harvest from Farms are all marinated in fear. Their blood is bitter. Unpleasant. However, the hormonal condition humans call love is quite delightful on the palate. Such a flavor pairing is worth seeking out and even keeping them alive to dine on only occasionally."

"If she believed she was in love, then why did he have to tranq her?"

Both the Dean and Sebastian swiveled to look at Carter. "She freaked out when she saw the Collabs patrolling after dark," he said. "She had second thoughts."

The Dean frowned. "Won't that change her . . . flavor profile?"

Carter gritted his teeth at the casual way the Dean talked about Lily's blood. Like she was bottle of wine instead of a person. It took everything in him not to throw himself across the room and finish the beating Sebastian hadn't delivered. Instead, he gave a bored shrug. "I'm not worried. Once she wakes up, I'll be able to convince her I did it for her own good. She'll believe me."

The Dean seemed to be considering whether or not he believed them. Had he bought it? Impossible to tell. Every instinct in Carter screamed to take the girls and run. Or let Sebastian kill the Dean. Yes, it would tip their hand to Roberto, but at least they'd be off this damn Farm.

That calculating gleam was back in the Dean's eyes. "You seem pretty confident."

Carter smiled. "I'm persuasive. She's gullible. It'll work out."

Unless her subconscious was listening in on this conversation. God, he hoped she couldn't hear what he was saying. Not only would she kick his ass, but she'd never trust him again.

Basically, he just prayed she didn't wake up while the Dean was still here. He had no idea how her skills as an *abductura* would be affected by the tranq dart. Would they be deadened or heightened? If it was the latter, he'd have to get her out of here fast.

Finally the Dean turned back to Sebastian. "It seems to me that if this Green is more delicious than any of the others, then she should be worth more."

Sebastian narrowed his eyes. "Our bargain is made."

As if on cue, Lily stirred. She groaned and rolled toward her sister.

The Dean and Sebastian both pivoted toward Lily. Mel shot Carter a look that seemed to be begging him to do something.

So he did the only thing he could think of. He dropped to his knees in front of Lily. Her head was tipped back against the sofa, her dark hair tumbled over her shoulders. Groggy as she was, her face looked softer. The natural suspicion was gone from her eyes.

He swallowed the lump in his throat before reaching out to cup her face in his palm. He stroked her hair and said, "Hey, honey, you're waking up."

She blinked blearily at him, confusion heavy in her eyes.

"How do you feel, sweetheart?"

The endearment felt clumsy on his tongue. Lily wasn't a sweet girl. She was so much more complex than that. She was strong and feisty. She was brave and smart. Every once in a while she was disarmingly vulnerable. But she wasn't *sweet*.

A glance over his shoulder told him Sebastian was watching him with an expression of wary amusement. The Dean with obvious interest.

He brushed a strand of hair off her forehead. His fingers snagged in her hair and instead of pulling his hand away, he threaded them through the thick strands. God, her hair was soft. And faintly smelled of something fruity. The scent was fresh and clean and so unexpected he felt the punch of it deep in his gut.

She frowned for a second, looking at him like she wasn't sure she knew him, and his breath caught. If she didn't recognize him, they could be screwed. If she did recognize him and remembered he'd just shot her, they could be screwed for different reasons.

But slowly, the frown turned into a wobbly smile. "Carter?" she asked weakly. "Where'd you go during fourth? I thought we'd lost you."

He blew out a breath of relief. "I'm here now."

Something about the sentence made it stick in his throat. He'd been gone from her life so long, but he was here now. And he wasn't leaving.

Then she frowned again. "Wait . . . didn't—"

Before she could finish the sentence, Mel interrupted her. "Lil-lee?"

The fog in Lily's gaze evaporated and she sat up. Too quickly, apparently, because she winced and pressed a palm to her forehead. More slowly, she turned to Mel. "Are you okay?"

Mel bobbed in place. "Ladybird, ladybird, fly away home."

Carter nearly chuckled in relief. Yes, they needed to get out of there.

Lily rubbed at her forehead. "I don't . . . know that one. Jesus, for once can't you just tell me what you want?"

Mel looked pointedly at the Dean and her face crumpled into a frown. "Go," she said simply.

Lily followed Mel's gaze. Seeing the Dean, Lily frowned also. Oddly, she didn't even glance at Sebastian, but she seemed to recoil from the Dean. "Who are you?" she asked, the tranquilizer making her sound somewhat stupid.

The Dean leered at her. "I'm the Dean."

She gave a shudder of disgust. "You're awful. You should go away."

Carter sucked in a breath. He glanced at Sebastian to see if he'd caught it. The vampire's gaze had sharpened with interest.

Mel flapped her hands a few more times. "Ladybird, ladybird, fly away home."

Lily glared at the Dean. "Go away."

Hardly daring to hope, Carter watched the Dean, gauging the man's reaction. The Dean looked back and forth from Mel to Lily. Revulsion flickered across his expression as he looked at Mel. Yeah, he was that kind of person. After a second, he smirked at Sebastian.

"If this is the kind of food you've been reduced to, then maybe I should leave you to it," the Dean said.

Satisfaction surged through Carter. It was all he could do not to pump his fist.

The Dean chuckled as he walked out, seemingly convinced he'd decided to leave all on his own. "And Roberto thinks you're a threat. . . ."

Sebastian gave a self-deprecating smirk. "I never pretended to be a threat. I'm like everyone else, just trying to survive in this new world Roberto has created." He wrapped a hand around the Dean's arm and guided him to the door. "Can I assume you're amenable to my choice in Greens?"

The Dean shrugged. "As long as you work your magic on the computer, I don't care. I'm going now."

"Fly away home," Mel said again.

After sending another slightly repulsed look at Mel, the Dean left.

As soon as the door closed, Lily said, "I'm glad he left. I didn't like him." Her voice still had that dreamy, drugged sound to it.

Carter and Sebastian both blew out a sigh of relief. Sebastian locked the door. Carter moved to the corner behind the desk where he'd stashed his backpack before going out to search for Mel and Lily. He patted his pockets until he found his penlight and took it out.

"Did you see that?" he asked Sebastian.

"I did. I could barely keep myself from leaving," he said dryly.

"So you agree I'm right?"

"Let's just say I have renewed faith in your judgment."

Carter found the penlight and straightened. Lily was looking at Sebastian, frowning.

"Who are you?" she asked.

Carter knelt before her. "He's a friend. He's the guy I told you about from the school I attended. The one with all the military training." He tipped her chin up so she was looking right at him. "Can you focus on my left ear for a second?"

As soon as she did, he turned on the light and looked at her pupils. They contracted normally, and she jerked away. "Hey, what you're doing?"

"Just checking to see if the tranq is wearing off."

She looked at him, blinking. Wariness settled onto her face as her memories returned. "That's right. You shot me."

He held up his hands in surrender. "Only with a light tranquilizer and only so I could get you back to safety."

"You shot me in the back and dragged me to the Dean's office," she accused.

"Technically, only to the admin building."

"You lying, betraying sack of—"

Sebastian interrupted her. "I'd love nothing more than to listen to this witty repartee all night, but I have work to do or I'll never break into the computer system and clean out the records. And you should get her out of here. Before the Dean changes his mind and comes back for her."

"Should I cut out their chips before we go?" Carter asked.

"What?" Lily sounded horrified.

Sebastian ignored her. "I think not. If the program I'm about to install does what it's supposed to, they'll blank out at dawn when we leave. Besides, if the Dean decides to track them, I want him to think the girls are exactly where they're supposed to be."

"What do you mean when we leave at dawn?" Lily stood on wobbly legs and gave Carter's shoulder a weak shove. Mel followed her sister's cue and stood as well, but she didn't so much as glance at him. "I'm not going anywhere with you."

Sebastian rolled his eyes in exaggerated boredom. "Carter, take her away and explain this to her. We can't have her fighting you the whole way out. You have until dawn or we'll tranq her again."

"If you think—" Lily started to say, but then she took a step forward and her legs gave out.

Carter caught her and wrapped an arm around her waist. "Understood." He nodded to Mel. "Come on, let's go."

"No," Sebastian said offhandedly as he rounded the desk and sat back down. "Leave the other sister here."

"But—"

"You seem barely able to control one sister, let alone both. Besides, this way Lily will be motivated to return."

Carter studied Sebastian, taking in the vampire's pale skin and humorless eyes. He looked about as human as could be expected. "Back then with the Dean, how close were you to losing it? Because I'm not going to leave her here if you're on edge."

"Please." Sebastian waved dismissively. "I was putting on a show."

"When was the last time you fed?"

"I'm fine."

Carter gritted his teeth and debated. Lily would hate this. She might be woozy and light-headed now, but as soon as they left the building the cold night air would probably knock the last of the tranquilizer out of her system. Then she'd be friggin' pissed.

Still, Sebastian had a point. It would be easier for the two of them to move across campus without being caught. And keeping Lily away from the Dean had to be the top priority. Finally Carter nodded. "Okay." He turned to Mel. "Stay here, okay? Sebastian will take care of you until it's time to leave. And he has more gum."

To his surprise, Mel just looked at Sebastian, her head cocked to one side. Then she sat back down, flapping her hands a few times. She started humming to herself. A classical tune that he didn't recognize, but that made Sebastian's mouth curve into something that almost looked like a smile.

Carter looked around the room one more time, at Mel humming in her spot on the sofa and then at Sebastian pulling up some file on the laptop. With a shrug, he led Lily to the door.

"I'm not leaving her here," she protested weakly, but her feet stumbled along beside him.

"Come on," he coaxed her. "Just think, you have all night to tell me what a dick you think I am."

As they walked out the door toward the elevator, once again the fruity scent of her hair hit him in the gut. Six hours alone with Lily didn't sound bad at all. As long as he could convince her he wasn't a lying sack of shit. And keep her from trying to kill him.

CHAPTER THIRTEEN

MEL

The blue pills are earplugs. They muffle everyone's music. Or maybe more like water muddling all the noise. I'm sitting applesauce on the bottom of the pool, holding my breath, resisting the urge to push to the surface because it's peaceful down here without all the noise.

Carter is the snare I didn't see coming, despite the macaroni I kept hearing. Never thought we'd be bunnies to his Trickster. He's more Bugs than kitty cat.

Can't tell yet if *his* Benedict will be like eggs or like Arnold. If he's just coddling us or serving us up for the silent shark, this man who is not a man.

Not a *hu*man, anyway.

Don't ask how I know. There's not just one thing about him. Or even two. Though the two pointy teeth certainly don't help.

Makes my skin crawl and my blood slither. Like it's trying to retreat farther into my body to get away from him. Like the iron in my blood is repulsed by him.

I listen, waiting to hear his music, now that we're alone, now that Lily's frantic drumbeat is gone and Carter has taken his Rachmaninoff. I expect movie-villain music. Dark and sinister. Darth Vader's imperial march. *Jaws*'s ominous bass drum. Perhaps even Beethoven's Moonlight Sonata. Or even something innocent that somehow sounds creepy. Itsy-bitsy-spiderish.

Instead, I hear nothing.

No human music.

No Tick wild cacophony of grating notes. Not even the buzzing of inanimate objects. Just nothing. Silence. Silence like I've never known. Vast. Deep. Terrifying. Exhilarating. Smothering in its expanse. Like an avalanche of void. Like the death an atheist expects. Nothing.

A nothing so vast I can hardly breathe. And I feel it eating at me.

His presence makes me feel thin. Not model slender. But worn, like an old cotton housedress. Thin like a specimen pressed between two plates of glass. Like a bug squashed beneath the marching boot of a soldier.

Thin and worn and silence like I've never known.

This is how I know he is not a Tick.

They are as pitiable as they are inhuman. They are fear personified. Their emotions and minds given over to rage and hunger. They are all noise. He is none.

If he is not a Tick, does that make him a Tock?

CHAPTER FOURTEEN

LILY

As Carter led me out one of the side doors into the darkness, I tried to pull myself out of his arms, but his hands were tight around my biceps. My feet stumbled slowly behind the rest of my body, like they were the last parts of me to wake up. He tugged me close and whispered, "Stop it."

Right now, with his body right behind mine, with his voice in my ear and his breath in my hair, this was the moment to be brutally honest with myself.

I wanted Carter. I had always wanted Carter from the very first moment I'd seen him. He was my first crush. My hardest, longest, fiercest crush.

No, if I was being honest, he was my *only* crush. Because I'd never felt about any guy the way I felt about Carter.

And when I'd known him in the Before, I'd constantly been looking for hints that he might like me, too. I'd cherished every word he'd said to me, even when I'd been too shy to answer. I'd dreamed up countless, ridiculous scenarios in which he'd find me alone somewhere, pull me into his arms, and declare his eternal love. I'd searched desperately for clues that he might be into me.

It was stupid. I was an idiot. I knew that. But I couldn't help it.

Pathetic, right?

This one time in biology, he'd dropped his pencil on the floor between us during a test. The thirty seconds it had taken him to bend down and pick it up had been excruciating. I imagined his hand brushing my leg as he bent down. I imagined his hand on my ankle. On my thigh. By the time he actually scooted his chair back and bent to pick up the pencil, I'd practically been trembling.

And then the unimaginable had happened. I was wearing a miniskirt and his hair brushed my leg as he bent over. I could have sworn I felt every hair on his head where it touched my skin. It took him forever to find the damn pencil. Hours, it seemed. I was aware of everything. Every thump of my pounding heart. Of the fact that I'd shaved my legs just that morning and they smelled like mango lotion. Of the way my blue toenail polish was chipped.

But I was especially aware of everything about him. The way his hair in back was darker than his blond bangs and short enough that I could see the dip in his neck. The way the navy cotton of his T-shirt stretched across his shoulders.

Then he sat up so slowly, I thought I was going to die, right there, in biology. And poor, stupid Coach Ballard would probably never notice because he was too engrossed in whatever stupid game he was playing on his iPad.

As he straightened, Carter had flashed me one of those crooked smiles. "Mango, huh? Nice."

After that, I was done. The test was a wash. I couldn't think of anything but Carter. The phyla of the animal kingdom were a distant blur. When the test came back two days later, my grade was as crappy as I'd expected. I got all of the first seventeen questions correct. And all of the last thirteen wrong. It was my first failing grade. That wasn't even the bad part.

No, the bad part had been realizing that his grade was identical to mine. Carter had copied me. I'd been so into him, I hadn't even noticed he'd been cheating off my test. The bastard had played me. We both ended up getting zeros.

This was why I couldn't trust him. Because I couldn't trust myself where he was concerned.

Now, as Carter led me away from the admin building, I made myself remember that day. That endless moment when I'd gotten caught up in the fantasy of Carter falling for me and then gotten so badly burned. I needed to remember that moment, because I could not let that happen again.

I only wished I'd had this little heart-to-heart with my past self after third meal. I should never have trusted Carter to begin with. He was handsome and charming and a player. If I let him, he'd play me again. Hell, he already had played me again.

He had shot me. In the back. That was what I had to remember. Not that his fingers had felt frickin' amazing twined through my hair.

"Let go of me," I hissed under my breath, giving my arm another tug. I had to get away from him. Now, before I did something else stupid.

"Look." He spun me around to face him. "Even though it's night, there are still plenty of Collabs around. You keep this up and one of them will notice."

I used the nearness to my advantage, jerking up my leg and kneeing him in the groin. He grunted in pain, doubling over. His grip loosened and I ran for it. Security lights were mounted on the building, casting ovals of light on the grass. I ran for the shadows, toward a clump of trees. I stumbled, lost my footing, and nearly fell. I ducked around the corner of a building—one of the dorms, I think—pressed my back to the trunk of a broad tree, and stood there panting, considering my options.

The exertion made my head pound. I couldn't keep running in the dark. Twisting my ankle wouldn't help Mel.

Oh, God. Mel.

I'd left Mel in the admin building.

I'd had no choice. I would go back for her. But how?

I rubbed my palm against the sudden ache in my chest, wishing it was only the exertion that made my heart feel like it was about to pound out of my rib cage. But I knew it was more than that. It was fear. And despair.

I *would* go back for her.

I had to. But first I had to find a way to give Carter the slip. And then I had to get back into the admin building. And then I had to . . .

I couldn't think about all the *and thens*.

I listened for his footsteps, following me, but heard nothing but the quiet buzz of the lights and the rumble of the generator in some nearby building. Off in the distance, I heard some Collab call to another. A burst of raucous laughter. Then silence. But beneath the hum of night sounds, there was an edge in the air.

I needed to find somewhere to hide. I pushed off from the tree and was moving toward another shadowy spot when Carter grabbed me by the arm and pulled me toward him.

"You didn't really think that would work, did you?" Carter asked, his voice low. As dark as it was, I could still see the annoyance on his face. Kneeing him in the groin had pissed him off.

"It might have if I'd moved faster." I wrenched at my arm, trying to get free and keep him from grabbing the other arm. "Let me go."

"Not a chance." He bit out the words. "Not until you let me explain."

"Explain what? You're a Collab. You set us up." I kicked at his legs, fighting against him with everything I had. "You made me leave Mel in the admin building!"

Then suddenly, he whirled me around, pulling my back against his chest and wrapping both arms around me. "Stop it before you hurt yourself."

He held me with my arms pinned to my sides. But my legs were still free and I hopped up, walking my legs up the trunk of the tree I'd been hiding behind. I kicked my legs out, hoping to knock him off balance; instead he merely stumbled back a couple of steps, muttering curses under his breath.

He carried me physically to the side of the nearest building, spun me around, and pushed me back against the wall. His entire body was pressed against mine, pinning me there, completely immobilizing me. His legs bracketed mine. His hands were clamped on my arms. When I tried to scream, he slapped a hand over my mouth and leaned close.

"Things aren't what they seem—" I bit his finger. He jerked back his hand and shook it. "Damn it!"

"No shit, things aren't what they seem!" My anger was a tangible thing in my body. It pressed against my skin until I felt like it might actually burst through. "You seemed like a friend, but you're a stinkin' Collab! You—"

He ignored my rant and leaned even closer to me, pressing the side of his face to mine, so that my mouth—my one weapon left—didn't have anything within biting range. When he spoke, his voice was low and so close I could feel his breath warm on my ear.

"Stop it! You just left the Dean's office. No one walks out of there alive. No one's supposed to, anyway. So it'd be great if we could get undercover before a dozen or so Collabs find us and drag us back there. Let me explain."

His words were slow and steady in my ear, seductive almost,

because I couldn't *not* listen. He made it sound like he was in danger, too. And there was a note of real urgency in his voice. It made me want to believe him.

I tried to push down my fear and panic over Mel, that choking sense of betrayal. I tried not to notice that he smelled good—damn it! Something woodsy with just a hint of mint. Not that long ago, Scruffy had had me pinned to the ground. I'd felt trapped. Panicky. With Carter, it was different. I felt safe.

I could not let myself do this. I needed to get a little perspective here. A little distance. Like, a little distance between his body and mine so I could *think* again.

"Okay." I bit out the word. "Explain."

He stepped back, freeing me from the cage his body had created. "Sebastian isn't like them. He isn't—"

"He isn't what?" I sneered. "A collaborator? Someone who would hand kids over to save his own life?"

"He isn't what you think he is. Neither am I. This is what we do. We travel from Farm to Farm. He convinces the Deans to let him come in and overhaul their computer systems. To delete the files of any Greens that have escaped or haven't made it or whatever. In exchange, we get to walk out with Greens. It's how we get paid. We're rescuing people. We aren't Collaborators."

My instincts roared at me not to believe him. He'd shot me in the back, for God's sake. But at the same time, he looked disarmingly serious, his gaze meeting mine, his eyes begging me to listen to him.

What if he *was* being honest? What if getting out of here was as simple as putting my trust in him? What if I didn't have to do all this on my own?

I wanted to believe that. There were a lot of things I wanted to believe right now. I wanted to believe that Mel was safe. I wanted to believe that Carter was trustworthy and that maybe, just maybe, he could help us. I *wanted* to believe those things so badly that I couldn't trust myself to see the truth.

When it came to Carter, I had a history of deluding myself. I couldn't make the same mistakes I'd made in the Before. I needed to be stronger than that. More logical.

"If you can get me and Mel out of here, if that's your big plan, then why didn't you just let us go?"

"Because on your own, they'd hunt you down and kill you."

"You don't know that for sure," I protested.

"Yes, I do. Trust me. I know more about the security measures on a Farm than you do."

"I've been watching—"

"Okay, you know about the chip in your neck."

My hand went to my neck, to the spot that was scanned four times a day when I entered the dining hall. "Of course. It's how they figure out when we miss meals and what our blood—"

"Each chip has a micro GPS locator. They start sending out a signal the second you leave the Farm. They'd catch you ten minutes out. Escaping from a Farm is a crime punishable by death, punishment to be administered instantly at the discretion of the local Dean. And that's if it's the Collabs who catch you. I don't know for sure, but I think the chip's frequency bugs the Ticks. Or at least attracts their attention. People with active chips usually don't live long enough for the Collabs to find them."

At his words, my heart started pounding in my chest and a wave of nausea washed over me. It had never—not once—occurred to me that the chips might be anything other than dehumanizing storage devices.

I sagged against the wall, dropping my elbows to my knees as I struggled to pull air into my lungs. Bile filled my throat and I had to concentrate to keep from puking right there.

I felt Carter's hand on my shoulder. "You okay?"

"I could have killed us. We would be no better off than those Greens outside the fence. Mel would be dead."

"You didn't know." He crouched down beside me and tipped my chin up so that I looked him in the eyes. His touch was warm and solid. Reassuring. "You see now why I had to stop you? If I'd let you escape, I would have been sending you to your death."

"But now that I know"—my mind was racing again—"about the tracking devices, I mean, now that I know, we can try again. We can—"

I broke off abruptly. Mel was still in the Dean's office. There was no way I could get her out on my own. Whatever else happened, I needed Carter. And—it seemed—Sebastian.

Carter was shaking his head anyway. "It's more complicated than that. You're just going to have to trust me." He blew out a breath. "Look, I'm not going to talk about this here. We're too exposed."

"Too exposed? Who talks like that?" I asked.

His mouth twisted into a little smile. "Military school. Remember?" He scanned the area then nodded toward one of the buildings sitting off the quad, maybe fifty yards away. "I'm taking you over there. You're not going to bolt again, are you?"

He shook his hand absently, rubbing his thumb over the spot where I'd bit him. I had to shift my gaze away from him, almost ashamed that I'd done that. Besides—after so long on the Farm, so many months of being invisible, of having almost no human contact—it was seriously weird being the center of someone's attention. Being touched at all.

I felt a little shiver go through my body. I pushed th too, burying it even deeper than the anger.

When I didn't answer right away, he kept talking. "Look, trust me, okay?"

Then abruptly Carter stepped away from me. He flicked open his blue Collab jacket and pulled out my shiv. Flipping it over in his hand, he held it out to me, handle first.

It was the second time he'd given me back my weapon.

"Here," he said, nudging it toward me. "Take it. If you have this, will you come with me? Just somewhere I can really explain. If I don't convince you, I'll let you walk away."

I took the shiv, holding it close to my side. "I'd feel better if I had the tranq gun, too," I muttered.

"Bet you would." He actually chuckled. "But a Collab and a Green walking across campus after curfew is suspicious enough, even if she's not the one holding the rifle." He swung the rifle off his shoulder, popped open the chamber, and removed the dart. "Look, I'll take the dart out, then you know I can't tranq you again."

I snatched the dart out of his open palm, dropped it onto the sidewalk, and crushed it beneath my shoe before he had a chance to stop me.

He just looked at me, flabbergasted. "What the hell, Lil? What if I need that later? Collabs are only issued two at a time."

I smiled. "That's how I know I can trust you not to shoot me in the back again."

He gave a beleaguered sigh and gestured for me to start walking.

I felt better with him weaponless and with the shiv in my hand. I still couldn't beat him in a physical fight—not without trying to kill him—but at least things were a little more equal now. Still, I kept a couple of feet between us, but he didn't try to grab me again. He led me to a drab building squatting on the edge of campus, just past the water tower. It wasn't far from where we'd been, but the walk felt interminable. With every step, my logical mind took back a little more real estate in my brain.

At this moment, the only thing I could do was hear him out. The first door he tried when we reached the building didn't open, but he walked around the side, tried another, and jimmied it somehow, and it swung open. I didn't see exactly what he did to the knob, which was frustrating, because that might have come in handy later.

It turned out to be some sort of maintenance building. A hallway led to an enormous open room filled with massive equipment chugging away in the background, all pipes and steam and meters and whatnot. It must have been the air-conditioning building for the whole campus. By the door we entered, there was a deserted break room.

Carter reached around and flicked on the overhead fluorescents, which flickered dully to life to reveal a sink and cabinetry along the outside wall, some storage lockers, a time punch, and a long, scarred table surrounded by cracking vinyl chairs. Against the far wall stood a pair of vending machines. The light on the Coke machine was still on, as it dutifully chilled the drinks inside, patiently waiting for some long-dead maintenance guy to come plug in his buck for an ice-cold can of soda.

After all these months on the Farm, I'd assumed that every corner of the place had been picked clean of anything valuable. A swarm of locusts had nothing on us Greens. If there was something we could eat or trade or use, I thought we'd found it. But apparently, much as we had Dr. Estleman's stash of birth control pills, we'd overlooked the maintenance buildings.

Entranced, I crossed the room to stand before the machines,

for a moment all the angst and fear of the past twenty-four hours receding into the background of my mind.

Some emotion that I hadn't allowed myself to feel in months—nostalgia maybe—clutched at my heart as I stared through the glass at the neat rows of sodas and snacks. I pressed my hand to the glass, feeling like I was looking through a portal to another world, one sweetened by candy-coated chocolate and high-fructose corn syrup.

We had junk food aplenty on the Farm, but it was the same thing every day. I'd eaten so many damn corn chips they didn't even taste right anymore.

I heard Carter moving to my right and I jerked away from the machine. Carter slid out one drawer after another, digging around for something. After a few minutes of searching, he triumphantly held up a clear plastic cup with change rattling around in the bottom. Walking toward me, he poured the money out into his palm, picking over it.

"Two dollars and thirty-eight cents. Enough for a Coke and a snack." He stopped beside me, considering the machines. "If I remember right, you're a Dr Pepper girl."

How had he remembered that? Before today, it had been nearly two years since I'd seen him. Even then we'd never eaten together. I'd sat in my quiet corner of geeky kids, while he'd been at the table of popular kids on the other side of the cafeteria.

For a second, I just stared at him, baffled. "Yes. A Dr Pepper would be great."

He fed about half the change into the tiny slot. A coil within the machine rotated, pushing the plastic bottle off its little ledge. Carter reached his hand through the slot and pulled out the soda, then handed it to me. Then he stepped over to the candy machine. "What else do you want?"

I raised the bottle of Dr Pepper in silent toast. "This is enough. You should get yourself something."

Nodding, he picked out Rolos from the candy machine.

A moment later, he pulled out one of the blue vinyl chairs for each of us, angling them so they faced each other just slightly, and he dropped down into the one nearest the door. I stood there, stone still, just watching him as he stretched his long legs out in front of him.

He'd never refastened his jacket and it hung open over his pressed white shirt. The shirt was looking a little worse for the wear. It now bore wrinkles and smudges of dirt, mostly in the places I'd elbowed him. He let the tranq gun drop to the floor by the chair as he peeled off a layer of the wrapper on the Rolos and popped one in his mouth.

I set the shiv down on the table as I lowered myself to the chair. Then I twisted the cap off the Dr Pepper. Habit had me glancing at the inside of the lid. I laughed.

Carter's eyes popped open and he straightened.

I tossed the cap onto the table between us. "I won a thousand bucks." I held the bottle up, reading the label, listening to the fizzing of the carbon bubbles. "All the Dr Peppers I've drunk in my life and I never won jack. Today must be my lucky day."

Somehow the words didn't sound as bitter and ironic as I meant them to. Suddenly I was just tired. Or maybe it was the tranquilizer still pumping through my blood.

I took a sip. As the soda rolled over my tongue, I felt a rush of gratitude. Carter may have just beaten the crap out of me, he may have shot me in the back, but he'd bought me Dr Pepper. I know it was effed up, but somehow, it balanced out.

Carter smiled, that odd, twisted smile of his. "Maybe." Then he set the Rolos down on the table and pushed them toward me. "You want the rest?"

I looked from him to the Rolos to my Dr Pepper. "That isn't fair. I got the soda."

We must have realized the absurdity of the conversation at the same moment because we both kind of laughed.

I reached for the candy, then asked, "You sure?"

"Yeah," he said. "I've been on the outside more recently than you. I've probably had all kinds of stuff you haven't."

At some point, the Rolos had melted a little and the caramel had leaked out to sort of glue them to each other, but I managed to pry one free. "About that . . ." I asked, just before popping it into my mouth.

"Yeah, about that." He gave a little shrug, then scrubbed his hand over his newly shaven jaw, like he was trying to figure out how to tell me something difficult. "You said you had questions."

Hell yeah, I had questions. Thousands of them—some hugely important. But oddly, the one closest to the surface was: why had he remembered I like Dr Pepper? Why had he gotten so upset when he found out he'd gotten the date of our birthday wrong? Why did he keep acting like he cared for me? Not in a generic, I'm-clinging-to-the-remnants-of-my-past kind of way. But like he actually *cared*. About me.

The way he was acting was seriously messing with my head. Yeah, sure. The hot guy from school coming to rescue me, that was a nice fantasy. But it was *fantasy*. Not real. One hundred percent guaranteed to crush your soul. It was like the pencil thing all over again.

Carter was playing me. I had something he wanted and he was charming me to get it. Last time it was my test answers;

this time it would be something else. I just hadn't figured out what yet.

But I knew this: I wasn't going to just sit back in my chair and swoon like I had last time. I was going to call him on it. "You know I can't just trust you, right?"

"I don't see why not."

Okay, so a braver woman than I might have actually reminded him of the pencil incident, but I couldn't do that without tipping my hand to the fact that I'd been all weak-kneed crushing on him before. I wasn't that bold yet. So instead I said, "I can't just blindly believe that you're going to be able to get me and Mel out of here. If it was just me . . ." I shrugged. "Maybe. But if we're going to go with you, you have to tell me everything."

"What can I say to convince you that I'm on the up-and-up?"

"Why don't you just start at the beginning and I'll stop you when you've won me over."

CHAPTER FIFTEEN

LILY

"What is out there?" I asked abruptly. I know I'd asked him to start at the beginning, but suddenly I couldn't wait to hear the truth. And I didn't even wait for him to answer. "We can see through the fences, but we never see any people. Never hear anything beyond the Farms other than the Ticks at night. Are there any people left out there? Any towns, cities? Anything?"

Carter's gaze dropped away from mine. He frowned and rolled a Rolo across the table with his forefinger.

"Nothing?" I asked.

"Not in the big cities," he said slowly. "I haven't been everywhere. I don't know for sure. There are Farms in every state I've been in. Lots of them. In the Farms, I've heard rumors—"

"Rumors about what?"

"Just people guessing mostly. We know there are factories. Someone's making the food Greens eat. Someone delivers it. Adults who are Collaborators. We've turned some of them, but only a very few. There must still be farms—real ones that grow food—down in the valley and out in California. But in the part of the country I've seen . . ."

He shook his head.

I couldn't imagine the Dallas metroplex empty. There had to

be at least five million people in the area. How did that many people just disappear?

I didn't ask about my mom. I'd known in my heart that she must be gone. My mother was a fighter. She would have fought to the death to protect us. To get us back. She would never have given up once she realized the Farms were not the sanctuaries everyone believed them to be. I wasn't ready to talk about her yet—I didn't know if I ever would be.

I leaned back in my chair. "Okay. Now you can start at the beginning."

Carter looked at me for a long minute, screwing up the corners of his mouth, like he was testing out what he wanted to say. Finally he blew out a breath, met my gaze, and said, "Here's the part you're not going to want to believe."

"Okay, hit me."

"Vampires are real." He said it straight-facedly, like this was supposed to be shocking news.

I arched an eyebrow. "Not the mutated genetic freaks that ate their way through the Southwest. But real honest-to-God vampires? Like, the mythical monsters who don't like garlic and sparkle in the sun?"

I waited for him to laugh. He didn't. His gaze was completely serious when he said, "They don't sparkle."

"O-okay." I popped another Rolo in my mouth to give myself time to process. "Yes, we have all these Ticks now and some people call them vampires because they're really strong and hard to kill and have a moral compass that points straight to *hmm, humans are yummy*. But you're talking about something different, aren't you?"

"Yes." Never once had his gaze wavered, which made me uncomfortable when I was the first to look away.

"Have you seen one of those vampires yourself?"

He must have heard the barely contained sarcasm in my voice, because this made him smile. "Yes. With my own eyes. I've seen the fangs. I've seen one eat. They aren't like Ticks. They're smarter. Maybe smarter than we are. And cunning. And completely amoral. By our standards, at least."

I studied Carter, the tension in his shoulders. The stubborn set of his jaw, like he was daring me to call him on it. Like he was expecting me to argue with him about the existence of vampires.

The Ticks had a clear scientific origin—at least according to the CDC. Scientists at the Genexome Corporation had been tinkering around with epigenetics. They'd been using certain benign mircoorganisms to switch genes on and off, trying to cure a whole host of diseases and disorders, including autism. Because of the autism link, I'd actually been following their work even before the outbreak. They'd been able to affect brain development, tumor development, and birth defects. Their work was amazing. Until it had gotten out of hand and a supposedly harmless microbe was accidentally released as a pathogen that turned about one percent of the population into horrible monsters. Anyone who was exposed to the pathogen had a one-in-a-hundred chance of morphing into a Tick overnight.

After thinking about it for a minute, I asked, "So are the Ticks and the vampires related?" He frowned and I rushed on. "I don't mean, like, by birth. But genetically. Do tweaks to the same epigenes create vampires and Ticks?"

Carter looked surprised. "You believe me?"

I waggled my hand in an *eh* gesture. "A year ago, I'd have thought you were bat-shit crazy. But now? Who's to say what is and isn't believable? You could tell me that the UN was run by opera-singing, alien werewolves and I couldn't argue with you."

Carter's lips curved in what might have been a smile, but before he could respond, I sat forward and tapped the table with my forefinger.

"What I want to know is what any of this has to do with the Farm. With me and Mel. Does knowing any of this help get us out?"

He leaded forward, too. "This has everything to do with the Farm. They're all part of a plan. To take over the world."

"The vampires have a plan to take over the world?" I asked. I felt a bit dumb, gasping in surprise at every twist to the story and incredulously repeating all the important bits. But somehow Carter's version of things made sense. I felt like Dorothy at the end of *The Wizard of Oz* when the green curtain is pulled back to reveal the truth.

Carter shook his head. "They're not all in on the plan. Vampires don't work like that. That's one way they're different from Ticks. Ticks are pack animals. They stick together. Vampires are the opposite. They're fiercely territorial about their kine and—"

"Their what?" I asked.

"Their kine." Carter said the word more slowly, toying with a bit of Rolo wrapper as he did. Like he didn't want to look at me. "Their livestock."

"Oh, livestock. The humans they feed on." A sort of sick feeling roiled in my gut. I'd been donating blood to feed the Ticks for months now. I thought I was long past being creeped out. So why did that word—kine—send a shiver through my body?

Maybe because it wasn't the sort of word Carter could have just come up with on the fly. It was an archaic word, but one he knew well enough to slip into conversation. And it lent a sense of truth to his story about vampires. Vampires who—according to him—were just as deadly as Ticks, just as fast, just as strong, but were also smart. *Smart.*

The Ticks' diminished brain size—their lack of mental capacity—represented the one advantage humanity might have over them. Someday, we might have a chance of winning against an enemy that was as dumb as stegosaurs, but if they got smart, we'd be screwed.

I took another gulp of Dr Pepper because I needed that sugar burn on the way down to keep me grounded.

"Do they have . . . like, ranches or something?" As soon as I asked it, I realized how stupid that sounded. I was on a Farm. I was a Green. That was as livestock as it got. "I mean in the Before. There couldn't have been Farms before. Right?"

Carter gave a terse shake of his head. "No, there weren't Farms. Vampires think of all the humans in their territory as their kine. As belonging to them. The way a medieval king would think of the deer in the forest as belonging to him. But if a vampire accidentally makes another one then—"

"Wait a second. What do you mean accidentally? Isn't it, like, you get bitten by a vampire and if he doesn't suck all your blood, voila, you're a vampire?"

"Not exactly. The only people who turn have a very rare gene. They call it the regenerative gene. Less than one percent of the population has it. Only people with that gene become vampires. But if they're bitten by a vampire and exposed to a vampire's venom, they *always* become vampires. And once a vampire turns someone, he has to share his territory. Which means—"

"Less livestock," I supplied, talking past that sick, squelchy feeling in my stomach.

"Exactly. And one vampire decided he'd had enough. He decided to build an army and take over the U.S. Roberto started by—"

"Did you say Roberto?"

Carter nodded. "Yes. Roberto De La Cruz. He's the vampire who—"

"Roberto?" I said again.

Carter's mouth flattened in annoyance. "Yes. Roberto."

"So there's an evil vampire trying to take over the world . . ."

"Yes."

"And his name is Bob?"

"Yes." Carter huffed with impatience. "Roberto—"

"Bob." Laughter bubbled up inside me. It was the juxtaposition that did it. The dehumanizing brutality of people as *kine*, up against the benign banality of the name *Bob*.

"Bob," I said again. And then dissolved into giggles.

It was inappropriate. Completely. And it pissed Carter off. I could see that.

"This isn't funny." Carter frowned.

"I know," I gasped. "I know it's not. It's just . . ."

"Just what?" Carter asked when I was laughing too hard to talk.

"Bob is the least scary name. Ever." I wiped tears from my eyes. "My grandfather's name was Bobby. And there's Bob Hope. Bob Dylan." I could feel more laughter well up inside. "Bob Newhart. SpongeBob. That gelatinous guy from *Monsters vs. Aliens*."

I lost the battle again; I dropped my head onto my folded arms to hide my lack of control.

"Why is this funny?" Carter bit out the words. His voice was terse and angry.

"It's not." I pushed myself up, wiping my eyes on my sleeve. "That's the thing. If you were making this up, you'd have come up with something else. Something that sounded scary. Like Vlad or Damien or Dante." Suddenly I wasn't laughing anymore. "But his name is Bob."

The harsh lines of Carter's face softened. "It's Roberto. But yeah, I probably would have gone with Damien or something."

I nodded, swallowing back my emotions. Carter just looked at me, an intensity in his gaze that unnerved me. Suddenly I felt so damn vulnerable. I wasn't one of those girls who looked pretty when I laughed. Or when I cried, for that matter. My face got all red and splotchy. Never mind that I hadn't seen makeup in half a year.

And none of that mattered. Not really. "So," I said after a minute. "Roberto. He did this."

"Yes. He wanted to build an army that would destroy modern civilization. He wanted to take back what he thought should be his. The Aztecs once worshipped Roberto as the god Tezcatlipoca. They offered him daily blood sacrifices and thought he was all powerful. He wanted to be returned to his former glory."

"So why not just bite a bunch of people? Why not make his own vampire army?"

"Because most people he bit wouldn't turn into vampires. They would just die. Besides, he didn't want a vampire army. He'd never be able to control them. No, he needed something else. Something like vampires, as strong, as fast, as difficult to kill, but something he could easily control."

I gave a snort of derision. "Yeah, how'd that work out for him? I mean, the Ticks I've seen don't seem like they're under anyone's control."

Carter gave a shrug. "That's where our intel gets dicey. We're not sure if this is what he really intended to happen or if the Ticks have gotten out of hand. But. . ." Carter's words trailed off and he shook his head.

"What?" I prodded.

"Well, we know some of what Roberto wanted because of

things he told Sebastian, but I can't imagine that this was his end goal. Either things in the Genexome Corporation went really wrong, or this is just a stage two in a multi-stage plan. Which means things could get worse."

I let that vile thought roll around in my gut for a while before I pushed it away and went back to something Carter had said. "What about the Genexome Corporation? All those scientists? Do they work for Roberto?"

"It's buried pretty deep, under about five dummy parent corporations, but yeah. He owns it."

"Those scientist at Genexome, they must have started with vampire venom and—"

"Actually, we don't know that for sure. And we have no way of knowing if they knew what they were working with. But, yeah, it's a pretty good guess that Roberto supplied them with a sample of his venom and they used that as a starting point."

I felt the Rolos trying to creep back up my esophagus. The idea that the Tick outbreak wasn't accidental, that someone had done this on purpose was repugnant. I dropped my head back to my arms, resting my ear on my sleeve, feeling suddenly more exhausted than I could believe. I just sat there, staring at the cheerfully glowing Coke machine. Something that had no right to exist in this horrific new world. It occurred to me then that this might be the last time I ever drank a soda. Or ate candy. And if it was, then I resented the hell out of this Roberto guy. I really didn't want to puke up the last Dr Pepper I ever drank.

Slowly, I realized that Carter still hadn't answered the basic question: what did this have to do with anything? What did it have to do with the Farm or with me and Mel or escaping?

But as soon as the question drifted through my mind, the answer was there behind it. I remembered what Carter had said just now about things Roberto had told Sebastian. Suddenly it was as if the fog of the tranq rifle had lifted and I could see the truth that should have been so obvious from the second I opened my eyes in the admin building.

I pushed myself up. "He's one of them, isn't he? Sebastian's a vampire."

For a long moment, only the gentle hum of the Coke machine filled the room, but eventually Carter spoke, his voice as soft as someone trying to coax a spooked kitten out of hiding. "He is. But he's different."

"Different how? Like Edward Cullen different? Like Stefan Salvatore different?"

"No. Nothing that . . ." He searched around for a word. "That romanticized. He's a vampire. He drinks blood. But he's on our side."

"Our side? We have a side?"

"I do and I'm hoping you're on it, too." He pulled his chair closer to mine. He propped his elbows on his knees. "That guy I mentioned before, the guy with the military background from school. That's Sebastian. The school was sort of an . . . investment for him. He was there when the Ticks hit the school. After we lost the school, Sebastian expected us to scatter. But those of us who were left stayed together."

"I thought you said there weren't many left."

"Forty-three guys. Out of over five hundred."

"Oh." Less than ten percent.

Christ. So those were the odds.

He raised an eyebrow, like he was asking if I had any more questions. I gave my head a little shake and he continued. "We found a stronghold that we can defend, most of the time anyway."

I almost interrupted to ask about the stronghold—how they

were actually able to defend it—but restrained myself. I could ask more about that later. I needed to get my sister off the Farm and to safety in Canada. Carter's stronghold wasn't my concern.

"Working from our base camp," Carter continued, "we've been mounting a rebellion."

"A rebellion?" I was so surprised that I couldn't let it pass.

"Yes."

"Against the Ticks?"

"Yes."

"Forty-three guys against an unstoppable army of bloodsucking monsters? Are you kidding?"

Carter straightened a little, glaring at me with defiance. "There's almost a hundred of us now. But, yeah. It's just us against the Ticks. Well, us and Sebastian."

"Sebastian, the vampire," I said doubtfully. "Shouldn't he be on Roberto's side? How can you trust him?"

"I don't trust him. But I understand him. And we need him. He can sense when other vampires are around and when Ticks are, too. It's like he's got this spidey sense or something. He's thrown in with us because he hates Roberto and he's pissed about what Roberto has done."

"Why? I don't get it. Haven't the Ticks just made it simpler to corral humans? Hasn't he made Sebastian's life easier?"

"No. You're thinking about it the wrong way. In the Before, Roberto and Sebastian each had separate territories. They stayed out of each other's way. When Roberto created the Ticks, they destroyed that. They don't care about territory. The pathogen that created them doesn't, either. Sebastian went from being the only vampire in a territory with tens of millions of people to a territory where the only free-roaming kine are the Ticks."

I released a strangled laugh. "So this guy, who's all pissed off about losing his kine, this is the guy you trust?" And then another thought hit and I jumped out of my chair. "This is the guy you left Mel with?"

Carter stood also and reached out a hand to me. "Hey, calm down. Mel will be fine."

"The hell she will! You left her with a vampire!"

"He's not going to hurt her. I promise. In all the time I've known him, I've never seen him eat a person."

"Oh, well, that's a resounding recommendation. You've left my defenseless sister alone with a bloodsucking monster who hasn't murdered when you've been around. You're right," I quipped. "When you say it that way, he sounds like such a stand-up guy."

"Look, I got you away from that Collab, right? Maybe I've earned a little bit of trust here."

"Okay, fine. I trust you. Now let's go get my sister."

"We can't do that. We've got to leave her there with Sebastian for now."

"Why?"

He placed a hand on my shoulder and gently eased me back into the chair. "This is what Sebastian and I do. It's what we've been doing since this all started." Standing beside my chair, Carter shucked his jacket. "Sebastian and I, sometimes other guys, too, travel from Farm to Farm, offering to upgrade their security. The new software fixes a few surface problems, but when the system is rebooted, it allows us to delete a couple of files permanently."

Before I could ask what he was doing with his shirt, he dropped it on the ground, then tugged the white T-shirt he wore beneath it over his head.

"I've been in and out of more Farms than I can remember." He turned his back to me and knelt, tracing his finger across a scar on the left side of his neck, just across the spot where my chip was in my own neck. "This was Colorado Mesa University. It was just a quick in-and-out. Me and three other guys. We didn't know what the chips did yet. It was tight. My buddy Mike didn't make it." His finger moved down another inch to another scar. "This one was down in Durango. By then we knew the chips were trouble, but we hadn't figured out a way around it. Sebastian hadn't figured out the computer program for turning the chips off. But even that's not fail proof, so we still just cut the chips out every time we leave a school. That way I can get a new one put in at each Farm and no one questions that I'm a Green." He moved on to one of the scars on his right shoulder. "This was in the Oklahoma panhandle. It was the first time we felt confident enough to get Greens out. We rescued five people one of my guys knew back in the Before. Three of them joined us. Two headed west."

He kept talking, listing off Farms and how many people he'd helped rescue and from where. His words became a blur of states and numbers. I could barely hear him past the thoughts tumbling through my mind.

He had done so much in so little time. All those scars. I'd seen them earlier, but hadn't put it together. I never would have dreamed that each half-inch red spot was from a chip implant. My hand went instinctively to his back and trailed a fingertip across one raised scar and then the next. Every one of them represented a Farm he'd gotten into and out of. And the incalculable risk he'd taken. Lives he'd saved.

Suddenly I realized his voice had trailed off.

"Why would you do this?" I asked, my voice sounding breathless. "Why would you risk your life like that?"

"I've been looking for—" He broke off abruptly, swallowed, then finished. "For people who will fight."

My fingers kept shifting over the muscles of his shoulders. His skin was warm beneath my hands, his muscles hard beneath my touch. I was awed by his strength. Not his physical strength, but his will. His courage. The sheer audacity that brought him back to this fight over and over again. He had been free. He could have run for the hills and never looked back. Instead, he'd stayed and fought. He'd faced death countless times to save other people, some of them strangers.

I stopped counting his scars at a dozen. He'd stilled. The muscles of his back were tense beneath my hand. His head was dipped down and he wasn't even breathing.

I jerked my hands away and fisted them in my lap. He exhaled then pushed himself to his feet. Without turning around, he grabbed the white T-shirt and yanked it over his head, shoving his arms through the sleeves. He didn't even glance over his shoulder as he tucked the hem into his pants and pulled on his Collab jacket. Every movement seemed jerky and tense. Like he was angry with me.

"Do you believe me now?" he asked.

"I'm . . . I'm sorry," I said.

He half turned to look at me, his fingers still on his buttons. "Christ, you don't even know what you're apologizing for, do you?"

I felt myself shrink back into the chair. "I accused you of being a Collab. I was so sure that you'd betrayed us. I'm . . . I'm sorry."

He gave me a long, steady look. Like my apology didn't even begin to cover it.

I leapt to my feet. "Maybe I haven't been out fighting in the great rebellion, but it's not like I'm some Collab."

He just shook his head as he picked up the tranq gun and slung the strap over his shoulder.

That look never left his eyes, like I'd disappointed him, like maybe, after all he'd been through tonight, this was his breaking point. This was where his patience with me had run out.

I knew I could never join his rebellion. Taking care of Mel had been the priority drilled into my mind from the time I was a child. Those had been my mother's last words to me as we'd boarded the bus to come to the Farm. Not "I love you," not even "Take care of yourself," but "Keep Mel safe." Still, I couldn't blame my mother. Mel needed someone to take care of her. I'd always been so independent. Even as a kid I hadn't liked to rely on anyone else. But Mel needed Mom. She needed me, because I was all she had now.

"I don't suppose it's occurred to you that just keeping me and Mel alive has been a full-time job. If I'm so focused on getting her out and going to Canada, it's because I don't have any other choice. I have to do it because there's no one else here who can."

I expected some kind of reaction to my impassioned speech, but Carter just blinked and asked, "What's in Canada?"

"Safety, I think. One of the last things I saw on the news before Mel and I were shipped here was a story about Canada closing its borders." For the first time it occurred to me that I might be wrong about Canada. Or maybe I just hadn't let myself think about it. I leaned forward. "Do you know if Canada is still . . . there? Were they successful in keeping the Ticks out?"

"I don't know," Carter said quietly. "I haven't been that far north. I haven't met anyone who has, either. The Canadians aren't here fighting for us, I know that much."

I ignored the bitterness in his voice. As far as I was concerned, getting to Canada was still our best bet. "If we can get there, maybe we'll be safe from the Ticks. And the vampires," I added with chagrin.

"That's all you care about, huh? Keeping Mel safe?"

"I'm all she has. She has to be all I care about."

"Mel isn't the only person who cares about you," Carter said, his voice pitched low.

Under other circumstances, in another world, I might mistake that for a come-on. Or maybe another dropped pencil. Some way of luring me in. But no matter how I played through it in my mind, I couldn't think of anything Carter could want from me. And I was really tired of being so suspicious all the damn time.

So I decided to give him a little credit. Maybe he meant it exactly the way it sounded. Maybe he cared about me—no, I wasn't going to get caught up in some fantasy that he'd been nursing a crush on me all this time—but maybe he'd meant everything he'd said that afternoon about being glad to see me because we'd known each other in the Before. Maybe it was just nostalgia. Maybe I was just his can of Dr Pepper. So I could buy that he cared about me on some level.

"I admire what you're doing," I told him. "But not everyone can be a hero."

He gave a little nod, and I couldn't help thinking he was disappointed in me again. He picked the last of the Rolos up off the table and slipped them into his pocket. Then he nudged the chairs back into place around the table and picked up the foil wrapper, removing nearly all signs that we'd been there. "That's a shame, Lily. Because you'd make a pretty kick-ass hero."

"Will you still help us get off the Farm?" I reached for his arm automatically, but regretted it the moment I felt him tense under my touch. "Even if we're not going with you back to your mysterious stronghold?"

He stared at the spot where my hand rested on his arm. He closed his eyes for a second, then looked up at me.

I expected to see frustration in his eyes. Instead I saw humor. "You bet your sweet ass I am." Then he grinned. That same shit-eatin' grin I remembered so well from the Before. "It's a long drive to Canada from here. That'll give me, what, about twenty hours to convince you."

My heart thudded desperately in my chest. "You'll go with us? You'll bring us all the way to Canada?"

After all his talk about the rebellion, I hadn't dared hope he'd help us get to Canada.

He studied me for a second, no doubt seeing the pleading hope on my face. "Absolutely. There's no way I'd get you out of here and then let you fend for yourself against the Ticks. What kind of a jerk do you think I am?"

"I don't think you're a jerk at all," I said quietly, suddenly feeling awkward and very unworthy of that Dr Pepper he'd given me.

An hour ago, I'd been sure he'd betrayed us. A half hour ago, I'd been convinced he was crazy. Now, I was ready to trust him with my life. The thought was terrifying.

Despite that, I had no idea what Mel and I would face outside the Farm. But I did know this: having Carter on our side would greatly increase our chances of surviving.

"So what's next?" I asked.

"Next, we find somewhere you can catch a couple hours of sleep. Dawn's more than five hours away and you've still got the tranq in your system."

"I'm fine," I protested.

"You may feel fine right now, but you'll be sharper if you sleep off the rest of the tranq."

"Can't we just stay here?"

"No. No one's messed with the soda machine, so the building is probably unused, but we don't know that for sure. And I'd rather be somewhere you're familiar with."

"I guess it's back to the science building then."

"If that's the place you know best, we might as well use it to our advantage."

I picked up my bag and slung it over my shoulder, preparing to leave. A single Rolo sat in front of my spot. I hadn't eaten it yet and Carter hadn't cleared it away with the trash. Quickly, I pulled off my backpack and dug in the front pocket until I found an old empty Altoids tin. I popped it open and carefully placed the Rolo inside. As I slipped the tin back into the pocket of my hoodie, I realized Carter was watching.

"You're not just going to eat that now?"

"I don't . . ." Suddenly my throat felt tight, so I pushed the words out quickly. "I don't know when I'm going to have candy again." If I'd *ever* have candy again. "I think I'm just going to keep it. For now."

Carter frowned and gave the candy machine a thoughtful look. "You want me to get the rest of the candy out of there for you?"

"We're out of money," I pointed out.

Carter chuckled. "Oh, come on, I could break into that thing in less than a minute."

"Then why didn't you do that earlier?"

"I was trying to convince you I was trustworthy. Violence and theft didn't seem like the way to go."

"But you'd do that for me? You'd commit candy robbery for me?"

Standing next to me, he gave my shoulder a playful bump with his own. "I broke into a Farm for you. Of course I'd break into a candy machine for you."

My breath caught at his words. "I thought you just broke into this Farm and you happened to find me here."

He shrugged it off. "Yeah. That's what I meant. You want the candy or not?"

Was this another dropped pencil? I slanted a look at him, but his expression looked perfectly casual. Concerned only about the candy.

I touched his arm, then nodded toward the door. "Let's leave it."

He didn't question me about why and I was glad of that. I didn't know if he'd understand. I didn't know if *I* understood. But somehow it comforted me to know that this machine was here, quietly chugging, doing its job. A silent monument to the culture that once was. It made me sad to leave its familiar red glow. It wasn't like me to be sentimental about that kind of thing.

CHAPTER SIXTEEN

LILY

I thought escaping from the Farm would be the hardest part of my day. It wasn't. When Carter suggested I try to get a few hours of sleep before dawn, I thought he was crazy. He wasn't.

By the time we made it back to the closet in the science lab, I was starting to crash from all the sugar in the Dr Pepper, despite how jittery I'd been all evening. Or maybe because of that. Carter wedged the chair from his room under the door to the science lab. In our closet, he set the chair against the door and then sat down, his back to the door.

Suddenly I felt nervous being alone with him. Sure, I'd been alone with him all night, but this felt different. More intimate, because this was essentially my bedroom. Besides, now I knew the truth about Carter. He wasn't just some crush from the past trying to charm me for his own questionable purposes. He was a hero. Maybe the bravest person I'd ever met. Or the stupidest, if there was a difference.

The room was lit with the single-bulb gooseneck lamp I'd snagged from Professor Bajaj's office. It was funny. After six months of living in this building I felt like I knew all of these people.

For the first minute or so we were in the room, I didn't quite know what to do with myself. I'd thought I'd already said good-bye to this room when we left it earlier. I'd never expected to be back here.

Finally I sat on the mattress Mel and I kept on the floor, before toeing my shoes off. I scooted into the corner, resting my back against the wall and crossing my legs. Crisscross applesauce, they used to call it in school.

"You should lie down," Carter said. "Try to get some sleep."

He'd stretched out his legs in front of him and crossed his arms over his chest, and his eyelids were drooping. Like he was nearly asleep himself.

"You should lie down," I countered. "You need sleep, too."

"I'll be okay."

"Military school," I chimed before he could say it. "I know."

Regardless of how much training he'd had, he was exhausted. For whatever reason, he was determined to guard the door. After a few minutes, I lay down, pulled the blanket up—the ratty one we'd decided to leave here—and flicked off the light, plunging the room into darkness. Lights off in a windowless room was really, truly dark. Sure, I'd gotten used to it over the past few months, but the night felt even more encompassing with Carter in the room with me. I could hear his breathing, which had slowed but not yet evened out. I heard every shift he made in the chair trying to get more comfortable. Every creak of the mattress as I tried to find a more natural spot.

"You'll fall asleep faster if you stop moving around so damn much," Carter said, his voice laced with laughter.

"I can't help it," I muttered. "This is weird."

"Weird how?"

What was I supposed to say to that? Weird 'cause I wasn't used to sleeping with a guy in my room. Watching over me, for Pete's sake. But that would be admitting how aware I was of him.

I went for the half-truth rather than embarrassing honesty. "I haven't slept in a bed by myself in six months. It's weird not having Mel here." Which was at least partly true. Mel slept sprawled out like a starfish and I'd gotten used to wedging myself against the wall. "And it's cold."

That part was wholly true. I hadn't bothered to get out the other blanket or the sleeping bag from Joe and now I was regretting it.

Then I heard Carter shift again and the chair squeak. Four footsteps later, I felt the mattress dip as he sat down on the edge. I heard him take off his boots. And then the rustling of fabric that I assumed was him taking off his Collab jacket. "Scoot over."

I literally couldn't breathe. No air moved in or out of my lungs as I wiggled into the corner and lifted the edge of the blanket. He slid under the covers.

Even though he didn't touch me, I was acutely aware of him lying there beside me. He must have been lying on the very edge of the mattress, because he left a gap of several inches between us. I could practically feel the energy bouncing off that no-man's-land.

At some point I must have started breathing again, because his scent wrapped around me, seeming to sink into my very skin. His body just radiated heat. Suddenly the blanket enveloping us felt like a heavy down comforter.

Every muscle in my body was tense. There was no way I was going to fall asleep. Probably ever again.

I just lay there—I didn't know how long—pressing my back against the wall and trying not to move.

"You're still not falling asleep," he muttered, his voice sleepy.

"I can't help it. This is—"

"Weird?" he finished for me, his voice amused, despite sounding groggy.

“Maybe if you talked to me.”

“Oh, great.”

“Hey, you’re the one who said we should try to remember what we loved about the Before.”

“That’s true.” I heard a rustle I took to be him rubbing at his eyes. “I did say that.”

“So . . .” I prodded. “Tell me something you liked in the Before.”

He was quiet for so long I wondered if he’d fallen asleep. Then he said, “I liked sitting next to you in science.”

I gave his arm a little sock. “That’s so lame. Don’t do that.”

“Don’t do what?”

“That thing where you try to charm me to get your way. Just be honest.”

“Okay.”

“So? One thing you liked in the Before.”

“You always smelled like homemade cookies.”

“Excuse me?”

“I mean, I never had anyone bake me homemade cookies, so I don’t know for sure. But you had some lotion or something, I guess, that made me think of cookies.”

“Brown sugar vanilla,” I whispered.

“Huh?”

“That was the lotion I used. And sometimes mango madness. But that wouldn’t make you think of cookies.”

“Yeah. I remember the mango, too.”

Was I crazy or could I hear his smile in his voice?

“And you were funny,” Carter said.

“What?”

“In class. You were always muttering crap under your breath. Giving Coach Ballard a hard time.”

"The man was an idiot," I said now, partly to cover how surprised I was that Carter remembered these things about me.

"That he was. You were merciless."

"He was barely qualified to teach P.E. Forget honors biology. Someone had to tell him how to pronounce all the stages of mitosis."

"I think you made him cry once."

"I did not."

I heard Carter chuckle. "Yeah, I'm pretty sure you did."

"Great, now I feel bad."

"Nah. The guy was a jerk." He was so tired he was starting to slur his words now. "Making him cry only made me like you more."

Another one of those long, awkward silences passed. This time, I was sure he was going to reach for me—at least my hand. But then I heard his breathing even out. He was asleep.

I lay there for a long time, just listening to him breathe. It felt like hours before I relaxed enough to drift off, and when I woke up Carter was gone.

I jerked to a sitting position, then fumbled for the phone in my pocket that I kept charged just so I'd have a clock. Four twenty-three. I tugged my shoes back on. If it wasn't yet time to head back over to the admin building, it would be soon. However, when I opened the door connecting the closet to the lab room, Carter wasn't there.

Shoving my arms through the straps of the backpack, I all but ran across the room to go look for him. I flung open the door into the hall and ran headlong into Carter's chest. I jerked back and we stared at each other in the dim light for an instant before we both spoke at the same time.

"Where did you go?"

"Good, you're up."

We each broke off, but he recovered first.

"I've been patrolling the halls. Good thing, too." He wrapped a hand around my arm and started leading me out of the room. "Did you leave anything behind? Or do you have all your stuff?"

"No. Yes. Wait, what's going on?"

"Collabs are searching the building. They're down on the second and third floors now and working their way up. That's not normal, is it?"

He'd been pulling me along the hall. I assumed we were going to the stairwell, but he stopped in front of the elevators. My brain was still foggy. "What? No. It's not normal." Collabs in the building? "They do inspections, but never in the middle of the night."

"Damn it," he muttered. "That means they must be looking for you."

"How do you know they're not looking for you?"

He sent me an exasperated look. "You wanna debate it now or do you wanna wait until after they've caught you?"

"I thought you had some sort of a deal with the Dean. I thought he was supposed to just let us walk out of here."

"We did. He was."

"So what changed?"

"I don't know." Carter sent me a thoughtful look. "If we're lucky, he just decided he might be able to cut a better deal with Sebastian if he holds on to you. Once we get you off campus, he should lose interest."

"And if we're not lucky?"

"We'll worry about that after we get out of here."

"How did he even know where to find me?"

Carter's eyes dropped to my shoulder.

Surprise made me clamp a hand to the spot where my chip was lodged. "They can track these even if I haven't left the Farm?"

"Yeah. If they want to find a particular person, they use the GPS locator."

"And you think the Dean wants me back badly enough to bother with that?"

Carter looked chagrined. "I think he must. He wouldn't send all these Collabs to find you if he wasn't serious."

I thought about the scars on Carter's back. Even though the thought made me a little queasy, I said, "Then let's cut it out. Destroy it."

Carter shook his head. "There's no time. We've got to be across campus to meet Sebastian in less than an hour. I'm not cutting you open right before a car trip with a vampire."

"You said he was safe. Would he—"

"No. But I don't want to make it any harder on him than it has to be. Or to take any unnecessary risks. It's better to leave the chips in for now."

"Not if they're tracking me with it."

"At the other Farms I've been on, there's only one tracking device. It's expensive and kept in the Dean's office. Most Collabs don't carry walkie-talkies or sat phones or anything, so it's harder for them to coordinate a search. Plus, he only knows you're in the building. Not exactly where in the building you are."

Carter sounded like he knew what he was talking about. I shut down the rest of the questions I wanted to ask. "How many of them are there?"

"I saw eight. I assume there's at least one more pair on the first floor guarding both of the staircases."

"Did they see you?" I asked. He was still in his Collab uniform and probably could have just walked past them.

He shot me a look like I was an idiot. "I made sure they didn't see me. I didn't want to risk talking to them."

That sounded really serious. "Okay, what do we do?"

"Is there another way out of here?" Carter asked, his voice low and hushed. "We need another option."

My brain seemed to stutter along at half speed for several long moments. Collabs. In the building. And here we were, trapped on the seventh floor.

Just then, the floor numbers above the elevator doors blinked to life.

Carter looked over his shoulder and saw it also. "Guess we won't be taking the elevator."

"Yeah. Not this one." Then it hit me. "Come on," I said, heading down the hall at a trot. "There's a service elevator."

I led Carter through the twisting corridors, away from the classrooms and lab rooms at the front of the building to the maze of tiny offices. I stopped at the wide swinging door that led into a room that was part staff room, part maintenance room. Barely bigger than our storage closet, it had a couple of tables. Some Green had taken the chairs long ago. One wall was lined with floor-to-ceiling cabinets. The microwave that had once sat on the counter was now in our closet. The far wall was dominated by the no-nonsense doors to the service elevator.

I reached out to punch the down button, but Carter grabbed my hand before I could.

"Hang on."

I followed his gaze to see him staring at the line of numbers above the elevator doors. For a long moment, nothing happened, the glowing number one assuring us that the elevator was down on the first floor, where it had been these past six months. But then, just as Carter was letting go of my hand so I could push the down button, there came the unmistakable sound of the elevator cables creaking to life. The one blinked out and the two lit up.

Carter cursed under his breath, glancing at me. "Any other ideas?"

My mind raced from one ridiculous plan to the next. "Um . . . drop a bomb down the elevator shaft to cause a distraction?"

Carter's eyebrows shot up. "A bomb?"

My cheeks reddened, but thankfully Carter didn't seem to notice. He backed away from the elevator doors and started searching the room.

"My mom liked action movies. We watched a lot of those old Bruce Willis movies when I was a kid."

Carter just smiled, barely paying attention to me as he opened the various cabinet doors. "I don't know if I should be offended or glad that your violent streak isn't limited to me."

"Nope, not just you, apparently." I glanced nervously at the elevator.

The two blinked out. The three turned orange.

"Um, have you got some kind of plan going on here," I asked, "or are we just waiting until they get here and greeting them face-to-face?" He didn't say anything, but tried the door to the broom closet opposite the cabinets. "It's kind of short notice, but I might have time to brew some tea. Put out some cookies." The door was locked. "Maybe some—"

Carter backed up a step and rammed the door with his shoulder. The wood buckled with a thunderous groan.

"Holy crap!" I exclaimed, jerking my hands up to my face, like if I blocked the noise from my ears then the Collabs wouldn't hear it, either.

The doorjamb splintered but the lock held.

"You know, unless they're deaf, they can hear that."

"You have any better ideas?" he asked, stepping back so he could ram the door again.

"Yes! I have the keys!"

"The keys? Seriously?"

"Yes." I slipped my backpack off, unzipped the front pocket, and started digging around inside. "I searched all the offices right after we moved in. Clearly Professor Bajaj—whoever he was—was a total control freak. Plus, he was the head of the department."

I found what I was looking for and held it up so Carter could see the key ring with eight keys hanging from it. Each had a little paper tag dangling from it, labeled "Master Key 1st floor," "Master Key 2nd floor," and so on. Like I said, control freak. You gotta love that about a man. Makes it so easy to pilfer his belongings later.

I found "Master Key 7th floor" and jammed it into the lock.

Carter looked inside. "Shit. Just more brooms."

"What were you expecting? A door into the magical world of Narnia?"

He smirked. "Good point. I was just hoping for a solution that doesn't involve bombing them. We'll consider that our last resort."

Carter backed out of the broom closet and shut the door. He let his shoulders sink into the wall in a defeated sort of way. We both looked at the row of numbers above the elevator. The Collabs had made it to four. Who knew what floor the others were on? However many of them there were, they were getting closer. And we were out of options. Unless we wanted to parachute off the top of the building, we were stuck here.

"We've got to hide." He grabbed my hand and started pulling me toward the door, but he stopped short. Slowly he reached out and swung the door away from the wall. Pointing to the hatch that had been hidden behind the open door, he asked, "What's that?"

"That's the garbage chute."

"The . . . what?" He shot me a look of either confusion or disbelief.

"The garbage chute. You know, you open the door and drop a bag of trash all the way down to the basement. Or, I don't know, maybe it's a laundry chute or something."

"All the way down to the basement?" he asked with his eyebrows so high up his forehead they'd disappeared beneath his bangs. He looked from the hatch door in the wall to me and back again.

"Oh, no," I muttered, the significance slowly dawning. "You can't be serious."

He yanked on the handle, pulling it open so the door dropped flat against the wall. He stuck his head through the opening and looked down.

"You cannot be serious!" I repeated, panic starting to gnaw at my gut. I threw out the first objection that came to mind. "That opening is only, like, two feet by two feet. We wouldn't even fit."

He eyed me. "You'd fit. I might."

"It's a seven-story drop!"

"Good point." He grinned, not looking at all like I'd convinced him.

Behind us, the elevator cranked to life again. It had nearly reached our floor.

Carter closed the hatch to the garbage chute, then carefully opened the maintenance room door so that the hatch behind it was nearly invisible. Then he opened up the broom closet and pulled me inside.

The closet was dark, with only a thin strip of light coming from under the door. My eyes adjusted as I kept fumbling with the keys, making them rattle. Finally, I felt Carter's fingers pry them out of mine. I let him because I was too afraid of making noise.

The room was tiny and so dark I could barely see. I felt Carter's presence behind me. I was all the more aware of him because I was starting to feel jittery from the adrenaline. Even though we hadn't heard the ding from the elevator—so I knew the Collabs hadn't made it to the seventh floor yet—I felt like they'd be able to hear my pounding heart the second they stepped out of the elevator.

I took a step away from the door and felt the backpack bump into Carter. I turned and took a step to the side, only to feel it nudge something else. Mop handles slid and clattered against the door.

"Crap," I muttered.

I tried to look over my shoulder and turned another ninety degrees, but I bumped something else.

Before I could do any more damage, Carter grabbed my shoulders and pulled me closer to him.

"Come here, before you knock anything else over. Jeez, and you were worried about me making too much noise."

He must have been leaning his back against the shelves, because his legs were stretched out in front of him a little and I ended up standing between his legs. I gripped the straps of the backpack, waiting for my eyes to adjust. Even without seeing, I could tell my face was just a few inches from his chest.

"Hey, I'm not the one who decided to put us into the tiniest closet on this floor," I said defensively.

"Oh, yeah, I'm sure you could have found something better—"

"Professor Estleman's office is right around the corner. She has a storage closet almost as big as the one Mel and I lived in. And then there's that one, too. And—"

"Okay, I get the point."

My eyes had adjusted to the dim lighting. Our chests were maybe five inches apart and his lips were right at eye level. It was odd, standing so close to him, trying to be so perfectly still and quiet. I was too aware of the way his legs were stretched out on either side of mine. I could hear every breath he took, could feel his exhalations against my cheek.

Then, somewhere in the building, the heater cycled on. The silence in the room wasn't quite so deafening.

"Could you really build a bomb?" he asked.

"Don't get too excited," I quipped. "I mean, I couldn't build, like, a nuclear missile or anything. But when Mel and I first started planning our escape, I figured out how to build a Molotov cocktail."

"And . . ."

"And, it's doable. There are all kinds of chemicals locked in the chem lab's safety cabinet. I could come up with something."

"Are we talking a lot of fire and noise?"

"Yeah," I whispered. "Something to distract people, if that's what you want."

"I'm impressed."

"I've lived in a science building for the past six months with almost nothing to do except read and explore," I blurted out. "I'd be pretty stupid if I couldn't come up with something that would explode after all this time."

"Good point." Again there was that humor in his voice.

Was he making fun of me? I took an instinctive step back.

Before I could bump into anything else, he reached out and grabbed my arms, pulling me toward him. He released my arms, dropping his hands to my hips. "Hey, don't go too far," he murmured.

"Um, just out of curiosity. Couldn't we just stay here until they leave to go look for me somewhere else?"

His hands seemed to tighten infinitesimally on my hips. "That does sound nice, doesn't it?" His voice was low and intimate. I squeezed my eyes closed. "But I don't think so. We need to get you out of here and across campus in less than an hour."

Then he shifted his legs, straightening. I opened my eyes to see him dipping his head. He reached his hand up and traced his thumb down my cheek. "Lily . . ."

Then he stilled when the elevator door finally dinged. The Collabs had made it to our floor. Carter's gaze sharpened and he cocked his head to listen toward the door.

". . . why we're looking here," one of them was grumbling.

"Who knows? The Dean's a jackass for dragging all of our asses out of bed to search for one stupid Green."

Their footfalls were heavy and dull. The sound of the door opening. Then the first guy said, "Hey, do you think the Dean will let us play with her a bit first?"

"Dude, she's not a Breeder."

"Yeah, but that doesn't matter if he's just going to feed her to the Ticks anyway."

The second guy let out a bark of laughter, like what his buddy had said was actually funny or something.

The voices faded as the Collabs left the room.

Suddenly the air in the tiny broom closet felt heavy. Sure, I'd known the Collabs had to have been searching for me, but hearing them say it was something else entirely. I felt a jolt of panic as suddenly the danger I was in became all too real.

For a long moment, Carter was as silent as I was, and for some reason I didn't understand, I wasn't looking at him anymore but was staring at one of the stupid mop handles. I forced myself to look at him. I could barely see him in the dark, but I could feel the tension in his body.

"So . . ." I started, wanting to change the topic away from the Collabs and what they planned to do to me if they found me, ". . . what are you going to do with this bomb I'm supposed to build?"

"I'm going to get you out of this building."

Before I could ask what exactly his plan was, he edged around me and used my key to unlock the door. "Stay here. I'll be back to get you in a few minutes."

CHAPTER SEVENTEEN

LILY

Since the staff room was at the end of the back hallway, there was only one direction Carter could have gone to follow the Collabs. I crept down the hall, practically holding my breath, my ears straining for the sounds of Carter getting his ass kicked. Or worse, his ass knocked out.

Yeah, he was tough—I knew that better than anyone—but there were at least two Collabs. And his tranq rifle was out of darts. I would never forgive myself if he ended up hurt just because I hadn't trusted him enough not to shoot me in the back again. Of course, I also wouldn't have been able to forgive myself if I'd missed the chance to take the dart and then he'd shot me later, so I guess it balanced out.

I reached the spot where the maintenance hall met the building's main hall and stopped just shy of the intersection, listening. Still nothing. Back pressed to the wall, I crouched low and peered around the corner, fully expecting to see the Collabs and maybe Carter, too, but the hall was empty. Where were they?

I cursed Carter as I tiptoed down the hall. Suddenly, a thud came from one of the rooms on my right, followed quickly by a yelp and a scuffle.

I broke into a run and skidded into the room only a few seconds later to see Carter leaning over the two Collabs, both of whom were knocked out on the floor.

"Wow," I said.

Carter looked up at me. The angle made his bangs hang over his eyes and for a second he looked so much more like the boy I'd known back in the Before, it almost made my heart catch. He quirked an eyebrow; either he was surprised to see me standing there or it was some sort of commentary on my reaction.

"That was fast!" I said.

He stood. "Yeah. Mili—"

"Military school," I finished for him.

"I told you to wait in the closet for me to come get you," he said as he dug something out of his back pocket.

"Right. Next time you want me to stay in a closet while you go out to face the bad guys by yourself, you'd better lock me in. 'Cause I'm not just going to hide while—"

He pulled a couple of cable tie handcuffs out of his back pocket. "I left you behind for a reason. I—"

"I can handle myself."

"I know you can handle yourself." He gave a little rub at his neck to remind me exactly how well he knew it. "But I also knew I could handle these guys alone. And I knew I had to do it quietly, because we don't want anyone else coming up here."

"Oh." I stood there for a moment watching as he rolled the first Collab onto his stomach and fastened the cable tie around his wrists. "Why can't anything ever be easy with you, Carter?"

He barely glanced up at me. "It was easy. I told you to stay put. If you'd stayed put, that would have been easy."

"No, that would have been stupid."

"Look, it's my job to keep you safe and—"

"It's my own job to keep myself safe. I've been doing that quite well for the past six months. So don't treat me like I can't take care of myself. Next time you're planning on rushing off to save the day, tell me your plan first."

"Fine." By now he'd bound the wrists of the second Collab and had moved on to binding their feet, too. "Next time I'll tell you what I'm going to do. Now can you tell me where the nearest closet is that I can lock these guys up in?"

"Right across the hall."

I rushed across to make sure it was unlocked. By the time I made it back, he had his arms hooked under the armpits of the first Collab and was dragging him to the closet. I went back and grabbed the second. The guy was heavier than I would have thought. Or I was weaker.

Carter came up behind me. "Hey, let me get him."

I stood up, sucking in a deep breath as I did, but my head still swirled a bit.

Carter grabbed the other guy and dragged him across the hall. I must have looked as newborn-deerish as I felt, because he asked, "When was the last time you donated?"

It took me a second to remember. The days tended to blend together without weekends to divide up the time. "Five days ago. Maybe four."

He cursed under his breath. "I shouldn't have tranqed you."

"No, you shouldn't have."

"Yeah. Sorry about that." He got Collab number two into place beside his partner. "You should take it easy until the rest of the tranq wears off."

I nudged my foot toward one of the Collabs. "Are they going to be okay?"

"They'll be fine. Someone will realize they're missing. Either tonight when they don't report back or tomorrow when they don't report for duty. Their supervisor will activate their chips and send someone to look for them." He grabbed my hand and started walking down the hall. "How long will it take you to make a couple of those things?"

"Maybe twenty or thirty minutes. I think I've got everything I need back in the room Mel and I lived in."

Thankfully anything I could possibly need had once been stored there. I was as familiar with the contents of that room as I'd once been with my bedroom at home. Of course, since Mel had worked her magic, things were not where I'd left them. But most of the bottles of chemicals were the same color, so finding them shouldn't be too hard.

A few minutes later, we were back in the storage closet, and I was rounding up ingredients. The sooner Carter and I were out of here, the sooner I'd be back with Mel.

After helping me carry a tray of bottles out to the lab, Carter asked, "You good here, or do you need me to stay?"

I glanced up from a bottle of benzene. "Where are you going?"

His evasions might have annoyed me, but I didn't really like the idea of being in here alone when there were still four Collabs prowling around the building looking for me.

"I was going to search this floor. Try to find some rope."

"No need." I nodded toward the backpack as I continued to sort through the items I needed to make the bombs. "I've got some in there. Check the middle pocket."

A minute later, he'd found it and was stretching it out in arm lengths to estimate how long it was.

"About thirty feet," he said, shaking his head. "Not long enough. Where did you get this? Was there more of it?"

I'd covered a bottle brush with a paper towel and was using it to clear out the bottles I'd selected. I didn't want anything in there that I didn't put in. So I didn't look up at him as I answered. "One of the geology professors had a bunch of rappelling gear. I guess she took students—"

"Where's her office?"

"Down on the third floor."

"Damn," he muttered.

I smiled as I moved on to the next bottle. "But I brought all the rappelling gear up to the storage closet as soon as I found it."

His face broke into a smile. "You're a genius."

"Thanks," I quipped, without letting his compliment go to my head. "But you'll have to search the storage closet to find it. The last time I saw it, it was in a gray and blue backpack. I have no idea if Mel took it out of the pack or not."

I returned my attention to the task at hand. By the time I was screwing the lid onto the second jar, Carter came out of the storage closet holding a single harness. His expression was grim.

I picked up a towel and began wrapping the first of the bottles in it. "I'm guessing it's not what you wanted."

He held up the harness. "There's only one."

Dread wormed through my stomach. While I was concentrating on making the bombs, it was easy not to think about what Carter was planning, but staring at the harness in his hand, it was harder to ignore. "I thought you wanted rope."

"A couple hundred feet of rope would have worked in a pinch. This is better."

And here I'd been hoping he was just going to use it to tie up the Collabs.

"Why exactly is this better?" I carefully wrapped the next jar in a towel. I tried to keep my voice lighthearted, to hide my fear of heights. "We're not actually going to be repelling out any of the windows, are we?"

Carter ignored me and tapped a fingertip on the jar. "How's this work anyway?"

I let him distract me for a few minutes, partly because he'd need to know how this was going to work and partly because I wanted to be distracted.

"The jar contains mostly methanol thickened with benzene. But I added in a pyrophoric compound that will ignite the fuel when it's exposed to air. So basically, you throw the jar and run. The jar breaks, there's fire, fumes, bad stuff."

"A pyro what kind of compound?"

"Pyrophoric," I said, feeling a little . . . well, maybe not smug, but at least pleased with myself. Since coming back into my life, Carter had one-upped me over and over again and he'd been so damn competent and calm while doing it. But I'd made mistake after mistake. I felt like I'd been twisted inside out and turned upside down. But this, this was stuff I knew and liked. In this one small arena, I had an edge over Carter. I liked feeling like I brought something to the party, too. And for once, my geekiness was useful.

He looked at the jars as if baffled. "If it ignites when it's exposed to air, how did you get it in the jars?"

"Since I didn't have a glove box or a Schlenk Line, I flushed a syringe with inert gas—" Carter's eyes were starting to glaze over, so I cut straight to the point. "Very carefully. I did it very carefully."

"In the movies, when someone makes a Molotov cocktail, they just light a rag on fire. Why not do that?"

I snorted. "You think they let us Greens have matches?"

"I have matches."

"Oh." And just like that, my geekiness was no longer useful.

Then Carter grinned broadly. "But this is much cooler. Perfect, actually." Carter picked up the first jar and set it just outside the door to the closet Mel and I had shared. Then he carried the second one over to the door leading out into the hall. He stood there a moment, seeming to gauge the distance.

I realized what he was thinking and had to swallow past a lump in my throat. He was going to throw one jar at the other. Either he'd hit the second jar and the explosion would be bigger or he'd miss, but the fire would blow up the second jar a few seconds later. "You think you can throw it and hit the door frame?"

He nodded. "Yep. I figure between the books and the mattress, there're plenty of things that will burn." He turned to me. "I want you to wait by the fire stairs. Will you do that for me?"

My heart was suddenly racing. I wanted to argue with him about who was going to throw the actual bomb. This was my idea; I should be the one to take the risk.

Yeah, I was . . . oh, eighty percent sure this would work. But it wasn't like I'd actually tried it before. I had no actual experience in demolition. And if I was wrong . . .

"Carter, I don't know. Maybe this is a bad idea."

He flashed me a smile. "No. It's a great idea. It's gonna work."

"I could do it."

"Naw." He eyed the corner again. "I can throw farther than you can. Just go wait by the stairs and I'll be there in a minute."

I felt my throat closing up. "Okay. Be safe."

I couldn't stay and watch, even if I wasn't supposed to be heading for the stairs. I ran all the way there, my adrenaline fueling my speed. And then I waited, heart pounding, back pressed to the wall beside the door.

I heard the explosion a second before Carter turned the corner and I saw him running down the hall. I'd already opened the door and he ran in behind me, slamming the door shut. He pulled me against his chest, just as the second explosion rumbled down the hall.

"Perfect timing," he said softly. "I thought you said the explosions would be small."

"I thought they would be. It's not like I took Blowin' Shit Up 101 last year as an elective. I tried to—"

"Shh."

Carter pushed me away from him and opened the door just a crack. I leaned forward, straining to hear whatever had caught his attention. It was footsteps. At least a couple of people thundering down the hall.

We waited. Listening. And in those few moments, it hit me. I'd just blown up the room where Mel and I had lived for the past six months.

Everything I'd known was gone. There was truly no going back.

CHAPTER EIGHTEEN

MEL

There is a sweet, blessed peace in Sebastian's silence. I know it's wrong. I know the noise he doesn't make is a sign of his not-rightness. Still, there's a kind of relief in it. Like death.

But the longer I'm here, the less oppressive his silence is. His not-noise feels like the weight of water. Tranquil. Maybe he's just sitting at the bottom of a different pool.

He's not a talker, this one. Still, I can feel his attention. It presses against my skin, making me aware, but not nervous. I feel his hunger, but he hasn't bitten yet. Which makes sense, because even the hungriest sharks leave their pilot fish alone.

I wonder at his quiet. Even at peace most people jangle. I've met no one yet this blank and quieter than hushed.

His silence allows me to hear the noise of the others, far beyond this room. The Blue ones rumbling around the building all thump, thump, thumpity thump thump. Why do they all sound the same?

And then there's the Ladybird, plump as a pigeon up in his office. His music is sour and rotten as dead fish on the shore. Do pigeons even eat fish? Bet he'd eat anything. Wish he'd flown farther.

Which makes me think of Carter. I worry about Lily, sluggish as she is. Will she see Carter's truths? Will he tell her? God knows she won't hear them. She's moving too fast to hear anyone's music but her own. She's so set, but I know he could make her settled. I tried to sync their noise into music, but they both pushed back. Too obdurate to be obliging.

Silly Lily. How can she resist someone who brings gum and sounds like math?

CHAPTER NINETEEN

LILY

Sure, as soon as Carter set the bomb down outside the storage closet, I knew our room would be in the blast zone. But knowing that and hearing the boom were two different things. There should have been something cathartic about blowing up the room that had been both my sanctuary and my prison. But I also felt a pang in my heart. I was already missing the sanctuary that room had provided, even if it had never really been safe.

I didn't have time to analyze the feeling. There were footsteps pounding past the door. Collabs running toward the explosion to investigate.

As soon as the footsteps passed, Carter edged over to the railing. "Pebbles?" he mouthed.

I was confused for only a second, thinking of cereal I'd loved as a kid. Then I nodded and reached into my pocket. I did the usual routine and watched as the pebble bounced down the stairs. Silence followed. I looked over at him and he held his head cocked to one side, still listening. Then finally he nodded and we moved.

My feet pounded on the stairs, seeming way too loud. Like I was a thundering elephant. Behind me, Carter might have been lighter on his feet. I couldn't hear anything over the pounding of my heart and the slap of my shoes on the metal treads. It was more than fear that drove me forward. We were almost out. Almost free. We'd made it down one flight and then another and another.

He stopped me on the second floor. "Okay, here's where it gets tricky. Wait here for second." Then he seemed to remember what I'd said earlier about needing to know where he was going and he turned back to me. "I'm going to go out into the hall. Do a quick surveillance to make sure there aren't any Collabs out there and then I'll come back for you. If I'm not back in five minutes—"

"Just come back," I said.

"Okay."

Carter slouched his shoulders a bit and his features settled into an expression of insolent disinterest. Suddenly, he really looked like a Collab. Even though the difference between this Carter and my Carter was minor, the effect was huge. I hadn't realized until that moment how much a part of him that tough military posture was.

Before I could marvel at it, he swung the door open and slunk out into the hall. I waited in the darkness, counting my heartbeats. He came back quickly and ushered me out into the hall. We all but ran to the staff room on the second floor.

Once we were there, Carter slipped his backpack off his shoulder, unzipping it as he walked. I watched with trepidation as he pulled the harness and cables from the bag.

"We're not really going to use that, are we?"

"We're not. You are." He pushed open the door to the second-floor staff room and dread slammed into me.

"I so don't want to do this."

Carter dumped his pack against the wall and swung the rope over his shoulder. He passed the harness to me. "Put this on. Your legs go through here." He indicated two hoops in the harness. "This strap goes around your waist. Snug, but not tight. The belay goes in front."

I stood there mutely for a minute, watching him move around the room, holding a carabiner in one hand, tugging on various things with the other. The doorknob. The cabinet handles. Even the handle on the hatch to the trash chute. He seemed to dismiss each one. Mounted on the wall opposite the trash chute was a coatrack with a row of two-pronged hooks. A single canvas tote hung from a hook. He pulled the tote off, letting it fall on the floor, then gave the hook a tug. It held. He tugged again. Then he held it with both hands and hung on to it as he climbed up the wall, letting it support his entire weight. He let go and dropped to the ground.

He opened the carabiner and slid it around the base of one of the hooks. Then he glanced over his shoulder and realized I was still standing there holding the harness in my hands. "Hey, you okay?"

I swallowed. My voice quavered when I spoke. "I don't like . . . small spaces."

"You did just fine in the closet earlier."

Yeah, but I'd had him there to distract me. And, yeah, I'd lived in a tiny closet for months, but this was much tighter. And vaguely reeked of garbage. Yikes. "Sure, that was the same. I also don't like being trapped. Or heights."

He came to stand in front of me, placing his hands on mine. "You'll be just fine."

"Why not just take the stairs the rest of the way down?"

He must have seen through my question to the fear beneath. His tone softened. "Because thirty minutes ago, there were Collabs all over the first floor. I wouldn't ask you to do this if I didn't think it was the safest, fastest way to get you out of the building."

I looked down at the harness in my hands, then back up at him. I nodded, but couldn't talk past the dread lodged in my throat.

He reached out a finger and tipped my chin up so I was looking at him. "Hey, you're kick-ass. You can build bombs and beat the crap out of a guy. Don't wimp out on me now. You can do this."

When he looked at me like that, I almost believed I could.

He held out the harness and I automatically stepped into it. As he buckled it on, he spoke simply and calmly. Like he was trying to soothe a horse. Or a spooked Green. "You're going to rappel down to the basement. All the offices down there have high windows that open at ground level."

"How did you—"

"Yesterday, before fourth meal. I did a little exploring. Go to the nearest room with an exterior wall. You should be able to climb out. Wait for me in that spot for another fifteen minutes. If I'm not there by then, you bail. Go straight to the place by the fence where I found you last night. Sebastian and Mel will meet you there."

Panic started clawing its way free of my throat, but I ruthlessly shoved it down. I couldn't think about the possibility that he might not come find me. That we might be leaving the Farm without him.

"What exactly are you going to be doing?" I wanted to sound strong and fierce, but my voice came out weak.

"I'm a Collab." He spread out his arms to indicate his outfit. "Hopefully, I'm going to just walk out of here."

I wasn't sure what terrified me more, the idea of rappelling down a trash chute or the thought of leaving Carter.

I didn't want to abandon him. I didn't want to think of his fate if he got left behind. But even more terrifying, there was a tiny part of me that was afraid I couldn't do this without him. He'd been back in my life for less than a day and—

Holy crap, had it only been a day?

How was that possible? How had I become so reliant on him in such a short period of time?

That thought gave me courage. I had to be strong enough on my own. If the past six months had taught me anything, it was that I couldn't rely on others. I had to be strong. Not just for me but for Mel.

Carter tightened the strap around my waist, talking as he tugged on the bits of gear. "This is your brake." He held out a piece of aluminum made up of two circles, one on either end, with the rope threaded through it. "Keep your brake hand right here and squeeze the rope to stop. You loosen your hand, the rope slips through. Pretty simple. You don't have far to go and the space is tight. It would be almost impossible for you to free-fall, okay?"

"Got it. Squeeze to stop."

"The hook on the wall should hold. You only have to go down two flights. And it'll be pretty tight. At the bottom, you just step out of the gear, climb out the window—"

"Yeah, I got it." I cut him off abruptly. I could not stand here thinking about the possibility of plummeting to my death. Or the possibility that Carter might get caught. Instead, I'd think about Mel.

The belay attaching my harness to the rope was right at gut level and he gave it another tug, testing its strength. The action pulled me a step closer to him. He handed me the brake and the extra rope.

"You'll be fine."

"Right." I tightened my backpack straps and then turned to face the trash chute.

"One more thing—"

I turned back to face Carter, only to find him right behind me. The line stretched from my belay to the hook in the wall and back to the brake. All my gear was still between us, but he was standing so close his hip bumped against the belay.

"Can you do me a favor?" he asked.

"Um . . . sure."

"As soon as I walk out that door, I want you to concentrate on one thing."

"Okay."

"I want you to think about the Collabs not seeing me. Them just letting me walk by. Just think it over and over again, okay?"

"Yeah. Sure." But I wasn't sure. "You want me to, like . . . pray for you or something?"

He looked surprised, so I knew that wasn't actually what he'd meant, but he nodded and smiled. "That'll work."

"'Cause you don't seem the type to believe in prayer."

"I'm the type who believes in whatever works." He fiddled with my belay and brake. "Here, give yourself a little slack."

I fed some of the extra rope through the figure-eight brake, just enough to give me room to climb into the garbage chute. The hatch door was at about chest height. Carter dragged the table over to the wall. "Step here. You should be able to wiggle in from here."

It wasn't as easy as I'd hoped. Climbing feetfirst into a waist-high tube that's two feet by two feet, isn't easy under any circumstances. The harness and belay only made things more awkward.

I went through the hole on my belly. Once my feet were in, Carter stood up and held on to my arms, easing the rest of me in. With the backpack, my torso hardly fit through the opening.

My heart pounded in my ears. I wiggled my butt farther into

the trash chute and felt the rope go taut. Licking my lips in concentration, I felt for the brake.

"Hey, you okay?" Carter asked, giving my arm a squeeze.

"I'm climbing into a trash chute and about to plummet to my death. Do I look okay?"

He chuckled. "Hey, trust me. This is going to work."

"It better," I grumbled, easing a few more inches in.

He bent close to me. "One more thing—"

"Yeah, yeah," I said, trying to look down the chute past the bulk of my backpack. "I'll pray for you or whatever. Just go."

"That wasn't my one more thing."

I looked up at him. He slipped a hand behind my head and leaned down, planting his lips on mine in a fast, fierce kiss.

It was over entirely too quickly. Before I could respond he lowered me the rest of the way into the trash chute.

"I'll see you outside the building under the tree."

I nodded and then realized he probably couldn't see me. "Okay."

My hands were shaking. No, my whole body was. I didn't want to be trapped here in this stinking trash chute. I wanted—quite desperately—to be back in that closet with Carter's arms around me in those few moments before the Collabs arrived. Now he was gone and I might never see him again.

I felt the walls of the trash chute closing in on me like my own regrets, so I did the only thing I could think to do. I released the brake and started the long drop down to the bottom.

There wasn't a lot of wiggle room in the trash chute. The harness squeezed tight on my legs and butt. I'd probably have bruises tomorrow. If there was a tomorrow. Assuming this rigging held and I didn't go plunging to my death in the basement of the science building. And if the Collabs didn't catch me on the way out.

And if I made it across campus to meet up with Sebastian, Carter, and Mel.

God damn it. I was tired of these lists of ifs.

All I could do was inch my way down, knowing that eventually I would reach the basement. Of course, I had no idea what was waiting for me in the basement.

To distract myself, I started keeping my promise to Carter.

"Please let no one see him," I muttered, alternately squeezing and releasing the brake. "Let him just walk right out of there. Let him be invisible. Please. Please. Please."

Realizing I'd been squeezing my eyes shut, I forced myself to open them. Was it a little lighter in here? I glanced down. Though I was unable to see the ground below, I could see a faint square of light coming from around the hatch door below me.

Then, from somewhere above me, I heard a voice.

I breathed out slowly, trying to hear past the sound of my own blood rushing in my ears. Then I felt the rope thrum beneath my hand, the way a spider can feel the vibrations of a fly landing on her web. Someone, up above me in the maintenance room, had grabbed hold of my rope. As taut as the rope was, I didn't think anyone would be able to get the carabiner off the coatrack. Still, someone knew I was in here. Or they would soon.

I hung there frozen for a minute, my gaze pinned on the small square of light above me, unable to move, paralyzed by the irrational feeling that whoever was up there wouldn't notice me if I was still.

Then something dark blocked out the light. A head poked in through the hatch.

"Hey," a voice called, "is someone down there?"

The voice was rough and unfamiliar. Not Carter's. The faint hope that it might be him up there vanished completely.

He would be far away by now. Probably already outside the building, making his way to the stadium. I was on my own.

The head disappeared for a moment, but the rigging was so loud, I didn't dare go farther down. Still, I had little hope that he'd left.

A second later, the head was back and the bright beam of a flashlight cut through the darkness. It followed the rope down through the trash chute to my location. The light landed on my upturned face, blinding me for an instant. I closed my eyes, turning my face away from the light.

"I found her!" the voice called. "Hey, I found her!"

Shit!

I was out of time. Descending cautiously had gotten me only halfway there. I released the brake again, keeping my eyes closed, ignoring the sick feeling in the pit of my stomach as I dropped several feet at once.

"Hey! Stop!" the voice called again.

The rope slipped beneath my hand as I descended and I felt it twang oddly.

Then I did stop. What was going on?

I looked down, trying to gauge how much farther I had to go. The rope shifted under my hand again. I looked up, but could see nothing. The rope twitched back and forth. My heart leapt as I realized what that movement meant.

The Collab up on the second floor was trying to slice through my rope.

CHAPTER TWENTY

CARTER

Carter strolled past all the Collabs on the first floor and walked out of the building so easily, it seemed like proof that Lily really was an *abductura*. Not that he needed proof. Spending a night in her company, having her inadvertently messing with his emotions, that was all the proof he needed that she was exactly what he'd promised Sebastian she was. An *abductura* capable of controlling the thoughts and emotions of others.

Which explained perfectly why he'd been such a mess for the past day. The last thing he should be doing right now was kissing Lily. He had one job. Get her off the Farm and away to safety. Kissing her, cuddling her in the closet, reminiscing with her about the past, and falling asleep beside her so he could wake up with her draped across his chest were not on the agenda.

It didn't matter how the hell he felt about her. It didn't matter if he wanted to do all those things. His job was to keep her safe. And he couldn't do that if he was distracted by wanting to be with her. He kept talking about military school for a reason. Defense and strategy weren't the only things he'd learned there. He'd learned focus and determination. He would keep her safe, even though he wasn't keeping her safe for himself.

Worse still, because of the effect she had on him, he knew every emotion she felt for him. But he knew her personality well enough to guess how she would react when he told her the truth. When he explained that she was an *abductura* and what that meant and why he'd been searching for her, she wasn't going to be happy about it. She'd probably resent the hell out of him for it. She might even hate him for it. On the bright side, he thought grimly, at least then he wouldn't have to worry about his feelings for her anymore. But he had to get her off the Farm and to safety before he could come clean.

Then, just as he was walking around the corner to the south side of the building, he walked straight into a Collab. And the guy already had his tranq rifle drawn and raised.

It happened so fast, Carter barely kept himself from slamming into the barrel of the rifle. In the second it took him to sling his own rifle off his shoulder and bring it up, the other guy cocked his weapon.

"What are you doing here?" the Collab shouted.

Carter eyed the other Collab. The guy looked tweaked. Nervous eyes. Twitchy fingers. Adrenaline pounding. A nice little cocktail of paranoia and fear.

If this guy was freaking out, was there something wrong with Lily? Was he picking up on her emotions? Was she nearby but in danger? If so, why hadn't he felt it?

"I'm doing the same thing you are," Carter said, trying to keep his voice slow and calm, despite his fear for Lily.

"Yeah? What's that?" The twitchy Collab jerked the barrel of the rifle, like he couldn't decide where to shoot Carter.

"The Dean sent me."

The Collab's eyes narrowed in obvious suspicion. "He sent twelve of us. You weren't there."

A Collab with a brain. Just what he needed.

"He sent me to see what was taking so long."

"Why didn't the Dean radio me and tell me he was sending you?"

If this Collab had a radio, that meant he was high ranking. He had more than a brain then. Now would be the perfect time to just shoot the guy with his tranq rifle. If he still had darts in it.

Since shooting the guy was off the table, Carter started edging closer, but before he could dodge around the rifle, a blur of motion rocketed into the Collab, knocking the guy clear off his feet. The guy grunted in surprise as the tranq rifle flew out of his hands. Carter almost felt sorry for him. He'd been on the receiving end of one of Lily's tackles not that long ago. She was stronger than she looked.

But Carter didn't spare the guy any sympathy. Especially since the Collab managed to twist on the way down and land on top of Lily with a sickening crack.

Dropping his own useless tranq rifle, Carter dashed for the Collab's, praying it was still fully loaded. He snatched it up from the ground, lined the Collab up in the sights, and fired. After a long second, the Collab drooped forward.

Carter reached out a foot and gave the guy a firm shove off Lily. Without lowering the rifle, he asked, "You okay?"

"Took you long enough," she grumbled, struggling to wiggle her legs out from under those of the fallen Collab.

Carter gave the Collab another nudge with his toe, watching to see if the guy moved. He didn't. "The guy was like a bull elephant. I didn't want to have to shoot him a second time."

Lily sat up, rolling her shoulder as if working out a kink. "Ah, man. What a jerk." She used her foot to scoot herself away from him, maybe with more enthusiasm than she needed to. Then she stilled. Slowly, she reached behind her to feel at the back of her shirt under the backpack.

For a second, she was so still, Carter half expected that she'd pulled her hand away and her fingers would be bright with blood. Instead, she jerked her hand around and shucked her backpack while scrambling to her feet. It wasn't until she let it fall to the ground that he put the clues together. She'd been carefully guarding that backpack since the moment they'd met. As she grabbed his hand and began running away from it, he knew there could be only one reason why. She must have made a third jar that she'd kept in her backpack. The crunching noise he'd heard had been it breaking.

If the glass jar had broken, then her bag was now soaked in methanol. Her bag was so tightly packed that the bomb hadn't yet been exposed to air. That was the only reason it hadn't already burst into flames.

They ran through the darkness, trying to put as much distance between themselves and the backpack as possible. It caught fire just as he pulled her around the corner of the next building over. Without the breaking glass, it was less dramatic, but he bet a flaming backpack in the middle of campus would still attract plenty of attention. Out of breath and heart racing, he pulled her to a stop, leaning against the building and clutching her to his chest.

He let himself drop his head to hers and just rest his cheek against her hair, breathing in the scent of her.

Christ, that had been close. Too close.

He'd gotten almost a hundred Greens out of Farms. He'd faced Collabs, manipulated Deans, killed Ticks. In the past six months, he'd done all kinds of crazy crap he never would have thought himself capable of doing in the Before. And he was pretty damn good at it.

So why was he having such a hard time keeping this one girl alive and safe? Was it just because he actually cared about her?

Did these close calls just seem closer because it was Lily and not some Green he barely knew? Or was he somehow screwing up?

When he'd first told Sebastian about Lily, Sebastian had wanted to send one of the other guys in after her. But Carter had insisted he be the one to come get her out. He knew her. Knew she wouldn't just trust a stranger to get her off the Farm. But had Carter made the wrong decision? Was he too close to her to keep her safe?

Of course, it didn't help that she questioned him at every turn. That she didn't trust him. That she was cautious enough to sneak an extra bomb into her bag without telling him.

But he had to admit, if he was in her shoes, it's what he'd have done. If someone he'd barely known in the Before showed up out of the blue, offering a ticket out, he wouldn't trust the guy, either.

By nature, Lily was cautious, suspicious, and loyal. Those were exactly the qualities he loved about her. They were what was going to make her a great *abductura*. But right now, those qualities were making his job that much more difficult.

Finally he forced himself to let her go. "Let's see your hands. Did you get . . . what kind of fuel was that? Methan—"

"Methanol." She brought her hands up to her face and sniffed them. "Yeah, I got a little on them."

"Let me see if I've got a rag or something to clean them off." He slung his bag off his shoulder and dug around until he found a package of baby wipes.

She blinked at them in surprise and then chuckled. "You have the weirdest stuff in that bag." But she took the wipe and used it on her hands as they started walking. "How much time do we have?"

"We need to move fast, but we'll get there." He nodded back

the way they'd come. "Besides, at least the Collabs will be distracted for a while."

She groaned. "Everything I owned in the world was in that backpack."

"Then maybe you shouldn't have been carrying around an explosive combination of liquids in a glass jar."

Clearly annoyed by his observation, she shot him an evil look. He probably deserved it for giving her hell when she was down.

"I'm just saying, you wouldn't have lost the backpack if you'd just trusted me."

"I'll keep that in mind the next time someone's forcing me to rappel down a trash chute."

"I got you out, didn't I?"

Her gaze softened. "Yeah. Thanks for that."

"Let's get out of here. It'll be dawn soon and we still need to get across campus."

He pretended not to notice the expression in her eyes. He didn't want her thinking he was some kind of hero. It would be easier on both of them later if he kept his distance now. When she found out the truth, she was going to hate him.

CHAPTER TWENTY-ONE

LILY

After the rapid descent in the trash chute, getting out of the basement of the science lab had been pretty easy. Yeah, my fingers had fumbled getting out of the harness, and sure, I'd been terrified that the Collab was going to figure out my escape route and cut me off before I could scurry out the ground-level window, but strangely, both of those fears paled compared to my panic when I'd rounded the building and saw the Collab attacking Carter.

My nerves still buzzed with adrenaline as we made our way across campus. This was it. We were getting out. Assuming Sebastian kept up his end of the bargain and met Carter and me at the rendezvous point, Mel and I would be off the Farm.

After all these months of planning, we were really going to do it.

Dawn was near and as we made our way across campus, the outlines of the buildings and trees slowly became more clear, dark shapes looming against the lightening sky. We didn't see any more Collabs. Not after the last bunch of them that rushed past our hiding spot, heading toward my exploding backpack. Despite that, dread began to crawl up my spine like the itsy-bitsy spider that had come back out now that the sun had dried up the most recent batch of obstacles.

Slowly the truth dawned on me. As terrifying as being on the Farm was, I was scared to leave. To stay meant certain death, but it was a certainty I knew and understood. Beyond these walls . . . was something else. I had no idea what would happen once we were out.

Yes, I'd seen Ticks on TV, back when there was TV still, before everything went completely to crap. Right when the Before was becoming the Before. I'd seen the same blood-chilling news footage everyone had seen when the Ticks started appearing. The pathogen that transformed ordinary people into Ticks spread quickly across the Southwest and Midwest. Most people merely got sick for a few days. But some people's bodies transformed, almost overnight, into something no longer human. Something bloodthirsty and animalistic. Something the police couldn't stop or control. It had been terrifying. The idea that any one of us could turn into a monster capable of massacring our families and friends.

And since coming to the Farm, I'd even glimpsed them outside the fences. Especially this winter, with night coming early, you could sometimes see the hulky shapes lurching through the darkened streets of the town, their movements somehow both unnatural and graceful all at once. And, of course, I had heard their howls.

But I'd never seen one up close. The thought of what they must be capable of terrified me. But I was more afraid to stay. I didn't want to be a placid cow. I wanted to fight for my freedom.

Mel was waiting for me somewhere out here in the darkness and Carter's hand held mine. He pulled me forward, one step after the other, as we crept through the night.

Carter led me past the cafeteria toward the north side of campus, toward the football stadium near the same tree Mel and I had hidden behind a mere eight hours earlier.

To distract myself from my fear, I asked, "Now what?"

"Now we wait."

Carter wore a watch, and when he checked the time, the light-up face flashed briefly in the darkness.

"How long?"

"Five, maybe ten minutes." His voice sounded tense and I wondered if he was worried about Sebastian. If he was, then Mel would be in danger, too.

"I thought this guy was former military," I whispered.

"He is. Why?"

"Well, shouldn't it be 'T minus three minutes' or something? You know, something more—" I broke off when I spotted a shadow moving in the distance down by the gymnasium.

"Shh," Carter hissed.

"I see it," I breathed back, barely loud enough for him to hear it, let alone anyone else.

As soon as I focused on the movement, I realized it couldn't be a Collab. The creature was low to the ground, about the size and shape of a medium dog, but it didn't move with the cheerful gait of a dog. It scuttled and scurried, zipping side to side in the shadows. It didn't see us until it was maybe twenty feet away. Then it paused, looking at us, its whiskers twitching and its orange teeth gleaming in the moonlight.

I stepped back, pressing my spine against the tree, hoping the creature would move on. It ducked its head and scurried off toward the lush vegetation over by the gymnasium.

I'd never seen a nutria on campus before. I'd seen them outside, though. Mel used to pull me over to the north fence and show me their fried corpses.

The Farm was surrounded on all four sides by twelve feet of electrified chain-link fences. On the north side, there were two fences, one separating the football stadium from the rest of campus—that one was never electrified—and then another fence on the far side, between the stadium and the river. That was the one that got turned off each night because of the nutria. If a nutria had gotten onto campus, it must have come through a hole in the fence.

Before I could mention it to Carter, I heard a low buzzing noise.

He cursed under his breath and bent down to his leg. He removed something from a case strapped to his calf. The item was gray and rectangular. About the size of a can of Coke. It was so unexpected it took me a minute to recognize it.

"You have a phone?" I asked in a whispered hush.

Waving my question aside, he spoke into the phone, keeping his voice as soft as mine. "Carter here."

He was silent, listening for a long moment, while I stood beside him grinding my teeth. I realized that was what I'd seen him do on the way into fourth meal. He'd gotten separated from us because his phone had rung and he'd been unable to answer it in front of all the Greens. I wondered what that call had been about almost as much as I wondered about this one. Then he hung up without saying anything else.

"You have a phone?" I repeated as soon as he hung up.

Of course, I had a phone, too, but mine didn't work. His did. Which meant it had to be a satellite phone or something.

I don't know why it surprised me so much. What else didn't I know?

Instead of answering my question, he grabbed my hand and tugged me in the direction of the stadium fence.

"This way. They had to bail and they're already waiting for us on the other side."

"They're waiting for us?" I asked stupidly. Then I realized he was leading me toward the exact same hole in the fence that I'd made just last night.

The hole was bigger now, the chain link stretched out as though several people had already climbed through. Carter pulled the cuffs of his sleeves down over his hands to protect his palms and grabbed the edge of the chain link and pulled it out of the way so I could climb through.

Crawling on my hands and knees, I grumbled, "After all that, we're still just sneaking out through the back fence?"

"What did you expect?" he asked, leaning down to unsnag a bit of sweatshirt that got caught on the fence.

He was close enough that I felt the warmth of his breath on my cold cheek.

"I don't know. Something a little more elaborate. Smuggled out in a car trunk or airlifted out in helicopters."

On the other side of the fence, I stood, then mimicked Carter's actions with my sleeves and the fence. The other side of the fence curved inward and I grasped that edge and pulled, leaving room for him to wiggle through. The thick wire of the fence was stiff and cold, even through my sleeves. It took all my strength to make enough room for him to squirm his big shoulders through the hole.

Once through, he stood and dusted off his hands. "Right. 'Cause helicopters wouldn't attract any attention."

"If you two are finished, we could use your assistance over here."

Sebastian.

I recognized the voice instantly. I'd never met anyone else who spoke with such icy clarity. Or with that fancy-schmancy accent.

He stepped out of the darkness and I felt Carter stiffen beside me. A moment later, I realized I'd done it, too.

Sebastian gave a slight incline of his head, nodding in the direction he'd just come from, and both Carter and I started moving. Sebastian fell into step beside us and, a few moments later, the second fence—the one between the stadium and the river—came into view. The hole in this fence was much larger. I expected to see Mel there, waiting for us.

"Where's Mel?" I asked.

"She's waiting on the other side of the fence," Sebastian said smoothly.

"She wouldn't leave without me," I said, trying to put into words the sudden choking panic I felt. "After all these months, she wouldn't just walk out of the Farm with a stranger. I know that!"

Sebastian stalked up from behind me and grabbed my elbow. His fingers, sharp and painful on my arm, propelled me forward. Under his breath he cursed in a language I didn't recognize. "Yes, my pet, she's out there. I had just as much trouble with her. You have my word."

At the fence, I dug in my heels.

"He wouldn't leave her. Trust me," Carter said.

But it was hard to trust someone dragging you somewhere by force, even if it's somewhere you're desperate to go.

"Lil-lee?" Mel's voice called out. "Lil-lee?"

The fight left my body at the sound of her voice coming from somewhere nearby. She was, as Sebastian had promised, already outside the fence. The hole Sebastian had cut was ten feet or so from the corner. This side of the fence was only a few feet away from the cliff that dropped forty feet down to the Red River. Looking out through the chain links to my left, I saw the street that ran along this side of the Farm. Across it was a deserted restaurant that had once overlooked the river. And beside it were abandoned shops and fast-food places. Beyond the row of commercial properties, I could see the hulking shapes of an apartment complex. On the street nearest the fence, Mel stood in front of an SUV. The doors were open, and the overhead dome light cast a little glowing circle through the darkness.

Now that I'd seen Mel, I couldn't wait to get out. I released my grasp on the fence, the edge of the metal sharp against my palm.

Carter and I tumbled through the hole in the fence.

His arm tightened around me for a second before he released me. "Try not to plummet to your death."

There were only a few feet between the fence and the drop-off. Suddenly I wasn't so eager to try swimming across the Red River. I wrapped my hand firmly around the fence, weaving my fingers through the links. I looked down the line of the fence and saw shapes moving beyond the end of it. Dawn was lightening the sky and I saw two figures waiting with Mel and the outline of the vehicle. Only then did I hear the hum of a motor, a sound that—like the elevator—was only distantly familiar now.

"Lil-lee?" Mel called again from her spot near the car.

It wasn't light enough for me to identify anyone but Mel. Her jerky motions and flapping hands made her unmistakable.

I swallowed past my relief. "I'm coming, Mel. I'm almost there."

After my near fall I was unwilling to let go of the fence, so I crept along, hand over hand, toward the corner where the fence ended maybe ten feet away. Determined not to look down again, I kept my gaze on Mel.

She stood just beyond the edge of the fence, flapping her hands, birdlike, as she looked from me to whoever stood behind her. I glanced back at Carter and was surprised that he wasn't beside me, but had hung back and was talking to Sebastian in a whispered hush. The odd, slanting light of dawn made Sebastian's features stand out in sharp relief, as though he was straining or in great pain.

Beside the car, Mel called out again, "Lil-lee?"

Whatever was up with Sebastian, it wasn't my problem. "I'm coming."

Her head twitched nervously in the direction of whoever stood beside her, waiting at the car.

I watched her as I walked; it was better than looking down. Besides, she was outside the Farm. We'd gotten out. We'd really done it.

Then several things happened in quick succession. From across the river came a high-pitched, anguished squeal. As if something had caught a nutria. The sound sent a terrified chill down my spine. Nutria were new enough to this part of the world that they didn't have many natural predators, but there was one predator that would hunt anything.

Mel—who must have been as freaked out as I was by the noise—started walking toward me.

Carter called out, "Stop her! On that side, the fence is electrified."

I knew that, of course. Mel knew it, too. She wouldn't have touched the fence. But whoever was with her assumed she didn't know. One of the people ran forward and grabbed her from behind. I didn't know who it was. Maybe someone from Carter's resistance. Whoever it was, they didn't use a gentle touch on the arm, which would have been enough to stop her, but a full-body hold.

She screamed in panicked outrage. She kicked up her feet and they both were knocked over. Mel kept screaming, like only Mel can scream, one long wail. Like an opera singer cast in a horror movie.

Then, from across the river came an answering howl. Not the fearful screech of a nutria, but the inhuman wail of a predator that has sighted its prey. It was the bay of a Tick and it was coming for us.

CHAPTER TWENTY-TWO

LILY

This escape plan just kept going from screwed up to worse.

Mel's scream cut off abruptly. Either she'd run out of air or she, too, had recognized the howl and panic had choked her. But the grunts and moans of a struggle still came from whoever had tried to hold Mel back.

Carter was right behind me now. "Keep moving," he barked.

I'd only stopped for a moment and sure as hell didn't need to be told twice. I moved as quickly as I dared, hand over hand, still not letting loose of the fence entirely. Knowing what was on the other side of the river, I wanted to risk swimming across even less.

Then another howl joined the first. And another. They yipped and yapped, like dogs, dissonant and eardrum piercing. Still moving, I glanced across the river. They were there, right at the edge of the river. Outlined against the dawn sky, they were all shadow and darkness. Their chests were massive and bulging with muscles, their arms out of proportion with the rest of their bodies. The disparity made them look clumsy, but they moved with surprising agility, dancing along the bank, desperate to attack us but unwilling to jump into the river to get to us. Even in the darkness, even from so far away, their features looked horrific. Or maybe my mind was superimposing the images I'd seen on TV onto the

Ticks across the river. I imagined I could distinguish the grotesquely distended jaw. The inhumanly large teeth.

One of the Ticks held something in its fist. A lifeless, decapitated nutria, I realized with a jolt of revulsion. It shook the nutria's body in frustration.

I jerked back around, my hands suddenly pouring with sweat, despite the cold. I couldn't look at them. My heart clenched at the very wrongness of them. My hands trembled and my fingers slipped on the icy metal. Another howl split the frosty air, this time much closer. From this side of the river.

Carter was right at my side, keeping me moving.

"Get them in the car!" he shouted to whoever was still struggling with Mel. To me, he said, "Keep going."

"What do you think I'm doing?" I snapped.

"I think you're panicking. Let go of the fence. I'm not going to let you fall."

I didn't let go, but tried to move faster.

There was more howling. Closer.

We were only a few feet away from the edge of the fence now and Carter grabbed my hand before I could grab the fence again. "There's a gap and insulators between this fence and the other one, but that corner post is electrified. You have to let go now."

For a second, I stood there looking from the cliff to the electrified post. Just once, I wanted to face a dilemma where at least one of the options wasn't a horrible death. I swallowed hard and edged toward the corner. I could feel Carter's hand around my arm, but it offered little reassurance. If either of us slipped, we'd both go.

Ten heart-pounding seconds later, I was at the post. The electricity pumping through the fence hummed like the sound you hear walking past a mountain laurel in the spring when it's buzzing with bees. I held my breath as I crept past, felt it pulling at me, trying to suck me into it. If I so much as brushed the metal, the force of the jolt would propel me off the cliff, no slipping required.

Then we were both around the fence. Carter's hand was at my back as we ran for the car. The howl of a Tick came from somewhere on this side of the river. Too close. I could hear the thundering of its uneven gait as it plowed toward us. Ahead, the doors of the car were open. One of the people had climbed inside. The other was trying to force Mel into the car. She was struggling and making a soft keening noise of protest, much softer than the wail of the Ticks that flooded the air.

"I'm here!" I yelled to Mel. "Get in the car, Mel."

Whoever had been trying to get her in abandoned the job and hopped in, slamming the front passenger door behind him. Then we were there at the car and Mel, Carter, and I all seemed to tumble in through the rear passenger door.

It was some kind of crossover SUV with plenty of legroom between the seats. Still, my calves rammed the running board and my shoulder clipped the seat as I landed on Mel. Carter just grabbed the arm of the seat in one hand and the edge of the door in the other as he jumped onto the runner.

"Go! Drive!" he yelled to the driver even though he was barely in the car.

And for just an instant, I thought he was being overly dramatic. But then the driver threw the car into reverse just as something slammed against the back of the vehicle. Tires squealed as the Tick we'd hit yelped in pain.

Mel scrambled out from under me and I jerked my legs the rest of the way into the car. I scuttled farther in on my hands and knees, desperate to make room for Carter. Another creature hit the car just as he got the door closed. And then another. This one landed on the roof and the sound of crunching fiberglass seemed to echo in the momentary silence.

Then there was the roar of tires and several people shouting at once and Mel whimpering and I could barely hear any of it over the thundering of my own heart.

Mel had folded herself into the tiny space of floorboard behind the driver's seat. She had her legs pulled tight to her chest. I was beside her, on my knees, my arms braced on the nearby seats as the SUV picked up speed, bumping over the uneven ground of the field near the fence. Carter was right behind me, still shouting orders to the driver I hadn't even seen yet.

"Faster! Get on the road. It's just ahead."

"Stop yelling at me!" screeched a panicked female voice.

"There's one on top," he said, ignoring her. "You're going to have to shake it off."

As if to punctuate his order, the creature scraped its nails across the roof of the SUV. A hand slapped the window above Mel's head. It looked so perfectly human, I nearly cried out.

"Take a hard left. Now."

The driver started to turn, but Carter stepped over me, half knocking me down so I went face-first into the seat. I couldn't see anything but cream leather upholstery, but he must have jerked the steering wheel from the driver, because the SUV made the hard left Carter had ordered. For a second the car spun and the tires squealed. The sound of something sliding across the roof followed, punctuated by an inhuman yelp as it was flung off.

A moment later the SUV bumped and jerked and landed on smooth road. The engine roared as the driver accelerated.

"Where do I go?" she asked in a trembly voice.

Carter panted, stepping back over me and then dropping into

the open seat. "Just drive. West for now. We'll cross over the river in the next town."

"I don't know—" She broke off, clearly on the verge of tears.

"Away from the rising sun." He placed a hand on my back, his touch gentle.

"West? Don't we want to go north?"

"We won't go west for long. The safest place to cross the river is about an hour away." He searched my face. "You okay? Sorry I knocked you over."

I straightened, unkinking my body. "I'm fine. Mel, how are you?"

She just looked at me, shaking her head, her eyes wide and terrified.

"We should all get buckled in," Carter said. "You two take the middle row. I'll climb in back."

He climbed over me to the third row of seating and a second later I heard the clicks of buckles coming from the front seat and the back.

Numbly, I knew he was right, but I didn't have the energy to move, let alone coax Mel up into the seat. She sat on the floorboard, her bright pink backpack still on her shoulders. I barely spared a thought for the mysterious passenger and driver. I pulled the armrest up on the seat beside me and sank into it, legs wedged between the seats to leave room for Mel. Her low keening had subsided and she rested her head on my knees. I hesitated for a second, then let my hand rest on her hair. I waited for her to flinch, but she didn't. For once she needed to be touched. I knew how she felt. I wanted to pull her into my arms and hug her tight, but for now, this would do. It was better than nothing.

I slouched there, staring blankly at the empty seat beside me for several heartbeats before its significance registered. Then I sat bolt upright. "Oh, my God, Sebastian! Where's Sebastian?"

"He stayed behind," Carter said from the backseat.

I ripped my gaze away from the accusingly empty seat to glance back at Carter. There wasn't a lot of room in the third-row seat and he'd angled his legs across them. The seat belt was strapped across his lap. His eyes were closed, his head tilted back. If I hadn't just heard him speak, I would have thought he was asleep.

"What do you mean he stayed behind? He stayed with those—" But my voice shuddered as revulsion crawled up my throat and my mind raced. How many Ticks had attacked our car? Was it three? Four?

I knew better than to hope that we killed any of them, even the one the driver had thrown off the roof.

"We have to go back for him! Turn around."

I felt the driver ease off the gas, then Carter sat up and barked, "Don't slow down. Don't turn around. We can't go back."

Realizing Carter was the one I had to convince, I shifted over to the empty seat so I could talk to him better. "We can't just leave him there."

"Sebastian chose to stay behind." Carter scrubbed a hand down his face, then straightened, opening his eyes. For an instant, his gaze flickered to my hands. "He stayed behind because . . . somebody needed to close the hole in the fence."

"The hole in the . . ." I started to ask, but I let the question trail off. The hole in the fence was five feet tall. No way was anyone going to be closing that hole. Not without serious equipment. Not while three or four Ticks sat by and patiently waited to gobble him up. "That doesn't make any sense."

Then I glanced down at my hand and the smear of blood on my palm. "Oh."

He hadn't come because of me.

"Don't worry about it," Carter said gently, following the direction of my gaze. He reached out and took my hand in his, running his thumb across my palm as he studied the cut. He fished a clean rag out of his pocket and dabbed at the blood. His face looked lined with worry. Or maybe just exhaustion. "Someone needed to stay behind. With that many Ticks around and a hole that big, they would have found it. Even as dumb as they are. Sebastian stayed behind to make sure the Collabs got the hole closed and the fence turned back on. He didn't want to leave the Farm vulnerable."

"But—" I frowned, thinking it through, remembering what Carter had said about Sebastian. He so didn't seem like the type to sacrifice himself to save a Farm full of Greens. "Will the Dean try to capture Sebastian?"

Carter snorted. "I'd like to see him *try*."

"Was that the plan all along, for Sebastian to stay behind?"

"No. The plan was to climb into a sedan and cheerfully drive off into the sunrise. Even leaving this way, we should have had a clean getaway. This close to dawn the Ticks should have all been off trying to find nests for the day. Looking for somewhere quiet and dark. I don't know why the plan went all to hell." Carter scrubbed his hand down his face again.

I looked down at my hands. The bleeding had stopped. I'd thought my hands were just sweaty, but . . . "I must have actually cut myself on the fence as we were leaving," I mused aloud.

Mel's hair was shiny and smooth where I'd stroked her head. In the milky morning light, that was the only sign that I'd gotten blood in her hair.

Trying not to freak Mel out, I casually reached over and tapped the front-seat passenger on the shoulder. He and the driver had been quiet until now. "Hey, can you check and see if there are any napkins in the glove box?"

"Um . . . sure." The guy hadn't said a word before now, and I'd been too preoccupied to notice him. But as soon as he spoke, I recognized him.

"Joe?" I leaned forward and around the seat to get a look at him. I hadn't thought much about the driver and other passenger until now. I guess I just assumed they were other people Carter knew. Though now that I thought about it, it made sense that whoever was on the outside of the fence was someone Mel knew. That was how Sebastian had gotten her to leave without me.

"Yeah." He nodded. "Um, hi, Lil." Then, without even glancing at me, he started rummaging in the glove box.

After our escape, after running from the Ticks and nearly not making it, his "Um, hi" seemed a little anticlimactic. Frowning, I looked at the driver. Surprise rocked me back in my seat. McKenna Wells.

For a long moment I didn't get it. I just sat there, looking back and forth between Joe and McKenna. Then I started sifting through the conversations I'd had with him yesterday. There weren't that many dots, but it took me way too long to connect them.

If Joe was here now, it meant he'd cut a deal with Sebastian. A deal that most likely had involved giving up our location so Carter could come find us. He hadn't really believed I could get them all out of the Farm. Or maybe he just thought I wouldn't do it. Either way, Joe had put his faith in Sebastian instead of us. Joe had sold us out.

I sank back in my seat. "Holy shit, Joe. I mean . . . I can't believe . . ."

I couldn't even make myself say it aloud.

Joe had dropped his head into his hands. Then he straightened and thrust his hand back toward me, clutching a fistful of napkins. It took him a moment to speak, but when he did, his voice was firm. More resolved than I'd ever heard it. "I did what I had to do. I told you she was pregnant. I had to protect my baby."

And instantly, all those words I couldn't force out came gushing to the surface. "You betrayed us, Joe. You fucking betrayed us. You betrayed . . ." I felt Carter's hand on my shoulder. I shook it off. "Christ, I can see you turning me in. But how the hell could you betray Mel? How could you—"

"Come on, Lily. This isn't—" Carter tried to interrupt me.

I ignored him. "How could you? It's Mel, Joe. Mel. What kind of monster would—"

"Lily, stop." Carter's voice was low. His tone, serious.

"No! I'm not going to stop." My own voice rose, tinged with hysteria. Joe still held the napkins and I swatted them away. They drifted to the floorboard unnoticed.

With her head still resting on my knees, I could feel Mel tensing. One of her hands gripped my leg so tightly it was like her muscles had seized up. Suddenly I felt panicky and claustrophobic.

McKenna represented everything I hated about life on the Farm. She'd gotten pregnant *on purpose*. She was trading the life of her unborn baby for a few more months of her own life. The idea was so revolting I couldn't even think about it. The Breeders were the very worst of what was left of humanity. And Joe had betrayed us for one.

My whole body started trembling. Part of my brain knew it was shock setting in. Knew that my anger was only a thin veneer covering my fear. I'd taken a gamble with Mel's life and if Carter hadn't been here to save us, we would have lost.

If Joe had turned us in to anyone other than Sebastian, Mel

and I would be in the Dean's custody now. Or we'd already be dead. Because of Joe.

"I'm not going to pretend this is okay or forgivable." I glanced at McKenna. I expected her to be yelling back at me, but instead she just looked whipped. And pathetic. Maybe I should have pitied her, but I was still too angry about what Joe had done. "The one person on the Farm I thought I could trust betrayed me to protect a Breeder."

"Lily, that's enough."

But it wasn't enough, because now we were all stuck in a car together. How was I supposed to trust them for the rest of the drive? If we found ourselves in danger again—and I wasn't fooling myself, we would—how could I believe that Joe wouldn't throw us to the Ticks just so he could keep McKenna safe? How could I possibly protect Mel under those circumstances?

I felt the panic rising in my throat, something wild and uncontrolled. "I'm not going with them. Mel and I will find another way to Canada."

Trying to calm myself, I looked out the window at the passing fields. A farmhouse sat on the field to the north. A sprawling ranch style with a three-door garage. The kind of place that would have a couple of extra trucks somewhere. This SUV wasn't the only way to get to where I wanted to go. "McKenna, pull over the car."

"Don't pull over the car, McKenna," Carter said.

"Pull over."

"Don't listen to her, McKenna. Don't do it."

"Pull over the car!" I ordered.

The fact that there might be Ticks around barely occurred to me. All I knew was that I had to get out of that car. I had to move.

And there was a chance that the ranch house in the distance would have a truck I could steal.

"Stop the car!" I demanded.

The car skidded to a stop in the middle of the road. I pried Mel's hand off my leg, thrust open the door, and tumbled out onto the road. Carter hopped out after me.

He reached for my arm, but I shook it off.

"What exactly is your plan here?" he demanded. "You want to walk to Canada?"

I wrapped my arms over my chest, suddenly cold in addition to shaken and emotionally bruised. Mel had clambered out of the SUV after me, but she stood by the door, her head cocked to the side as she watched me unravel.

Unkempt fields bordered the road on either side. The sun hung low in the sky, casting everything in an eerie pink light. Everything looked too pretty, too soft, for the world as it was now. An icy wind blew down the road, cutting through the many layers of my clothes.

"No, I'm not going to walk to Canada," I snapped. "I'm going to that house. It'll have a car Mel and I can steal."

"Oh, really?" Carter's tone rose to match the belligerence in my voice. "You're really going to drag Mel across that field to look for a car? What if there's not even one there?"

"It's a farm. It'll have cars. Or trucks. Something."

"What if they don't work? What if they don't have gas?"

"I—"

As desperate as I'd been to get out of the car, I knew he was right. The car felt toxic, Joe's betrayal a poison in the very air. Now that I was outside, my new plan seemed ridiculous. So I just stood there, shivering.

"Don't be an idiot," he said. "Get back in the car. This isn't helping anything."

"It's helping me," I said.

"Hey, I just risked my life to get you out of that Farm. You're crazy if you think I'm going to let you just wander off on your own."

"And you're crazy if you think I'm getting back in that car."

Carter blew out a breath of frustration. "Lily, be reasonable."

"No, you be reasonable." Instead of sounding angry, suddenly I just sounded sad. "You don't understand. Joe was our friend. He was the one person I knew I could trust. I didn't trust anyone on the Farm. But I trusted him. And he sold us out. For what? A piece of ass."

"You don't know that's all she is to him."

I groaned. "Don't be like that."

"Like what?"

"So understanding."

"How should I be?" he asked. "Should I pout like a child, too? Would that help?"

I glared at him. "How can you expect me to ride with them? If I get back in that car with them, I'm putting Mel's life and mine in their hands. I'm trusting them not to feed us to the Ticks the next time it means protecting themselves. How can I do that?"

My throat closed over the words as I said them, because it was what I would do. I didn't like to admit it—hell, I didn't even want to think about it—but it was what I would do. If we were in a life-or-death situation and saving Mel meant tossing Joe or McKenna to the Ticks, I'd do it. Probably without thinking twice.

What kind of monster had I become?

Carter reached for me again. He wrapped his hands around my arms and this time I didn't pull away. Some of the anger leached out of his eyes, but his voice held that same ferocity. "Think about it this way. If you get back into that car, you're also trusting me to keep you safe. To keep Mel safe. And I promise you that I'm not going to let Joe betray you again."

The look in his eyes all but sucked the air out of my chest. His words didn't sound like empty reassurances. They sounded like a pledge. I thought about all the things he'd done in the past twenty-four hours to protect me. Not just from Collabs and Ticks, but from himself as well. I'd wrestled with him twice now. First in the science lab and then again when he'd taken me out of the admin building. Both times, I'd fought with everything in me. Other than knocking me against the wall to keep me from strangling him, he hadn't hurt me at all. Okay, with the exception of shooting me with the tranq rifle. Other than that, he'd been so gentle with me. Way more so than I had coming. He could probably snap me like a twig, but he hadn't.

He was stronger, tougher, and faster than me, but he hadn't used it against me. I found the thought deeply unsettling, but I wasn't sure if it was his overt strength that bothered me or his inherent gentleness.

Instead of considering the question, I said, "Just think how you'd feel if it was your sister he'd put in danger."

"I'd want to kill him." Carter's voice was low and harsh. "But I'd try to remember that Joe's not the enemy. We humans—those of us that are left who are human—we have to try to stick together. We can't be at each other's throats over crap like this. That's what the Ticks are for."

He said that like he was trying to make a joke, but his voice was still too tight. Like he really did want to kill Joe over this betrayal.

Which confused me for a second, until I remembered Sebastian. And how Sebastian had stayed behind. *To fix the fence.* Which may or may not have been a euphemism for throwing himself on the sword while we escaped. Clearly Carter believed that Sebastian could survive being attacked by Ticks. Whatever Sebastian was—no matter how strong and fast—he was still just one guy. Against God only knew how many Ticks. There was no way he could have survived. But even if Sebastian hadn't been attacked by Ticks, even if he was still alive, he was still back at the Farm and he wasn't with us. And Joe was inadvertently responsible for that, too, because Joe was the one who had tackled Mel and got her started screaming. So maybe Carter really did want to kill Joe.

"I . . ." Suddenly everything I should say seemed like an embarrassing excuse. Or woefully insufficient. So I just said, "I'm so sorry."

Carter looked at me then, surprise clear on his face. "About what?"

"Sebastian. I'm sorry he got left behind. I'm so sorry."

Then Carter let out a bark of laughter, the kind that didn't sound amused at all. "Sebastian isn't my friend. I thought I made that clear. And I'm not worried about him. He knows how to take care of himself." He met my gaze then, for the first time since we'd left the Farm. He frowned, like he was worried. "You, on the other hand . . ."

"Right. I can see why you'd be worried about me." I gave an embarrassed laugh. "I'll try to behave."

"You may not want to get back into that car with McKenna and Joe, but it's the only option we've got. That's the only car we have and we can't leave them here. Please don't ask me to do that."

The note of pleading in his voice shocked me. Like he was really worried I was going to demand we leave McKenna and Joe on the side of the road. Like he was almost afraid he'd actually do it if I did ask.

I blew out a long, slow breath, which misted in the cold morning air. "I won't ask you to. But I'm not going to trust them, either."

"Fair enough."

When Carter and I climbed back in the SUV, Joe and McKenna had traded places, so that now Joe was driving. Mel sat in the passenger seat behind him, buckled in and facing forward, perfectly still, which was the way she liked to ride in a car. I half expected Carter to offer to drive. I would have felt way more comfortable with him in the driver's seat.

But Carter climbed back to the third row, stretching out his legs as he had before. He couldn't have been comfortable, but he looked too tired to care.

Once I'd climbed into the seat behind McKenna, closed the door, and snapped the buckle, Joe asked, "Where to now?"

"Keep heading west," Carter said without opening his eyes. "Next town over, there's a bridge across the Red River. There's a Baptist church on Main, just south of there. Pull into the parking lot. Sebastian will meet us there."

Part of me wanted to ask how long we were going to wait for him, because I couldn't imagine that Sebastian was actually going to make it. Even if he was still alive, how could he have followed us? But before I could think of a way to frame the question, Carter was already asleep.

CHAPTER TWENTY-THREE

LILY

I hadn't exactly been paying attention as we drove away from the Farm. I'd been too occupied by other things to look around at the tiny college town where the Farm was located. Now, with Carter asleep in the back, Joe driving, McKenna fidgeting in front of me, and Mel sitting stonelike beside me, I had nothing to look at except the scenery. I simply didn't have the energy to try to make sense of Joe's betrayal.

So instead, once I'd wiped the blood out of Mel's hair, I stared blankly out the window, my eyes searching for any indication that life outside the Farm had continued. I saw no other cars on the road. No signs of life from the farmhouses we passed. The cotton fields were as overgrown as the manicured lawns of the quad had been. The cotton was still in its even rows, the bolls left to rot on the stalks. It had been planted last spring, in the very end of the Before, and no one had tended or harvested the fields. But I'd never been through this part of north Texas before and it was possible to pretend the sense of desolation was normal. With that lie firmly in my mind, I drifted off.

I don't know how long I slept, but when I woke, Joe had pulled the SUV to a stop and was cutting the engine. Blinking, I straightened in my seat. Mel's eyes were closed, but I couldn't tell if she was sleeping or not. Even asleep she never seemed fully relaxed. Carter must have woken earlier than I, because he'd crept between my seat and Mel's and was leaning over the center console, talking to Joe in a hushed tone.

". . . no," he was saying, "but this isn't what I expected, either."

Joe mumbled a response. The only word I caught was "plan."

Carter's tone was irritated when he said, "We never said this was a foolproof plan. Sebastian promised to get you out. He did. Be glad it wasn't me, or I might have left your ass outside the fence and let you fend for yourself."

His response made me feel better—it was nice to pretend I had someone on my side. Part of me wanted to hear where their conversation was going, but McKenna must have realized I was awake, because she glanced over her shoulder at me before saying, "Are you sure that church thing really works?"

Carter looked back at me for a second before he shifted his weight and moved toward the bench seat.

It hadn't been that long ago that I'd been freaking out at the side of the road and something about the way he looked at me now made me uncomfortable. I wasn't used to losing it in front of other people. All alone in my room, sure. In front of family, maybe. In front of Carter, not so much. Why did my emotions always seem so close to the surface around him?

Pushing aside my awkwardness, I asked, "Where are we?"

"The parking lot of the Vidalou First Baptist Church."

"Where the hell is Vidalou?"

"Small town on the Texas-Oklahoma border. We're about a mile from the river."

After all the months of living on the Farm and being constantly told that we were safer there than anywhere else in the world, it seemed wrong to be just sitting in the car in the middle of the day, where anyone or anything could just . . . pounce. Even though I knew the Ticks weren't active during the day, I still felt strangely unprotected.

Funny, when I was on the Farm, I'd never really believed all that propaganda, but now that I was out, I realized more of it had sunk in than I'd thought.

"Are we safe here?" I asked. "Because it's a church?"

"Exactly. Vampires can't come on holy ground," Carter said.

The building in front of us didn't look anything like holy ground. In fact, it looked like it had been a car dealership back in the fifties and then sat empty for three decades before being repurposed by the Holy Rollers. However, an enormous sign had been mounted above the plate-glass windows. The sign was shaped like a steeple. It didn't look like a house of worship, but it certainly referenced an old-fashion clapboard church. The words "Vidalou First Baptist Church" had been painted on the windows.

"Vampires? So does it apply to Ticks, too?" I asked. "Or are we safe only if the cast of *Twilight* decides to attack?"

Carter sounded exasperated. "Just trust me, okay? I have more experience with them than any of you do. Vampires, Ticks, whatever. They don't come on holy ground."

"I don't get it," I said.

"Thank you!" McKenna snapped. "That's what I've been telling him."

If I listened for it, I might have heard the fear behind her sneer, but I didn't let myself. I didn't want to sympathize with her. I couldn't. I had to hold my distrust close to my chest because letting either McKenna or Joe in was a mistake I couldn't make.

"I'm not agreeing with you." I turned to Carter. "It just doesn't make a lot of sense. The Ticks aren't really vampires. They're genetically engineered mutants. Everything about them can be traced back to specific changes to their epigenetics. There is no gene for avoiding holy ground."

"I don't really understand it, either, but Sebastian has a theory. It's not that the Ticks are physically unable to cross onto holy ground, it's that some part of their brain remembers what it meant to be human. Religion is one of the things that separates humans from animals. They're horrified by things that remind them of what they used to be. Therefore they fear holy ground."

"Even if the holy ground used to be a Ford dealership?"

In the front seat, McKenna snorted and I instantly regretted my sarcasm. Negative bonding with her was not part of my plan.

Surprisingly, it was Joe who answered in that quiet stoner voice of his. "It's not the shape of the building that makes something holy ground. It's the faith of the people who worship there. That big cartoon steeple sure looks like a church to me."

"Yeah, I don't think these people's faith in God did them a lot of good when Ticks swarmed through their town," I grumbled, still not sold on this whole sacred-ground thing.

"Hey, even God can only do so much," Joe said. "People are responsible for this. Human choice got us here."

I hadn't pegged Joe as a spiritual kinda guy and the sincere faith in his voice made me uncomfortable. So I turned to Carter and asked, "Does Sebastian avoid holy ground, too? Is it horrific to him?"

"It's why newer vampires don't go on holy ground," Carter answered. "It's hard to say with Sebastian. He's been a vampire for almost two thousand years. I doubt he remembers what it was like to be a human. And there weren't churches here then anyway."

Two thousand years. Wow. That was unsettling. It made me even more aware of his otherness. Surely the holy-ground thing wouldn't actually apply to him, then. "Forget the theory. I think maybe it would be better if—"

But then I couldn't bring myself to say it out loud. Sebastian was probably dead. Staying here waiting was putting us all at risk.

"If what?"

I placed my hand on Carter's arm. "I know you think Sebastian is capable of anything. But—" Again I shied away from saying the most likely explanation aloud. Even though he was a vampire, he was just one vampire. Against . . . how many Ticks had there been? A lot. I went for the best-case scenario. "If he did manage to close the fence, then, mostly likely, he's still in the Farm. He's probably not getting out anytime soon. Certainly not soon enough to meet us here. He's not coming."

Carter didn't argue with me. He just let me talk, like he could sit there all day and my arguments wouldn't sway him.

"She's right—" McKenna started to say.

"Don't try to help." I cut her off. "You're only going to make things worse."

As soon as the words left my mouth, I knew that was why I didn't want to think about what might have happened to Sebastian. I couldn't shake the very real fear that everything I'd done had made things worse. My brilliant plan to save Mel and myself had put everyone else at risk.

"So what's the plan?" Joe asked, glancing nervously out the windows. "How long are we going to wait here?"

"Sebastian won't be long. While we're waiting, I'm going to see what I can find."

"You're going to get out?" I looked out my window and then Mel's. The town outside our car looked deserted, but there was an eerie stillness to the morning air. "You can't just wander around town. There could be Ticks out there."

"I won't be gone long. There are cars parked out on the street. I'm going to go see if any of them have gas. By the time I'm back, Sebastian should be here." He nodded toward the door. I kept my legs stretched out, refusing to let him pass. "Move over and let me out."

"No," I said simply. "This doesn't feel right. You shouldn't go."

"We need to get gas wherever we can," he argued. "I'll be fine. I'll find some supplies, I'll find Sebastian. I'll be right back."

I didn't want Sebastian to be dead, but even more than that, I didn't want Carter to climb out of the car to go looking for him. What if Carter never came back?

My outstretched legs didn't stop Carter. I guess I hadn't really thought they would. He turned to Mel.

"Let me out, okay?" he said.

Mel looked right at him. She rarely met even my gaze, so it surprised me. But instead of letting him pass, she asked, "Itsy-bitsy spider?"

Carter frowned for a second but put the pieces together faster than I did. "Yeah. I'll find Sebastian and bring him back."

That must have been answer enough for her, because she opened the door and tucked her legs onto her seat so he could easily pass.

He hopped out of the SUV and went around to open the back and pull out something. When he came back around, he was carrying a pair of gas cans.

He tapped Joe's window and Joe swung the door open.

"Whatever you do," Carter said to Joe, "don't let Lily and Mel out of your sight. If I'm not back in fifteen minutes, leave without me. Head for Utah."

"Utah?" I asked. "What the hell does that mean?"

"It's a state. Just north of Arizona." Carter winked at me.

"I thought you were supposed to be smart. It also happens to be where the base camp is. The group sends out enough patrols that if you go to Utah, someone will find you. If they can't convince you to stay, then at least someone there can get you where you're going."

With that, he swung the door shut and sauntered off across the parking lot.

"You know," I mumbled into the silence that followed, "that whole if-I'm-not-back-in-fifteen-minutes thing gets really old. Besides, Utah is really big."

Which, I supposed, was just a sign of how confident he was that he'd be back in fifteen minutes.

Beside me, Mel gave a snort. If anyone else had made that noise, I would have thought it was laughter, but even in the Before her sense of humor had been strained. You had to really talk her through a joke before she understood it was supposed to be funny.

But McKenna must have interpreted it as a laugh, too, because she joined in. "I know, right? Even I know where Utah is."

It took all my willpower not to flick her on the back of the head. What little willpower was left I used resisting the urge to get out of the car and follow Carter. If Sebastian was out there, how did Carter think he was going to find him on his own?

Inside the car, silence was thick in the air. Mel gazed out the window, looking at who knew what—maybe nothing. Her hands twisted in her lap nervously and after a minute, I got her Slinky out of her pink backpack and handed it to her. After that, the steady *sllluuunk, sllluuunk, sllluunk* filled the car.

"Does she have to do that?" McKenna complained.

"Yes. She does," I answered. For once, Mel's Slinky soothed me as well as her and I began to relax.

The wait seemed interminable. I checked the clock on my

phone three times, only to find that just a few minutes had passed. How long would it take to siphon gas from a car into a gas can? At first, I prayed time would pass more quickly. Then, as five minutes turned into ten, I prayed it would slow down. Carter still wasn't back. At fourteen minutes, I stopped closing my phone and just stared at it as it ticked down the seconds.

Joe started fidgeting. "We should—"

"Shut up." I cut him off. "We're not leaving."

"It's almost time."

"I don't care. We're not leaving." I unbuckled my seat belt and opened the door.

"You can't go out there," Joe protested.

"I'm just looking for him." I stood on the running board and looked over the top of the SUV first in one direction and then in the other.

I saw and heard nothing. Until a chilling howl split the air.

Inside the car, Joe cursed. McKenna yelped. Mel clenched her hands, her Slinky suddenly silent.

Heart pounding in my chest, I scanned the street in every direction. Nothing. No Ticks, but no Carter, either.

"Damn it," I muttered. "Where are you?"

Then another howl rent the air.

"Get back in the car." Joe started the engine. "We gotta go."

"We're not leaving Carter," I protested.

"He said to leave in fifteen minutes. It's been fifteen minutes. And there are Ticks out there."

I hopped to the ground and stuck my head in the car. There was no way I was going to climb in because then Joe would just drive off. "Exactly. There are Ticks out there. And he's alone, looking for supplies. For us."

In her seat, Mel was getting twitchy, first looking out her window and then twisting to look out the back. Suddenly she grabbed something from the back floorboard and held it up. Carter's backpack.

"He told us to go," Joe argued. "It's what he would want us to do."

"He doesn't even have his backpack! He has nothing to defend himself!"

"He probably found Sebastian."

"You know that's a long shot. Sebastian is probably dead!" I yelled. "We can't leave Carter!"

Inside the car, Mel had slipped her Slinky onto her wrist like a bracelet. She was clutching her backpack and Carter's.

The Tick howled again, closer now. And then another howl joined the first. Shit. They were coming this way. I searched the street again, but still saw no sign of Carter.

Damn it, where was he? Didn't he hear them? Why wasn't he hauling ass to get back here?

"Lily, we have to go." Joe shifted the SUV into drive. "Get in the car. It's time."

"No." But my protest was weaker now, because I knew he was right. We needed to leave. It was what he'd told us to do. It was what we had to do to save ourselves. It was what I had to do to protect Mel. But I couldn't make myself do it. I couldn't force myself to climb into the car, knowing the second I did, Joe would drive off, leaving Carter behind. Leaving Carter to die.

CHAPTER TWENTY-FOUR

MEL

I know the Ticks are coming before anyone else. Their jangled cacophony shatters everyone else's music. I know Carter is near, too, but not close enough. Sebastian is with him—his quiet all noise, none of it right, none of it music, but louder than any I've ever heard.

This happened before, too, at the river. His emotions like the concussion blast of a bomb.

Time moves slowly in the car with Joe like a beaver wanting to go, go, go. Lily's the easy one now. Stay, stay, stay. For once she listens to my music. Everyone fighting and I'm the odd girl out. Always the odd girl. Time is tick-tocking and I've nothing to do.

The Ticks have no music, only noise, and they can't stand the sounds the rest of us make.

I feel them getting closer. Feel their anguish. Their hunger. It's not just thirst that brings them here, when they should be sleeping. There's something else, too. Like a mosquito buzzing in their collective ear. Or a nursery rhyme chanting in their collective brain.

I feel our panic rising and even I can't slow the rhythm of the song.

CHAPTER TWENTY-FIVE

LILY

"Get in the car," Joe said again.

I could feel the tears streaming down my face. I didn't know what to do, but I knew I couldn't leave Carter.

The howl of the Ticks—more than two now—grew steadily louder, heading at us from the west. As they got closer, we could hear their higher-pitched yips and yelps. Wherever Carter was, he'd be completely defenseless. They would swarm over him and devour him.

I put one foot back in the car and dipped my head in to say, "I swear to God if you drive off now I'll—"

But I never finished the thought. I broke off when I heard the roar of an engine. Tires squealed as a vehicle pulled around the corner. It was a long van, the kind schools used on field trips, that seated maybe twelve to fifteen people. The name of some unfamiliar school district was painted on the side. I noticed all this because my eyes were glued to it as it came barreling down the street. Sebastian was behind the wheel, but I couldn't tell if Carter was in there with him.

The van slid to a stop at a slant perpendicular to our SUV. The side door of the van flew open and Carter was inside. Relief flooded me.

Thank God.

"Come on, get in!" he ordered.

He didn't have to tell me twice. I grabbed my bag and Mel's hand and pulled them both out of the SUV. Carter hopped out of the van to make room for us to clamber in. Sebastian dashed around the front of the van, then threw open the back of the SUV and grabbed the bags that had been stashed in back. I got Mel settled onto the second row of the bench seats and snapped a buckle across her lap, then looked out of the van to see if Carter needed help. Sebastian was tossing bags to Carter, who was throwing them in the back of the van.

Somewhere—too close—the Ticks howled. And then I heard an ominous crunching sound, like something had run into a car out on the street.

Only then did I realize Joe and McKenna hadn't made it into the van yet. He was helping her out of the SUV.

"Hurry up," I yelled.

They were maybe two feet away from the van when I heard another loud crunch and the whole SUV shook. The Tick sprang on the top of the SUV and in one feral leap soared over the back of the SUV, the open door, and Sebastian to land in a crouch behind McKenna and Joe.

"Spear!" Sebastian yelled.

I reached out a hand and grabbed Joe, who was closest to me, and hauled him into the van. He pulled McKenna with him, but she moved more slowly. The Tick scraped a nasty clawed hand across her back. She screamed in anguish. Joe spun and launched himself at the Tick.

Carter charged around from behind the van, two long wooden sticks in his hands. He tossed one to Sebastian and then closed in on the Tick with the other. He slammed the spear through the Tick's back. The Tick arched its back, yowling in pain, its gangly arms stretched over its head as it spun, trying to reach the stake piercing its heart. Its flailing arms smacked Joe and he fell, bashing his head on the floorboard on the way down.

McKenna was screaming, but whether in pain or panic I couldn't tell. Carter dragged Joe into the van. Another Tick launched himself over the SUV and Sebastian thrust the other spear up through its heart and tossed it aside as if it was nothing.

A third Tick came screaming around the SUV and Carter scrambled to slide the van door closed. An instant later the beast slammed into the closed door.

Something clattered on the roof of the van and then Sebastian slid effortlessly through the window into the driver's seat. He looked like he wasn't even breathing hard.

"All in?" he asked, his voice calm.

Carter looked first at me, then at Mel before answering. "All in."

As Sebastian drove off, another Tick hit the back of the van. Their indignant howls echoed through the air as they chased us. But they didn't stay on our tail long. They loped behind us for a few long strides and then fell back.

"Who's hurt?" Carter asked. "Lily? Mel?"

Struggling to pull air into my panicked lungs, I looked at Mel. "We're fine."

I could hardly believe it. We were okay. We'd all made it into the van. And Carter had made it back. He was okay. He wasn't dead somewhere, his heart already ripped out of his chest and drained of blood.

Relief rolled through me and I had to tamp back my tears. And the urge to throw myself into his arms. God, I'd been so afraid.

It took me several deep breaths to get my emotions back under control enough that I could even think to check on anyone else.

Carter and McKenna were both looking at Joe, who sat dazed on the floor of the van, his back leaning against the front passenger seat, his legs tucked up against his chest. He held his hand against the back of his head and his eyes looked glazed.

Carter had one knee propped on the first bench seat and other leg down on the floor in the narrow space between the seat and the door. He'd whipped out that penlight of his again. I vaguely remembered him shining it in my eyes when I'd first woken up in the admin building.

"You're tracking fine and I don't see any blood," he said. "Your head is going to hurt like hell, but unless you puke or pass out, I think you'll be okay."

McKenna was on the first bench seat, one hand on Joe's arm, the other holding his hand. It was the first time I'd seen her actually touch him. The first time I'd noticed any genuine signs of affection from her.

I forced myself to look away, because it seemed strangely intimate. Like something too personal to witness.

Instead I looked up into the front of the van where Sebastian drove. Although he'd looked perfectly peaceful just moments after fighting the Ticks, now his expression was taut and strained. His hands were clenched on the steering wheel. He glanced up into the rearview mirror and met my gaze.

I recoiled against the seat, barely containing my gasp. His pupils had contracted. Instead of the round pupils of a human, his had shifted into slits, but they weren't the oval slits of a cat or a snake. Instead the edges were scalloped, like the petals of Venus flytrap. For the first time, he didn't look like a human. He looked like a monster.

I jerked my eyes from his, wanting to look anywhere but into his unsettling gaze.

That was when I saw McKenna's back. The fabric of her sweatshirt had long rips torn through it and blood was beginning to seep through.

I gasped. "McKenna! Your back!"

Joe looked up. Carter whipped his head toward me.

"McKenna, you're bleeding."

As soon as I said the words, I looked back at Sebastian. Carter did, too. And then Joe and McKenna. Even Mel was watching him, perhaps even more carefully than I had. We all sat there, just staring at the vampire as the implication rippled through the van.

Sebastian kept driving, not even slowing down. He kept his gaze pinned on the road, though I could still see his bizarre pupils in the rearview mirror.

"It's fine," he said quietly after a minute.

"Are you sure?" Carter asked.

"I have to be, don't I? We have only one car. Unless you're suggesting I ride on top of the van."

"We could pull over," I suggested, remembering how careful Carter had been about the cut on my palm, a cut that was tiny by comparison. "You could wait outside while we bandage her."

"I'm fine," he said, his voice terse. "Believe me when I assure you that I am the least of our worries right now."

"But—"

"Tell me, child, has your hunger ever been so out of control that you've devoured everything in your path with no thought of the consequences? I think not. I am no different. I will control myself."

I blew out a breath, half thinking of telling him that he'd obviously never seen me alone with a bowl of cookie dough on a Saturday night. But if his brittle tone was any indication, this was not the time to crack a joke.

Instead I glanced at Carter, who returned my gaze steadily, seeming to read the question there. Slowly he nodded, as if to tell me that he was okay with this turn of events.

"McKenna, we'll go to the back of the van. Get you cleaned up there." As Joe helped her move, Carter turned to Mel, who still had his backpack held on her lap. "Mel, can you find my first aid kit?"

I nearly told him that I would do it, but Mel cheerfully unzipped the bag and started looking. I scooted to the edge of the bench, ready to follow Carter back and help with McKenna's wound, but before I could stand, he crouched down beside my bench.

"Why the hell didn't you drive away?" His voice was dense with anger.

"What?" I asked, recoiling in surprise.

"I told you to leave."

"But—"

"Fifteen minutes, I said. You were supposed to leave after fifteen minutes."

"Joe—"

"Don't try to pin this on Joe. He was driving, but you were the one standing outside the friggin' car. If he stayed it's because you told him to."

His anger stirred my own. After the terrifying last few minutes, adrenaline still pumped through my veins. "I wasn't going to pin this on Joe. I made the decision to wait."

"It was past time to leave, Ticks were bearing down on you, and you made the decision to wait?"

"Yes!" I bumped up my chin. "I was waiting for you, you dumb ass!"

"Well, you shouldn't have!"

We kept our voices low, but we were nose to nose now and the car had gone silent around us.

"You would never have left without me," I hissed. "And there was no way in hell I was going to leave without you."

Suddenly Carter sat back. As if my words had hit him in the chest. "Jesus, Lily!" He scrubbed a hand down his face.

"Don't think you're the only one who gets to save people. Carter, I—"

"Stop," he said, cutting me off before I could say any more. He met my gaze, but there was no longer anger in his eyes. Or fear. Just tired resolve. "You can't think like that. It is not your job to save anyone but yourself."

"But—"

"I don't care what you feel. Or what you think you feel. You have to keep yourself safe. That is the only important thing. Do you understand me?"

"No, I don't understand." I wanted to cry again, but even more than that, I wanted to curl inside myself. I couldn't look at him now, but my gaze was on his hands and I saw him clench them into fists. Like he wanted to reach for me but wouldn't let himself.

At least that was what I wanted to believe.

"Carter, I—"

"No, God damn it! You have to promise you'll never risk your life for mine again." I didn't answer and a moment later, he stood. "If you can't promise me that, I'm getting out of the van now."

My head jerked up. "What?"

"Sebastian, pull over the van."

"What the hell?" But Sebastian was already starting to slow the van. "No! Stop! I promise." The van was still coasting and Carter already had the door open. I launched myself at his back. "I promise! I'll never risk my life for you again!"

Carter looked back over his shoulder and he seemed to be considering whether or not to climb out. Somewhere in the distance, a Tick howled.

"I won't! I swear! Just get back in the van!"

He studied my face and I didn't even care that tears were streaming down my cheeks.

Finally Carter closed the door. Sebastian watched from the rearview mirror and didn't start driving again until Carter had met his gaze and nodded.

I wanted him safe so desperately I knew I'd never be able to keep my promise.

* *

I didn't offer to help with McKenna. Mel handed Carter the first aid kit, while I slumped on the seat, nursing my bruised emotions. What was his problem? Did he have some kind of martyr syndrome? He got to run all over the country rescuing people, but no one was allowed to return the favor? No one got to help him? Or maybe it was just me he was trying to drive away. He hadn't yelled at Joe. No, he blamed me.

He must have realized I was starting to . . . what? Fall for him? It seemed crazy when he'd only been back in my life less than twenty-four hours. But his presence hit my emotions fast and hard, just as it had when we'd first met. Clearly he didn't feel the same way. Well, if he wanted me to back the hell away from him emotionally, I could do that. It wasn't like I'd ever see him again once we got to Canada anyway. But he couldn't stop me from trying to protect the people I cared about. He could yell all he wanted, but if Mel was in danger, I was going to do everything I could to help.

I glanced over at her now. I knew she was physically okay, but I wasn't sure how she felt about the Ticks attacking. I expected her to be staring blankly out the window the way she usually did in the car, but instead she was watching me. Her head was tilted to the side, a slight frown on her face. She slid the Slinky off her wrist and held it out to me.

I let out a huff of surprised laughter. Yeah. I needed soothing right now. I took the Slinky from her and gave it a few *sllluuunks* before handing it back. She seemed satisfied. Oddly, I felt calmer after that. Still hurt. Still bruised. But quieter.

I wiggled down a bit so my head rested against the back of the bench, for the first time in months feeling . . . I don't know. Like she was in this with me. Not just someone I had to take care of. Like she was my sister and not just an appendage I was lugging around.

Behind me, I heard Joe ask, "So a wooden stake through the heart really works?"

"As it turns out, any stake through the heart works," Sebastian answered from the driver's seat. "It doesn't kill them instantly. Just immobilizes them until it's removed. Once they've been staked, they can bleed to death or starve to death. Or you can cut off their head."

"Oh. That's pleasant," I said.

I thought I heard McKenna make a gagging sound. Or maybe she was wincing from the pain of having Carter treat her injury.

Sebastian ignored us and continued talking. "Wood has the advantage of being plentiful, light, and easy to carve."

"What else works?" I asked.

Carter looked up from where he'd been swabbing McKenna's back with antiseptic wipes and glared at me. "You don't need to know what works, because from now on you're staying clear of the fights, damn it."

"Everyone needs to know what works," I countered. "Once you drop us off in Canada, you won't be there anymore to boss us around, and excuse me if I'd like to know how to kill these things."

Carter opened and closed his mouth a couple of times like he was trying to think of something to say and failing.

"So what kills them?" I met Sebastian's gaze in the rearview mirror. As unsettling as it was, I did it to convince him I was serious. "Guns don't, right? Otherwise the police and National Guard could have taken care of the infestation before it even left south Texas."

Sebastian was silent for a long moment, like he was trying to judge how serious I was. "No. Guns generally don't work. Large-caliber assault rifles, sometimes. Buckshot at close range will slow them down. But the stake through the heart is your best bet."

Involuntarily, I imagined what it would actually take to thrust a stake through the heart of anything. The physical strength. The willpower. Plus, if you were close enough to stake a Tick through the heart, wouldn't it be close enough to rip your heart out?

I swallowed my nausea, closing my eyes to block the image. "Isn't there anything that just . . . scares them off?"

"They are like any primitive beast. Fire frightens them, if you have enough of it."

"You would have thought," Joe mused, "that with all the things the army and the police tried back in the Before, they would have tried spears and fire, too."

I didn't open my eyes, but said, "I don't know about spears, but they did try fire."

"Well, obviously they didn't," McKenna said in her most obnoxious know-it-all voice. "Because all the news reports said the Ticks couldn't be stopped."

But I could picture the news segments in my mind. Hours and hours of footage of that initial wave of Ticks. The way they swarmed through the Southwest. I could see the images of first the police, then the National Guard, then the army. All our lines of defense, decimated one after another. There were huge losses on our side in every attack. Worst of all, some of the men and women didn't die, but turned into Ticks themselves. And in my mind, I could practically hear that chick from the local news station Mom used to watch. Marena something. "The CDC is working around the clock to try to find a cure. . . . Nothing seems to affect them. . . . People are advised to stay indoors at all costs. . . . Teenagers in particular seem to be at risk. . . . The government is recommending teenagers be relocated to fortified camps. . . ."

I opened my eyes and pushed myself up. I angled my body sideways so I could easily look from Sebastian in front of me to Carter behind me. "So why do spears and fire work? Everything we know about Ticks says they can't be killed. Not with guns, not with poison gas, not with bombs, not with flamethrowers. Now you're telling me all we need are some matches and really big pencils?"

"Everything *we* know?" Sebastian asked drolly.

"Okay," I conceded. "Everything I know. But I know a fair amount. How could everything in the news have been wrong? Were we all lied to?"

Carter and Sebastian exchanged a look—another one of those whole-conversation-in-a-single-glance kinds of looks. Like they were disagreeing about how much to tell me, and I wasn't sure which of them came down on the side of total honesty.

Finally Sebastian said, "Let's just say the media didn't know the whole truth. They rarely do."

There was obviously more to the story than that. I would have to get Carter alone at some point and try to get the details from him. And if he didn't give them, then I'd need to talk to Sebastian.

But I wasn't going to push it now, when Mel was listening. Instead I asked hopefully, "Are the Ticks getting weaker?"

"Ah . . . would that that were true. But sadly, they are not getting weaker. Only better fed. A lion that's not hungry will not bother chasing antelope."

I shuddered at the thought. Beside me, Mel looked just as disturbed. We'd been lucky.

"What would have happened if they had been hungry?"

It was Carter who answered. "We have a full tank of gas and a van that can go faster than they can run."

That actually hadn't occurred to me. "Jesus, how fast can they run?"

"Thirty-five, forty miles an hour."

"Holy crap," Joe said from the background.

I sank back against the bench seat thinking. Despite all my preparations, now that we were off the Farm, I felt woefully unprepared. I hadn't thought about having to siphon gas or defend against the Ticks in the daytime. I hadn't planned on having to kill them. How could I possibly keep Mel safe? I didn't have large-caliber assault rifles or buckshot or an endless supply of pointy broom handles.

The van fell silent as we crossed into Oklahoma. Carter finished bandaging up McKenna's back. Then he opened one of the windows in back and threw the bloody antiseptic rag away.

After a long moment, I said, "I was a Girl Scout."

I didn't necessarily expect a big reaction, but Mel did smile. She knew what I was getting at.

"So was I," McKenna said.

I laughed at that. I don't know why it was funny. But I had completely forgotten that once, long ago, McKenna and I had been in the same Daisy troop when we were kids. "Yeah. You were. You remember summer camp?"

I turned and looked at her in the back of the van. She frowned, her cheeks flushing red. "Yeah, sure."

"I went every summer for eleven years."

From the front seat, Sebastian said, "I'm sure your Scouting experiences are very impressive."

I ignored him and said, "My point is, I took archery every summer for eleven years. I can shoot a bow and arrow. If a stake can immobilize a Tick, will an arrow work?"

Carter blew out a sigh. "It would. If we could get one."

"Stores—" I started to ask.

"They've all been looted," he answered. "All those fishing, hunting, survivalist places . . . they got hit early and hard."

Frowning, I sat back. Mel sat there humming, staring out the window. I didn't place the song right away, but it was homey and comforting. Now that I'd seen the Ticks in action—not once, but twice—I knew I needed some way to defend myself and Mel. I couldn't just sit back and let Carter and Sebastian rescue us. I wasn't ready to give up the idea of the bow and arrow. If it was an advantage I had, I was going to find a way to use it. Which was when I realized she was humming "She'll Be Coming 'Round the Mountain," a song Mom had always sung during road trips to our uncle Rodney's. Once again, Mel was one step ahead of me.

"Do we have a map?" I asked.

"Of course. Would you like to see it?"

I choked back my *Well, duh*. "Yes, please."

Sebastian handed it back and I unfolded it on the bench between Mel and me. After a few minutes of searching, I found the tiny town of Vidalou that we'd just left. With my index finger I traced a path to the main highway that headed north up through Oklahoma.

Mel leaned over the map and looked with me. After a minute or so, she pointed to a spot just east of the Oklahoma-Arkansas border. I nodded. "That's just what I was thinking."

"What?" Joe asked, leaning forward to brace his arms on the bench in front of him.

I still didn't want to talk to Joe—I knew I could never trust him again—but at the same time, the experience in Vidalou had changed things. It brought home so clearly how right Carter was. We humans had to stick together. We couldn't tear into one another. The Ticks were all too eager to do that for us. So I turned and looked over my shoulder.

"I'm wondering if we can take a little detour on the way to Detroit."

"Detroit?" Sebastian drawled. "I wasn't aware our travel plans had changed."

Carter cleared his throat. "Yeah. I didn't have a chance to mention that. Lily doesn't want to go to Utah. She wants to seek asylum from the Canadians."

"Ah." The way Sebastian said it, it was a sort of that-explains-everything "ah."

I looked at him. I felt that same shiver of apprehension I always felt. I considered backing down, but something told me that backing down now was the wrong thing to do. That he was judging me in this moment, waiting for me to fall short of some unspoken standard.

I didn't like being judged any more than I liked people who manipulated others. "If you have an opinion, Sebastian, share it now."

"Only that it should be interesting, if the person who is supposed to be leading the rebellion is in Canada."

"I never asked you to come with us."

"Oh, I did not mean me. It hardly matters at all where I am."

"Fine. Carter then." I glanced at him to see him clenching his fists again.

"Ah. I see." To Carter he said, "Then you didn't—"

Carter interrupted Sebastian. "I didn't think it was smart to debate where we were going until we were off the Farm." His tone was fierce. "Getting them out was the most important thing. I figured we could debate where to go next once we were all out."

Neither man said anything for a few minutes. When I couldn't take the tension in the car any longer, I said, "I never asked anyone to come with us. At the next town, you can help us find a car and we'll get to Canada on our own."

"I'm not trying to convince anyone," Sebastian said. "Merely commenting that I was unaware our plans had changed."

"Why does she get to decide?" McKenna asked.

"I'm not deciding for everyone. Just Mel and me. It's the logical destination. North Texas to Detroit is just about the closest border. Once we get there we can throw ourselves on the mercy of the Canadian government." I shot her a glare from under my lashes. "No one's going to make you come with us."

Joe and McKenna exchanged a look. One of those things couples do where they seem to say a lot without ever saying anything at all. Then Joe gave a terse nod.

I couldn't help the little flurry of jealousy that went through me at their bond. And the truth was, I'd been hoping they'd decide not to come with us. But since that didn't happen, I said, "I'm just wondering if we have time to drive through Alpena, Arkansas."

McKenna snorted. "Why would we want to do that?"

"Our uncle Rodney has a cabin outside of town. He's one of those redneck gun-nut types. He'll have weapons. Bows and arrows. Mop handles we can whittle down," I added with only a little sarcasm. "Besides, he probably even has antibiotics. Which McKenna might need."

Carter sat forward. "One of those survivalist gun-nut types? The kind who might have, oh, an arsenal of weapons and food stockpiled?"

"I don't know about an arsenal, but he's the only guy I know who fills his own shotgun shells."

Sebastian smiled. "Looks like we're going to Arkansas."

By the time I'd found the approximate location of Uncle Rodney's place on the map, exhaustion had started to sink in. We still had a long day of driving ahead of us. I figured at some point it would be my turn to take the wheel. So I closed my eyes and tried to get some rest, but as I drifted off to sleep, one thought haunted me. If the Ticks we'd just encountered weren't hungry, then why had they chased us at all? And why were they out in daylight? They were supposed to be nocturnal.

I thought about what Sebastian had said about lions. It was true, a pride of lions who were well fed wouldn't chase an antelope. But they would chase off another lion.

CHAPTER TWENTY-SIX

CARTER

They stopped to siphon gas again in Muskogee. By then it was around noon. Sebastian assured him there was a nest of Ticks sleeping in a barn outside of town, but they were unlikely to wake. It was a tedious thing. Driving to residential neighborhoods and walking through them, house by house, looking for cars that might still have gas in the tank. The town itself was completely deserted. Nearly every home showed signs that its occupants had left quickly, but no clues remained as to where they'd gone. They found a few cars with gas in their tanks. They stopped again in Fayetteville, Arkansas. It made for slow going, but they'd learned that anytime the Ticks weren't around, they had to take advantage of it. Each time they stopped, he and Sebastian siphoned gas while the others searched the nearby houses for canned food and supplies. Even with Sebastian's assurance that the Ticks were asleep, Carter tried to insist Lily wait in the car. She merely rolled her eyes and muttered, "Don't be ridiculous."

By Fayetteville, McKenna refused to get out of the van. She looked so battered and worn, no one blamed her. Carter kept expecting Mel or Lily to rip apart at the seams. To come to him in tears. Neither did.

However, he still worried about taking the detour to Alpena and not because of the extra hours it would take. He only hoped

Lily and Mel would be strong enough for whatever they found there.

Since she knew the way, Lily took over driving on the outskirts of Alpena. Sebastian moved to the middle row and lay down for a few minutes of sleep.

Mel sat in the passenger seat beside Lily, humming "She'll Be Coming 'Round the Mountain." Carter sat on the first bench, right in the middle so he could lean forward and talk to Lily.

"You sure you want to do this?"

"Of course." But her voice trembled slightly as she said it.

"Searching for supplies in abandoned houses is one thing. Ransacking the house of someone you knew, somewhere you stayed, that's going to be something else entirely."

She glanced over her shoulder as she slowed down to take a sharp right onto a steep, tree-lined drive. "Do you say that from personal experience?"

"Some. We passed through Dallas on the way to your Farm. I didn't go to my parents' house, but we drove past the building my dad's company was in."

"But not your parents' house?"

"No," he said, suddenly aware of what not going might say about him.

She nodded like she understood exactly what he was talking about. But part of him knew she couldn't. Yeah, sure, her parents were divorced. But he remembered seeing her mother at school events, looking tired and frazzled, but there for her kids. He'd never had anyone in his life who'd been there for him like that.

"Yeah," she said finally. "I get why you wouldn't want to see it. I've been the same way. Avoiding facing the hard facts."

He didn't disagree with her, even though that wasn't the reason he'd avoided going home.

Then she frowned, tilted her head to the side as she seemed to consider. "No, not avoiding it. I know my mom probably isn't . . ." Her voice cracked a little on her words. "There is nothing that woman wouldn't have done to get us out of there if she knew what was going on in the Farms. But until I know for sure, until I have proof, I'm just not going to go there. I don't need to obsess about what happened or how it went down."

"I don't obsess about it," he said flatly. "But I know my parents. They're the kind of people who buy themselves out of any tough situation. You can bet the second the Ticks got too close to home, they bailed. They're probably on some lush tropical island right now, worrying about how the vampire apocalypse has affected their portfolio."

"That's"—Lily blew out a breath—"that's pretty harsh. You can't really believe that." She met his gaze and after a second of him not backing down, she looked away. "You've never really had anyone in your corner, have you?" She looked like she wanted to cry.

He couldn't bear to see that. He'd never wanted her pity. "I do now," he said, and then, because he was afraid of what she might read in his words, he explained. "Up in Utah, I've got nearly a hundred kids who have my back. People who would fight to the death with me. People I'd trust with my life."

And suddenly it hit him how much he wanted her to be one of those people. He wanted her with him in Utah for reasons that had nothing to do with the rebellion. He wanted her there for her courage and for her fierce, unshakable loyalty. He wanted her there for himself.

And he knew then that part of him wished she wasn't an *abductura*.

She was quiet for several long minutes. He could tell she was trying to think of something to say. Something that would bridge that awkward revelation of his.

Finally she must have decided to ignore it completely, because she said, "My uncle Rodney, he used to do all kinds of crazy crap. He'd hunt wild boar with only a bowie knife. Stuff like that. If anyone could have made it, he did."

Carter felt something crack inside his chest for her. "Lil, don't—"

"I'm not saying he's going to be there. Just that he would have made it to safety or gone down fighting. The sight of his empty house isn't going to freak me out."

A moment later, the sloping driveway evened out to a grassy yard. A small clapboard house sat in a clearing beside a covered carport. There was no car in the drive.

Carter woke Sebastian so the vampire could use his spidey sense to feel around for Ticks. He gave the house the all clear and they piled out of the van.

McKenna—who'd mentioned needing a potty break about a dozen times already—went straight for the front door. She hesitated on the porch.

"The door's been busted in," she called. "Looks like we're not the first people here."

Carter glanced around, expecting to see disappointment on Lily's face, only to see her and Mel disappearing around the side of the building. He called out to Joe. "Go with McKenna and make sure the house is clear before she uses the bathroom."

He didn't wait for Joe to answer before trotting off after Mel and Lily. He found them around the back of the house, standing over a stack of wood. It was the better part of a cord of wood that covered a good eight feet by four feet of the ground. It looked like it had been culled from the surrounding forest, if the variety of branch size was any indication. A tarp covered the wood and a pallet of plywood kept it off the ground.

"Do you want to start a fire?" he asked. "It's not a bad idea, if we want to stay here for the night."

Mel turned and looked at him. She pointed at the wood and said, "There's no place like home."

"Um, sure."

But Lily dropped to her knees and angled to look under the pallet. She stood up, dusting her hands on her jeans. "Hey, can you help me move this? Uncle Rodney always kept the woodpile beside the doors to the storm cellar. I think before he left for wherever he was going, he must have moved the wood on top of them to hide them from anyone passing by. If we can just shift the whole pallet over . . ."

Before waiting for him to answer, she went and grabbed one side of it, like she could get started on her own.

"Hey, Wonder Woman, you're not going to be able to budge that thing."

She smirked. "I can if you help."

"No. Even if Mel helps, the three of us aren't going to be able to move a cord of wood."

"Together—"

"Why don't you go inside the house and make sure Joe and McKenna know we're out back?" She looked ready to protest. "I'll move the wood myself. That way, whatever's down there, I see it first. If he's down there and alive, I'll get you right away. If he's down there but . . ." He couldn't think of a tactful way to say it and he didn't need to. From her expression, he knew she got his point. "Then you don't have to see it. Besides, Sebastian can move the pile more easily than any of us."

"Oh, yes," Sebastian grumbled with irritation as he came

around the back of the house. "That's what I'm here for. The heavy lifting."

Lily ignored Sebastian completely, but seemed to be considering Carter's words. Finally she nodded and left for the front of the house with Mel, guiding her sister with a single finger on Mel's elbow.

Sebastian followed Carter's gaze. "You know, I get the feeling she doesn't like me."

"Why? Because you're a bloodsucking monster?"

Sebastian placed a hand dramatically to his heart. "Sometimes your words hurt."

Carter ignored him and knelt down to start moving the wood. Despite what he'd told Lily, he didn't expect Sebastian to help. It would take much longer for Carter to move it himself, but he'd never asked Sebastian for anything without him wanting something in return.

Sebastian must have seen Carter's ruse for what it was, because he didn't offer to help but leaned his shoulder against a nearby tree and stretched his legs out in front of him. "Is that why you haven't told her she's an *abductura*? Because she doesn't like me?"

"I haven't told her because she freaked out after I tranqed her. She wasn't in a particularly trusting place."

"Ah."

Moving it mere inches at a time, Carter was able to pull the pallet of wood to a new spot. The pallet must have been on skids, because he was able to move it even though the corners of the two-by-four frame dug into the moist earth, leaving a trail.

"And so you've decided to keep her in the dark. So that she won't . . . freak out?" The modern slang sounded awkward on Sebastian's tongue. "Because you are running out of time to convince her. Even if we stall and stay here tonight, we should be in Canada by dawn the day after tomorrow."

Carter ran a hand through his hair. "You're right. I know, you're right."

"I would be happy to—"

"No." He said it more forcefully than he meant to. To hide his discomfort, he squatted beside the cellar door latch and pretended to examine the lock. "I know you get impatient with us humans and our silly emotions, but she wasn't ready to hear it. I'll tell her soon, but it has to be me who tells her."

Sebastian didn't answer right away and Carter looked up to see the vampire tilting his head to the side as if listening to the conversation in the house. After a second, he returned his attention to Carter and whispered, "You'll stay here tonight, examine your own motives, and then find a time to tell her. Don't test my patience any longer."

"Or what? You'll refuse to go to Canada with us?"

Sebastian smirked. "Of course I'll go to Canada. I'll go wherever she's going to be happiest. A happy *abductura* broadcasts more strongly. But you, my boy, can't lead your little revolution from Canada. If you're content to leave me alone with your *abductura*, I will certainly oblige you."

Carter stood and stalked over to get in Sebastian's face. "This fight is yours as much as it is ours. And don't pretend for a second that you don't want to bring down Roberto just as badly as I do."

Sebastian straightened so that the distance between them was mere inches. "Obviously." He enunciated the word with all the crisp perfection of a British schoolchild. A sure sign his temper was short. "If undermining Roberto's plans was not of the utmost importance to me, I would not be reduced to playing fetch and carry for a disorganized group of teenage kine."

Carter gave a harsh chuckle. "Yeah. You hate having to work with us at all. The feeling is mutual. We're both stuck with each other. Neither of us has a choice here. But just know, if you touch Lily or Mel, I will find you and take you down. If you so much as breathe in their direction—"

Sebastian chuckled. "See, this is the advantage of dealing with teenage kine. Your emotions are so close to the surface, it's quite amusing."

Carter had to grit his teeth to hold back the urge to punch Sebastian. That would be sheer stupidity. Sebastian—maybe all vampires—had a short temper and deadly outbursts. You didn't pick a fight with a vampire unless you already had a stake halfway through his heart.

Instead, he breathed out and changed the subject. "How long has it been since you've eaten?"

Sebastian's eyes had a dark, glazed look that Carter didn't like. He looked hungrily at Carter's arm. "Why? Are you offering?"

Carter gritted his teeth and resisted tugging on his sleeve. "No. I fed you last month." That was the one scar he hadn't shown Lily. The shallow, inch-long cut on his inner wrist, where he'd bled a pint into a cup for Sebastian. The guys in the rebellion took turns feeding the vampire, but none of them liked it. Thank God he didn't drink directly from humans anymore.

Sebastian was exceptionally paranoid about accidentally turning a new vampire, even now when the vampire territories of the Before were gone. Maybe especially now.

"I know you don't like the premixed blood on the Farms, but you should have eaten there. Since you didn't, you should go hunt tonight."

Sebastian smiled. "Excellent advice. I'll follow yours if you follow mine."

"I'll worry about Lily; you worry about quenching your thirst."

"The forests around here have been overhunted already. I will hunt, but I have little control over the outcome of my night's work. I may find nothing worth eating. You, however, know exactly what you should do and have the means to do it." Sebastian's enlarged canines gave his smile a nasty wolfish appearance. "You should act quickly before she slips out of your fingers and you find yourself walking to Utah alone."

With that, Sebastian sauntered back to the van, hopefully to be useful and actually carry something in. Carter watched him walking away, still gritting his teeth. He took out his frustration by kicking the latch on the door. Pain spiked up his leg, but it was worth it.

"If you're having trouble with the combination," Lily's voice said from behind him, "try Elvis's birthday."

"What?"

"Eighteen, nineteen, thirty-five. My uncle was a big Elvis Presley nut." She and Mel were walking down the back steps of the porch. "I once heard him tell my mother that's what he always used for his passcodes. January eighth, nineteen thirty-five."

"Oh. Okay." Carter dropped to his knees again and spun the tumblers into place. "Where are Joe and McKenna?"

"McKenna wanted to take a shower. Uncle Rodney was on well water and the house has a backup gas generator. Joe thinks he might be able to get it started. He said it runs on propane, so we couldn't use the gas in the van anyway."

The combination lock clicked open and Carter slid the shank free of the latch and slipped it into his pocket. As he stood to lift the door, Lily hung back, looking fragile.

As much as he hated to admit it, Sebastian was right, damn it. It was time to tell her the truth. Joe and McKenna were occupied.

Sebastian wouldn't interrupt them. As for Mel . . . hell, she seemed to just know things. It was possible that she'd already figured out the truth. He couldn't think of any nursery rhymes that conveyed *You have the power of mind control*, but that didn't mean she hadn't been humming one.

Of course, whatever they found on the other side of this door would certainly affect their conversation in the next hour.

There was another wooden door beneath the steel one, and beneath that a short flight of stairs into the underground storm cellar. Another steel door. This time with Priscilla Presley's birthday as the combo.

Joe had gotten the generator on and it was humming loudly from the other side of the house. When Carter reached for the light switch on the wall, an overhead fluorescent flicked on.

Based on Lily's crazy-redneck description, he expected the cellar to be stocked with all kinds of survivalist gear. Dehydrated food, gas tanks, bottled water, rifles, that kind of thing. And it was. It was just also decorated like a shrine to Elvis. Uncle Rodney had mounted a classic velvet Elvis painting on the wall opposite the door. Beneath it sat a turntable and a collection of LPs surrounded by unlit candles.

Other Elvis paraphernalia was scattered throughout the twenty-by-twenty-foot room—an Elvis wig, a pair of blue suede shoes, a TV and VCR and what had to be every movie Elvis was ever in.

There was a bed against one wall, well-stocked shelving on the other. A ratty recliner in front of the TV.

For a long moment Carter just stood there, blinking at the bizarreness of it all. He called out twice, but there was no answer. No lingering smell of death to ward them off.

Lily walked past him, smiling. It was one of the first genuine smiles he'd seen from her since he'd found her again. There was only a hint of sadness to her expression. Or maybe it was nostalgia. Maybe she hadn't held any hope that her uncle would be down here.

She gestured to the Elvis shrine. "Weird, huh?"

"This is the man who hunted wild boar with a bowie knife?"

"Yep." She crossed straight back to the velvet Elvis. On a table beside the LPs was a framed photo. She picked it up and looked at it.

Curious, he followed her and looked over her shoulder. It showed two little girls, two women, and a man. This must be Uncle Rodney. The two women looked enough like Lily—but probably thirty and fifty years older—that he figured they were her mother and grandmother.

"This was taken at Grandma's house, out in Nebraska. We were ten. We spent summers there after Dad left."

Only then did he notice the lines of strain around their mother's eyes. The protective way Uncle Rodney draped an arm over his sister's shoulder. Mel looked off into the distance. Lily was leaning against her mother and clenching her uncle's hand. She looked small and frail. Helpless and vulnerable in a way she didn't anymore.

Lily reached to put the picture back, but she stopped and picked something up off the table. An envelope that had been waiting beneath the picture frame, five pieces of Dubble Bubble gum sitting beside it. On the front of the envelope were scrawled the letters *R & L & M.*

Lily carefully slid the envelope open and pulled out a page of lined notebook paper. Carter let her read it in silence. A moment later, she handed it to him.

Dear Rachel, Lily, and Mel,

I wish you had followed my suggestion and come up to stay here when the first wave hit Texas. I know those damn fools in the government said it was best to stay in our homes, but when have they ever known their asses from a bunch of skunk holes?

I took the rig down to Texas last month, but could find no sign of you. A friend has suggested heading east and I suspect it's about time for it. On the off chance you make it up this far, I've left supplies for you and the girls. As always, what's mine is yours,

R

He handed the letter back to her. She gave a loud sniff and swiped her eyes with the back of her hand. She immediately went to where Mel was sitting cross-legged in the recliner and handed her the letter to read as well. Mel took the letter and laid it across her knee. She'd found an old Rubik's Cube and toyed with it as she read. Her Slinky, her first love, sat on her other knee and whenever she got stuck on the Cube, she pulled on the Slinky a couple of times.

He turned around in time to see Lily carefully tucking the photo into one of the pockets of Mel's backpack. Then she unzipped the main compartment and dug around until she found a hairbrush and a small, ragged-looking stuffed animal.

It was odd, this surge of protectiveness he felt for her in that moment. The unexpected affection he felt for the man in the picture. If he didn't know better, he'd rationalize it away. Say it was normal to be fond of the relatives who had cared for Lily during a tough time in her life. He might even chalk it up to relief at having found a safe haven for the night. But he did know better.

This rush of affection he felt, it wasn't his own. These sentiments were Lily's. She broadcast her emotions so clearly, he felt every one of them. Because she was an *abductura*, she had the power to force her emotions on others. Because she didn't know about her powers yet, she did it unintentionally whenever her feelings were running high, as they had yesterday and today. All her fear, her panic, her relief at getting off the Farm, and now her fondness for her uncle. Her pleasure at finding some sign he was okay and, yes, even the hope she'd claimed not to have. He'd felt that, too.

He was keenly tuned in to her emotions—as was Mel—but Joe and McKenna were susceptible, too. He suspected Sebastian was also, though the vampire would never admit it.

Sometimes he resented the things she made him feel. Not the feelings themselves, but her blithe ignorance. She had him tied in knots half the time and she didn't even know it. But she didn't do it on purpose. She no idea what she was.

And it was time he told her.

He squatted down beside her and placed his hand on hers. "Lily, there's something I have to tell you."

"What is it?" She looked up. He got hit again by that surge of protectiveness. That bone-deep knowledge that he'd do anything in the world to keep her safe. And in that moment, he was equally sure that this wasn't going to be easy for her to hear. He didn't want to place this burden on her shoulders. He couldn't even think of what the hell to say.

He cursed under his breath and scrubbed a hand down his face. "I . . ."

She leaned closer to him and put her hand on his arm and even though the cellar had a dank, musty smell to it, suddenly all he could smell was the fresh, fruity smell of her hair. But it wasn't her touch or even her scent that kicked him in the gut. It was the look in her eyes.

And he was about to destroy that trust.

Because he wasn't just a guy who had rescued her from a horrible situation. He was a guy trying to save the human race. And he needed her to do it. Even if it meant she hated him for it.

CHAPTER TWENTY-SEVEN

MEL

This rabbit hole feels cozy and we're not trapped even though Carter's still acting like Bugs. Uncle Rodney understands about music even if he worships a dead god.

Uncle Rodney knows it's not just about the sounds, but the rhythm and beat. The notes *and* the silence. How I hear it, anyway. What Carter is not saying, more than what he is. Or maybe he's more deaf than I thought and even he doesn't hear what's not there. Doesn't he know he'd catch more bunnies with Rachmaninoff?

Elvis gets it. The King isn't in the velvet; he's where the velvet is not. The after-burnout image. It takes both to make the picture. But there's beauty in the inky velvet, too. Not just the nothing counts. Rubik knew it, too. If I make those colors sing, will Lily hear it?

I can try. I have all night to find the music. The pink gum helps.

The shark is gone—out tocking after Ticks. Finding food before it finds us. But part of me misses his watery silence. Who will pilot *us*, if we're not pilot fish to his shark?

CHAPTER TWENTY-EIGHT

LILY

Carter was doing that weird stuttery thing. I knew he was trying to tell me something, and he just could not seem to spit it out. My heart started thumping nervously. He dreaded it. Whatever he needed to say, he absolutely dreaded having to say it aloud. Which so could not be good.

"Oh, God," I muttered, standing. "You're not a vampire, too, are you?"

He gaped at me for a minute and then burst out laughing. He stood and then pushed his hair back out of his eyes. "No. God, no. Here's the thing. It's not an accident that I found you on the Farm. I was looking for you."

"What?" I asked, figuring I'd heard him wrong. Or just misunderstood.

"You're special, Lily. There's something about you. Something I don't think you even know." He searched my face for an instant, then turned away. "I'm doing this all wrong." He looked up and gestured to the velvet Elvis. "It's like Elvis."

"Huh?"

"Elvis!" Carter's tone had *Eureka!* all over it.

"You lost me," I admitted.

"Did you ever see Elvis perform?"

"No," I said, stating the obvious. "'Cause he died, like, two decades before we were even born."

"Not live. I mean like in a movie or on TV. Footage of him with all those screaming fans."

"Sure, I guess." I walked over to Mel and carefully showed her the brush to let her know what I was planning. She didn't flinch away or scream. Which meant she *might* be okay with me brushing her hair. When she kept twisting the Rubik's Cube, I laid the stuffed squirrel on Mel's knee next to Uncle Rodney's letter and picked up a section of hair.

Carter was going on and on like I was supposed to follow his conversation. "Girls and women, even some men—obviously your uncle Rodney—acting like crazy people. Over a singer. Yeah, he was good, but did he really deserve all that craziness?"

I didn't know how we'd gotten on this topic, or why Carter suddenly seemed so excited about Elvis. I tried to joke. "Don't let Uncle Rodney hear you talking that like. Especially not in front of the shrine."

"He was the kind of guy people build shrines to. The vampires have a name for people like him."

"Rich? Talented?" I ran the brush through just the bottom inch. When it came to Mel having her hair brushed, you had to do just as much as you could and be happy with the progress you'd made.

Carter laughed, but I couldn't tell if it was in relief or at my lame joke. "No. The term they use is *abductura*."

"Abductor?"

"No, *abductura*. Not one who steals. Literally, one who leads. There have been *abducturae* throughout history. King Arthur—the real guy—apparently, he was one. Martin Luther King. Martin Luther, for that matter. And Elvis."

"That's a lot of Kings. What are you talking about?" It felt like it was time to take a big step back from this crazy-ass conversation. I stopped brushing to turn and look at him.

"There are other, more recent examples. Adolf Hitler. The Beatles. Steve Jobs."

"I don't mean to be rude, certainly not when you're settling into full-on history-teacher mode, but is there a point to today's lesson?"

Carter's cheeks reddened, like he was chagrined. "Yes, the point is, all these people—people who have this incredible charisma or power. It isn't an accident. They're not just lucky. Or talented. They're not just politicians around at the right time and place; they have an actual gift. They can make people feel the emotion they're feeling. It's a power they have over others."

"Like a superpower?" I asked dubiously, running the brush through a section of hair. Her hair—like mine—was thick and had just a hint of wave to it. She messed with hers more, so it always looked a little off, but it was still pretty.

"Exactly!"

"Cool. So Hitler was one of the X-Men? Great."

Carter's blush deepened. "I told you I was saying this all wrong. If you think about it, it'll all make sense."

This was so not the conversation I'd been expecting and my annoyance came through in my voice. "I don't need to think about it to know that this is the stupidest, most ridiculous fantasy I've ever heard. People don't have superpowers."

"Why not?"

"Because . . . because it just doesn't make any sense. If people—if anyone—had this power back in the Before, why didn't everyone know about it? Wouldn't it have been studied and reported on? Why weren't there scientists analyzing these so-called powers?"

"Who says there weren't?" Carter asked quietly.

My hand stilled on Mel's hair and I noticed suddenly that she'd stopped working on the Rubik's Cube. She was listening, too. "Were there?"

Doubt started to creep in.

"Not many, but some. The vampires have known about it for centuries. Apparently they tried to re-create the powers of the *abducturae*, but it doesn't work."

I frowned as I shifted from disbelief to confusion. "But how . . . Why don't people know about this? I mean, I'm still not saying I believe you, but if this is a real thing and scientists have been studying it, then why wasn't the news of it everywhere?"

"What purpose would that serve?" Carter asked. "What would happen if the entire population knew that there were a few special people who could control the emotions of everyone else?"

I thought about it for a second. When I spoke, dread dropped my voice to a low whisper. "There would be fear. Paranoia. No one would know who to trust. Every bad decision you made you would blame on someone else."

"Exactly. So instead, the truth was kept hidden, usually even from the people who had the skills. Very few *abducturae* know the gift they bear."

"If someone did know . . ." My voice trailed off.

Carter pressed the point. "If someone did know, they would have tremendous power at their fingertips."

I studied his face then, dread starting to churn in my empty belly. "What kind of power? I mean, it's just a localized thing, right? Like at an Elvis concert. Other people share the emotions of the *abductura*. That's it."

Carter jumped in to explain. "It's more than that. Human emotion affects everything we do. Every decision we make. According to Sebastian, an untrained *abductura* will affect the people immediately near him or her. Someone who knows what they're doing could affect the decision making of the entire country. Martin Luther King inspired an entire nation. Hilter convinced Germans to do unthinkable things. An *abductura* can heighten someone's emotional experience and inspire him to greatness, or they can convince someone to act in a way that's contrary to his personality. To his beliefs. To his very nature. Trained soldiers can be overwhelmed by panic. Police officers can be crippled by fear. Brave men and women can be convinced their fight is hopeless. Parents who would otherwise die to protect their young can be talked into leading their children to internment camps. And it can all be done with the subtle manipulation of emotion."

I felt the blood rushing in my ears and I set down the brush. "What are you saying?" He didn't answer but waited for me to fill in the blanks. "That that's the reason the Ticks took over? Because some *abductura* made us surrender?"

"Did you never wonder how we got to this point so quickly?" Carter asked. "You start with half a dozen victims in an unpopulated area of New Mexico. Within six weeks, there are Tick outbreaks in every major city in the South, Southwest, and Midwest. Within three months, the government is mandating internment of all teenagers. Less than a month after that, the government falls completely. It took the Ticks less than six months to conquer the U.S. No nation in the history of the world has fallen that quickly. Do you really think a bunch of animals with brains the size of kiwis were responsible for that?"

"The Ticks were unbeatable. It was smarter for the government to try to placate the Ticks rather than kill them off completely. We had to try to contain . . ." I trailed off, realizing I was only parroting the propaganda that had played on the news.

"What do you think now?" Carter prodded. "Now that you've seen them in action? Do you still believe they are unbeatable?"

I frowned. "They were crazy fast. And obviously strong. But we made it out. If the six of us were able to get away, then trained soldiers should have been able to fight them off. . . ."

This, I realized, was the answer to the question I'd asked in the van. The question neither he nor Sebastian had wanted to answer.

After a long moment, I kept talking. "So that vampire Roberto, you're saying he's one of these things? He's an *abductura*? He just convinced humanity that these things couldn't be killed?"

"No," Carter said. "There are no vampire *abducturae*. That's what I was saying earlier. As far we know there are several human traits that don't survive the change. That's one of them. We know it's not Roberto."

"So there's a *human* who is working with Roberto?" All that blood that had been rushing around in my ears dropped into my belly, making me feel light-headed.

"Yes," Carter said. "He's extremely powerful."

"I can't believe a person would do that."

I felt horror rising off me, like steam. A bone-deep revulsion rolled through me.

Carter was watching me closely and I could tell he half expected me to freak out. "So you believe me? About the *abducturae*?"

I blew out a sigh. "I don't know what to believe anymore." Then I paused, my mind clicking away. "But if you're right, then it changes everything. We could destroy the Ticks without ever fighting another one. All we'd have to do is find this *abductura*. Take him out and the Ticks lose their advantage."

Carter shook his head. "Impossible. There'd be no way to get close to the *abductura*. He's probably the most closely guarded person in the country."

"We could try," I said.

Carter grinned. "We?"

Okay, so, yeah. I was starting to think of this as my battle, too, but I couldn't let myself get distracted.

"Is it hopeless, then?" I asked.

"Not at all. The *abductura* working with Roberto isn't the only one out there. All we need to do is convince another *abductura* to fight on our side."

I frowned, picking up the brush again and returning to Mel's hair. It soothed me and her. I heard the *click, click* of her turning the sides of the Rubik's Cube punctuated by the occasional *sllluuunk* of her Slinky. "That's what you've been doing at the Farms, isn't it? You haven't just been helping Greens escape." I looked up and met his gaze. "You've been searching for an *abductura*."

"Yes." His breath seemed to catch and I got the feeling that he was waiting for me to figure something out. Suddenly I didn't feel smart, but incredibly stupid.

And sad, too. Because once Carter dropped us off in Canada, he'd be back in the fight. Searching for his *abductura*. It was what he had to do. I knew that. But I realized that some tiny part of my brain had been hoping I could convince him to stay with us once we found safety. Now that I knew what he was really doing, I knew there was no way that would happen.

"I'm sorry you didn't find what you were looking for at our Farm."

"But I did."

"What?" My hand stilled, the brush stuck in midstroke. For a long second I just stared at him blankly. Then I looked around, half expecting to see McKenna or Joe in the room.

He did chuckle then. "No. Not them. You. I came looking for you."

I waited for Carter to deliver the punch line of the joke, but he didn't say anything for a long time. He just stood there, waiting. Maybe waiting for me to speak. Maybe for the full impact of what he'd said to cut through the fog that seemed to envelop my brain.

I just looked at him. "You're not serious, right?"

He placed his hand over mine. "Yeah, I am." Finally, he asked, "How you doing there, Lil?"

I let out a snort of disbelief. "Oh, I'm great." Suddenly the dank walls of the storm cellar seemed to close in on me. "You know, besides the fact that I'm trapped with a delusional wack job."

Carter arched an eyebrow. "I seem delusional to you?"

"Hey, you're the one who thinks Mel and I are the wonder twins. You tell me."

My voice sounded less quippy than I meant it to and more like I genuinely wanted an answer. I shot Carter a look. I expected him to look away. He didn't.

After a minute, I gave a strangled, nervous laugh and suddenly found that I couldn't look at him. So I wandered off a step or two to stare at the shelves and shelves of supplies. And to think, once upon a time, I'd believed my uncle Rodney was crazy for being this prepared. Now it turned out he was the right amount of prepared, and I'd thrown in with people who were way crazier than he was. My laughter turned sour in my stomach. So I was thankful when Carter interrupted my thoughts.

"Something funny?" he asked.

"There aren't a lot of benefits to having a sister who's autistic and parents who are desperate for any cure that will help her, but one of them is that you learn to tell when people are lying to you.

The bad liars, they can't hold your gaze. But the charlatans, they'll look you right in the eye while they sell you some crazy-ass 'cure' for five grand a treatment."

I glanced back at Carter. He still met my gaze, not even flinching. "That means either you think you're telling me the absolute truth or you're a sociopathic liar."

His gaze dropped for a moment and his lips curved into a wry smile. "Which do you think it is?"

"I can't—" I broke off, shaking my head and staring mindlessly at the black flocking on the Elvis painting. "That person you described? That person who is charismatic and persuasive? That person who other people can't help but follow? That's not me. I don't have any of those characteristics."

"Maybe you do and you just don't see them yet. Many *abducturae* are older than you when their talents develop. Still, you may not see it, but I do."

"I don't—"

"Do you remember what happened at the Dean's office? You told him to leave and he did."

"Maybe he needed to go somewhere. Besides, I barely remember that. I'd been tranqed."

Instead of looking apologetic, Carter frowned, clearly puzzling through something. "Yeah. I've been wondering about that. If maybe being tranqed made you stronger or just let you tap into your powers better. Something was definitely up there."

Somehow his obvious confusion over the incident wriggled under my skin, making me feel queasy. "No. There was nothing up. He probably just had to leave."

"No." Carter shook his head. "The Dean was in the middle of important negotiations. There's no way he'd just walk out. You told him to go and he did." I didn't even know what to say to that. I just floundered, mouth gaping for a moment, and then Carter continued talking. "And then there's the riot outside the cafeteria."

"You weren't even there for that!" I accused.

"When it started, I couldn't get close enough to get you out." His voice was taut with regret. "By the time you got yourself free, I was already late to meet with Sebastian and had to use the fight as an excuse for disappearing anyway. But I saw the fight. You and Mel got separated. Some guy harassed Mel and all of a sudden you were freaking out. A crowd of maybe two hundred docile Greens exploded into violence in less than a minute all because you were afraid for Mel and you panicked."

"Here's another explanation. It was two hundred teenagers who've been trapped on a Farm for six months against their will. Sometimes they just lose it. The miracle is that it doesn't happen more often."

I thought the argument was a sound one. I thought I'd see a chink in his resolve. Instead he sighed, as if exhausted.

"Yeah, that is the surprising thing, isn't it?"

I shrugged. "I don't even know what you're talking about."

"Think about it, Lil. What have you been doing since you arrived at the Farm? What's been the one thing you've focused all your energy on?" His voice was gentle, like he was trying to soothe a skittish colt.

"Keeping my sister safe," I said, my voice sounding more spooked-horse than I wanted it to.

"You've been keeping her calm."

"I've been protecting her."

"I've watched you do it. You soothe her. You do everything in your power to keep her relaxed."

"Hey, that's what I have to do! Have you ever seen Mel in a full-on meltdown freak-out?"

"Yeah, I have."

"The rocking and moaning. The hair pulling and occasional screaming. That crap would have gotten us dragged to the Dean's office. It'd be disastrous even if there weren't any Collabs around. Greens wouldn't put up with it any better. We'd have both been dead."

"I'm not criticizing you." He put a comforting hand on my arm. "There are other Farms in the country where the Greens aren't docile. But the closer you get to your Farm, the—"

I shook his arm free. "I get what you're saying. You're saying I'm responsible for the way the Greens acted on the Farm. You're saying that all those kids were placid cows because of me. You're saying they just blindly accepted their fate because of *me*. You're accusing me of being worse than any of the Collabs. Being worse than the Dean."

"That's not what I'm saying."

"That's exactly what you're saying."

"You didn't know what you were doing." He was clearly trying to placate me, but I wasn't in the mood for it.

"What you *think* I was doing," I corrected him. "I still don't believe you."

"Lily—"

"I can tell you really believe this. But it doesn't make sense to me. Not one bit. And then to top it all off you basically accuse me of"—I paused, choking on the lump in my throat—"of sedating the Greens and turning them into easier food."

"Think about it this way. If you did all of that unintentionally, then imagine what you could do if you put your mind to it. Imagine the things you'd be capable of if you learned how to use your power. Humanity wouldn't have to just roll over and be farmed as food. We could fight back. You could convince people to fight. You could lead us."

"No, I can't! Do you even hear yourself? You want me to brainwash people into fighting? The U.S. military—the strongest military in the world—could not beat the Ticks. But you want me to brainwash a bunch of teenagers into trying to fight them? I'd be sending everyone to their deaths." My breath started coming in rapid bursts. It was like I couldn't get enough air into my lungs. Like they'd just stopped working. I covered my face with my hands and pushed aside the thought of what Carter wanted me to do. "I don't want that kind of power." Somewhere in the background, I heard several rapid *sllluuunks*. The sound calmed me. "Even if I did, I still have to think about Mel. Getting Mel to safety is my first priority."

"But—"

"No. That's what matters. Keeping her safe. Getting her to Canada."

I couldn't let myself be distracted by anything else. I couldn't even let myself consider the possibility that what he was saying was true. It just wasn't. He was wrong.

He couldn't be right. I *couldn't* be responsible for all those deaths.

"Lily—" He reached out to me, but I dodged around his hand.

"I don't want to talk about this again. Ever. I'm going to get Mel and take her back up to the house. I want a shower while there's still hot water."

Carter must have known there wasn't any point in arguing with me, because he let me go.

I let Mel shower first while I looked through the kitchen. I wasn't looking for anything in particular. Just opening and closing cabinets. Staring mindlessly at what remained of Uncle Rodney's life. It wasn't until I was standing in the tiny, mustard yellow shower, with warm water washing over me, that I let myself really think about what Carter had said. I still didn't believe he was right about me being an *abductura*. The idea was absurd.

No, that wasn't what bothered me. What bugged me the most was that he believed it so completely. And it explained everything about his behavior in the past couple of days. How protective he'd been of me and Mel. The way he'd yelled at me for putting myself at risk in Vidalou. The fact that he'd come to rescue us at all.

This was the friggin' pencil and the biology test all over again.

I squirted a glob of Uncle Rodney's cheap shampoo onto my palm and scrubbed it into my hair, scraping my nails across my scalp. Getting upset because a boy didn't like me was about the stupidest thing imaginable under the circumstances. It so did not matter. But it still hurt. It hurt because I wanted him to like me, but also because I thought I was past hoping for things like that. I didn't like being wrong about myself.

* *

I managed to avoid being alone again with Carter for the rest of the night. Staying busy was easy.

Sebastian had disappeared down the mountain on foot to "patrol the perimeter." There was plenty to do before sunset. Uncle Rodney had brought most of his supplies with him, but true to his note, he'd left some things. A month's worth of MREs—meals ready to eat, like soldiers eat in the field. Divided among the six of us, it would be enough food for more than a week. Certainly plenty of food to get us to Canada. There was the bow but only four arrows, far fewer than I'd hoped for. But that was okay. It gave me hope that Uncle Rodney—wherever he was—had figured out that arrows could hurt the Ticks. Several rifles. Hunting shotguns. Water purification tablets. All kinds of things we'd find useful. It took over an hour for Joe, Carter, and me to pack everything we needed into duffel bags and load them into the van.

McKenna was exhausted and spent the time watching old Elvis tapes. Mel played with her Rubik's Cube. As I walked in and out with supplies, I noticed that she was frowning a lot and seemed distracted. Normally, working the Cube she'd had at home back in the Before relaxed her and she moved through it over and over again quite easily. Today, though, she seemed to be having trouble making the pieces line up.

I could sympathize. By the time we were done packing the van so we could get an early start in the morning, it was nearly dusk. Carter went off to find Sebastian. I quickly looked for a place to sleep while he was gone. McKenna had claimed the storm cellar's only bed, so I piled blankets on the floor and lay there curled on my side. Mel came and lay beside me and I was comforted knowing she was near.

I didn't believe Carter was right about me. It felt wrong. I couldn't explain it any other way. I just had this gut-deep feeling that he was wrong.

But I wasn't sure why. Maybe it was because of the comic-book quality of the power he described. Or maybe I just didn't *want* that kind of power. If I was an *abductura*, then that changed everything. Forever. I wouldn't be able to go to Canada to safety. I would have to give up any hope I still clung to that there might be a normal life for me somewhere. I just wasn't ready to do that based on Carter's hunch that I had this weird power.

And I certainly didn't want that kind of power, because I wasn't strong enough to lead humanity in a war against the monsters.

Even though my mind was racing, the normalcy of Mel's

presence calmed me. I kept my breath slow even when Carter came in and talked to Joe. Apparently Sebastian had sensed a nest of Ticks about thirty miles to the west when we passed through Fayetteville, but he didn't think they'd be a problem. His Tick ESP had longer range than their sense of smell. They wouldn't smell us as far away as they were. Sebastian would stay awake throughout the night. If they headed our way, he'd know and there'd be plenty of time to warn us. They talked for a few more minutes. Once Joe went off to lie down beside McKenna in the bed, I sensed Carter standing over me. I kept my breathing deep and even. After a minute, he walked away. At some point, I rolled over to stare at the ceiling. I felt Mel's fingers brush against my hand. She was never a touchy person, but I turned my palm up, some part of me hoping she'd take it. She carefully placed her stuffed squirrel in my hand. My fingers closed over the lovey and I squeezed tight. I must have actually fallen asleep after that. When I woke, I still held the squirrel and I'd never been more sure of Mel's love.

I sat up and tried to quietly stretch the kinks out of my body. A couple of blankets hadn't been enough to offset the hard concrete floors, or the abuse my body had taken in the past two days, and my muscles ached.

Everyone else was still asleep and I moved quietly so I wouldn't wake them. On the bed, McKenna lay curled against Joe. They looked unexpectedly cozy so close together on the twin mattress. Carter lay stretched out on the floor beside the cellar door, his head propped on his backpack. I would have to step over him to creep out the door, so I sat down near the Elvis shrine and pulled my shoes on.

Before I left the cellar, I went to stand in front of the shrine. I pulled the Altoids tin out of my pocket and removed the Rolo. I put it at the base of the velvet Elvis painting. I let my fingers rest beside the Rolo and sent up a silent prayer of thanks for Uncle Rodney. I'd looked all around the cellar but hadn't found a pen. Uncle Rodney hadn't been big on writing. But I got my sweet tooth from him and I knew he'd appreciate the Rolo. If he came back through, he'd see it and know I'd been there.

Then I went the rest of the way up to the steel door. I pushed it open a mere inch, listening to the sounds of dawn, the irregular *drip, drip* of condensation falling from the trees, the chatter of birds. Before I could decide whether or not I heard anything sinister, the door was wrenched from my grasp and opened. Sebastian stood there, door in hand.

"I was just coming to wake you."

"Me?"

"All of you. We need to get back on the road. The Ticks I felt last night were heading back to their nest from hunting, but something caught their attention and now they're heading this way."

"What?" came Carter's voice from behind me. I turned to see him standing in the doorway. He looked surprisingly alert for someone who had been asleep just a moment ago and I wondered if I had woken him up when I stepped over him. "I thought you said they wouldn't catch our scent from that far away. They shouldn't be coming anywhere near us."

Carter walked up the steps and I automatically stepped aside to let him pass.

"The Ticks shouldn't be able to track us from that far away," I said. "We aren't even downwind from them. They shouldn't have caught our scent."

Sebastian looked from Carter to me and then said, "Lily, you should go wake the others."

"I will. As soon as you tell me why those Ticks are heading this way when you said they wouldn't."

"I was just wrong."

I stepped closer to him, despite the little tremor of fear that skittered down my spine. "I'm not being unreasonable here. I'm not blaming you, but you acted like this spidey sense of yours was infallible. If it's not—if it's something that only works sometimes—then we should know about it."

Sebastian's lips peeled back from his teeth in a wolfish expression. The sound emanating from his throat was almost a growl. That sense of unease I often felt in his presence exploded into fear. Before my fight-or-flight instinct could kick in, Carter stepped between us.

"Lily, calm down. His instincts are good. He's never wrong when it comes to locating the Ticks."

"Except this time," I pointed out, my panic abating now that I wasn't looking right at Sebastian.

"He wasn't wrong about their location; he was wrong about their decision making. That's not his spidey sense. He made a guess about what he thought they would do in the night based on his understanding of their psychology. Besides, something else may have attracted their attention."

"What would do that?"

Neither man answered, but they exchanged a look that said there was something they both knew and didn't want to tell me.

"Don't keep me in the dark about this. Whatever it is, tell me now."

Carter blew out a breath and said, "They might be tracking the chips."

My hand flew to the spot on my neck. I remembered what Carter had said about the chips emitting a buzzing sound that annoyed the Ticks. "I thought you said the computer virus or whatever it was would deactivate our chips."

"It was supposed to," Sebastian said simply.

Sebastian and Carter exchanged another look.

"Damn it," Carter muttered. "He really wants her back."

"He must."

I looked from Carter to Sebastian. "Who wants who?"

For a long second, neither of them spoke and I got the feeling they were trying to decide how much to tell me. Finally Carter blew out a harsh breath. "The Dean. He really wants you back. The Ticks shouldn't even know we're here. Even if the chips were left on, we're not really close enough for them to hear the sound."

"So the Ticks really *can* hear the chips? They can hear us coming?" I asked

Carter held up a hand, like he could ward off my growing fear. "It's just a theory Sebastian has."

"There are some electronic devices that . . . annoy me," Sebastian said. "I can hear the signal they emit. It's like a constant buzzing. We think maybe the chips and the GPS locator buzz for the Ticks. It may vary based on the frequency of—"

"Less science lesson," I interrupted, "more planning. If the Ticks are using the chips to hunt us down, what do we do? Should we cut them out now?"

"I don't think they're after us, precisely," Sebastian said. "I think they're following someone else. The Dean must have sent Collabs out to follow us. With the right receiver, the chips have a fifty-mile range. It's more important right now that we get a head start on those Collabs. Who knows how close they are."

"Oh, great. So in addition to the Ticks chasing us down, we have a Collab—"

"Or more than one," Sebastian interjected. "If the Dean has any sense at all."

"Okay, or more than one, on our tail." I blew out a breath. "So he's chasing us and the Ticks are following him, right?"

"Right."

"Any chance we could get lucky and they'll catch him before they get to us? Maybe they'll fill up on Collab and drop out." The thought made me feel a little queasy and I hated even saying it aloud. I didn't want the Ticks to kill anyone. Not even a Collab.

"Well, that would be lucky, wouldn't it?" From Sebastian's sardonic tone, I could guess just how unlikely he thought that possibility was. "But Ticks don't eat Collabs. The Deans feed them daily doses of progesterone to make them unappetizing."

"Eh." My revulsion slipped out unintentionally.

"Exactly," Sebastian agreed. "Progesterone is unappetizing enough. It's why Ticks avoid girls who are pregnant." He glanced pointedly back down the cellar steps to where McKenna still slept. "But the combination of progesterone and testosterone is practically revolting. To them."

I thought about the birth control pills that had been in the backpack that blew up. Would they have provided another layer of defense against the Ticks?

Before I could ask Sebastian, he continued, "The Ticks would have to be starving to even be tempted. However, the Collabs could easily be luring them closer to us."

"Is he luring them closer to us on purpose?" I asked.

"Unlikely. The Dean wants you back." Sebastian's tone was casual. As if this wasn't anything we really had to worry about. "He sent the Collabs to get you. Unfortunately, most Collabs don't have any idea what they're really dealing with."

I snorted. "They're idiots. I could have told you that much."

"The question is, how badly does the Dean want you back?"

"Do you think he knows what she is?" Carter asked.

I nearly growled in frustration. "Please don't tell me you both think this is all because the Dean thinks I'm an *abductura*."

"You had better hope, young girl, that that is precisely what he believes. Because if it is not, then there is only one other reason for someone to be tracking you."

A chill chased my confidence down my spine. "And what is that?"

"That it is not a Collab tracking you at all. That Roberto has learned about you and is coming for you himself."

"What, you think this Roberto guys wants another *abductura* for himself?"

"No, my dear. Roberto already has a very powerful *abductura* in his employ. It is how he's controlling humanity. If he wants you, it is so he can kill you."

CHAPTER TWENTY-NINE

CARTER

The way he saw it, there was an upside to everything. Whenever things went to hell all at once, it helped to look for that upside. In this particular case, Lily was talking to him again. She still didn't believe she was an *abductura*, but at least she was no longer treating him like a pariah. As silver linings went, it was pretty damn dingy.

Especially given that the big black cloud threatening to rain on their parade just seemed to get bigger and bigger. For starters, Sebastian hadn't hunted the night before; that had been obvious when the vampire had growled at Lily. Sebastian didn't enjoy feeding off Ticks, but he often did it. Carter had seen him singlehandedly take on packs with four or five Ticks in them. It didn't bode well for their progress today that the only packs he'd found had been too large to attack.

However with Collabs and Ticks already tracking them, Sebastian's hunger was the least of their worries. They'd left Uncle Rodney's house and been in the car for six hours, pushing the van to its limits. Naturally, they'd debated cutting the chips out as soon as they realized the Dean might be tracking them. But to do that, they'd have to leave Sebastian behind. Maybe he could have driven another car, but who knew how long it would take to find and hotwire a car. Even if the car they found had gas, it was too precious a resource to use traveling in two separate vehicles. At the time, they thought they had enough of a head start on the Collabs to justify keeping them in and just making a run for it. But now they were still being followed by Collabs. They'd attracted the attention of God only knew how many Ticks. And even with the pedal all the way to the floor, Carter knew they weren't going to get much more out of the ancient van.

Hands gripping the steering wheel, Carter slowed down to take yet another hairpin turn on the windy road. The tires slipped to the right as he pulled out of the turn. The road opened up ahead of him and he took advantage of the straightaway by flooring it, coaxing another five or ten miles an hour out of the vehicle.

Watching the speedometer creep up, Carter blew out a long breath, hoping to slow his pulse. He could feel the adrenaline pumping through his blood, but couldn't tell if his own intuition had kicked in or if he was just responding to Lily's fear.

She sat in the front passenger seat beside him. Hands gripping the edge of her seat, she alternated between glancing at the speedometer and twisting in her seat to look out the back window.

"Can this thing go any faster?" she asked.

"It's an aging fifteen-seater school van. What do you think?" He glared at Sebastian in the rearview mirror. "This was really the best you could find when you were looking for a car?"

"I'm sorry, Air Force One wasn't available. Personally, I was quite happy just to have found something big enough to comfortably seat all of us." Sebastian leaned forward so he was nearly between the two front seats. "By the way, you might want to consider slowing down. Vehicles such as this aren't very fuel efficient at high speeds."

"Maybe. But I'm pretty sure the Collabs behind us aren't concerned about fuel efficiency."

"I only point it out because we're rather close to running on empty."

Carter glanced down at the fuel gauge. Unfortunately, a look in the rearview mirror showed him another car not that far behind them sliding out of the last turn. He huffed with annoyance, even though he hadn't meant to.

Lily glanced back, too. "Oh, shit! That's them, isn't it? They caught up to us!"

From way back in the van, Joe asked in a sleepy voice, "Hey, anything new?"

Beside him, McKenna stretched her arms overhead. "Are we there yet?"

Lily looked irritated. "Canada is a three-day drive from the Farm. No, we're not there yet."

"Then why are we slowing down?"

Lily leaned over the console between them to get a better look at the speedometer. "She's right. We're slowing down. Why are we slowing down?"

"We can't outrun those Collabs. Whatever lead we had six hours ago, we've lost. We'll probably run out of gas before they do. It's better to stop now, where they can see us doing it on the straightaway, and try to talk to them."

"You want to talk to them? Are you frickin' crazy?"

"No. But thanks for the vote of confidence. I'd rather we talk to them now, while someone fills up the gas tank, than run out of gas and have the Ticks eat us all while we negotiate." He sent Sebastian a look in the mirror. "I assume you don't have any trouble talking to them while I fill up the gas."

Sebastian gave a grin that showed off more of his teeth than he usually showed. "Not at all. I'm quite sure I can make them see reason."

"What about the rest of us?" Lily asked with an eager fidget in her seat. "What do we do?"

"It wouldn't hurt to have Joe up in the front seat ready to leave again in case we get company," Sebastian said.

"What about me?"

"Young lady, I recommend you stay in the van, sit still, and try to restrain your emotions."

Lily practically growled.

"He's right," Carter said as he let off the gas. "The situation is tense enough as it is. We don't need you out there spewing emotion all over."

She snorted. "I don't—"

"It doesn't matter whether or not you believe it. Is this the time and place you want to test it out?"

Grumbling, she sat back and flung her arms across her chest.

Keeping his eyes on the car in the rearview mirror, Carter pressed his foot to the brake and gave the steering wheel a sharp turn, angling the van across the road as it rattled to a stop. The oncoming car would have to stop and he'd be able to keep an eye on the action as he filled up the tank. Struggling not to let Lily's annoyance with Sebastian influence him too much, he swung open his door. "Let's do this."

He jogged around the nose of the van and met up with Sebastian at the back, where the vampire was already unloading the gas cans.

"You sure you can handle two Collabs on your own?" he asked.

"Don't be insulting."

"Just don't do anything too vampirish."

Sebastian arched an eyebrow. "Please don't tell me you haven't told them that yet, either."

"They know, but try not to freak them out, okay? Remember

that happy *abductura* comment you made? I'm thinking no one's going to be very happy when they see you go all Vlad the Impaler on a couple of Collabs."

"Don't be ridiculous," Sebastian scoffed. "Vlad of Wallachia was in the Order of the Dragon and most decidedly not one of us."

"Can we save the history lesson for later and settle on a game plan?" Carter remembered how freaked out he'd been the first time he'd seen Sebastian in battle. It had been terrifying and it hadn't mattered that Sebastian had been defending him and his classmates. Carter continued, "Look, if you think she can handle any more shocks in one day, then go ahead and rip the heads off these guys when they step out of the car. Otherwise, keep it together and have a little discretion."

Yeah, he was pushing it, talking to Sebastian that way. If they were alone, Sebastian would backhand him for it and probably send him flying with a broken neck. Thank God for their audience and for the fact that Sebastian needed him. For all his smooth manners, Sebastian didn't deal well with humans. Hunger strained his diplomacy skills to the limits.

In answer, Sebastian growled low in his throat, baring his teeth in an expression no one could mistake for a smile.

"I'll play nice. But don't forget how fragile *all* humans are."

"I won't." He almost reminded Sebastian that he knew better than most that vampires had a few fragilities of their own, but instead he said, "Just don't forget how much you need Lily and we'll continue to get along just fine."

Sebastian sneered again before turning his back on Carter and walking out into the road to wait for the rapidly approaching sedan.

Carter didn't stand around to watch, but unscrewed the cap on one of the cans of gasoline and started dumping it into the van.

The four cans they had held a total of eight gallons. *Maybe* enough to keep them moving through the night. If they were only going about forty or forty-five, which would be fast enough to outpace a Tick, but not fast enough to outrun a sedan. Not that the van could do that anyway.

He glanced over his shoulder to see Sebastian standing in the dead center of the road fearlessly staring down the oncoming car. For a second, Carter's pulse raced. This whole don't-look-like-a-vampire gambit would only work if the driver slowed down the car and didn't just barrel over Sebastian.

But—what the hell?—the car wasn't slowing down. If the car did hit Sebastian, chances were good it would also barrel into the van.

Carter tossed aside the now-empty gas can and darted for the driver's-side window. He slapped the glass, getting Joe's attention. Joe cranked down the window.

"He might not stop. Start the car and be ready to get out of his way. If everything goes bad, you ditch us and leave."

"Dude—"

But Carter didn't wait to hear what Joe was going to say. Instead, he raced back to the gas tank and started pouring in the second of the gas cans. The glug-glug-glug of the gas seemed slow compared to the pounding of his heart. Whatever else happened, he had to get as much gas into the van as he possibly could.

Sebastian, too, must have realized the car wasn't going to stop. He started running. Not away from the car, but toward it. That must have gotten the driver's attention. Apparently it was one thing to ram a person just standing in the middle of the road and another thing entirely to drive into someone crazy enough to play chicken with a car.

The driver turned the car into a spin just as it reached Sebastian. He kept running, leaping onto the hood with unnatural grace. With one hand he grabbed the luggage rack on top of the car. The sedan—caught in the tailspin—slid across the road closer and closer to Carter as if in slow motion. The momentum of the car nearly flung Sebastian off, but he held the luggage rack in a death grip and struggled to swing his legs back up onto the hood.

Watching the car spin toward him, the glug-glug-glug of the gas can seemed unnaturally loud. Then it slowed. Gluuug-gluug. Glug. Glug. He dropped the empty can and leapt out of the way as the car slid to a halt, scraping the side of the van.

Carter landed hard on the asphalt, tucked into a roll, and tumbled into the ditch beside the road. For a heartbeat, the impact radiated through every muscle of his body as the wind was knocked right out of him. The glug-glug sound he'd been so focused on still thrummed in his ears.

His bones creaked and his muscles trembled too much to force his legs to stand—nearly being bisected between two cars did that to a guy—so he scrambled back along the opposite bank, trying to get high enough to see over the crest of the road.

The van wobbled from the impact, rocking back and forth. The van's passengers were scrambling out the door. Joe must have still been in the driver's seat, because Carter could hear him cranking the engine over and over, trying to get it started.

Carter pushed himself up, willing his legs to hold him. He had to get Lily, Mel, and McKenna back into the damn van. And then he had to get Joe out of the driver's seat so he'd stop flooding the engine.

He climbed out of the ditch and back onto the asphalt just in time to see Sebastian punch his hand through the sedan's windshield to grab the Collab in the driver's seat. He pulled the screaming guy out through the hole he'd made. Glass sprayed the car and the road, glistening in the late afternoon sun. The screams stopped a moment later when Sebastian twisted the guy's neck and tossed him aside like he was a rag doll, not so much out of disdain as necessity. The corpse was scratched and bloody from its windshield extraction. Even though the Collabs were pumped full of progesterone to make them unappetizing, Sebastian must not have trusted himself around the smell of that much blood.

So much for the plan where Sebastian tried to act normal. With vampires there was no fight or flight. When their lives were threatened, when their adrenaline got pumping, there was only fight. Fight and kill. There was no logic. No intellect. Only their gut reaction, which was to destroy everything in their path. If that killer instinct had overtaken Sebastian, none of them would be safe.

"Sebastian!" Carter called, hoping he could pull the vampire out of the frenzy before he lost all control.

Sebastian's head jerked up. He was crouched on the hood of the car like a giant spider, his every muscle tense, poised to attack. His normally pale skin had gone a ghastly white, and his eyes were glazed, yet somehow focused.

In the moment it took Sebastian to get ahold of his bloodlust, the doors of the sedan flew open and two people tumbled out. The first was a Collab, his blue uniform bright and unmistakable in the sunlight. The other man climbed out of the back of the car. He was squat and fat, like the toad he was. The Dean.

Shit.

Deans never left the safety of their Farms. This guy really did want Lily and Mel back. And Lily and Mel had climbed out of the van, like they were eager to return with him. They were still on the far side of the van and he hadn't seen them yet. Carter started for them. He couldn't yell at them to get back into the van without letting the Dean know exactly where they were.

Thankfully, the Dean seemed unable to tear his gaze from the broken body of the Collab that Sebastian had just killed. Both he and the other Collab seemed in shock.

Before Carter could move toward Lily and Mel, Sebastian went unnaturally still, then his head whipped around to look out across the field to their west. "Incoming," he hissed.

Carter followed Sebastian's gaze. He could see nothing but the faint shimmer of sunlight on windblown grass, but if Sebastian said Ticks were coming, they were.

"How many?" Carter asked, even as he looked around for a weapon. Now the Dean was the least of their worries.

"Two in the lead. Faster than the others. A dozen more behind."

"Do something!" the Dean ordered the Collab, pointing at Sebastian.

The startled Collab fumbled for his weapon. Carter didn't bother to watch. There was nothing a Collab could do to hurt Sebastian. He was torn for only a moment between protecting the girls and giving backup to Sebastian. Lily would know to get Mel and McKenna back in the van. If he was extremely lucky, she'd have the sense to stay there with them. True, she hadn't stayed out of a fight yet, but all those other times she'd been alone. Surely she'd stay with Mel. She'd promised him she wouldn't risk her life for his. As much as his instincts urged him to protect Lily, the best chance they all had for survival was if Sebastian could take out the two closest Ticks.

Carter looked around for something—anything—Sebastian could use as a weapon. They had weapons in the van, but Carter would rather find a weapon out here if he could. If he went for the bow and arrow, knowing Lily, she'd climb out and try to fight off the Ticks herself. The fence nearby was barbed wire stretched between cedar posts. He leapt across the ditch and grabbed the first post he came to. It was cast in cement and solidly planted in the ground, but looking down the fence line, Carter could see that every other post was thinner, more spindly. A veritable arsenal of wooden stakes. He ran for the thinner post a few feet away.

Behind him, he heard the rapid gunfire of untrained panic shooting. The Collab must have unloaded an entire clip into Sebastian. Which, Carter knew, would only piss the hell out of the vampire.

A piercing howl ripped through the air just as Carter reached a thin cedar post. At first he thought it was Sebastian's battle cry. Then another howl joined the first. The Ticks were close. The post didn't lift straight out of the ground, but it wiggled in his hands. Backing up a step, he kicked at it, rocking it several inches to the side. He kicked again. Just as he raised his foot for another blow, Lily appeared on the other side.

"If we go back and forth, it'll come out faster." She didn't wait for his answer but kicked the post toward him.

"What are you doing here? Get back in the van!" He kicked the post toward her, his anger at her mule-headedness giving his kick extra force.

"I got Mel and McKenna back in. Joe's starting the van again. I came back to help." She kicked the post again.

"You can help by getting your ass back in the van." Another kick.

"Right. 'Cause you and Sebastian are playing it so safe." Her final kicked knocked the post clean over and he stared at it, stunned for a second.

"You promised you wouldn't—"

"Bite me." She dropped to her knees and pulled on the post, finally freeing it from the ground. She held it out to him.

He grabbed it, closing his hand over hers. "Please. Get back in the van. I'm begging you."

Using his hold on the post for leverage, she let him pull her to her feet. "Come back to the van yourself."

"I will. Give me twenty seconds. I swear I'll follow."

She nodded, then turned and ran for the van.

He sprinted up the side of the ditch and around the rear of the van just in time to see the sedan jerk into reverse. It barely missed him before the Dean threw it into drive and skidded off. The Collab—the one that was still alive—chased after the car, yelling and shaking his useless weapon. Carter looked around for Sebastian.

Sebastian was crouched over the shape of the broken Collab on the side of the road. The starving vampire had succumbed to his hunger.

Closer now, the Ticks howled in outraged hunger of their own. Sebastian seemed to blend into the corpse; they were an obscene mixture of Sebastian's black clothing, Collab blue, and bloodred gore. Then Sebastian reared up over the corpse and threw back his head, and his howl joined the chorus of the Ticks.

Carter skidded to a halt, maybe twenty feet from the monster Sebastian had become, his mind racing through his options. Running for the van, ditching Sebastian altogether, was the most logical choice. It was the short term, best-odds bet. But in the long run, they needed Sebastian's spidey sense to guide them around the nests of Ticks. Besides, he just didn't want to leave a man behind. Even if that man had lost himself.

Of course, on the other hand, getting eaten by a vampire had never been on his personal to-do list. And twenty feet away from a feeding vampire was a lot closer than he wanted to be.

Holding the fence post like a bat, he spun on his foot and threw it, like a discus, straight at Sebastian. He didn't wait to see if it hit. He didn't wait to see if the blow snapped Sebastian out of his bloodlust. Carter turned and ran.

As he reached the van, his feet slipped out from under him and he skidded across the blacktop. Again, that glug-glug-glug echoed in his ears. This time, it was accompanied by the pungent scent of gasoline fumes. The two spare cans of gas were now slowly leaking fuel onto the blacktop.

The first of the Ticks hit the road just as Carter reached the side of the van.

The Tick bounded straight over Sebastian in a single leap. It took a giant running stride toward Carter, but skidded to a halt several yards away. It cringed back, wrinkling its nose. For an instant, it looked almost human as the creature considered him.

He didn't know if Ticks had gender. He'd never even thought about it before. But he could tell now that in its human life, this one must have been a woman. Now, her body was covered in patchy hair, several inches long. Shrunken, shapeless breasts flapped against her massive chest. Her hips were broader than a human woman's, her shoulders equally broad. The proportions were all wrong on her arms, because the muscles were approximately the size of his thighs.

But it was her face that was the most grotesque. Her jaw jutted out at an unnatural angle. Her teeth, massive leonine chompers, were so big she couldn't even close her mouth. Her nose was broad, her nostrils flared, the better to scent prey. The look in her eyes, calculating, assessing, almost human—but not—sent a chill of revulsion straight through to his soul.

Then she leaned closer, sniffed again, literally turned up her nose, and spun away from him. She galloped down the road after the Collab the Dean had left behind. The whole exchange took only a second. A second during which Carter's heart had stopped beating and lay frozen in his chest.

He glanced down at that gas covering the ground and his clothes. They'd undoubtedly miss the extra gas later, but for now, he wanted to kiss the ground on which it had spilled. It had saved his ass.

Beside him, the van backed up, turned, then roared forward, screeching to a halt with the open side door next to him.

"Get in!" Lily yelled.

"Sebastian—" he started to protest.

They both looked out over the blacktop to where Sebastian was only now standing up. He picked up the cedar post Carter had thrown. For an instant, it looked as though Sebastian was about to chase after them. Then he spun as another Tick leapt out of the field. Sebastian swung the post, using it like a bat to knock the Tick away. The crack of impact resounded through the air like a thunderclap. With a canine yelp, the Tick crashed to the ground.

Sebastian strode over to the whimpering Tick. He nudged it indifferently with his foot until it rolled over, then he stepped on its shoulder, pinning it to the ground. Raising the post high above the Tick's chest, he let out a ragged battle cry. Then he brought the post down, driving a three-inch hole into the beast's chest.

Beside him, Carter heard Lily whimper in horror. Somewhere else in the van, someone wretched.

Sebastian loped away from the Tick, running to catch up to the van with unnatural speed and grace. Carter gripped the interior handle of the door, ready to slam it closed. If Sebastian was still in the grip of his bloodlust, the door wouldn't provide much defense, but it was better than nothing.

Carter looked around the van for something with which to fight Sebastian off if he had to. One of the shotguns had been slid under the first bench seat. Maybe it would kill him; more than likely it wouldn't. But it would definitely be the end of their bargain. Carter was reaching for it when he saw the expression on Sebastian's face.

As he ran for the van, he flashed a grin. His eyes looked human. Carter stepped away from the door. Just as Sebastian hopped through the opening, the van drove past the other Tick. The Collab's crushed body lay spread out on the road. Hunched over the body, the Tick held the Collab's heart in her hands, drinking the Collab's blood as it pumped right out of the aorta.

The Tick looked up, her blood-soaked fur glistening bright red. Carter slid the door shut. Then he sank to the floor of the van, leaning his back against the door.

Sebastian had sat on the closest bench, but he was hunched over, wiping blood from his face and hands. Carter nearly asked why Sebastian had eaten the Collab's progesterone-laced blood, but figured the question might freak Lily out even more. She sat on the center bench, her back pressed to the wall of the van, her legs tucked up on the bench, her arms wrapped around them. Her skin had gone pasty white. He could see her chest rising and falling in rapid bursts as she struggled to pull air into her lungs. She displayed all the classic signs of shock.

Frankly, he didn't blame her. He'd been pretty freaked out himself the first time he saw Sebastian eat.

Carter moved to the back of the van, looking for one of the duffel bags that might have a blanket or coat he could use to warm her up. He'd just unzipped one of them when Sebastian spoke.

"You need to turn around. You're driving south."

Lily lifted her head off her knees. "We're chasing the Dean."

"Why?" Sebastian asked. "However badly he wants you, I can assure you that we've convinced him you're not worth the effort."

However, even as Sebastian spoke, Carter looked around the van. Dread filled his stomach. Something was wrong. Someone was missing.

Before he could even form the thought, Lily spoke.

"He has Mel. She—" Her voice broke over the words. He could tell she was in shock because no emotion at all radiated from her. It was like she was just gone. "She left the van on her own and the Dean grabbed her in the confusion. We have to go get her back."

CHAPTER THIRTY

MEL

I'm no pilot fish after all. I should stick to conducting orchestras, but even then I couldn't make the Ladybird sing.

I thought I had him and could make him fly, fly away, but I guess his lady is stronger than his bird. Is that why his music makes no sense? He's all dissonance and strife. Too at odds for the one he is, but still not two.

He's not plump and useless like I thought. Who'd have guessed his arms were as strong as his will? And now I'm truly caught. He wouldn't let me go, and Silly Lily won't, either. She'll pilot the others here and then he'll win. If I could really make the music play, I'd drive them all away.

CHAPTER THIRTY-ONE

LILY

How the hell did I let this happen?

After everything I'd done to protect her, everything I was doing to get her to safety, how *the hell* had I let Mel get taken by the Dean?

I didn't realize I was asking the question aloud until Carter sat down beside me, took my hand in his, and said simply, "This isn't your fault."

My skin prickled with icy shards of panic and his touch nearly hurt. I didn't jerk my hand away but only because I relished the pain. I was only vaguely aware of the rest of my physical surroundings. The road rushing past the window, Joe driving in silence, McKenna in the seat beside him looking fragile in her terror.

"She's my responsibility," I said, my voice shaky.

I couldn't make myself meet Carter's gaze, but looking at the floorboards didn't help because that was when I realized she hadn't even taken her pink backpack with her. She been captured by the Dean and she didn't even have her Slinky.

"She's my sister." I spoke only because it was better than crying. "If it isn't my fault, then whose fault is it?"

"It's everyone's fault," Carter said simply. "In a group, we're all responsible for everyone. She isn't your burden alone."

"As charming as this guiltfest is," Sebastian interrupted, "I hope neither of you will mind if I voice my own opinion on the matter."

I couldn't bring myself to look at him. The image of him—of what he really was—was too fresh in my mind.

Of course I had known he was a vampire, but in the confusion of our escape from the Farm, it was easy not to think about. His inhuman qualities had slipped in and out of my awareness. I pushed them to the back of my mind. Let myself pretend he was . . . if not human, then something very close to human. I no longer had that luxury.

He was monster.

Like them, but not.

The Ticks' appearance was a pure, physical representation of their nature. Merely looking at them repulsed. Sebastian was the opposite. The handsome facade, the urbane speech, the outward trappings of a civilized human. Those were the things that made him grotesque.

"Has it occurred to you, Lily," he continued—either unaware of my bone-deep revulsion or unconcerned with it—"that Mel is as much her own person as you are. Perhaps it is not anyone's fault but her own."

"Don't you talk about her." Fighting a wave of nausea, I pushed myself to my feet, only to have the motion of the van knock me back down. "I don't even want to hear you mention her name."

"Lily—" Carter reached for me again.

I recoiled. "Stop!"

There was another truth I couldn't avoid. Carter had told me Sebastian didn't eat people. He'd sworn to me that he was safe. I saw now that he was about as safe as a domesticated tiger. Which was to say, he wasn't safe at all.

"I can't . . ." I stammered, suddenly unable to form a thought, much less a sentence. "I can't—"

"Yes, you can." Carter grabbed my hand again and this time he didn't let me pull away. "You can handle this, because you have to. Don't think about it. Block it out, if you have to. Ignore it. Pretend it didn't happen. Do what you have to do to make peace with what Sebastian is, because we need his help. If we're going to get her back, we need him."

I wanted to protest. I wanted to scream. I wanted that monster out of the car and as far away from me as possible. Instead, I made myself look at him.

He looked much like he had before the attack of the Ticks. His clothes were more wrinkled, but the blood hardly showed. His skin was still unnaturally pale, his lips too bright a red.

Maybe Carter's approach would have worked. Maybe I should have just blocked out my memory of the truth. But I didn't want to forget what he was capable of. I wanted the image of him crouched over a body drinking human blood to be the first thing that came to my mind every time I thought of him. But knowing his nature and letting myself fear him were two different things.

Yet Carter was right. We needed him. Sebastian's spidey-sense would tell us where the Ticks were. And he was obviously more than capable of killing them. He might be the only chance we had of getting Mel back.

Underneath my revulsion was a seed of something else. Fear, maybe. Not fear of him but fear of myself.

I'd said all along that I would do anything to protect Mel. Would I kill to get her back? If I planned to kill the Dean, if I thought about it logically before acting, was that any better than Sebastian killing someone in a fit of bloodlust? Was I just as much a monster as he was?

* *

With every passing minute Mel and the Dean got farther and farther away. Our van was slower and older. Worse still, the sun was setting. We weren't driving on fumes yet, but we would be if we tried to drive through the night. If we ran out of gas before dawn, we'd be dead.

The debate over our next move whirled around me with little or no input from me. I sensed the others watching me, waiting for me to protest. I didn't have the energy or the will to voice my thoughts. Even I knew we had to stop to regroup. I wasn't happy about it, but I wasn't stupid, either.

I needed a plan. Something other than find a church and wait until dawn. That wasn't acceptable. But sitting in the van, listening to the others' hushed conversation, I just couldn't think of what to do next. My every thought was on Mel.

Poor Mel, who couldn't stand to be touched even by me. Who didn't like strangers. Who didn't even have her coat with her.

I squeezed my eyes shut and swallowed past my despair. After all I'd gone through to get her the coat. And then I hadn't even made her wear it.

It seemed like I'd made nothing but bad decisions since we'd left the Farm. I'd been wrong so often. And yet I was the person they expected to lead some rebellion? Didn't they see how many mistakes I made?

Mel would be a better leader than I was. She certainly figured things out faster. She was braver, even though she was probably very afraid right now.

And I hated to admit it, but Sebastian was right. Mel had made her own choice. She must have gotten out of the van because she'd thought she could help. How could I criticize her? I'd gotten out to help. Why did I treat her like a child when I knew she was smarter than I was, more observant? Yes, more fragile in some ways, but stronger in others.

All those months on the Farm, I had treated her like she was a burden. I had acted like some sort of saint for taking care of her. God, that must have irritated her. Suddenly I thought about how her speech patterns changed on the Farm. I had assumed it was stress, but maybe it wasn't. After all, she'd started talking again when Carter showed up. Carter, who'd always treated her like an equal. Maybe I really *was* the problem. Why had I always treated her like she was a burden, when we were really in this together the whole time?

Of course, I knew the answer already. I protected her because she needed me. And also because I needed to. We had both lost everything. In this crazy new world where kids were food and monsters were real and maybe I had a superpower or maybe I didn't, she was the only thing I clung to. She brought focus to my life, but hope as well. Because every version of the future that I saw was drenched in despair, but Mel saw the world with different eyes. Just as she'd seen the spot in the fence that allowed us to escape from the Farm, she might see a path to a better future.

I don't know how long I sat there yearning for my sister, but when I felt a hand on my shoulder, it was dark outside the windows of the van and we were slowing down. We were in another tiny town. The run-down strip malls and dilapidated houses looked much like those of the other towns we'd passed.

Looking up, I saw Carter beside me. "What's the plan?" I asked.

"Find a church. The four of us hunker down for the night. Sebastian's going to look for other cars that might have gas. Try to siphon enough to fill up the van. If he can pick up the scent of the Dean's car, he'll try to follow it."

I nodded and didn't comment on what he didn't say. That Sebastian couldn't come into the church with us. That whatever it was about holy ground that protected us from Ticks would keep out Sebastian as well. Or maybe it was him the church walls would protect us from.

Maybe the thought of him out there should have comforted me, but it didn't. He may have more intelligence and control than the Ticks, but I'd just seen him eat a person. A Collab, yes, but still . . . I couldn't think of it without my stomach churning.

The building we stopped in front of was a squat, ignoble structure of dingy redbrick topped with a cheap-looking white roof. Only the stained-glass windows and thin obelisk protruding from the peak distinguished it as a church rather than something else, like a VFW hall or a senior center. Even the aging Impala parked in front seemed forlorn. As holy ground went, this place seemed awash in despair.

If the strength of the building's fortifications against evil was based on the faith of the people who had once worshipped here, then I couldn't help wondering if we hadn't been safer back in the parking lot in Vidalou.

Sebastian directed Joe to pull the van up onto the curb, right beside the church's back door. Night had fallen and beyond the van, the streets were dark.

"Take what you need on the first trip," Sebastian said. "You can't come back to the van for anything. Move fast. Once you're in, stay in the sanctuary as much as you can. Carter, do a perimeter sweep for open doors or windows. Don't even think about coming out until at least an hour after dawn."

McKenna and Joe both nodded seriously, apparently content to take orders from someone who less than an hour before had eaten a person.

Carter asked, “How many and how close?”

“A whole nest west of town. I’ll try to lure them away from you, but I can’t make any promises.”

Before any of us could ask exactly what that meant, he slid open the van door and hopped out. “Don’t forget to move fast.”

And with that, he disappeared into the night. Far off in the distance, I heard a yelp and a howl and I couldn’t help thinking they sounded hungry.

“You three stay here and get the gear together,” Carter ordered. “I’m going to get the door open.”

Joe abandoned his spot in the driver’s seat and moved past my row toward the back of the van. Carter left the door open, so the overhead dome gave him a little light to work by. I watched for a moment as Carter pulled a small case from one of his pockets and flipped it open. A moment later he pulled out a collection of tiny metal prongs. Lock picks, I assumed.

Joe had collected his backpack and McKenna’s shoulder bag. Since my own bag was a casualty of my brush with bomb making, I grabbed Mel’s. My fist clenched around the pink rubber handle on the top of the bag. It was the backpack of a little girl. It even had the little tab on the front where you could attach a matching lunch box. God, I’d hated it when my sister had carried that backpack to high school. Now it was all I had left of her.

My heart ached as I held it in my hand. Somewhere in here was Mel’s worn and ragged stuffed flying squirrel. She couldn’t sleep without it and I wouldn’t sleep until she had it back. Whatever else I did, I was going to get her back.

Once I'd hopped down out of the van, Joe called, "Hey, Lily."

I turned back only to have him shove another two bags into my arms. I humphed in surprise.

"Carter's bag and our food. Remember, only one trip."

"Oh, thanks." I grunted—the food bag had to weigh twenty pounds—but Joe had already turned around to help McKenna from the van.

By the time I made it up the steps to the church's back door, Carter was swinging it open. "Wait here. I want to do the security sweep before the rest of you come in."

I didn't argue. It wasn't what Sebastian had told us to do, but I was still iffy on this whole holy-ground-is-sanctuary thing. Carter was gone only a few minutes. He held open the door and nodded down a darkened hall.

"The sanctuary is down that way, straight ahead. Leave the bags there. Bathroom is on the left if you need it."

I dumped the food bag and his backpack where he directed me to, but kept the pink bag clenched in my hand. Even though Carter had just said it was clear, my heart pounded as I crept down the hall.

The building was musty, with the lingering scents of air freshener, old carpet, and stale coffee. There was nothing familiar or welcoming about the church. Only the strong sense that I was the invader. That I was the one it was trying to keep out. Maybe it was because I didn't belong here. Maybe it was because we'd never been churchgoers in my family. Or maybe it was this "gift" that Carter and Sebastian claimed I had. Maybe I was as much an aberration as Sebastian was. Or maybe I was just a little bit afraid of the dark.

Whatever the reasons, my steps were slow as I made my way

down the hall. McKenna, however, made a beeline for the bathroom and dashed through the door like a woman who'd drunk a forty-eight-ounce soda during a *Lord of the Rings* movie.

Carter jogged up behind me, his Maglite cutting a swath of light through the darkness. He held his penlight out to me. "Here. This will help."

I bit my tongue against my natural response and instead said, "Thanks."

"I'll be right out here as soon as you're done."

I wanted to tell him not to bother, but hey, his flashlight was bigger than mine and I was tired anyway.

The bathroom was dark except for my tiny penlight. McKenna must have needed to pee too badly to care, because she was already in one of the stalls.

I held the light in my teeth and peed on a toilet for the first time in twenty-four hours, nearly weeping for joy at the sight of the toilet paper roll. I made a mental note to search the closets for more toilet paper before we left. I flushed without thinking, but then was surprised that the toilet worked. It was weird to think that somewhere nearby a water treatment plant still operated, but I was thankful. We could refill our water jugs.

When I left the stall, the light was still clamped in my teeth. I was surprised to see McKenna standing near the sink, drying her hands slowly. I let my mouth gape so the penlight dropped into my hand. I'd spent most of the past couple days pretending she and Joe didn't exist. I didn't want to think about either of them. That was a rabbit hole of emotion I didn't have the time or the energy to go down.

I tried to remember the McKenna I'd known in the Before. "Careless" was the best word to describe her. Carelessly beautiful and confident. Carelessly popular. Like it was never any work to be charming, funny, or cruel, depending on who she was with and what that person could do for her.

Now she just looked . . . worn, I guess. I couldn't reconcile the person she used to be with the one she was now. Did she have the same difficulty with me? Was there anything left of either of those girls?

McKenna wore a pair of black leggings and a bulky cable-knit sweater. Her skin was pale, her hair pulled back. The dark hollows under her eyes a testament to how uncomfortable the long car ride had been for her. One hand rested on the bulge of her belly. I'd never thought of McKenna Wells as the type of girl who'd be whipped, but that was how she looked. Like life had beaten her down.

Maybe I looked that bad, too. Without meeting her gaze, I walked around her to the sink. I set the light on the counter, shining it away so I wouldn't have to look at my reflection and find out.

The water from the sink wasn't at full pressure, but thankfully there was soap in the dispenser and I gave my hands a quick, much-needed scrub in the trickle of water.

"I'm sorry about Mel," McKenna said. There was a quiver in her voice.

I grunted in reply, turning the water off.

"When you went back out to help Carter, she was in the back of the van. Just sitting there. I made sure of it when I went to sit next to Joe. One minute she was there, the next she was gone. I—"

"It's not your fault." I didn't say it to ease her guilt. I just couldn't listen to her apologies. I didn't want to feel sorry for her or responsible for her. I didn't want the connection between us to be any stronger. "She's my responsibility. Not yours."

I reached past McKenna to pull a paper towel from the dispenser.

"I'm sorry about Joe, too," she said softly.

I pretended not to know what she meant. I dried my hands, then turned the water back on and wet the paper towel.

"When he said he could get me out, I didn't know what he had planned."

I scrubbed it over my face and neck. I shook it out and refolded it to expose a clean side, then ran it over the back of my neck and arms. I tried to ignore her, but damned if she didn't keep talking.

"I had no idea that he'd turned you in to—"

"What did you think he'd done?" Whirling on her, I balled up the paper towel and shot it past her toward the trash can in the wall. It missed. I ignored it. "You can't tell me that you thought you guys could just waltz out without putting anyone else in danger. That you thought—"

"Why not? You thought that." She bumped up her chin and took a tiny step closer to me. "When you went to him to get that stuff for Mel, did you think about how much trouble he'd get in if he got caught? Did you worry about his safety?"

"That's different!"

"Why?"

"Because I didn't do this for myself. I did it for Mel. She's—"

"And he and I did it for our baby. You think that's any less noble?"

"I—" Whatever argument I was going to say got caught in my throat. Because she was right and I didn't want her to be.

Protecting an innocent baby. A baby, for God's sake. No. That was probably more noble than protecting Mel.

But it was McKenna Wells's baby. A Breeder's baby. I couldn't let myself care about a Breeder's baby. None of us knew what was going to happen to all those Breeder babies. The possibilities were so horrific, if I stopped to think about them, I'd completely unravel.

Suddenly I wondered if this wasn't the root of all this anger I'd been carrying around toward Joe and McKenna. I didn't want to care about their baby. If I did, would I have to start caring about all those babies? All the Greens? All the kids?

It was so overwhelming. The weight of millions on my shoulders. And if Carter was right and I was an *abductura*, then how could I ignore that responsibility? I couldn't. If he was right, then I'd have to fight. I'd be in it forever. I would go from being responsible for myself and Mel to being responsible for the life of every teenager in the United States. Christ, was it any wonder I didn't want this?

I fought against a rising tide of panic.

"I don't have time for this." I grabbed the light and pushed past her toward the door.

"If it makes any difference at all," she said from behind me, "it really is Joe's baby."

For the first time I considered the possibility that she really cared about Joe. I thought about when Joe had hit his head in the van and how she'd tended to him first, even though her own back had those terrible scratches on it. I paused, my palm against the open bathroom door, listening without turning around.

"In the Before, we'd hang out sometimes. Mostly during the summer. We'd smoke a little and, you know, hook up. Matty was away at football camp all that summer, so you know . . . I know it's Joe's."

Matty had been McKenna's boyfriend. The quarterback. The other half of the school's golden couple.

I glanced back at her. Her hands were clenched in front of her belly, her head ducked. A lock of dingy hair, blond except for the three inches at the roots, hung in front of her face. A single tear glistened on her cheek.

I looked from her belly to her face and back again. Ah, Christ. She was telling the truth. There was no other way to see it. No wonder her belly was so big. She wasn't showing it off. She was just much farther along than any of the other Breeders. No, scratch that. She wasn't a Breeder. She hadn't picked this.

She was tearing away the last shreds of my hatred for her. The ones I'd clung to so doggedly. I still didn't want to like her or befriend her. I still didn't want to care. I couldn't afford to care because I couldn't save everyone. I couldn't even keep my sister safe. How was I supposed to save the world?

She looked up. "I just wanted you to know. In case it makes any difference at all."

I wanted to tell her it didn't.

I also wanted to promise I'd do anything I could to get her to Canada.

And I kinda wanted to walk back into one of the stalls and puke because suddenly the weight of this *abductura* thing was so heavy on my shoulders it was giving me acid reflux.

I didn't do any of that. I just set the penlight down on the counter and walked out.

CHAPTER THIRTY-TWO

LILY

After I left the bathroom, I stood there leaning against the wall beside the door for a second, just getting myself back under control. I felt ragged and thin. Tired beyond belief. And I didn't have any shred of a plan that would actually get my sister back. When I opened my eyes, they adjusted quickly to the darkness. I heard McKenna at the bathroom door and I scurried away.

I was looking for somewhere to hide for a minute and I slipped into the door just across the hall. It must have been the church office because there were a couple of desks and some ancient computers. Bulletin boards with old flyers on the walls. To the left of the door was a long console table with fake flowers, cloying potpourri, and a fan of summer camp pamphlets. A basket sat on the far end with something inside. Walking closer, I frowned. Why had Carter left the keys to the van in here?

For a second, I considered taking them. I could take the van and leave. Go after Mel. But I wouldn't do that. Even knowing they'd most likely be able to find another car in the morning, I couldn't leave them vanless overnight.

I picked up the keys to bring them back to Carter, only to realize they weren't for the van. The Chevy logo on the key was the same, but there were a couple of other keys on the ring. And the Chevy one looked older. Just a key. No unlock button.

I held the mystery keys in my hand for a second, thinking about the Impala in the parking lot, when Carter stepped through the doorway.

"There you are."

"Sorry. I just . . ." I hesitated. I didn't want to tell him about the key. I knew what he'd say. He'd never let me go alone and I couldn't ask him to go with me. That would put him at risk as well as Joe and McKenna.

So instead, I slipped the key into my pocket and said, "I just needed a moment."

He nodded his understanding. "About Mel—"

I interrupted him. "There's running water."

For a second, he looked like he wanted to say something else, but instead he nodded. "We should fill up our water bottles now. Who knows how long it will stay on. Come on, the sanctuary is this way."

I fell into step beside him, only vaguely aware of Joe coming out of the men's restroom and waiting for McKenna beside the door to the ladies'. She must have needed a minute to herself, too.

"I'll get Joe and McKenna settled in the sanctuary and you can drop off Mel's bag. Then we'll look for more bottles. We shouldn't drink any of the water until we've boiled it or used those purification tablets."

He rattled off a list of other things we needed to do. Double-check that the windows were secure. Look for supplies. Search for candles.

By then we'd reached the double wooden doors to the sanctuary. He held one open and let me pass. A couple dozen wooden pews formed V-shaped rows facing the pulpit. Carter had already deposited some of the gear in the empty floor space between the front row and the choir seating.

Joe and McKenna filed in after us. Carter pointed to the seats. "The seat cushions are worn, but if we stack enough of them, they'll make a decent pallet. McKenna, you should get off your feet and lie down. Sleep if you can."

I blew out a breath and forced a smile. "Okay," I said. "I'll stay here with her while you and Joe do . . . all that other stuff."

"No." Carter nodded Joe in the direction of the cushions. "Joe, you stay with McKenna. Lily, you're with me."

"What? Why?"

I glanced around, but Joe was already shoving bench cushions under his arms and McKenna was waddling toward the pulpit.

Carter pinned me with a look before grabbing my arm and steering me back out to the hall. "You're with me because I need you here. Where I can keep you safe."

"Why wouldn't I be safe in the sanctuary?"

Carter didn't glance in my direction. He pushed open the swinging door that led into the church's kitchen. "Oh, come on, Lily. Don't play dumb. I know exactly what you're planning to do."

My mouth gaped as he started looking through cabinets. "I don't know what you're talking about."

He pointed to the row of cabinets. "Look over there. We're looking for water bottles, matches, food, first aid. Anything like that."

Shrugging, I opened a cabinet and started poking through the sort of cheap, overused kitchen utensils that were common to church kitchens. "I'm not planning anything."

He slammed a door shut. "You were going to wait until we were distracted, then you were going to go look for Mel on your own."

I snapped my mouth shut. Shit, he knew me better than I knew myself.

"Well, okay. But it wasn't a plan yet."

"Then why'd you grab the keys from the church office?"

Double shit. Did nothing get by him?

I slammed one cabinet shut and moved on to the next. I hit the jackpot with a cabinet full of candles. Everything from scented jarred candles to ceremonial candles to a whole big box of white Christmas Eve service candles. The kind that aren't meant to burn for long. Cheaply made and quickly thrown away. A symbol of hope that would have been freely handed out in the Before, but that wouldn't burn long enough to do us much good now.

Still, I pulled down the big box first and then started loading the other candles inside on top of the cheap Christmas ones.

"Look, it wasn't a plan. Not yet. Just more of an instinct."

"That's what your gut tells you to do? Ditch us and storm off your own? Headlong into danger?"

His side of the kitchen had gone suddenly quiet and I got the feeling he was watching me. I didn't know what to say to him. The truth was, I no longer knew what to do. I'd strayed so far off the path I'd set out on, I wasn't sure I could make my way back.

My hand clenched around a peppermint-scented Yankee Candle. I ducked my head. "My instincts tell me to protect my sister. They tell me that she's out there. Alone. And scared. In the hands of a man who's betrayed the entire human race. And he's not even the worst thing out there. There are monsters that will kill her in an instant." I dropped the candle into the box, not caring that it was heavy enough to smash the more delicate candles beneath it. "And if you think I can just hunker down in the safety of this church while she's out there at the mercy of the Ticks, then you're completely delusional."

I felt Carter's hand on my shoulder and his touch stripped away the layers of numbness that had coated my emotions since the Dean took Mel. The nonstop adrenaline fest of a day. The constant fear. The bone-deep betrayal. The burden. The fear. The cost of just living in this world. It all hit me at once and I cracked under the pressure like one of the cheap Christmas candles. And suddenly I wasn't just exhausted or scared. I was damn near hysterical.

"Don't worry," Carter was saying, though I could barely hear him past the blood rushing in my ears. "We'll get her back."

I shook his hand off my arm, but he didn't let go. I fought against him for a moment, but then my anger faded into sobs.

I don't know how long I stood there, crying in Carter's arms. But I cried until my throat felt raw and my legs gave way under me. I felt him slide us to the floor and cradle me in his lap. Vaguely I became aware of his hand stroking my hair and his arm strong and solid at my back.

It felt good sitting there in his arms. Too good. I pushed him away.

"Lily—"

I didn't want to talk about my emotional outburst, so I got up and shoved my hands into my pockets and headed for the kitchen door. "Since there's food here we can bring with us, I'm going to go get some of the backpacks to put it in."

Carter reached the door before I did. He held out his hand. "Give me the keys." He sighed. "You know I can't let you go out there alone."

"I'm not asking you to go with me. McKenna and Joe need you here."

"Leaving right now would be stupid. You don't even know where they are."

"They're heading back to the Farm, right? I'll follow them."

"Yes, we know he headed south, but you don't know that's where they're going. The Dean doesn't want Mel; he wants you.

He'll stay nearby. But until we know where they are, leaving the church would just be stupid. You don't even know if the car will start." He looked me right in the eye. "But if you're leaving, I'll go with you."

Damn it.

I didn't want him to risk his life for me again. By offering to come, he'd all but guaranteed I wouldn't go myself. I gritted my teeth, yanked the keys from my pocket, and dropped them into his hand. "Fine. We'll wait until morning."

A few minutes later, I carried a couple of backpacks into the church's kitchen and dumped them on the counter. After I set them down, I realized that one of them was Mel's backpack. The pink flowered one. My hand shook a little when I unzipped it. I'd kept Mel's backpack light on purpose. I hadn't wanted her to have to carry too much. I knew she wouldn't complain even if the pack was too heavy for her, just as she wouldn't complain about the cold. So there was still some room where I could pack in some supplies.

The canned food we'd found was too valuable to leave. If I was going to head back for the Farm, I didn't know how much longer my trip was going to be. Mel and I would need all the provisions we could get. Still, I knew I couldn't ditch any of Mel's stuff. When I found her again, she'd need the clothes in the bag. She'd need her stuffed flying squirrel and her Slinky, too.

I unpacked the bag so I could put the heavier canned food in the bottom. Instead of putting her extra shirt back in the bag, I layered it under my hoodie. I did the same with one of the pairs of socks. That bought me a little more room and I started repacking the bag.

I left Squirrel and Slinky for last, so they'd be on top. Mel had

had Squirrel since she was five. We'd each gotten one in our stockings that Christmas. Mel had immediately become attached to hers and had carried it around as her snuggle for years. I'd loved mine, too, and had cuddled with it at night. Then when we were twelve, Mel had lost her squirrel at the Omaha airport. She'd cried so hard we got kicked off the plane and Mom had to rent a car to drive us back to Dallas. Once we got home, I'd taken my squirrel off the bookshelf, where he'd sat for the past few years since I'd decided I was too old to sleep with him, and given him to Mel. She'd cuddled him just like he was her own.

At the time, I hadn't minded giving up a loved toy so Mel could be happy and calm. I needed her happiness as much as I needed my own. On the Farm, I may have resented the burden of taking care of her, but it had given me purpose. It had kept me together.

What would I do if I didn't get her back? How could I live without her?

My hand convulsed on the stuffed squirrel and tears flooded my eyes. I made myself let go of the snuggly. I carefully tucked him inside the Slinky in the top of the backpack and brushed the tears away with the back of my hand. Then I zipped the backpack closed.

"You okay?" Carter asked from behind me.

I turned to see him walking into the room. I felt suddenly vulnerable, standing there crying over a stuffed animal. "I'm good," I lied and offered up a wobbly smile.

He studied me for a second and I caved under his scrutiny, turning back around to fiddle with the backpack, pretending to check the pockets for something.

He must have seen my feint for what it was, because he came

to stand beside me, resting his butt against the countertop so he faced me. "Are you?" he asked. He reached out to brush a tear from my cheek. "'Cause it looks like you've been crying again."

I let my eyes drift closed for a second. His hand felt good on my cheek. Warm and reassuring. I wanted to throw myself in his arms again. I wanted to tell him about Mel's squirrel and how worried she must be. I wanted to lean on him. Depend on him. Trust him to take care of me and to get Mel back, but if I lost it now, how would I ever get myself back under control enough to go out and search for Mel?

I couldn't tell him the truth, but at the same time I didn't want to lie outright. So I fudged and shared a half-truth. "I can't help wondering about the people who used to come to church here." I nudged a can of tuna with my finger. "About the people in the town. Wondering where they are."

Carter ran a hand up and down my arm. It was a touch that was meant to be comforting, but it only made me more aware of him. His body seemed to radiate warmth in the otherwise cold kitchen. His hands were strong and capable. He'd used them to keep me safe in a terrifying world.

I felt guilty for enjoying all of that when so many people had died. When my sister was out there, all alone with the Dean. I felt unworthy of taking comfort from him, but I still didn't push him away.

"You ever think about the world in the Before?" I asked. "You ever long for it?"

His mouth twisted into something that might have been a smile, but wasn't. "My life in the Before wasn't that great."

I turned to look at him, but his expression was distant. "Military school pretty tough?" I asked.

He chuckled then. "Yeah. But that wasn't what I meant." He

paused for a moment, like he was going to pick and choose what to say. Then the words rushed out of him. "You and Mel have always had each other. You've always been close. But I've never—" He shook his head. "I've never had anyone in my life that cared about me like that."

"Surely your parents . . ." I said weakly. But really, I didn't know jack about his family other than their general income bracket.

He snorted. "Yeah, my parents. Real winners. School was never bad. It was all the other stuff."

All the other stuff? All the wealth and privilege? But I guess even rich families can be horrible. Maybe they're even worse than others. I did know this: no matter what was going on in your life, if your family stuff was messed up, it affected everything. Suddenly I felt sorry for him because I couldn't even imagine what it would be like to have no one who cared about you. I would do anything for Mel and I knew, in her own way, she felt the same. Even though our dad bolted, I'd always known they both loved us.

Since he didn't seem to want to say more, I let it go. We were all allowed to keep our secrets.

Instead I asked, "So you think you'd still be in military school, then?"

"Yeah. I guess so."

"It'd be spring our senior year," I mused. "I'd be kicking back and relaxing."

"No, you wouldn't." He bumped his shoulder playfully against mine. "You're too type A for that. You'd be studying right up until the end. Trying to eke out the best possible GPA."

"Naw." I waved aside his assessment. "I wouldn't have to. I would have already gotten early admission. Into one of the great schools, too. Harvard or somewhere."

"Oh, sure. And a scholarship, I bet."

"Why not?" I agreed playfully. Then suddenly the game seemed more sad than fun. My tone grew pensive. "I guess we would never have seen each other again, though." I looked up to find him watching me, his expression serious. "I mean, in a world where there were no Ticks."

He brought his hand up to my face and brushed his thumb across my cheek. Only then did I realize I was crying again.

We were standing so close I heard it when he swallowed.

"I can't imagine a world where I wouldn't come find you after I left military school. You would have seen me again. I promise you that."

I felt something inside of me melt. At that moment, I wanted so badly to believe he meant it. His hand slipped up into my hair. Then he was pulling me toward him. I stepped over his outstretched legs and leaned against his chest.

The faintest pressure against the back of my head pulled me to him. I brushed my lips against his. His lips were smooth and dry. Not chapped, but like velvet. If I'd thought about it too much, I'd have pulled back. But I didn't let myself think. Instead, I lost myself in the warmth of his chest against my hands. In the strength of his legs bracketing mine. I let myself live the fantasy I'd been dreaming about for so long.

My hands slipped up to his shoulders. One of my fingers brushed against the scar on the back of his neck and I felt a tremor go through him. Had I hurt him? I might have pulled back then, but the pressure of his hand in my hair didn't ease up. The kiss was so gentle and patient. As delicate as whipped cream and just as delicious. Suddenly I wanted more than just the feel of his lips on mine. I wanted to taste him, to feel his body pressed against mine. I parted my lips, but before I could brush my tongue against his mouth, he straightened. Without ever moving his mouth from mine, he turned us both around and lifted me up to sit on the counter.

My whole world narrowed down to just Carter. His hands on my waist, my legs wrapping around his hips to pull him closer, my fingers in his hair. His tongue slipping into my mouth in a kiss so deep I couldn't tell where he ended and I began. Pleasure spiraled through my body and I shuddered with the need to get closer to him. To keep kissing him. Forever.

Something banged in the other room. There was a loud clatter followed by Joe shouting, "I'm okay. Just dropped one of the bags."

Carter pulled back slowly and dropped his forehead to mine.

"God, Lily, you don't know—"

My fingers were twined in his hair. I tilted my mouth, eager for him to kiss me again. I wanted so badly to stay there in the shelter of his arms, but he stepped back, keeping his hands on my hips but definitely, decidedly ending the embrace.

"This isn't the best time for this," he said. His fingers tightened, as if he had to force himself to let me go, and then he took another step back. He ran one hand through his hair and stuck the other in his pocket. "With Mel gone . . ."

For a moment I was only stunned. He was right of course. My sister was gone. Being held captive by a monster. This was so not the perfect time to be hooking up with my long-term crush. On the other hand, I needed him. I needed the comfort of his touch. The strength that came from knowing I wasn't in this alone. I needed to forget the horror that waited outside the church, if only for a few seconds.

I needed that. And he was rejecting me. I couldn't even fault him for it.

"You're right," I said, sliding off the counter to stand on the floor. I shoved my hands into my back pockets. "Of course you're right. This isn't the time."

"Lily—" He reached for me, but I instinctively flinched away from him. He pressed his lips into a line and nodded with resolve. "You're not even thinking straight. This isn't really what you want."

His voice took on that coolly logical tone. That military school voice of his. God, I was starting to hate that.

I whirled on him. "Don't tell me how I'm thinking. Don't tell me what I want."

His jaw clenched and I could practically see him drawing on those military school reserves of calm. "This is a tense situation. You're frightened and—"

"You're damn right I'm frightened. I'm scared none of us are going to make it through the night. I'm afraid I'm going to die. At eighteen. I'm afraid my sister is already dead."

"I promise you, we will get her back."

I almost wished he hadn't spoken instead of making promises he couldn't possibly keep. "You don't know that," I hissed.

"I do know this," he said. "I will do everything in my power to get her back."

"As long as it doesn't interfere with your plans for the rebellion." I knew I was being irrational, but I also knew there was a thread of truth to my words. Carter was in this for the rebellion. Even though he'd postponed things to take us to Canada, he'd done it because he thought he could convince me on the drive. "Because you'll do anything for the rebellion, right?"

"I'll do anything for you," he said fiercely.

"Yeah, right."

He reached out a hand and turned me to face him. "Do you

have any idea the things I've already done just to get you out of the Farm?"

"Um, yeah. I was there. I remember."

"No, I mean all the stuff you didn't even see me do. Do you have any idea what I did—what everyone in the rebellion did—just to *find* you?"

"I . . ." I shook my head. "No."

"There are Collabs—adult Collabs—who deliver food all over. We convinced some of them to join the cause. Bribed them to talk to other Collabs, to try to get information about girls who might fit your description. I've been in and out of twelve Farms myself just looking for you. Countless other guys have been in other Farms looking for you, too. Do you know how many people we've rescued for no other reason than they have long dark hair and they own a Slinky?"

"A Slinky?" I repeated. It was a stupid question, because I knew what he meant. I just couldn't imagine it.

"Right. A Slinky. That's what we had to go on. Twins, dark hair, and a Slinky." Carter gave a maniacal-sounding laugh. "In fact, there are now rumors in almost all the Farms that owning a Slinky is your ticket out."

"I had no idea."

"Of course you didn't. Because you're so focused on keeping Mel safe, you can't even see what's right in front of you."

"I . . ." Crap. What did I say to that? Why wasn't I better at this? "I don't know what to say, but it doesn't change anything. I still have to get Mel back."

He blew out a sigh. "Just don't put yourself in danger," he corrected. "I can't let you put yourself at risk. Don't ask me to do that. I have to protect you."

I started flinging open drawers until I found one that held dish towels, then I used one to wipe off my face. "I absolutely believe that your first goal is to protect me." I threw the towel down on the counter and whirled to face him. "I just don't like your motives. The only reason you give a damn about me is because you think I'm this *abductura* who's going to save the world."

I paused there, giving him half a second to disagree with me. Stupid of me, right? Hoping that maybe he was in this for more than these superpowers he thought I had.

Carter said nothing, so I kept talking. "I don't even care if I'm an *abductura*. I just want my sister back."

"You still don't believe it?" His voice was brusque, his hands on his hips.

"No. Of course I don't believe it." I threw up my hands in frustration. "There isn't anything special about me. I'm the normal one. No big secrets, no special powers. I could never even convince my mother to make me a birthday cake that wasn't gluten free. If I could have convinced anyone to do whatever I want, don't you think that just once I would have had a normal chocolate cake? Because when I was eight I really, really wanted one."

Carter dragged a hand through his hair. "I don't know. Maybe it doesn't work on cakes. Maybe it only works on important things. But I know—"

"How? How do you know? You're so certain that I have this gift that you broke into the Farm just to get us out. Why should I believe you about this when you haven't even told me why you think I am an *abductura*? And not just that crap you told me back at Uncle Rodney's about the Dean and the riot in front of the cafeteria. If you've been scouring the Farms for me, then you obviously had some other evidence before you showed up on our Farm. I need to know the real reason why you think I'm an *abductura*."

Carter turned away and continued searching the cabinets, as if he couldn't stand my scrutiny. At first, I thought he was dodging the question. Then, slowly, he started talking.

"You just don't see it," he said softly, without even looking up. "But when Sebastian first told us about *abducturae*, I just knew. It had been almost two years since I'd even seen you and I knew."

"How? Just tell me how you knew," I pleaded.

"I knew because . . ." His head tipped forward, like the answer to the question weighed on him. "Because from the moment I met you, I . . ."

"What?"

He turned, slowly lifting his eyes up to meet mine. "From the moment I met you, I wanted you."

The air left my lungs in a whoosh. My mind stuttered to a halt and it was a good thing he kept talking, because I would have just stood there gaping blankly at him.

"Do you even remember that day we first met back in the ninth grade?"

I did. Third week of school, third-period biology, six minutes into class. I was sitting at my normal seat in the back, reading a copy of *Scientific American* under the table. I know, I was a total dork. Coach Ballard was rambling on about mitosis—and blushing, for God's sake, because he'd just said mitosis was like sex, but on a cellular level—and, eew, teachers should so not make jokes about sex—when the door swung open and Carter strolled into the room. The moment I looked up from my magazine, it was like every cell in my body lurched toward him. Every cheesy insta-love cliché fit. Time stood still. The earth moved. My body quivered. I couldn't breathe. It all happened. I felt it. As Coach examined his schedule, Carter surveyed the room with the kind of lazy arrogance that only the very rich, the very popular, the very confident can convey in a single look. And then he met my gaze. And for one second I could have sworn he felt as shell-shocked as I did. But then he gave a dismissive smirk and looked away.

That was it. For over a month, that was our only contact.

"I don't believe you," I said numbly now.

"It's true."

"It isn't," I insisted. "That first day—not the first day of school, mind you, because rebellious Carter Olson would never do something as blasé as coming to school on the first day—you didn't give me a second glance. You didn't even know I existed until Coach Ballard moved you to sit next to me because you kept flirting with Lindsey Hannigan."

Carter crossed the few steps between us and took my face in his hands. His palms were surprisingly warm against my cheeks. "I was drawn to you from the moment I walked into that room. A guy like me, who'd gotten everything he ever wanted, who'd been in five different boarding schools before the ninth grade, I wasn't about to admit—even to myself—that I couldn't stop thinking about you."

There was some part of my brain—the part where fantasies lived, the part fed by teenage hormones and too many romcoms—that ate up every word he said like they were kettlecorn with crack sprinkled on top. What girl wouldn't want to hear this stuff? What girl hadn't spent hours fantasizing that the sexy, mysterious bad boy had been drawn to her the instant they met?

But the smart, cynical part of my brain that had kept Mel and me alive for the past six months heard the message under the smooth words.

I stepped out of his reach, instantly missing his warmth, even though I knew it was an illusion.

"Let me see if I've got this right. The reason you think I'm an *abductura* is because back in the ninth grade, you had a crush on me even though you thought I wasn't good enough for you? Am I understanding you right?"

He blew out a frustrated breath. "No, it wasn't just a crush. I'm not the kind of guy who gets crushes. I—"

"Oh, I get what kind of guy you are. I remember the ninth grade, too, Carter. You were arrogant and hot and instantly popular at our school. There were people I'd been in classes with for ten years who didn't know me but who knew who you were by the end of the day. But are you honestly telling me that *this* is the explanation that makes sense to you? You can't believe that you just happened to be attracted to someone who was geeky and shy. So instead you've bought into this ridiculous idea that I might have superpowers."

"It's not like that. You're making it sound ridic—"

"No, Carter, you're the one who's making it sound ridiculous. Do you have any idea how insulting this is to me?"

"I didn't mean to insult you." Anger edged his voice. "You asked. You're the one who wanted to know why I thought you were an *abductura*. That's why. An *abductura* convinces people to behave in a manner contrary to their nature. I know you have it in you to do that."

"I . . ." I fumbled. "I'm the daughter of a lawyer. I was raised making persuasive arguments. I'm just good at it."

I always had been. From the schoolyard squabble to the classroom debate, I could talk people around to seeing things my way. At least, I thought that was what I'd been doing. What if it had been something else? Something more sinister? What if I'd actually been imposing my will on others?

Carter stood directly in front of me. With one finger, he tipped my head up so I'd meet his gaze. "And I know that before I met you I was an arrogant and selfish asshole who didn't care about anything other than getting his own way and pissing off his parents. It was contrary to my nature to care about anything other than myself. But I cared about you. I wanted you in my life badly enough that I tricked Coach Ballard into making us lab partners. I befriended you. I fell for you. There were times when I couldn't even think because you were sitting right next to me."

"If you really felt that way, why didn't you just ask me out?"

"Because I was a fifteen-year-old punk of a kid who never let anyone close. Everyone I'd ever cared about had let me down and I was too damn scared of how you made me feel. If my parents hadn't shipped me off to military school, I would have caved."

"But you did get shipped off," I said numbly. It made me sad in some weird way. Yeah, thinking about the past always did. That life, that innocence, was gone forever. And some childish part of me always yearned for those things I'd missed out on. I'd never had a boyfriend. Never gone to prom. Never had one of those amazing, sweep-you-off-your-feet first kisses in high school.

Back in the Before, I'd thought I was above getting caught up in all that. I was the product of divorce. Too cynical to buy into those Disneyfied fairy tales. Now those romantic dreams seemed as gossamery as spiderwebs. Delicate and ephemeral, but no less beautiful for it. Why hadn't I enjoyed them when I could?

"Yeah. I got shipped off," Carter said. "Even after I left, I thought about you. And when I had the chance, I came for you. Not just because I knew you were an *abductura*, but because I wasn't about to leave you in a Farm. All those other Farms we went into and broke out of, I was looking for you. I couldn't leave you there."

I twisted my face away and stepped back from him as anguish

and revulsion mixed together in my belly to form a nauseating cocktail of self-doubt.

What was I supposed to do with this knowledge? All those years ago, Carter had a thing for me. The way he made it sound, he'd practically been obsessed with me. But he hadn't wanted it. I'd forced it on him. The thought filled me with self-disgust.

"All I know is this. As soon as I walked into that classroom, I saw the way you looked at me. I knew you were going to crush on me. And I knew I wasn't going to do anything about it. I wasn't interested. I'd been in and out of enough schools to know a guy like me could have any girl I wanted. And I also knew that a smart girl like you—no matter how pretty—was more work than I was willing to do. I had no interest in you at all. In fact, I was determined to stay as far away as possible. I was drawn to you despite that. I fell for you anyway."

My unease made me snappish. "What do you want me to do? Apologize?"

"No. You wanted to know why I was so sure you were an *abductura*. This is why. I stayed at Richardson High School longer than any school I'd been in since the third grade. Because you were there. Even though I never hooked up with you, I just wanted to be near you. And you were the reason I left. The way I felt about you scared the crap out of me. So I messed up on purpose. I stole my dad's Lamborghini because I knew it was the one thing he couldn't ignore. I knew he'd send me away and I thought I'd forget about you. But I didn't.

"There I was, stuck at that godforsaken school in the middle of nowhere, and you were the only thing I could think about. I friggin' pined for you like I was an eight-year-old with my first crush. Even after the Ticks took over, you were the one thing I cared about. When Sebastian told us about *abducturae*, I knew you were one of them. It was the only thing that explained how I felt. And I didn't even care. You may not believe that this is what you are. But I know it. And it doesn't even matter to me anymore. Even if you weren't the only one who could help us defeat the Ticks, I'd still have come for you. I still would have searched every damn Farm in Texas until I found you and got you out."

He paused then and looked into my eyes and then at my lips. "I'm tired of fighting this. I want to be with you and it doesn't matter to me why I feel that way."

With that, he cupped my face gently in his hands and started to lower his mouth to mine. He was going to kiss me.

I swatted him away because I couldn't bear to have his lips on me again. Not after the sweet, beautiful kiss we'd shared just a few moments before. Not now that I knew the truth. I had wanted Carter for years, but I never wanted him like this.

He reeled back a step. "What was that for?"

For an instant, my emotions fluctuated wildly. My anguish and self-disgust. My fear. My grief. It all flooded through me, threatening to pull me into the undertow. I fought back by calling on the one emotion I knew I could master: cold, exquisite anger.

"That's because you're an idiot."

"What is wrong with you, Lily? I just told you I loved you and—"

"No, you didn't. You just told me you didn't intend to love me. You didn't want to love me. You got yourself arrested to keep yourself away from me. That's not love. That's a compulsion. And, by the way, kudos on coming up with *the worst* pickup line of all time." I spun back and glared at him. "Did you honestly think I'd want to be with you after that? Even if there were no Ticks, even if Mel was safe in the next room watching reruns of *Star Trek*, even if unicorns and butterflies were frolicking—"

"Yeah," he interrupted. "I get it. You're not interested."

"No, apparently you *don't* get it. I could never be with someone who doesn't want to care about me but does because I've *made* him feel it. I don't want that. No one would want that."

He reached for me again, his expression anguished. "Lily, I—"

"Stop." I shook my head and stepped out of his reach. "I don't want to hear any more."

"But, Lily—"

"I believe you now. About being an *abductura*. At least you convinced me of that."

Ignoring him, I grabbed the backpacks and retreated into the sanctuary, where Joe and McKenna had set up an ad hoc camp.

When I walked into the sanctuary and saw the two of them together, I froze. They had made a pallet of the bench cushions. Joe was sitting with his back against the pulpit. McKenna sat in front of him, between his outstretched legs, resting her back against his stomach. His arms were wrapped around her, his hands resting on the top of her distended belly. His head was bent close to hers as he whispered something in her ear.

Suddenly they made sense to me, as a couple. When he'd first told me her baby might be his, they'd seemed so mismatched. Like Britney Spears and John Mayer. Just wrong. But now, instantly, I knew that together they were right. As mismatched as they might be, the baby connected them. The baby made them right.

I knew children didn't always do that. My parents had been right before us, but Mel and I had made them not work anymore. But in this case the baby did make them work together. And I could see so clearly that Joe loved both McKenna and his unborn child.

Watching them together, I felt sick to my stomach. And for the first time since the Farm, it wasn't because he'd sold us out to buy McKenna's escape.

This time it was jealousy that made me sick.

I didn't want to be an *abductura*. I didn't want this stupid power. I wanted that.

In the Before, McKenna had been high school royalty. She could have had any guy she wanted, but she chose him. At the Farm, Joe had been incredibly powerful. More powerful than any of the Collabs. He could have picked any girl, but he'd picked her.

Was it really so selfish of me to want the same thing? Just someone to choose me. All on his own.

I wanted someone who just loved me. Someone who would do anything for me. Not because he had to. Not because I'd made him feel it.

But I didn't have that. Instead I had a stupid power I didn't even know how to use.

CHAPTER THIRTY-THREE

CARTER

Lily was unnaturally quiet as they carried the supplies into the sanctuary.

He'd screwed up. Badly.

But what was he supposed to do? He couldn't lie to her. Clearly he shouldn't have told her how he felt. But what other explanation could he have given for how he knew she was an *abductura*?

He'd messed up beyond reason. The best he could hope for now was that a good night's sleep would improve her mood.

The problem was, before anyone got a good night's sleep, he'd have to slice them all open.

He carried the last of the supplies he'd gathered into the sanctuary, setting down the cardboard box on the bench closest to the pulpit. Joe had lit a few of the candles, casting the room in warm, flickering light. They'd lucked out and found some food. Mostly stale cookies and old Ritz crackers, but they'd hit the jackpot with five cans of tuna, and three of beans and wieners. Certainly nobody's favorite, but a good source of protein. He ate his quickly, licking the can clean.

Lily was still picking at hers, her expression grim.

He rifled through the med kit and gathered a collection of bandages and gauze pads, lining them up on the pulpit along with four individually wrapped alcohol pads. No one else noticed what he was doing until he pulled out his own supply kit and got out the tweezers and razor blade.

He ripped opened one of the sterile gauze pads and unfolded it. When he started heating the tweezers in the flame of one of the candles, Joe finally asked, "What's up, man?"

"The Dean found us. That means our chips are still transmitting." He held the end of the tweezers in a pair of needle-nose pliers, twisting them in the flame. "We're going to have to take them out."

Lily set her can of beans aside and stood. "If the Dean never ran the program deleting our chips, does that mean all our information is still in his computer?"

"Yes."

"What does that mean, exactly?"

"In the long term, it's hard to say."

If Roberto discovered Sebastian had been to the Farm and taken kids out, he'd know something was up. Until now, everything the rebellion had done had slipped under Roberto's radar. As far as they knew, Roberto had no idea that Sebastian was working against him and looking for an *abductura*. The Farms were set up to keep meticulous records of every person who came in or out. If the Dean hadn't erased those records, then Roberto might figure out not only that there was a rebellion, but also about Lily and Mel. Of course, none of that would matter if they all got eaten by Ticks the second they walked out of the church.

He'd deal with one crisis at a time.

"But there will be problems long term?" she asked.

"There might be. For now, we just have to get the chips out. Let's focus on that."

Lily nodded. "Okay, what do we do?"

"I'll cut out McKenna's first," he said, carefully lowering the tweezers onto the open gauze pad. Then he pulled the razor blade from its cardboard wrapper and heated it in the flame, too. "Joe and Lily, watch carefully. Whoever doesn't puke or pass out can do mine next."

Joe looked a little green, but Lily just nodded, watching his every move.

"We'll need to wash and sterilize the tweezers and the blade between people. How strong is your stomach, Lily? You think you can handle that?"

She swallowed hard, then said, "I'm good."

Once he'd had the razor blade in the flame long enough, he wiped it and the tweezers off with the alcohol pads. It wasn't perfect, but it would do. He hoped.

"Okay, McKenna, where's your chip?"

She walked over to him in mincing, hesitant steps. "Is it going to hurt?"

He looked at her pale, nervous face and thought about lying, but she had to be tougher than she looked. No one who'd survived for six months on a Farm was weak. Instead of offering her empty reassurances, he said, "The blade is sharp. The cut itself won't hurt much. If they put your chip in right, it's right below the surface. I'll work fast."

McKenna stepped closer, but clutched edged of her sweater together like she was warding off an attack. "If this is so important, then why didn't we do it earlier?"

"It's because of Sebastian," Lily explained. "The blood."

McKenna nodded, then turned around and loosened the neck of her sweater. "It's here." She pointed to a tiny raised bump where her neck met her shoulder.

He'd taken out enough chips in the past six months that he had the routine down pat. He worked quickly, blocking out everything except the task immediately in front of him. He didn't think of the person he was cutting open or the muscle he was digging through. He ignored the sounds of pain. The cries and tears from some. The rapid inhalation of others. He did it automatically now.

Swipe with the alcohol pad. A quick slice. Find the chip. Wriggle it out. Gauze to stop the bleeding. A butterfly closure. Two layers of gauze on top of that. Tape. And he was done.

Lily was silent and efficient by his side. Washing things and sterilizing them again so that he moved from McKenna straight to Joe and then on to her. After having her own chip cut out, she looked pale, but determined.

McKenna was still crying, silently. Joe was by her side on the floor, wrapped around her, trying to provide the warmth that her sweater couldn't.

Carter swallowed and glanced at Lily. "Guess it's you." He looked her over. She had a slight tremor in her hands as she held the razor blade in the fire. "You able to handle it?"

"I watched everything you did," she said. "I should be good."

He nodded, then pulled his sweatshirt up over his head, leaving it around his arms, and turned his back to her.

His heart pounded as he sat there. Not because he feared the pain—he'd had this done enough that he barely even thought about that—but because it was Lily doing it. Then he felt her hand on his back, her palm pressed against his left shoulder blade. This time, his chip was farther down his back. About two inches left of his spine. Her fingers moved slowly over his skin, seeking the raised spot where his chip was.

"Who did this the other times?" she asked as her fingers found the chip under his skin.

"One of the guys."

She stood there for a moment, her left hand framing the skin around his chip, the index finger of her hand lightly resting on top of the chip. He was painfully aware of the heat of her finger. Of how close she was standing and of the tension in her muscles. He could practically feel her gearing up to make the slice.

But instead she said, "If this thing Sebastian does with the computer deactivates the chips, why do you get a new chip each time? Why not just have one chip that gets turned on and off?"

"The first couple of times I didn't get a chip at all, but it turned out it's easier to blend in with the Greens if you've been processed as one." He blew out a breath, painfully aware of her hands moving with the shifting of his back. She didn't interrupt him, so he kept talking. "Whenever Sebastian comes onto a Farm, people notice. If I show up with him, like his assistant or something, everyone treats me like a Collab no matter how I'm dressed. But if he comes in, dragging some kids he just collected on the outside, and tosses us to the Collabs to be processed, then the Collabs treat me like crap. There are fewer questions. I blend better."

"But on our Farm, you dressed as a Collab."

"I never would have done that if you and Mel hadn't tried to escape. Sebastian had to send me out after curfew to find you and I couldn't wander around dressed as a Green, so I stole a Collab uniform from the admin building."

"So it's not just me you lie to," she said quietly.

"I've never lied about the important stuff." He hadn't lied about how he felt about her. Not that she'd been super happy with the truth, either.

"Don't the Collabs who put in your chips notice all the scars? You'd think that's a dead giveaway."

"At each new school, Sebastian insists on putting in the new chip. He does it when other people see it, but he does it himself. His eccentricities only seem to add to how much the Deans fear him."

Carter felt her hair brush against the bare skin of his shoulder and closed his eyes against the sensation. It was torture, feeling her hands on his back, her breath against his neck.

Lily gave a little huffing noise. "Right. They fear him because he's eccentric. Not because he eats people."

He swallowed, trying to concentrate on the conversation, then said, "I'm not stupid enough to think Sebastian is my friend. I told you that. Yes, he's a monster. Yes, he feeds off humans. But he's also our best shot at survival. And if that means playing nice with him until we get to safety, then that's what I'm going to do."

"Right. Because you're all about accomplishing your goals. No matter what you have to say to do it."

He turned and looked at her this time. Right in the eyes, so maybe she'd believe him. And he spoke slowly, repeating his earlier words. "I have not lied to you about anything important."

She looked right back at him, a glint of defiance in her eyes. And maybe something else, too. Maybe sorrow. "You've lied to me since the moment you walked back into my life."

"And how would you have taken the truth?" he demanded, suddenly tired of defending himself. "If I'd walked up to you that first day and said, 'Hey, Lily, remember me? I'm Carter. We used to flirt in biology. I snuck onto the Farm to rescue you because I think you have the power to incite a rebellion against the Ticks. By the way, I'm working with a bloodsucking monster that I'm pretty sure won't kill anyone.' Would that have worked for you?"

"I—"

"Yeah. I didn't think so. I said what I had to say to get you to trust me. I did it to protect you. In a perfect world, I wouldn't have to lie to you to do that."

"Yeah. Well, in a perfect world, I'd be at home on my couch right now watching *Jersey Shore*."

"Instead, this is what we're stuck with."

"Right." She didn't quite meet his eyes as she nodded. "Turn back around."

He turned back, dropping his elbows onto his knees to give her better access to his back. "Would you just cut the damn thing out and put me out of my misery?"

Sometimes she was so damn hard to read, it about killed him. She was tough and smart and single-minded and unlike any other girl he knew. He admired all of those things about her. But they were also all the things that were going to make it difficult for her to trust him again. And maybe impossible for her to forgive him.

He hadn't rescued her from the Farm just so he could hook up with her. He'd done it because the world needed her. And because he couldn't bear the thought of her in danger. Still, there was no denying he didn't just want her to be safe. He wanted her to be his. But saving her life had probably driven her away forever.

That was the moment she swiped the alcohol pad over his skin and then brought the razor blade down and made the cut. Her touch was slow but steady. She did what he'd told her to do, but he was still miserable.

He clenched his teeth against the pain as she dug under his skin for the chip and exhaled slowly when he felt her pull it out.

"I'm sorry," she said softly. Her hands were at his back again blotting with the gauze pad. "I'm sure one of the other guys would have done a better job."

"You did fine."

She pinched his skin together to apply the butterfly closure. "Where are the other guys now?"

"There were three guys with us at the last Farm, in Abilene. Carlos, Dwayne, and Joey. We got nine people. One of the girls was from Richardson High. She'd heard rumors, in the Before, that some of the kids from school had been brought to this Farm. So the twelve of them set off for camp and Sebastian and I went straight to your Farm."

By the time he was done talking, she'd finished patching him up. As she patted down the last of the tape, she asked, "Will this hold?"

"Huh?"

"Is this bandage strong enough that Sebastian won't"—the words caught in her mouth—"eat me the next time he sees me?"

"Yes. It'll hold. The cut should stop bleeding soon." He hesitated, before giving more details, but she was still looking at him with doubt, so he added, "It's the scent of fresh, flowing blood that—"

"I get it."

"You don't have to worry about him." He pulled his sweatshirt back down over his head. "He's been around for a long time. He has tremendous control."

"Yeah. I noticed that when he was devouring that Collab."

Even though his own stomach churned a bit at the memory, he had to defend Sebastian. "The Collab tried to ram him with a car. He killed the Collab to protect all of us. I'm not saying it was right that he fed off the guy afterwards. But it was a clean kill and I would have done the same to protect the group. Besides, I guarantee it was better than being eaten by a Tick."

Lily turned her back to him, making it impossible to read anything of her mood other than her tension.

"Look," he began, "I understand you're freaked out about all of this. I agree, the thing with Sebastian . . . it's messed up. He is on our side. And I'd rather be working with him than not. We don't have a lot of advantages when it comes to the Ticks. The fact that he can tell when they're near—we need that. And he's—"

"It's not him I'm worried about." She turned to face him, her expression resolute. "Don't get me wrong, I'm freaked out about that. Seriously. Freaked out. But for now, all I care about is getting Mel back. The way I see it, if this bandage"—she tapped a finger against the patch on her neck—"is enough to keep Sebastian from smelling my blood, then it should hold out against the Ticks, too. That's what I'm hoping, at least."

"By morning—"

"No. Not by morning. Now. If I go out there now, is the scent of blood going to attract them?"

Every muscle in his body tensed at her words. "We can't go back out there now."

"I'm not asking you to go with me." She turned away from him, busying herself with cleaning up the bloody gauze pads and other trash. "But I can't stay here overnight. It's already been too long. More than two hours since the Dean nabbed Mel."

"Exactly. He has a two-hour lead. And a faster car." He took the trash from her and dumped it into one of the brass collection bowls that had been tucked onto the shelf inside the pulpit. The chips he placed in a second bowl and set it on the bench. If the Dean was still tracking the chips, Carter didn't want to tip his hand to the Dean by destroying them now. "You're in no condition to go out there and look for her. You're tired. You need to rest."

She crossed her arms over her chest and stared him down. "I'm not just waiting here while my sister is out there alone with the Dean. That's not going to happen."

He pulled his matchbook from his kit and lit the contents of the bandage bowl on fire. "You think getting yourself killed is the answer? It's night. The Ticks will be everywhere. You'll be bait the second you walk out that door."

"You said—"

"Whether they can smell your blood or not, they'll be able to smell you. And they're hungry. The fact that one ate that Collab is proof of that."

"But—"

"I'm sorry, Lil." And he really was. "There's just no way we can go rescue Mel. Not tonight. Not when we don't even know where she is."

"But you've already proven that you'll say anything—even lie through your teeth—if you think it's going to keep me safe. So I can't trust your opinion on this. I can't let you decide."

He shook his head. "Yes, I've lied to protect you in the past. But I'm not lying now. Going after Mel would get you killed."

"She could be in danger and the trail is growing colder by the second. I'm not going to sacrifice her life for mine."

"I'm asking you to think about it. The Dean knows enough about Ticks to keep moving. He's got a fast car. I'm sure he'll keep driving. But it's you he wants. Not her. She's just a bargaining chip. The smartest thing we can do now is stay safe and hidden. We'll get some rest. Come up with a plan in the morning."

For an instant, Lily's determination faltered. He'd almost convinced her. And then his phone rang.

CHAPTER THIRTY-FOUR

MEL

Ladybird isn't a bird at all. Not even the vulture I thought. Worse than the Ticks, even. Orcas may kill for fun, but at least they eat their prey. They lost their music to disease. He gave his away.

His fear is an ugly sound, a primal screech that I can't hush and nothing, not even my own music, can make it stop.

Dread, like Chopin in B flat, creeps through me and I let it come; even slow notes might block his noise. I always thought death would be silence. Instead, it screams.

CHAPTER THIRTY-FIVE

LILY

Carter was right. I was exhausted. I'd caught only a few hours of sleep the night before. And even though the thought of my sister alone out there scared the hell out of me, everything Carter said made sense.

And on top of that, my head was actually starting to ring from my exhaustion. Just a low, thrumming sound. Like the phantom buzz of a cell phone.

Except, as soon as I heard it, Carter cursed.

His expression shifted from fierce determination to chagrin. Then he propped a foot on one of the benches, pulled up the leg of his jeans, and removed a cell phone from a case strapped to his leg.

Even though I'd seen him use it before, I'd forgotten he had it. That anyone might have access to that kind of technology.

He met my gaze as he listened to whoever was on the other end.

I raised my eyebrows in question.

He just frowned, then he looked away, concentrating on the conversation.

After a minute, he pulled the phone from his ear, covering the mouthpiece, and said the last thing I expected.

"It's for you."

I responded with a very elegant, "Huh?"

"It's the Dean," Carter said, meeting my gaze. "He wants to talk to you."

"Oh." I licked my lips, battling my confusion.

Carter pressed the speakerphone button then held it out to me. I took it, marveling at the feel of it in my hand. It felt strange and foreign, not just because it was bigger than my old cell phone, but because I hadn't held a phone of any kind to my ear in over six months.

"Hello?" I said into the phone, my voice shaking a little. I cringed. This asshole had my sister. I couldn't let him think I was weak.

"Well. Miss Lily Price." His voice was condescending and desperate all at the same time. "You are a young woman everyone seems to want."

"Lucky me."

"Do you have any idea how much trouble your disappearance could cause me?"

"I—" My urge to deny his words was automatic, but I cut myself off. The time to play ignorant was past. It no longer mattered whether or not I had this stupid power everyone claimed I had. Other people believed it. Assholes like this who were willing to use my sister to get to me. It had to stop now. "You better not have hurt my sister, or I will personally hunt you down and tether you out to a post at night."

The Dean gave a nasty sort of chuckle. "You're threatening me. That's cute. You're a seventeen-year-old girl. All alone in a world of scary monsters. No matter what extraordinary powers you might have, you don't have the slightest idea how to use them."

The Dean paused—for dramatic effect, I assumed. When he did, I glanced at Joe and McKenna. Neither looked shocked by the Dean's words. That meant at some point in the past twenty-four hours or so, Carter must have told them he thought I was an *abductura*. And that they must have believed him, which disconcerted me.

I didn't have to consider it for long, because the Dean kept talking. "I can protect you. You need me. But you're threatening me? What are you going to do, beat me up with your schoolbag?"

I could have told him the truth. I could have told him that I wasn't all alone. Whether I liked it or not, I had Carter here. And Sebastian—though I definitely didn't like that. Joe and McKenna had also come to stand nearby, listening to the conversation. Though their first loyalty would always be to each other, they would help me however they could. I believed that now. I also could have told him that I didn't have a schoolbag. I'd accidentally blown it up in the middle of the quad with the same kind of bomb that had taken a chunk out of the science building.

But if this skeezeball wanted to underestimate me, that was fine by me.

"Is my sister unharmed or not?"

"She's fine. But she's not the one I need. You have no idea how valuable you'll be to me."

"What are you doing to do? Sell me to Roberto?"

"Unlike your pet vampire, Roberto isn't the kind of man who buys what he wants. He's the kind who takes it. So, no. I have other plans for you."

I shuddered, instantly deciding I didn't want to know what those plans might be. If he, too, thought I was an *abductura*, he might very well plan on keeping me chained up somewhere just so he could use me like a microphone. The creep.

"If you want me, all you have to do is come and get me." My mind raced with sudden clarity. "You're still on the run. But you can't keep driving all night long. We have sanctuary. You'll be safe here. I'll leave with you in the morning."

"How stupid do you think I am, girl?" he asked with a sneer. "I've seen more of what these things can do than you can imagine. No way am I going out at night. Even though I loaded myself up with progesterone before leaving the Farm, I'm not going to risk it. Not even for you. No, you just sit tight. I'll call back in the morning and tell you where to come meet us. Sunrise is at six fifty-four. I'll want you here no later than thirty minutes after that."

He hung up before I could ask him anything else. I stared at the phone in disgust for a second before handing it back to Carter.

"What did the Dean say to you before you put the call on speakerphone?"

"Not much. He said he had Mel, cursed me and Sebastian a little bit, and then asked to speak to you."

"He didn't say anything that might have told you where he and Mel are?"

"No."

Joe stepped closer. "He said he wasn't going back outside. That implies he's somewhere safe right now."

"He could be in another church," McKenna pointed out.

"Or another Farm."

But Carter shook his head. "No, the Farms are all clustered together to make it easier to supply them. The closest Farm is about five hours away. Even if he really booked it, he wouldn't have made it there by sundown. And no Farm would open its gates at night."

"So they're in a church, right? Carter, is there anywhere other than holy ground humans can seek sanctuary?"

"Not that I know of. If we're going to look for her, we'll need a map of the area and a phone book with a list of the local churches."

"I saw a phone book in one of the cabinets," I said.

Carter fell into step beside me as I left the sanctuary. "I'll look in the office. They might have a map there."

Ten minutes later, we were back in the sanctuary. I'd found a couple of phone books fairly quickly. It took Carter longer to find maps, but eventually he came back with a local one and a state one. We laid them all out on the floor and set lit candles on the corners of the maps.

"Okay," Carter said, uncapping a marker with his teeth and then spitting the lid onto the floor. He marked an *X* on a spot on the state map not far from the Missouri border. "Here's where we had the showdown with the Dean on the highway. Here's where we are now." He put another mark on the map.

I had one of the phone books open on my lap and the other in my hands, thumbing through the churches section. "This is impossible. There are nearly thirty churches in this town alone. I had no idea small towns were this religious."

McKenna lifted an eyebrow. "How long have you lived in the Bible Belt?"

I frowned. She had a point. But knowing there were a lot of churches somewhere and devising a plan to search all of them in the next six hours were two totally different things.

Carter ignored McKenna's comment. "It's not impossible. We just have to put ourselves in the Dean's shoes. He'll keep his car in the parking lot, because he'll want it close. So we don't have to search all of the churches. We just have to drive past them."

Joe used his finger to trace a big circle encompassing the area around where we'd first encountered the Dean. "It was a couple of hours between when he grabbed Mel and when he called us. He could be anywhere within a hundred-and-fifty-mile radius."

"No." Carter tapped the *X* where we were. "He'd want to stay close to Lily. Remember, he's tracking the chips. He knows where we are. He said he'd call us at sunrise and tell us where to meet him. He was going to give us thirty minutes to get there. No way is he going to risk her going out before dawn. That means he's a half hour from here. Maybe less. That makes the radius more like thirty miles."

I blew out a sigh. That was more reasonable, but it would still be a lot of churches. All before morning. With less than a full tank of gas. And if we ran out of gas, we'd all be dead. And then so would Mel.

We spent the next twenty minutes marking the locations of churches on the map. McKenna and I would read out the addresses and Joe and Carter would painstakingly find the streets on the map index and then mark them on the map itself. It wasn't the first time I longed for a computer and an Internet connection, but it was the most desperate. What would have been a simple project on any mapping website was a chore that ate up precious minutes.

And the whole time, my mind raced through a hundred nasty scenarios that all ended with my friends dying in my quest to save Mel. Just a few hours before, I wouldn't have considered Joe and McKenna my friends, but somehow, watching them together now, I could almost forgive Joe for turning me in to the Dean. He'd done it to save his baby. How could I blame him when I knew I'd do the same if Mel's life was on the line?

As for McKenna, I felt queasy just thinking about how I'd treated her. And she wasn't even a Breeder. What did it matter that we never would have been friends in the Before? Somehow, in less than twenty-four hours, it had become impossible to hate either of them. What Carter had said by the roadside that morning was right. We were in this together.

Of course, Carter was a different story. I wasn't sure how I felt about him. But I knew I didn't want him risking his life for me anymore. Not because he thought I was the *abductura* who could save all of humanity and not because he felt compelled to love me.

No, I was the one the Dean wanted. And it was time I started fighting my own battles.

As we marked the last of the churches on the map, I put the phone book aside and said, "I appreciate all the help you've given me so far. But now that it's time to go, I'm going alone."

McKenna just stared at me mutely. Joe and Carter both broke into protest.

"We can't let you do that," Joe said.

"No way." Carter crossed his arms over his chest like he was going to physically stop me from leaving the sanctuary.

"I should go with her," McKenna said quietly.

Joe, Carter, and I all swiveled to look at McKenna. She stood off to the side, one hand rubbing the underside of her belly.

I saw her determination in her face and her absolute fear. I saw what it cost her to suggest it. To even consider it. And it all made me want to weep.

I'd been nothing but horrible to her and she was willing to risk her life to get Mel back. After all the horrible things I'd thought about her. How was it that McKenna was a better person than I?

There was a moment of stunned silence before Joe and Carter protested. My own protestations were caught in the lump of humble pie I was choking on.

McKenna held up a hand to ward them off and said, "The Ticks don't like pregnancy hormones. They should leave me alone, right? So if anyone should go with Lily, it's me. I should be safest."

"No!" Joe all but yelled it. "No way. You're not leaving this church. Not tonight. Not—"

"He's right, McKenna," Carter interrupted, more logically. "We don't know for sure that the Ticks won't go after you. I don't like that they attacked the Collabs today. Either they're hungry or . . . I don't know what."

"I've been thinking about that," McKenna said softly. "The Ticks attacked the Collabs, but not the Dean. Maybe he took their progesterone pills on the drive. Plus, Sebastian fed off that Collab, and didn't he say he didn't like progesterone any more than Ticks did? So the Collabs must not have taken their pills."

Carter looked impressed by her logic. I was, too. Clearly I needed to accept that there was way more to McKenna than I'd thought.

Still, Carter shook his head. "We can't risk it."

McKenna stuck her jaw out at a rebellious tilt. "Then I think we should all go. If we separate now, then who knows when we'll find each other again? The world outside this church is too scary to go it alone. We need to stick together."

Her tone was simple but firm. Joe looked like he wanted to argue. I felt like I wanted to cry. I hadn't wanted to be responsible for any more people. But now they were responsible for me.

I swallowed the lump in my throat and looked up to see Carter watching me.

"What do you say?" he asked.

"I can't ask you—any of you—to risk your lives for Mel."

McKenna's brow furrowed. "Wouldn't you do the same for us?"

Two days ago? No way. Even this morning, probably not. But now . . . yes, I would. Besides, there was a naïveté to the question that sucker-punched the last of my reluctance. Finally I nodded.

"Okay. We stick together."

CHAPTER THIRTY-SIX

LILY

It was five steps from the church door to the van and five steps back. Times six trips to carry all our stuff out and load it into the van. Divided by the three of us who were able to carry heavy loads. Twenty steps.

That might not seem like an eternity, but it was.

Twenty steps with only the van's interior dome light pressing against the darkness. Twenty steps with my ears tuned to every sound. The swoosh of the wind through the trees at the edge of the parking lot. The skittering of some creature's claws on the pavement. The rustle of something moving through the bushes.

Those were all normal sounds. Nighttime sounds. Innocent.

I wasn't afraid until my second trip. I'd just dropped off my load of bags in the back of the van when I noticed it. Silence. I stopped still. Carter, behind me, must have noticed it, too. I felt his hand on my back.

He leaned forward and whispered, "Move slowly. Maybe it's nothing."

But my heart was pounding, because it didn't feel like nothing. I crept forward, not even breathing until I crossed the threshold into the church. I expected Carter to be right behind me. He wasn't.

Joe was on his way out and I held up a hand to stop him.

"What's up?" he asked.

"I don't know. It's too quiet out there." I looked out the window beside the door, searching the darkness for Carter. It didn't take long to spot him. Standing at the back of the van, he held his Maglite at eye level and was shining it out at the tree line. I didn't see whatever spooked him, but a second later, he slammed the van door closed and dashed for the door. I held it open for him, throwing the bolt the second he was inside. A second later, the door shook as the Tick slammed into it.

I jumped back at the sound, nearly tripping over Joe and McKenna. My breath caught in my chest. An instant later, another Tick hit the door. Its misshapen hand thumped the glass. Then it pressed its face to the window.

"Holy crap!" McKenna gasped.

"Turn off the light," I said even as Carter was hitting the switch.

I didn't know how its vision was, but I instinctively didn't want it to have a good view of us. There was another thud on the door. Either a third Tick or one of the first two hitting it again.

"Back to the sanctuary," Carter ordered.

He didn't have to say it twice. He grabbed the last two duffel bags and we piled through the door, to huddle in the center of the room near the pulpit. Carter flicked the Maglite back on. We'd already blown out all the candles.

"What the hell?" Joe asked, wrapping a protective arm around McKenna. "I thought they couldn't come on holy ground."

"It's not that they can't," I reminded him. "It's that they usually don't."

Carter shoved a hand through his hair. "It's probably the chips. Either they followed us here or the blood from the chips attracted the attention of another pack."

"What do we do?" McKenna's voice trembled as she spoke and I didn't need the light to know she was starting to cry.

Carter blew out a sigh. "Just give me a minute to think."

"We can wait, right?" I said. "We just scrap the plan to sneak up on the Dean. We can wait until after dawn to leave."

I thought of Mel, alone with that monster, and had to swallow back my fear. At least she was okay. For now. The Dean might be evil, but he'd do everything in his power to keep himself safe. So that meant she was safe, too. Unless things got really desperate and he fed her to the Ticks to save himself. . . . No, I couldn't let myself think like that.

"Will that work?" McKenna asked, her voice high-pitched with fear.

"Will it?" I repeated, purposely blowing out a breath to calm myself. Not that I believed I was mucking with anyone's emotions. But there was no point in risking it. I found myself wondering if it would be easier to fight my panic if Mel was around. If I was focused on keeping her relaxed, would all the others chill out, too? When we were together, was I calm because I spent so much energy keeping her that way, or was the opposite true? Did I calm her down or did she calm me?

Carter frowned. "Maybe."

"Maybe?" I asked, watching him carefully. "This isn't the time to tiptoe around the truth. If you think it'll work, tell us. If you don't, we'll find another plan."

Carter's silence made my stomach flip over.

"Be honest," I said.

"Dude, if it's the chips that's driving them crazy," Joe interrupted, "can't we just smash the chips?"

We all glanced over to where the four bloody chips sat in the collection bowl on one of the benches.

"I don't know," Carter admitted. "The chips probably attracted them, but now they've caught our scent. If they're hungry, destroying the chips won't make them go away."

And they were probably hungry. He didn't have to say it. We all remembered the Tick eating the Collab out on the highway. If they were hungry enough they were here to stay.

"But they'll leave at dawn, right?" McKenna asked.

"Maybe," Carter said. Then he shook his head. "I don't think we should wait that long. The logical thing would be for me to take the chips and try to draw them away from the rest of you."

"That's not logical!" I protested. "That's insane."

"No. It makes sense. Think about it. That old Impala is sitting in the parking lot. I drive away slowly enough that they chase me. Then the rest of you head for the van and go get Mel."

"No. Absolutely not." I may be pissed as hell at him, but I didn't want him dead.

Carter met my gaze. "If it saves Mel—"

"Mel is fine for now. We still have other options."

"For now—" he started to protest.

"Yes," I said firmly. "Until we're out of options, no one's going out there."

For the first time I actually hoped I was an *abductura*. I desperately wanted to persuade them all to wait. As if in response to my statement, another crash came from the back door, followed by a blood-chilling howl. It sounded way too close.

Panic skittered up my spine. I swallowed it down. "I don't think this church spent enough on insulation."

Carter went to the side door and looked out into the hall. He turned back around and gave his head a little shake to indicate the door was holding. But for how long? Did we even have until morning?

I licked my lips and asked, "How many weapons do we have?"

"You still have your bow and arrows, right?"

"Yeah."

He nodded toward the bags he'd dumped on a bench on the way in. The shotgun he'd taken from Uncle Rodney's was strapped to the outside of one of them. "And I have my pistol. Joe, what do you have?"

"Just my nine-millimeter." Joe stuttered a bit over the word "my." I'd given it to him at Uncle Rodney's even though neither of us could really imagine him using a gun. Joe just didn't seem like the type.

But seeing the protective arm he kept around McKenna, I knew he would try. He would be what she needed him to be.

I swallowed. "We won't need the weapons. We'll wait. Mel will be okay until dawn. That's what the Dean said. We'll wait and see what the Ticks do."

Joe and McKenna both nodded. Carter clenched his jaw, but finally gave a terse nod also.

Then he hefted one side of the nearest bench, testing to see how easy they were to lift. To Joe he said, "Help me move this."

They moved benches in front of each door while the sounds of the Ticks throwing themselves at the doors continued. And spread. They kept up the attacks on the side door and another group started in on the front door. I checked the time on my phone too often. The minutes crawled toward dawn while I counted the thumps the Ticks made against the doors, trying to estimate how many were out there. It was thump-thump-thump on the side door and thump-thump on the front. I guessed five, but knew it was only a guess. Then I heard a sound that made my pulse race. The skittering of nails on glass. Nearby.

I checked the time on my phone again. The sun would be up about seven. It wasn't five yet. Shit.

Only then did I let myself turn toward the floor-to-ceiling stained-glass window at the end of the sanctuary. The screech of nails on glass echoed through the room. McKenna whimpered. I closed my eyes, unable to look at it again.

I couldn't watch, which was why I heard Carter stand up rather than saw him.

"Screw it. I'm not waiting for one of those things to break in here."

"Carter—" I popped up to my feet. I'd lost Mel already tonight. I didn't want to lose him as well. I couldn't.

"Look, I can do this. I can draw them away from the rest of you and you'll have a fighting chance." He dug the keys to the Impala out of his pocket and gave them a little shake.

"No." Joe and I said the word at the same time and it took me a second to realize he'd spoken, too. I turned to see him standing, McKenna's hand in his.

"No, dude. It should be me."

McKenna let loose a sob and buried her face in his shoulder. But she didn't question him or beg him not to go. It was like they'd done that silent communication thing again when I hadn't been looking. I felt another stab of envy for what I didn't have with Carter and for a moment that longing made me miss part of the conversation.

"I have a better chance of making it," Carter was saying.

"Which is why you're the one who should be with McKenna and Lily. Dude, if they're going to make it to Canada, it's going to be with you. You can get them out of this church and to safety. I might could do it, but you definitely can."

Carter was silent, like he wanted to argue.

He shot me a look, but I couldn't read it at all. There seemed to be regret there, but over what?

"Besides," Joe added, "you can cover me on the way to the car. You might actually hit something. If I tried to cover you, I wouldn't hit jack."

Finally, Carter nodded, but it looked like it took all his willpower to make himself do it. Even though I couldn't read his expression, I got the gist of it. It wasn't in his nature to let someone else fall on the sword for him.

But once the decision was made, he morphed back into the Carter I knew. The competent, in-control guy with a plan. I silently thanked God he had one, 'cause I sure as hell didn't.

"Okay, we're going to move fast. The Impala is parked in front, so Joe, you'll go out the main doors. McKenna and Lily, I want you waiting by the back door ready to run for the van on my signal, okay?"

"Okay," I said for both of us, because McKenna was crying too hard to speak for herself.

Carter scooped the chips out of the collection bowl but then stood there, looking around like he didn't know what to do with them.

I reached into the pocket of my hoodie and pulled out the empty Altoids tin and held it out to him.

He met my gaze. For the first time since he'd tried to kiss me. His expression looked so sad it made my heart ache.

Of course he was sad. He was sending Joe out into a night full of Ticks. He was sending a buddy out to his possible death. Joe was right. He was the logical choice, but all the logic in the world wouldn't make this right.

But Joe was volunteering. He was doing it for the woman he loved and the baby he'd made.

What was Carter doing this for?

Me. A girl he'd been forced to care about. Against his nature. Against his will.

Carter took the tin from my hand and poured the chips into it before snapping it closed.

"Keep these close," he told Joe. "If you get out to that car and you can't get it started, you leave the chips in the car and you get your ass back to the church. I'll be covering you the whole time. Drive slow enough to keep them on your tail, but don't let them catch you, you understand?"

Joe nodded, taking the tin like it was a life preserver. Maybe it was. Maybe it was the thing that would preserve the life of his child.

I felt Carter's hand on my elbow and realized numbly that he was guiding me away from Joe and McKenna so they could have a chance to say good-bye. I looked at them only once before letting him lead me away. Joe had dropped to his knees before McKenna. He was speaking to her belly.

I wanted to take it all back. To refuse to let him out of the church. To pretend that the horrible scratching of nails on glass meant nothing. But of course, it meant everything. Holy ground meant nothing to that Tick clawing at the stained-glass window. Just our luck to be attacked by Ticks who must have been atheists in the Before.

So I let Carter guide me over to the door leading out into the side hall.

Once I thought we were out of earshot, I said, "Maybe I should stay with you. I have my bow and arrows. I could provide additional coverage."

He shook his head, his gaze on Joe and McKenna. "No. McKenna's going to need you to calm her down. If you can keep her from freaking out and get her into the van when the time comes, that'll be help enough."

I didn't argue. This was a hell of a time to try out my skills as an *abductura*.

Carter gestured to the bench. "Can you get the other side?"

I rounded the bench and squatted to lift it up. The oak bench was frickin' heavy. With all my strength, I could barely get it a centimeter off the ground. My muscles screamed that I wasn't strong enough to do this. But Carter had thought I was strong enough. And he was on the other side, depending on me to pull my own weight, so I dug deep and lifted. Even while my heart was breaking.

* *

McKenna also was stronger than I'd thought. She let Joe go without a whimper of complaint, but once he was gone, she clenched my hand so tight I could feel my bones rubbing, but I might have clenched back just as hard. Waiting by the church door, we'd heard the concussive blast of Carter's shotgun twice in rapid succession and then twice more. The sound of the ancient Impala's V8 engine roaring to life seemed to meld with the frustrated howls of the Ticks as they gave chase.

Carter yelled for us and as McKenna and I ran those few short steps to the van, I prayed that Impala had a full tank of gas and that Joe would outpace the Ticks. We weren't that far from Canada. Maybe he'd make it there, even if he was traveling alone.

Once Carter, McKenna, and I were in the van, we were quiet except for McKenna's almost silent tears.

Carter drove, and I navigated with the map we'd marked, a penlight, and the telephone books I'd swiped from the church. Two hours and twelve churches later, it felt less like a rescue mission and more like a snipe hunt. Uncle Rodney used to send me and Mel out to hunt for snipes in the woods behind his house whenever we'd visit. We'd spend all day wandering around his property searching for the mysterious creatures. I was ten before I figured out it was just a way to get us out of the house. When I told Mel, she just looked at me like I was an idiot. It was the first time I realized she knew things I didn't.

Was this just a snipe hunt now? Were we just wasting our time, our energy, and our gasoline? Had we sent Joe out to face the Ticks alone for nothing? I was plagued by doubts. We should have waited until dawn. Maybe the Ticks would have found a way in, maybe not. Maybe they would have gotten sleepy and just wandered off on their own. Some logical part of my brain reasoned that Joe had made his own choice and that he'd done what was best for the rest of us. But the part of me that had known him since childhood grieved. And worried. Somehow, his sacrifice only drove home what danger we were all in. This was not some romantic cross-country road trip. We were fleeing for our lives.

What would Mel say if she was here?

We had just passed through another tiny town when Carter asked, "What are you thinking?"

I glanced over at him to see him rubbing his hand over his eyes sleepily. "What? You read minds now?"

He smiled. "You hum softly when you're thinking something through."

"No, I don't," I protested, but suddenly I didn't know if that was true or not. Did I hum? I didn't like having such an obvious tell and liked even less that he'd caught me in it. To distract myself, I answered him. "I was thinking about snipe hunts and wasted time. Joe. And I was wondering what Mel would think of all this driving around."

Carter pushed his feet under him and shifted so he was sitting up straighter. "What would she say?"

I tried to think of nursery rhymes about crossing things off a list. Or about counting, but I was tired and nothing came to mind. I shook my head. "She'd hate that we left him. She'd hate the idea that we'd sacrificed him for her."

Carter dropped his voice. "We had no choice. They would have made it in."

"You don't know that," I protested automatically. It felt like a familiar argument.

But this time, Carter admitted, "You're right. I don't know that. I don't know anything anymore. I thought we would be safe in the church."

He scrubbed his hand down his face again. The second time in only a few minutes.

"How long has it been since you've slept?" I asked. "You looked exhausted."

"I'll sleep when I'm dead."

"That's not funny."

"I didn't mean it to be."

"Carter—"

"This whole screwup is my fault."

"It's not!"

"It is. I was in charge. This was my idea. What could happen to Joe is on my head. If we hadn't agreed to take Joe and McKenna with us, he'd be safely back at the Farm."

"You can't think like that. He made his choice. Yes, he was safe at the Farm, but McKenna wasn't. And neither was their baby. He left for them, not because of anything you did or didn't do."

He drove in silence for a long minute and I could tell my words hadn't offered him much comfort. Finally, he said, "I wish I knew why the damn church didn't work. We can't afford to make that mistake again."

"Did you say the church has to look like a church? Maybe it just wasn't iconic enough."

I offered up the opinion thoughtlessly and didn't even realize he'd registered it until I felt the car slow down. As if dazed, Carter lifted his foot off the gas and the van slid to a halt in the middle of the highway.

"That's it."

"What?"

"The church wasn't *iconic* enough."

"That's what I said." I was starting to feel really stupid. Either he wasn't the only one who was tired or he'd figured out something I was missing entirely.

He put the car in park and turned on the overhead dome light. "Let me see the map." I handed it to him. He immediately unfolded it and started searching the circle I'd first drawn out on the map. "The problem is we've been hitting all these small towns. The churches are all like the ones we got stuck in—built in the middle of the last century. Like you said, those churches aren't iconic enough. Ticks have small brains. They wouldn't recognize the more subtle clues that a building is a church. We need to look in a bigger town, for a church that's been there at least a hundred years. Maybe more."

"Is it really that simple?" For the first time in an hour, I felt hope stirring in my chest. Maybe Joe hadn't risked his life for nothing.

Carter just shrugged. "Maybe. The Dean would know this stuff. And he has good reason to be afraid of the Ticks. He knows what they're capable of. He'd be extra careful."

I leaned over the map, too, and started looking. "Okay, where does that leave us?"

"Well I don't know for sure, but I think we should start here." He jabbed a spot on the map. "Decatur, Illinois. It's an older town and one of the biggest in the area. Champaign is also a possibility, I guess, but my gut says he'll go with something on the road south rather than north. Once he has you, he'll want to head back to Texas."

Since my gut said nothing, I folded the map so the route was visible and said, "Okay, let's go find us a church in Decatur."

CHAPTER THIRTY-SEVEN

MEL

Places have music, too.

Home always sounded like Beethoven's Ninth. School, like skate punk.

Only holy ground is quiet. Completely at peace. I wonder if that's why the Ticks avoid it. Do they hear its silence, too? Are they drawn to it, like I am, or repelled? If they can hear its silence, then what does that make me?

Should I worry that I'm like the Ticks? I long for cool, clear water that blocks out all of Ladybird's screeching and death's screams. I imagine the water. Here, I fold inside myself. Better than math. Better even than blue buttons or pink bubble gum. I find the silence of this place and sink into it. I push all the other noises away.

CHAPTER THIRTY-EIGHT

LILY

It was nearly six in the morning when we finally parked the car half a block away from St. Patrick's Cathedral in downtown Decatur, Illinois. St. Patrick's looks like a church. I mean, it looks like a *church*. It's a massive building made of white limestone with Gothic architecture. It has turrets and steeples and round stained-glass windows over the door so big if it had been a table you could have sat Arthur's knights around it. The church gleamed a ghostly white in the moonlight as it loomed over the surrounding buildings, all of which were aging with less grace than the church. It looked so iconically holy, I had no doubt that this was the place the Dean had picked to hide Mel for the night.

There was only one problem: we weren't positive they were here. Yeah, we could get out and check the building—as we had most of the others—but none of us liked getting out of the van if we didn't have to.

Not for the first time since we started the snipe hunt, I found myself wishing that Sebastian was here with us. The night was dark and silent. There were no signs of Ticks. But there was also no way of knowing they weren't out there. Waiting for us. If Sebastian was here, he would know. But we hadn't seen him since dusk, when he left to . . . do what? Carter wouldn't say. Hunt maybe.

Yesterday, when I'd first seen him devouring that Collab, I'd been so revolted, I didn't want him anywhere near me. Now I was wishing for even the meager security his prescience brought us. Our party of three seemed small and vulnerable.

"Are you sure about this?" McKenna climbed awkwardly from her spot in back to the first bench to ask the question.

"No," Carter admitted. "This could be another dead end. You got any better ideas?"

"Nope."

"Let's go get Mel back," Carter said, cutting the engine. "Everybody clear on the plan?" We'd hashed out the details on the drive here from the last church. We all chimed in with our agreement. McKenna was supposed to stay with the van. I was supposed to go in to distract the Dean. Carter was going to bring up the rear and take the Dean out with the tranq rifle he'd taken from one of the Collabs. A simple plan.

But it wasn't the first simple plan that had gone to hell tonight.

Just as Carter was swinging open the side door, there was the sudden clatter of something large landing on the roof of the van. McKenna screamed. Carter and I gasped. My heart seemed to explode out of my chest.

A second later—before Carter could even close the door—there was another creaking thud as the thing moved over the roof, then Sebastian swung in through the open door.

His countenance was unnerving in the light of the van's dome light. The last time we'd seen him, he'd been covered in human blood. A savage monster. Now he looked like a model in a Lands' End catalog. His dark hair looked freshly washed. Somewhere, he'd gotten new clothes and was now dressed in jeans and plaid button-up shirt. With a belt.

My startled fear morphed into anger. Joe had just driven off to face Ticks alone. Mel had been captured. We were fighting for our lives. And he had time to shower and accessorize?

"You're a little late to the party." He smiled at us, a nasty sort of mischievous grin.

It was the first time I'd seen his open-mouth smile. His vicious canines sent fear shooting through me.

The jumble of emotions fought their way out. "Where did you . . . How . . . ?"

Sebastian reached behind him and closed the door, throwing the van into sudden darkness. I was struck by the insane urge to yell at him.

Carter must have sensed it because he thrust an arm out in front of me. "Sorry we're late," Carter said, a bite in his voice as well. "We had planned on keeping cover until dawn. How did you get here?"

Sebastian smirked, like the answer should be obvious. "I followed them."

"You *followed* them?" I asked. "They drove off before us and when you left us you were still—"

What was the word for the state he'd been in? Yes, he'd been barking orders, like his usual arrogant self, but he'd just eaten a Collab. He'd been covered in human blood. He'd been monstrous.

From the front of the van, I saw McKenna visibly shudder.

But on the heels of that thought was another, equally disturbing thought. If he'd followed them, then how fast could he run?

Almost as if he could read my mind, he said, "I didn't chase them down. I followed their scent. Your sister's scent is unique. And the Dean is one of the few humans around who still eats the flesh of animals. I could track him for miles."

This time, I shuddered. I so had not needed to know that.

"Once I knew they were settled here for the night, I went looking for supplies." He swung a backpack off his shoulder. "I found a fairly well-stocked house nearby. You can thank me later."

Carter unzipped the bag to reveal more canned food. Something inside me ached at the familiar sight of a silver can of peas. Mel would have loved them.

Funny how something I'd yearned for so much just a few days ago, now I didn't even want. Losing my sister had changed everything for me.

I surreptitiously took the peas and tucked then into her backpack beside her squirrel.

Sebastian glanced around the van. "Where's Joe?"

McKenna let out a strangled cry and buried her face in her hands.

"I see. That's unfortunate. We could have used the extra man."

McKenna made another noise from the back. Just now, we needed her to keep it together. The idea flittered across my mind that I might be able to make that happen. I didn't want the power. But if I did have it, then wasn't this precisely the time I should pull it out?

I didn't even know how this would work, really, but I blew out a breath, consciously trying to slow my heartbeat and stay calm. Plus, I figured it wouldn't hurt to change the subject.

"Where are they? Are they in the church?"

"Actually, the Dean and Mel are holed up in the cafeteria of the school that adjoins the church. It's around back."

"Why?" Carter asked. "Why not the church?"

Sebastian gave a shrug. "I can't say for sure. But I suspect he's avoiding the church for the same reason the Ticks do. He is a man who's done unconscionable things. By now I suspect he's lost nearly as much of his humanity as the Ticks have. Walking into that church would terrify him."

"He didn't strike me as particularly religious," I muttered under my breath.

"It is the world's worst villains who believe the strongest. They have the most to fear from divine retribution."

I sat forward. "Enough philosophy. Is Mel safe here? Sacred ground isn't exactly guaranteed sanctuary."

"You are correct. However, they are safe in there. There is not a Tick around for fifty miles who would set foot in that building."

"If you knew they were safe, why didn't you come find us? To tell us that you'd found Mel and the Dean? We've been searching all over five counties. We've been worried sick. We've—"

Sebastian cut me off. "It didn't occur to me to come find you. Actually I assumed you'd found sanctuary and had the good sense to stay there. By the way, your sister is fine. Since you asked."

His voice was chiding. Like I was at fault for not wondering.

"I assumed that, because—" I started to say.

But Carter cut me off with a wave of his hand. "If you two are done bickering, can we discuss how we're going to get Mel back?"

Sebastian quirked an eyebrow. "Obviously the first step is to take this one back to safety." He shot Carter a disapproving glare. "You never should have let her leave sanctuary in the middle of the night."

Carter shrugged. "The Ticks trying to tear down the church doors didn't think we'd found sanctuary. And besides, did you really think I was equipped to talk her out of it? After all, I'm just a defenseless human. She's the—"

"I'm not an *abductura*," I growled, even though I'd just tried using my powers. Everyone ignored me. I cast a sidelong look at McKenna. She was drying her eyes and looking a little more composed.

Sebastian gave a beleaguered sigh. "Never send a boy to do a vampire's job."

"Go ahead. You talk her out of going in there."

I surged forward, as much as I could in the confines of the van. "You're joking? At a time like this? With my sister stuck in there with that slobbering, nasty man, you're joking?"

Carter held me back, his arm solid across my chest. "Calm down. Mel is fine."

"According to him. How do I know his definition of 'fine' doesn't include fava beans and a nice Chianti?"

"Ah, and I was starting to think you had no sense of humor at all." Sebastian smiled again and the sight of his incisors made my stomach lurch. Then he rubbed his hands together in almost gleeful anticipation. "However, she does have a point. We should get to it. Hopefully, we'll be in and out within five minutes and back on the road. Carter, you're with me. You girls stay here and try not to smell too much like food."

"I'm going, too." I spoke before he could even get his hand on the door handle.

"Of course you're not going." Sebastian waved a dismissive hand. "You've done enough damage already."

"I'm the one he wants."

"Exactly. *You're* the one he wants. If you waltz in there, there's nothing stopping him from killing Mel and taking you anyway."

"He told me to come alone. If you and Carter go in, and I'm not there, then there's also nothing stopping him from killing all three of you."

Sebastian laughed at that. Carter looked like he couldn't decide whether to be amused or insulted. "Come on, the Dean? Seriously?"

"Okay," I corrected. "He probably couldn't take out all three of you. But he got Mel to get in the car with him. She's wicked strong when she doesn't want to do something. So that means he's either stronger than he looks or a hell of a lot more wily. Besides—"

"She has a point," Carter conceded.

"Thank you," I said.

At the same time Sebastian said to Carter, "The last thing we need is her in there, out of control and spewing emotions all over the place. Besides, of course you're going to agree with her."

"Here's the deal. Neither of you can make me stay in here. We're wasting time. Carter and I had a plan. You can either use me as a distraction or you can try to leave me here in the van and wait for me to waltz in and screw up whatever plan you think you've got." I gave a shrug that was far more blasé than I felt. "What's it going to be?"

Carter gave Sebastian an I-told-you-so look.

Sebastian glared at me. It was the kind of look that sent adrenaline flooding into your bloodstream. "She better be worth it, because she's a real pain in the ass to deal with otherwise."

I felt a shiver of fear at his words. It was the first time one of them suggested that I might not be worth it. That I might not be an *abductura*. Maybe it shouldn't have bothered me. I didn't want to be an *abductura*, and I didn't believe I had these powers. But their thinking I did had lent me a sort of freedom. I had believed they needed me. And I had no illusions. If Sebastian decided he didn't have an *abductura* he could control, then Mel and I would be on our own. Or worse, we'd be dinner.

CHAPTER THIRTY-NINE

CARTER

The plan was a simple one, as rescue plans go. He and Sebastian would sneak in through the venting in the roof. Lily would wait fifteen minutes for them to get into place and then she'd call the Dean, tell him she was there, and—hopefully—walk in through the front door, therefore providing the distraction Carter and Sebastian needed to grab Mel.

Carter didn't like the idea of sending Lily in alone. But it was the best plan they had. Which was why it pissed him off when Sebastian didn't follow it.

Carter stopped and scanned the back wall of the building. "You said there was a ladder up to the roof."

"True."

"There's no ladder," Carter pointed out.

Sebastian grinned. "It is also true that I haven't spent the night removing all the screws on the ductwork so that we can move quickly through the ventilation system."

Carter fell into step beside Sebastian. "Okay, I'll bite. Why aren't we going in through the ventilation system?"

"Have you ever crawled through ductwork? Nasty business. Besides, I don't like dust. Also, earlier I picked the lock on the back door and going in that way will be much easier."

Carter gritted his teeth. "Let me be more specific. Why did you lie to Lily? Why not tell her the real plan?"

Sebastian paused and turned to look Carter squarely in the eye. "You, my boy, have not been paying attention. She doesn't trust you. She doesn't trust me."

"Not surprising, since we keep lying to her." It was all he could do not to deck Sebastian. In fact, he might have, if he'd thought doing so would cause the vampire even a twinge of pain. "You know, I've worked damn hard over the past couple of hours to convince her that I am trustworthy. Now you've blown it."

Sebastian crossed the rest of the distance to the building's back door. "Not necessarily. You're still trustworthy. I'm the lying jerk."

"You got that right," Carter muttered.

Sebastian swung open the door. "Don't worry. I'll make sure she blames me. And when this is all done and you've saved her sister, she'll throw herself in your arms and you'll be glad you aren't covered in dust."

"Just tell me why."

"Because Mel is not at all happy to be here. In fact, she's damn near catatonic. If you and I are lucky, we will get in and rescue the girl before Lily even sees her. If not, Lily will walk in and see what the Dean has done. Her emotions will be completely out of control. First she will lose it, then you will. I can't even guarantee that my own control won't slip. Is that what you want?"

Sebastian didn't give Carter a chance to answer, but disappeared into the darkened building, leaving Carter no choice but to follow him.

CHAPTER FORTY

LILY

I had every intention of following the plan. Really, I did. But as I approached the building, I could feel the hairs on the back of my neck prickling as trepidation tiptoed up my spine. I tried to dismiss it as nerves, but I knew something was really wrong as soon as I saw the human arm.

The school's front entrance had glass double doors. When I first approached, I thought someone had blocked the doors from the outside by threading a board through the two handles. The nearly full moon was low on the horizen. Even in the dim light of moon, I knew the shape wasn't right.

Part of the arm was covered in the tattered sleeve of a sweatshirt bearing the logo of the school our Farm had once been. The sleeve was from a hoodie identical to the one I wore. It might have been a cheesy Halloween prop, except for the unmistakable smell of rotting flesh.

I stood there for a moment while my mind struggled to process what I saw. I glanced back across the parking lot to where McKenna sat in the van, watching me. The parking lot was large, since the church and its grounds took up an entire city block. She'd parked the car under a pair of sprawling oak trees at the end of the lot, where it wouldn't attract attention.

I don't know why I looked back there, when she couldn't see

the arm from that distance, but somehow it comforted me knowing she was waiting in the van, ready to whisk Mel to safety.

Trying to breathe shallowly, I studied the arm, reasoning it through despite my panic. My brain felt sluggish. Like I was looking at the world through a bowl of Jell-O. Everything was wobbling and dense.

Why was the arm there?

Had Sebastian seen it? He must have. He'd been at St. Patrick's for several hours before we got there. And if Carter was to be believed, Sebastian's sense of smell was phenomenal. If he could scent Ticks from miles away, then surely he'd smelled this. Besides, he'd clearly told me to stay in the van until it was time to come in and provide the distraction. Had he been trying to spare me seeing the arm?

Not that any of it mattered. Not really. Because my sister was on the other side of that door. I could feel her fear pulling me forward. It pressed against the back of my head, drawing me to her, through the Jell-O in my brain. Maybe I'd been right all along or maybe her emotions were just that much stronger than mine. Any calming thoughts I might have sent her way got sucked into the undertow of her panic and were washed out to sea. Despite all my planning and my intentions. I had to get to her. I had to save her. I was the only one who could do it. But I'd have to take the arm out to get to her.

My stomach rebelled, pumping bile into my mouth. I swallowed it back. I didn't have time for puking or squeamishness. Walking closer, I sucked air in through my mouth, but somehow the stench seemed wedged up my nose. I raised my arm to my face and tucked my nose into the crook of my elbow, burying it in the fleece of my hoodie.

I couldn't watch as I did it. I just breathed out through my mouth, closed my eyes over my horrified tears, and reached for the arm. Even though I grabbed the shred of cloth, I could feel the skin slipping against the flesh rotting out beneath it. For one second, I was terrified I'd pull the skin completely off, but I tightened my grip and gave the arm a wiggle, too aware of the moisture seeping through the sleeve.

Finally it pulled free with a sickening squelch. I tossed it as far as I could, then dropped to the ground and wiped my hand on the icy pavement, heedless of the gravel scratching my palm. It barely helped. There was blood and God only knew what else on my skin and it wouldn't come off. I felt like I'd never be clean again. Like I'd never forget the feeling of that arm in my hand. Like the memory would eat at me forever, the way the constant stream of bile seemed to be eating my throat. Death was everywhere. I couldn't escape it.

I pulled my sweatshirt over my head and furiously scrubbed at my hand with the cloth. The bitterly cold air embraced the skin exposed by my few layers of clothes, but I didn't care. My thoughts reordered themselves slowly.

I used the sweatshirt to open the door handles—it was already ruined and I didn't want to risk getting more human juice on me—and then I stepped into the building, where I was met with a wave of panic and a sight so grisly I immediately dropped to my knees and puked up the Ritz crackers and canned beans I'd eaten earlier.

Carter was right. The Ticks weren't the only monsters out there.

CHAPTER FORTY-ONE

CARTER

Carter followed Sebastian through the back door straight into the building's kitchen. Utilitarian stainless counters lined the walls and silent appliances flanked the door. A professional oven on one side and a silent, still refrigerator on the other.

The air was dank and dense with the scent of rotting meat. Like maybe the refrigerator had been full of food when the town fell and it had been slowly decomposing over the past six months. The smell only got stronger as they crept out of the kitchen and down a pitch-black corridor. His stomach flipped over in his belly as bile surged up his throat. The air was thick with the scent of death and decay.

There was something so profoundly wrong about it that everything in him wanted to turn and run. Not only was the scent revolting on a gut-deep level, but it was illogical, too.

The kitchen in the other church smelled musty and unused, but it hadn't smelled like this. Whatever food had been stored in it had long since decayed. The kitchen here had been empty just as long. So it should smell no worse. Furthermore, the smell was stronger away from the kitchen.

Carter reached out a hand in the dark, grabbing only air for a moment before finally seizing the back of Sebastian's shirt.

"Wait." He had to force the word past his growing nausea. He sensed rather than saw when Sebastian stepped closer to him.

"Oh, how sweet. The poor human can't see in the dark and needs someone to hold his hand."

Carter ignored the jab. "What aren't you telling me?"

"I don't know what you mean."

"What's that awful smell? And why didn't you want Lily to come into the building? Even if you thought she'd try to grab Mel and leave, that wouldn't worry you. You'd be able to catch them. Which means you just didn't want her in the building. Why?"

In the darkness, Sebastian gave a beleaguered sighed. "I don't suppose you'd be willing to merely trust my opinion that it would be better if Lily were not around for her sister's rescue."

"No, I won't. What aren't you telling me? What has the Dean done to Mel that you don't want me to see? Is Mel hurt? Is she even still alive?"

"She is . . . still alive."

Carter cursed. "How badly is she hurt?"

"I can't tell. The Dean appears not to have hurt her physically, but . . . psychologically, she seemed unresponsive. Traumatized, if you will."

"Traumatized? By what?"

"The delightful scent you so keenly observed," Sebastian answered in a crisp, elegant accent. "Which, I promise you, smells even more revolting to me. So if you wouldn't mind, I'd like to proceed so we can leave as quickly as possible."

The tone of Sebastian's voice set Carter's nerves on edge. The vampire's diction got more and more proper the closer he was to losing control. It was his one tell.

"Give me the sitrep, so I'll know what to expect. Do it fast so we can get in and out quickly."

Again, Sebastian sighed. "Fine. You were dead-on about the Ticks not recognizing the cultural significance of all churchs. Sacred ground or not, it's not always identifiable enough for their tiny brains. But apparently the Dean knew that was a possibility. He brought along insurance."

"Insurance?"

"There is one thing that will absolutely ward off Ticks. Always."

"What is it?"

"As it happens, it works fairly well for humans and vampires as well."

Before Carter could demand more answers, they turned the corner into another hallway. The stench made the air feel thick with death. A row of windows near the ceiling cast wan beams of moonlight across the floor. Suddenly he could see the source of the smell. A trail of body parts littered the ground. Arms and legs mostly. His stomach rolled over as he fought against his nausea.

Sebastian's quiet voice broke through his battered senses. "Every predator alive is repulsed by the scent of its food rotting. A corpse more than a day or two old will ward off all but the hungriest of Ticks. Luckily humans and vampires can reason their way past their fear."

Carter let out a shuddering breath. "Lucky us."

Before he could say anything else, he was hit in the chest by a wall of fear so strong it nearly knocked him on his ass. From one breath to the next, he went from that eerie state of adrenaline-fueled calm to pure gut-wrenching panic. Sweat sprang from his every pore. The adrenaline in his veins turned against him, making his muscles shake. Every instinct he had screamed at him to flee.

Only Sebastian's hand gripping his shoulder kept him pinned in place. Even then, if he'd had any way of shaking him off and bolting, Carter would have.

Sebastian himself had gone unnaturally pale in the single ray of moonlight. His pupils had shifted from their normal round human form to creepy, scalloped vertical slits. But his expression lacked the deadly calm Carter had seen so many times before a battle. Even the vampire looked shaken.

The supernaturally strong hand on his shoulder tightened. "You must regain your control."

Carter nodded. Some tiny seed of his logical mind agreed one hundred percent. But that chunk of brain was a second away from abdicating.

They had to do this now. While he still had some control. Mel needed to be rescued and she had to be right on the other side of the door. And they were already too late. His overwhelming emotional reaction could mean only one thing. Lily had beat them to it.

CHAPTER FORTY-TWO

LILY

Only one thing kept me from losing it completely in the following minutes: I was nearly there. I'd have Mel back soon.

The doors to the school led into a foyer with a hall branching off in either direction. Just inside the door, I took the bow and quiver off and set them down. I couldn't bring them any farther for fear the Dean would see them and freak out. I only had four arrows anyway and didn't want to waste them on the Dean. I pulled the heavy Maglite from my back pocket and turned it on. I kept my shiv tucked through the loop in the back of my jeans. I could get it quickly if I needed it.

There was a storage closet off to the left and the door had been opened; all the sacramentals for a Catholic mass spilled out of the closet onto the ground. I couldn't tell if someone else had pillaged the church months ago, or if the Dean had done so when he'd first arrived.

I walked past the discarded implements of a faith I didn't practice and tried not to think it was a sign of bad things to come. If God hadn't protected this church and its holy regalia, then what hope did I have that he would protect my sister? But maybe that was what Joe had meant earlier about human choice. It was my choice to protect my sister, just as it had been his to protect McKenna.

Pushing aside the thought, I crossed the foyer and found the doors to the cafeteria that Sebastian had described. The second I walked into the room, I caught sight of Mel. Alive.

The room was empty except for Mel and the Dean. Mel's back was to the east wall, her gaze blank and unfocused. She wasn't rocking or stimming. I couldn't blame her. If the lack of movement allowed her to retreat into her own mind, then she was the lucky one. But she was still humming. This nursery rhyme I knew instantly. *Little Bo Peep has lost her sheep and doesn't know where to find them.*

Everything else in the room was so horrific, I couldn't look at it long. Five or six kerosene lanterns lay spread out in a half circle around where she sat and the Dean paced in front of her. Between each lantern sat a human head. Legs made up the second ring, one for each lantern and each head. The result looked vaguely like a mosaic of the sun, with the legs as the beams and Mel at its center.

The Dean paced between me and Mel, weaving his way between the heads and lanterns as if barely aware that one was a life taken and the other a risk. He tugged at his hair as he walked, intermittently rubbing at his eyes and muttering to himself. He wasn't looking where he was going. If he accidentally kicked one of the lanterns, the room could catch fire. But maybe he was too far gone to notice. Maybe he didn't care. Whatever madness gripped him, he was no longer the greasy, controlling man I'd seen in the admin building or even the one I'd spoken to on the phone just hours earlier.

I noted this all quickly. It only added to the terror pumping through my veins. I had to get out of here. To flee. I might have even done it, but my feet felt cemented to the ground. Beneath my fear, I felt a great surge of shame. Mel was trapped here, had been here for hours. I wanted so desperately to get her back to safety, yet still I had the urge to bolt. It took unimaginable will to keep from fleeing the room. My legs shook with the effort, but I made myself stay.

"Mel," I gasped out through trembling lips.

Both the Dean and Mel jerked in my direction as if neither had noticed my entrance, though I hadn't been quiet coming in the front door at all.

Mel broke off midtune, relief pouring off her. Hope. And something else as well. Shame maybe. In that moment, Mel, who was such a mystery, even to me who should know her best, was as crystal clear as a high-def CD.

She was embarrassed that she'd let herself get caught by him. Ashamed that she couldn't do more to save herself. Ashamed of her fear.

I wanted nothing so much as to run across the room to her and wrap her in my arms. For once she might have let me. She started to stand, but the Dean stepped in front of her.

"You came," he whispered. Then again, louder, "You came." He let out a laugh, shaking one finger in my direction. "You're a tricky girl. Early. But you came. I knew you would and you did."

I barely spared him a glance, but held out a hand to Mel. "Come here, Mel."

Mel moved to step around him, but he spun on her, surprisingly fast for such a rotund man. He grabbed her hair and tugged hard. Mel let out a screech of pain, stumbling toward him. Her body fell against his. She tried to push herself away, but his grip on her hair must have been too strong.

He stepped closer to me, dragging her along beside him. "Oh, no. Oh, no, you don't. You don't get to have her. Not yet. Not until I have you."

Mel kicked out at him ineffectually and he jerked her off the ground, her feet kicking out as she tried to regain her balance. One of the kerosene lanterns tipped over. Her foot inadvertently snuffed the flame, but the fuel glugged out onto the ground.

"Let her go!" I screamed, stumbling forward myself.

He ignored me, dragging Mel closer. "Stop right there!"

"Please," I begged. "Let her go. I'm here. Just like you asked."

"You came alone?" he demanded.

"I did." But as I spoke, my gaze flickered to the ground, to the rapidly spreading kerosene shining across the floor.

"What kind of a fool do you think I am?" He pulled Mel closer with one hand and with the other whipped a gun out from his waistband.

He forced Mel in front of him. Her foot landed on one of the legs and she slipped going down onto her knees, the extra leg trapped beneath her own. A high, keening sound pulled from her throat. The Dean never released his hold on her hair. Her neck strained backward, exposing her throat, and he wedged the nose of the gun into her jaw.

I whimpered as if it was my own neck. "I don't—" I had to shove the words out past my mingled fear and disgust. "—think you're a fool."

"It's a trick, isn't it? You didn't come alone. You brought him, didn't you?"

"I didn't!" My voice quavered and I prayed he couldn't hear the lie.

"You couldn't have made it here on your own. You didn't even call first. And you didn't throw up. You must have known. You must know about the Tick-proofing."

I had no idea what he was talking about and I shook my head mutely, but he didn't notice.

"Didn't you know that's what the bodies are for?"

"What? What are they for?" I asked. I looked from him to Mel, hoping for some sign . . . something, anything that would make this make sense.

Mel met my gaze. Her head was twisted to the side by the Dean's hold on her, but the panic seemed to have faded a bit. Or maybe shock had taken her, I couldn't tell which. But suddenly I knew I wasn't going to let this bastard win. He'd tortured my sister and I was going to bring him down.

"Did you even consider that's why I do it? It's a trick I learned from the Order of the Dragon. It's the only thing that really repels them. You didn't know that, did you? The scent of rotting humans repulses them even more than it does us. It terrifies them. Did you think I kept Greens tethered outside the fences because I'm a sadistic bastard?"

As he talked, I slipped a hand behind me, reaching for the shiv I'd wedged into the back of my pants.

He seemed to be waiting for me to speak, so I did. "I didn't—"

But then he cut me off immediately. "That's not who I am! That's not why I do these things! I'm protecting you all. The Ticks feed off the fresh blood, but as soon as the bodies start to rot, they leave. They stay away. It's the only thing that keeps them away!"

My hand tightened on the shiv. "You're sick."

Anger flickered across his face, but before the Dean could answer, there was a crash from the back of the room.

The Dean pushed Mel away from him and grabbed me, just as I was reaching for the shiv. Mel went sprawling across the floor in a tangle of too many legs. She knocked over two more of the kerosene lanterns. One flickered out, but the other stayed lit, its flame dancing across the fuel as it spilled.

The Dean pulled me to him, turning me so my back was

against his chest. One arm snaked around my neck; the other pinned my right arm to my side. The Maglite clattered to the ground as he jammed the pistol into my ribs just under my breast.

The flashlight spun across the floor, casting an odd arch of light around the room, like a pinwheel firework. I saw still shots from throughout the room: Mel sprawled on the floor, the flames spreading across the surface of the kerosene, a pair of legs standing in a dark corner of the room.

I didn't know who was there. Carter? Sebastian? Someone else?

The Dean had pulled me so our backs were to the front door now. Only three of the six lanterns were still lit, but fire spreading across the floor cast wild, flickering light into the shadows at the end of the hall, where shapes shifted and moved. Human speed? Or Tick speed? My muddled brain couldn't tell.

"You stupid bitch." Panic made the Dean's voice shake. "You lured me away from the body parts. You didn't bring in the arm, did you? Now we have nothing."

He tried to drag me back a step, but he hit the doors. I could hear the clicking of the door latch, but it stuck and he couldn't get out. He was taller than I'd thought and when his arm tightened on my neck, I struggled to pull air into my lungs. Even arching up onto my toes, black spots popped before my eyes.

I could feel him twitching behind me, as he looked about the room, turning from one corner to the other, spinning us both around.

Where were Sebastian and Carter? I cursed the fact that I'd come in early. I hadn't trusted Sebastian's motives, hadn't believed that he'd be able to get her out. But now she and I were in here alone. Still, I couldn't afford not to take advantage of our captor's momentary distraction. Not when flames were spreading across the floor.

I reached my left hand up, trying to gain purchase on his face, but though my nails scratched skin, he only yanked me farther off the ground. The gun rammed harder into my side. Oh, God, he was either going to shoot me or strangle me.

I arched to the side, trying to get away from the gun and free my windpipe at the same time. Something sharp and cold scraped the left side of my waist.

The shiv! In my panic, I'd forgotten I had it.

I dropped my hand, fumbling under my shirt. My sweat-drenched palm slipped on the handle. The black spots on my vision burst into stars as I yanked the shiv free of my belt loop. I heard the fabric of my shirt rip. I only had one shot at this. I hopped up, trying to loosen his grasp on my neck enough to suck in more air. I slammed one arm toward the gun, trying to knock it away from my ribs, and jabbed the shiv blindly toward his head.

I felt the pressure of the gun leave my ribs just a second before it fired. The roar of the gun almost blocked out his scream as the shiv connected with his face. I felt it sink into his skin. Felt the blade meet fleshy resistance and bone. Everything in me recoiled from the feeling, but I forced myself not to let go of the shiv. I pulled it free and dropped to the ground, landing hard on my butt.

His screams continued, seeming to blend with someone else's screams, maybe my own as air rushed back into my lungs. My head spun.

I tried to get my feet back under me, but the floor was too slick, my muscles were trembling, and my head spun. From somewhere over me, I heard a gun go off. Four shots in rapid succession. I waited for pain to bloom all over, but the aches in my body stayed the same: air-starved lungs, bruised butt, strained back and neck muscles. No gunshot wound.

I shook my head, trying to clear it. The air I pulled into my lungs was thick with smoke. The fire was spreading. The screaming continued. Mel.

Oh, God, Mel. Had the Dean shot her? Had that been the four—or was it five?—shots I'd heard? If he'd shot her, why hadn't he tried to grab me again?

Time had slowed to a crawl, but no more than a few seconds had passed. My ears still rang with the boom of close-quarters gunfire. Finally I got my hands and knees under me. I looked around the room, which was suddenly brighter from the spreading fire. The Dean lay sprawled in front of me; a horrible gash split open his cheek, but that wasn't what had killed him. He'd taken three shots to the chest and another to the forehead, and each was oozing blood that looked black in the light of the fire. Carter stood above him, the Dean's pistol in his hand.

Shaking, I sagged to the floor. Carter slowly lowered the gun to his side. For a second, he stood there over the Dean's body, just staring at it. Then he slipped the gun into the back of his waistband and turned to me.

He knelt down beside me, running a careful hand over my hair and face as if looking for wounds. "Are you okay?"

I nodded, my hand at my throat. I wasn't sure I could talk past my crushed windpipe and through the smoke.

"I was so afraid I wouldn't get to you in time. He had the gun on you." He pulled me against him, pressing his lips to mine in a quick, fierce kiss. "I thought I'd lost you."

I croaked out a single word. "Mel?"

"She's with Sebastian." Carter helped me stand, one hand at

my elbow, the other around my waist. "We've got to get you both out of here."

I glanced around the room. The fire was spreading rapidly. Then I saw Mel on the ground with Sebastian crouching over her.

"What happened?"

"The Dean's stray shot caught her in the leg. Sebastian's bandaging it now."

"Sebastian?" Panic shoved down the aches that had kept me immobile. "Sebastian, the vampire, is bandaging her?"

Mel was bleeding. I'd seen Sebastian with the bloody Collab. He hadn't been able to control himself. He'd devoured the Collab in his bloodlust. He'd do the same with Mel.

I shoved Carter away and stumbled across the room. My legs wobbled under me, but I pushed forward, through the smoke. A few steps from her, I slipped on the fuel-slick floor and crawled the rest of the way to her still form.

He was bent over her leg and, in the half-light, I couldn't see what he was doing. Ticks drank blood straight from the heart, but maybe vampires were different. Maybe they ate from the femoral artery.

Mel lay faceup on the floor. Her eyes were open, her breathing shallow, like she'd gone into shock. But she was still breathing and when I leaned over her, she turned her head to me and looked me right in the eye.

Her face was pale, her lips cracked and dry. She opened her mouth like she wanted to speak, but no words came out.

Muscles trembling, I clasped her arm briefly before looking down the length of her body at Sebastian. I was weakened, beaten. If he was feeding off her, I wouldn't be able to stop him. Not when he was so much stronger than I was.

He'd ripped off the entire left leg of her jeans, but he wasn't feeding. His shirt was off. He was wrapping the flannel around her leg. Only then did I notice that he looked unnaturally pale, even for him. His hands shook as he knotted the fabric.

He sat back on his heels, blowing out a strained breath. "It was just a graze. Went straight through. She didn't even lose much blood, but she was in shock even before he shot her." His lips were pressed thin, the skin of his face taut with tension. He hadn't fed off my sister, but it had cost him. Sebastian looked around the room. "We should leave. The fire's spreading."

With an effortless movement, he picked Mel up and stood. He held her as easily as he would a child as he sprinted toward the door.

Carter helped me stand and we stumbled after them. I couldn't wait to get out of this building. Away from the hell of death and torture.

Sebastian kicked open the door, but stopped on the other side. Carter and I came up behind him. At our back, the flames devoured the building, filling the night with the smell of roasted rotting meat. There was a creaking crash as part of the ceiling fell in. Smoke billowed out into the night air around us.

"Let's go!" Carter shouted, elbowing us past Sebastian's form. Then he stopped dead still as we saw why Sebastian had stopped.

Ticks.

A swarm of them had descended while we were in the building. They fanned out around the building maybe fifteen feet away as if held back by an invisible bubble. My eyes scanned the line of Ticks, automatically counting them up as I did. Ten. Fifteen. I stopped counting at twenty.

"Where the hell is McKenna with the van?" Carter shouted the question I had.

"I think we can assume," Sebastian said, his tone just as crisp as always, "that she felt Lily's panic and left without us."

I didn't point out that if McKenna had been out in the van by herself, surrounded by twenty Ticks, she wouldn't have needed to feel my panic. Her own would probably be more than enough.

I sympathized, but her desertion had completely screwed us. The van was gone. The building was on fire. We had no sanctuary and no way to escape.

CHAPTER FORTY-THREE

LILY

The horde of Ticks surged forward, but only a step or two. Then they tensed and stopped. Like dogs kept in the yard by an electric fence. They were testing the boundaries.

I'd never seen so many Ticks, certainly not this close. They all seemed about the same age—somewhere in their twenties or thirties. Carter had said that when vampire venom turned someone, it brought certain human characteristics back to the baseline. Perhaps age was one of those characteristics. Or maybe they'd just already killed off the young and the weak among them.

Despite the similarity in apparent age, there seemed to be much variety among them. They only vaguely resembled the humans they had once been. As though an artist had carved humans out of clay with a delicate hand and then a clumsy child had come along afterward and smashed them. Their frames were too bulky and broad, their arms disproportionate, but it was their faces that churned my stomach. The almost human quality to their features. Their eyes darting fervently under hair that was shaggy and unkempt. Their heavy jaws and bulging leonine teeth.

And then the one in the center tipped his head back and howled. It was the howl of a wild dog talking to his pack and the pack answered in a series of yips and yowls, a frenetic cacophony of hunger.

Instinctively, we all stepped closer to one another.

Only the sight of the church burning behind us held them at bay. It might scare the hell out of them, but it wouldn't be long before hunger overcame fear. They feared fire, as most wild animals did, which would be great if the heat coming off the building in waves wasn't about to roast us whole.

"Okay," Carter said, "anybody have any ideas?"

"My bow is right there." I pointed to the corner beside the door where I'd propped it before entering the building.

Carter turned, looking for it. He grabbed the bow and quiver of arrows and handed them to me. "That's, what, four arrows? I should have five bullets left in the pistol, which might slow them down if we get close enough. Any other ideas?"

We both looked to Sebastian. Who had vanished.

Mel now stood shakily where he'd been moments before. Behind her, the door to the church stood ajar. I looked back at Carter. "What the hell? He left?"

Carter's jaw tightened as he checked the clip in the pistol. "Frickin' vampires. If I make it out of this, I'm going to hunt him down and stake the bastard."

I gave a snort of derision as I looked out at the teeming mass of Ticks. "Yeah. I'm sure he's terrified."

The line of Ticks seemed to surge and wane in turns. They'd creep forward and then fall back again. None of them were brave enough to venture too close to the fire. Of course, they didn't have to. Behind us, the building was ablaze. The heat at our backs was almost unbearable. I could practically feel the hair on the back of my head singeing. I remembered the feeling from camping trips as a kid, when I'd sit too close to the fire while roasting marshmallows. I always had the sense to retreat before getting truly burned. We stopped going camping when Mom realized Mel didn't register the heat the same way. It wasn't a bad memory, though, as memories went. For my last one, I mean.

I skirted around Carter and went to stand by Mel. She hopped closer, standing on her one good leg, bracing a hand on the wall beside the door. She stared out at the Ticks, her head tilted to the side, and with her free hand she tapped her ring finger against her thumb. In some weird way, her stimming soothed me.

I don't think any of us expected it to end like this, but she was calm and that let me be calm, too. We were together, at least. I reached out a hand and brushed the back of her head, lightly, so maybe she wouldn't feel it. I didn't think I could bear to have her flinch away just then.

I felt Carter's hand on my shoulder. He was right behind me, solid and real. I leaned my head back against him and felt his breath ripple my hair.

"Dawn isn't far off," I said hopefully. "Do you think any of them will lose interest and go back to their nest at sunrise?"

"No. Not when there's fresh food around." He gave my shoulder a squeeze. "I have the five bullets. I could make our deaths fast."

But I shook my head. "No. We go down fighting. We take as many as we can with us." I looked over my shoulder at him and met his eyes. And I knew in that moment exactly what he was thinking. "Agreed?"

His mouth twisted into a grin. "Abso-freakin'-lutely."

What a fabulous guy. This crazy, brave, fearless guy who would face down Ticks at my side. Who would fight even when there was no hope of winning. How had I ever deserved a guy like this?

"Carter, I—"

Before I could choke out a confession, the door to the church swung open and Sebastian burst out. He held the massive stone altar propped on one shoulder, carrying it like it was a forty-pound bag of dog food. His other arm was full of . . . stuff. A processional cross, the bishop's crook, an incense burner. All the sacramental trappings I'd seen on my way into the church. He dropped it all at our feet, then swung the stone altar over his shoulder and set it down as well.

"Sorry to interrupt such a tender moment." He gave one of those ingratiating smirks of his. "I checked the back to see if there was any path through the building. The fire's spread too fast. You'd never make it out if we went that way. I brought anything we could use as a weapon."

Only then did I notice the singed smell in the air and smoldering of his clothes. He must have run through the entire building looking for a way through. Even as fast as he could move, the fire had burned him.

"But you could make it," I said. "You could take Mel. If you carried her, you could make it out the back."

He gave a snort. "Maybe. But it's you I'm not going to leave behind."

I thought then about telling them my theory about Mel being an *abductura*, but knew he wouldn't believe me. Instead, I nodded out at the Ticks, where they still stood, waiting as patiently as they could for the heat to drive us away from the burning building.

"You could carry us all out away from the Ticks. If you could carry the stone altar, all three of us would be nothing."

He chucked my chin gently. "You forget, they're as fast as I am. And they aren't carrying three humans. If we fight, we fight here."

As if to make his point, he once again picked up the stone altar and stepped out away from the burning building. He lugged the thing over his head and threw it right at the Ticks. It landed on a pair of Ticks with a thundering crash that literally shook the ground beneath my feet. The Ticks nearby yelped and skittered away. I saw at least one turn and flee into the distance.

Three down. We were still pathetically outnumbered, but with Sebastian at our side, at least we had a shot.

Sebastian didn't give the Ticks a chance to regroup, but blurred into motion, throwing himself into the line of them. I heard a savage crunch accompanied by movement too fast for me to see. Then a Tick dropped to the ground.

Okay, maybe we weren't totally and completely screwed. I dropped to the ground and started digging through the collection of sacramental paraphernalia. I wanted Mel to have something, too.

Carter grabbed a large wooden cross and began smashing it to shards.

"This feels wrong," I muttered, grabbing a vestment.

"I think the church or whatever will forgive us. If religion can't come down on the side of killing monsters, then what is it good for, right?"

The incense burner hung from a chain at the end of a heavily wrought pole. I wrapped the vestment twice around the incense burner, then knotted it. Standing, I held the burner out to the flames licking up the side of the building until the vestment caught.

Then I went to Mel's side. She stood staring out at the swarm of Ticks, watching the blur that was Sebastian fighting them. In the half darkness, I couldn't tell what was happening out there. The field of battle—there was no mistaking it for anything else—seemed to have been divided in half by the great stone altar he'd thrown into the line of Ticks. On one side, they were fighting Sebastian. One smart vampire against at least ten stupid Ticks. The Ticks that weren't engaged with him were growing restless, moving closer and closer to us.

I pressed the metal pole into Mel's hand. Alarmed, she thrust it away from herself, the flaming incense burner swinging wildly from the end.

"Mel, look at me." I hooked a finger and waved it in front of her face. She turned her gaze to me. "You stay close to me," I told her. "Unless I go down, and then you run. Got it?"

I didn't give her a chance to answer. I was one "Mary had a little lamb" away from losing it. I picked up my bow and notched an arrow.

CHAPTER FORTY-FOUR

LILY

I'd never fought in a battle before. Hell, in the Before, I hadn't even fought in a girl fight between classes. I wasn't the type. I didn't even like to play Call of Duty. Nothing I had done had prepared me for this.

Carter, Mel, and I edged away from the building back to back to back, in a tight triangle formation with Mel bringing up the rear, swinging her incense burner. Carter had his gun and an armful of wooden stakes improvised from the cross and I had my bow and arrows. Arguably, I was the best armed to take out the Ticks. But my bow and arrow skills were rusty and I couldn't risk shooting from too far away. Girl Scout camp was a distant memory and the bow felt clumsy in my hands. I wished suddenly that I'd taken the time to practice shooting back at Uncle Rodney's, but I hadn't wanted to risk damaging an arrow. With only four, I had to make every one of them count.

We were ready for the fight, but the Ticks weren't ready to rush us.

The Ticks weren't human. They weren't there to fight to the death. They were pack animals looking for a meal. We confused them and I could see it in their wild eyes. Any one of them was more than willing to fall back and let his or her fellow Ticks bite the dust if it meant living to eat what was left after the other Ticks had fallen.

So they edged closer to us, but none was willing to attack. Together, Mel, Carter, and I stalked farther away from the church, away from the blazing fire of what had been our last sanctuary. We had nowhere else to go. We, too, were just biding our time. Waiting for one of the Ticks to lose patience and rush us.

Finally it happened.

A Tick threw himself toward us. I saw him leap and I let loose the arrow, praying for accuracy. Another yelp. I must have hit his heart, because he fell to the ground, his body twisting grotesquely. The arrow protruded from his chest and his hands clawed at the shaft. To my left, I saw the red-hot blur of Mel swinging her incense burner. A Tick charged my unprotected flank. This one came in low, keeping his body close to the ground. I pulled another arrow from the quiver but didn't have time to notch it or let it loose. Instead I slammed it into his back as he reared up to pounce on me.

I reached for another arrow even as his blood spewed out of the wound. My palm was slick with sweat or maybe blood and the shaft slipped through my hand. I heard the thump of Mel beating off another Tick. The smell of burning flesh filled my nose. To my right I heard the sickening squelch of Carter staking one of the Ticks, followed by the thud of a Tick hitting the ground.

We'd gotten three. There were nine still out there, maybe a few less if Mel's fire had scared them off. Maybe more if any slipped by Sebastian or if they realized the meal was over here.

I didn't have time to think about it because another Tick was coming at me. I notched the arrow and let it loose. The Tick fell to the ground, but another was right behind it. My last arrow was gone.

Beside me I heard Carter stake another one. A second later, another Tick was flying through the air at me. I parried with the bow. She slammed against the wood, knocking me to the ground. My arms buckled, but I struggled to keep the thing off me. I shouldn't have been strong enough to support its weight over me, but somehow I found the strength. Even with the bow between us, the thing had longer arms than I did. She reached past the bow, straight for my heart. Then there was a flash of light beside her head, the roar of gunfire as Carter pressed the gun to her skull and fired. Her dead weight landed on me, crushing me. I rolled the body off me.

From all around, I heard yelps and yips, the sounds of Ticks being fought off or retreating. I pushed my elbows under me, struggling to get up. My bow was trapped under the body of the Tick. I was out of arrows. I was defenseless. Flashes of light caught my eye as Mel swung the incense burner. Carter was beside me, arm raised, his last stake in hand.

Straight ahead were three more Ticks. They dropped to all fours and charged us all at once. Their long strides ate up the distance between us and them.

Mel's incense burner had stopped swinging. Even the sounds of Sebastian's battle had died out. We'd fought off or killed all but the last three.

Then I heard the roar of an engine. The squealing of tires.

I was sure I must be imagining it. McKenna was gone. We had no vehicle. But then, headlights arced through the darkness. The van was barreling through the parking lot, straight at the Ticks. Would she get there in time?

She mowed down the first two, the force of the van's impact flinging them up into the air. I heard their distressed yelps, the crunch and thud of breaking bones. She swerved to ram the third as it dodged out of her way. The bumper clipped its shoulder. With a yelp it dashed in the other direction. The van careened to a stop right in front of me.

The driver's door flew open and McKenna stumbled out. Pale and wide-eyed, she surveyed the scene. Tears streaked her face and her chest rose and fell rapidly, like she was about to start hyperventilating. Her eyes darted around the parking lot, searching for Ticks.

"I'm so sorry," she gasped. "I don't know what happened. I was waiting for you. I swear I was. Then I heard the Ticks in the distance and I panicked. I kept thinking about—" She broke off, but it was a sentence she didn't need to finish. She kept thinking about Joe. "I just took off. I don't why. I—"

"It's okay." I pushed myself up on my elbows. "You came back."

"Once I got away from here, my mind cleared. I knew I had to come back." Her voice broke. "Joe wouldn't have wanted—"

"I know."

She reached out a hand to help me to my feet. I took it.

My body ached as I stood. My eyes scanned the parking lot. At my side, Carter was helping Mel to her feet. Across the parking lot, I glimpsed Sebastian, slowly rising from the ground. A corpse lay at his feet. His movements were slow and laborious, like it strained his every cell to stand again. I knew how he felt, even though the pile of dead Ticks at my feet was considerably smaller.

Somehow, miraculously, we were all still alive.

In the far distance, I heard the howling of a Tick. Then another. But they were far away. We had time to regroup and get in the van. Besides, the sun was starting to peek over the horizon. It was over.

"Carter, get Mel into the van," I said.

"Yeah, I'm on it," he grumbled, but his smile was wry. "Get yourself in the van. I want to get out of here."

Sebastian hobbled across the parking lot. His supernatural glamour had faded. He looked as exhausted as the rest of us. With barely a glance at us, he rounded the van and climbed into the back.

McKenna stumbled forward to slip an arm under Mel's shoulder. She and Carter helped Mel around the nose of the van. I was about to follow when I turned back and surveyed the wreckage one last time. Just a few feet away, the body of that last Tick lay, the whole side of her head blown off. My bow lay under her. I could see its tip sticking out. It had served me well and I didn't know if I'd ever find another one. I could make more arrows if I needed to, but I wouldn't have a clue how to make a bow.

Cautiously, I walked back over to the dead Tick. She looked really dead. Still, I kicked her first, leaping back out of the way in case she stirred. Her sightless eyes stared up at the sky, looking eerily human in death. Convinced she was dead, I crouched beside her and grabbed the tip of the bow. She was heavier than she looked and I had to sit beside her corpse, pushing against her with my feet, to pry it out from under her. I had just pulled it free when a Tick—maybe the one McKenna had clipped, maybe a different one, I couldn't tell—came bounding over the body and knocked me to the ground.

Every thump of my heartbeat lasted an eternity. My head snapped back and slammed into the pavement. Her pawlike hand was on my throat, cutting off my air and keeping me from screaming. I gaped in surprise up at the face of my attacker. Another female. Her hair was matted into long dreads; her eyes seemed to bulge out of their sockets. She opened her mouth, baring her teeth at me. Her jaw opened impossibly wide and it stretched her lips taut over the canines already too big to be held within her mouth. A thread of drool pooled on her bottom lip and began to drip down. Her mouth was easily big enough that she could have taken my neck between her teeth and snapped it like a dog shaking a chew toy. But that wasn't how Ticks drank their food. I'd known this for months. Ever since the first footage of Ticks showed up on the Internet—the kill shots being too violent for network news or even cable stations. I'd seen the footage. I knew what would happen next, but some part of me had never believed that it would actually happen to me. That this was how I would go.

It seemed so unfair that it would happen now. When I'd fought so hard to survive. When we'd nearly won.

Then the Tick arched her back and drew her arms over her head. Her hands were clasped. She was ready to slam them down onto my chest and crack me open like a clam.

I was as good as dead. Sebastian was the only one who might have been able to reach me in time, but he was already in the van. I couldn't watch, but turned my head toward the others. I didn't want the last face I saw to be the face of insentient violence. I wanted it to be a face of love.

I saw McKenna, someone from the Before I would have never considered a friend. Now she had saved my life—almost. I saw Carter. How could anyone have come to mean so much to me in just a few days? He was running toward me, but I knew he wouldn't make it in time. My gaze sought Mel. For me, hers was the face of love I was looking for. My sister. My other half. For so much of my life, she'd seemed like the less perfect version of me. In this moment, the opposite was true. All of my good qualities, without my petty resentments. Without my angst or anger. Just the love and joy. My father had been right. Having Mel as my sister was the greatest gift of my life. One I had never been worthy of.

Because I was looking at her, I saw the horror in her eyes as the Tick readied the killing blow. I felt Mel's fear. Her complete devotion to me. I saw the moment of decision. I felt her resolve. A feeling of peace and love spread over me.

Had the Tick been faster than Mel, I would have died suffused with that sense of love and contentment. I would have died in peace.

I don't know how she did it—how Mel moved faster than a Tick—but she did. Maybe her love was just that strong. Maybe the Tick was tired and weak. Whatever the reason, Mel did what no human should have been able to do. In that instant when the Tick's hands were arched overhead, ready to deliver the blow that would surely kill me, Mel acted.

She reached down to her leg and ripped off the bandage covering her gunshot wound.

Her fresh blood immediately started flowing. The Tick stilled above me. Her head tipped up to scent the air. She bounded off of me with a triumphant howl. In four loping strides, she was on top of Mel. The Tick's arms flailed and knocked McKenna and Carter out of the way.

Even though he was right beside her, by the time Carter scrambled to his feet, it was too late. The Tick had slammed her hands onto Mel's chest.

I leapt up, running; even though I knew there was nothing I could do, I ran anyway. My bow was still in my hand. Carter was there before me, gun in hand. He emptied the clip into the Tick just before I slammed the tip of the bow into her back. The bullets might have been ineffectual on their own. The attack from both of us was enough to kill her, but her clawed hands were already into Mel's chest. Her death spasm ripped Mel's sternum apart.

Carter brought one booted foot up and kicked the Tick off Mel. I dropped to her side, my hands hovering ineffectually over the gaping hole in her chest.

My own panic struggled to surface past Mel's utter peace.

Every instinct I had screamed at me to save her, but I didn't know what to do. I didn't want to hurt her. I didn't want to make things worse. Her chest was split clean open. Every one of her ribs was cracked. Her lungs were punctured in at least one place, probably more, judging by the blood pumping out of her chest. Even though the Tick hadn't yet pulled her heart from her chest, the Tick had killed her. There was no way Mel could survive. My sister was dying and there was nothing I could do to stop it.

And—damn it!—I still felt this eerie, unnatural calm. As if this was exactly what I wanted. As if this act of sacrifice brought me joy.

I fought it. Fought it with every cell in my aching heart, because I knew it was wrong. I did not want this. This was not the way it was supposed to happen.

I pulled my gaze from hers, looking up at the faces around me. McKenna and Carter both wore glazed, placid expressions. They were awash in Mel's emotions. As adrift in her sacrifice as I was. Just behind them stood Sebastian. The scent of her blood must have drawn him out from the van. Or maybe the noise. I didn't know because I could hear nothing past the roar of blood in my ears. He was no help, either, and I still couldn't bring myself to care.

I looked back at Mel, not at her blissful expression, but at her wounds. At the blood gushing from her body. At the slowing of her beating heart. I forced myself to look, because the thinking part of my brain wanted to be horrified by the wrongness of it. Of being able to see her heart.

Tha-dump, tha-dump, tha-dump.

Tha-dump. Tha-dump.

Tha. Dump.

Tha.

Dump.

And then nothing.

Her heart stopped. The strange euphoria softened at the edges as my sister began to drift away. Her heart had stopped. Her brain had only moments left. I forced myself to stand. Forced myself to shake off the effects of Mel's bliss.

"Save her," I said.

The others were still trapped in the prison of Mel's emotions. Carter blinked. Sebastian just looked at me.

"Save her!" I yelled. "You could do it! You could bite her and your venom would turn her. It would still work."

He just stared at me. Then slowly he shook his head. "It wouldn't."

I stalked around her body. I couldn't look at her again. Now that my mind was clearing, now that my emotions would soon be my own, I couldn't bear to see her.

I stopped in front of Sebastian. He stared down at her, his expression torn between the hunger that had driven him from the van and the wash of Mel's emotions.

I backhanded him across the cheek to get his attention. It was like slapping a brick wall, but he looked up at me.

"You have to save her."

He blinked slowly. "Even if I bit her, it probably wouldn't work.

Didn't he tell you, only one in a hundred turns. Maybe less. Chances of her having the gene—"

"You have to try! You want to anyway. You must want to drain her. So do it!"

"No. Even if she did have the gene, I don't want to do it. The responsibility—"

"God damn you. You bite her now! You have to do it!" And in that instant, I would have said or done anything to convince him. And I knew the one thing that would. It wasn't even a lie. "Don't you get it? She's your *abductura*. It isn't me. It never was. It's her. If you let her die, all of this has been for nothing. You have nothing without her."

He just stared at me for a moment, but his gaze flickered and I knew he was piecing it together, just as I had back in the church with the Dean. All the times my "powers" had worked. Every damn one of them, Mel had been there. The fight outside the cafeteria. The Dean's office. The things in the van. Even Carter. He hadn't loved me because I wanted him to. He'd loved me because she wanted him for me.

And finally, the panic the Dean had felt. He'd been trapped in that room with her for hours before we'd arrived. It was why he'd gone so completely over the edge before we even got there. Because Mel was losing it and he'd caught the brunt of her meltdown.

Sebastian's gaze came back to mine, his expression cold and resolved. His total lack of emotion matched my own rising panic. Mel had stopped transmitting.

"Then there's no point. There are no vampire *abducturae*. That's one of the qualities that the venom blanks out. Even if I could turn her now, there'd be no point. She wouldn't be an *abductura* anymore. Just another vampire. Another damn mouth to feed."

Sebastian's voice held not the slightest drop of warmth or understanding. Not even a hint of compassion. He was implacable. Unswayable. His decision was made.

I crumpled to the ground. It was over. Everything I'd done to protect my sister, and I'd failed. She was dead.

Carter stepped right over me. I watched in numb shock as he grabbed Sebastian by the arms and shook him.

Sebastian must have still been in shock himself, because otherwise he wouldn't have let Carter do that any more than he would have let me get away with slapping him.

Carter didn't stop shaking him until the vampire looked up at him.

"You have to do this," Carter demanded. "After all the things I've done for the cause. I've lied. I've killed. I've betrayed for you. All because you said it might make a difference. Now it's your turn. I don't care if you want to. I don't care if you think it won't work. And if it does work, I don't even care that it might not make any difference to the resistance. You do this. You have to do this one thing."

Sebastian just looked at him and asked in a perfectly calm voice, "Why?"

For an instant, Carter seemed taken aback. Then he let go of Sebastian's arms and stepped back. "Because, damn it, we're all in this together. This is our fight. All of ours. And you've stood on the sidelines, giving orders and making bargains, long enough. It's time for you to sacrifice, too."

My breath caught as I watched Sebastian, waiting to see if he'd knock Carter aside and just walk away or if the vampire would take orders from the human.

The wait was interminable. An eternity. And with every second, my sister's brain was dying.

Then, slowly, as if this were an everyday occurrence, Sebastian circled my sister's body and knelt down beside her across from me.

He looked at me over her corpse. "There is almost no chance of this working."

"I know." But any chance was better than none.

"And if it does, you will owe me more than you can possibly know."

Before I could answer, Carter's hand closed on my shoulder. "*I'll* owe you."

Sebastian smiled humorlessly. His fangs were fully extended; the sight chilled me. "You already do owe, my boy. You marked the wrong sister."

Then Sebastian ducked his head. I don't know what I expected. Him to bite her neck maybe. Or her wrist. Even her thigh.

But her heart was right there and that was what he sank his fangs into. There was the squelch of his teeth sinking into muscle. Then a horrible sucking noise that echoed in my ears.

Horrified, I scrambled back, crablike, on my hands and feet, but I couldn't make myself stop looking. Stop searching for signs that it was working.

Sebastian ate and ate. His skin flushed. His own chest rose and fell with rapid exultation. He didn't pause. Didn't stop for breath. Maybe he didn't even need to breathe.

Carter had said the change could happen even if the body was drained completely. It was all about that one gene. If she had it—if we had it—it would work no matter how much he drank. And he must have been starving, despite feeding the day before. I had no idea how long it had been since he'd fed before that.

The sun rose. Carter sank to the ground behind me. McKenna puked. Twice. And then finally retreated to the van and dissolved into tears. I nearly joined her. Surely if it was going to happen, it would have. But I couldn't make myself leave. Not until I knew for sure.

Then, finally, he sank back on his heels. Her blood covered him. An expression of absolute bliss shuddered across his face. He wiped his mouth with the back of his hand. When his eyes flickered open, they looked hazy and drugged. So contently full he might have been a newborn baby.

If all human emotion was just a hormone response, then he'd gotten a potent dose of her emotion at death. Her absolute peace with her decision. We'd all been hit with it when she'd transmitted it, but he'd actually drunk it. He'd consumed her loving sacrifice.

After a moment, he fumbled for the shirt she'd taken off to attract the Tick's attention. He scrubbed his face with the flannel.

I looked from Mel's broken chest back to him. "Did it work?"

He blinked sleepily. "I have no idea. You check."

He wasn't directly responsible for killing my sister, but in that moment, I felt such a profound hatred for him he might as well have done it himself. Had there been any stakes left, I would have buried one in his heart.

"Damn you! Did it work?"

"Lily," Carter gasped. "Look!"

I followed Carter's gaze to my sister's heart. Which twitched. And then beat. And beat again.

"You should close her ribs," Sebastian murmured. "Straighten them if you can. Make it easier for her. To heal."

I sank back on my heels, unable to move, but Carter followed

Sebastian's instructions. I had no idea how he did it. I couldn't even listen to it. I fled at the first crunch of her bones lining back up. I puked out my guts behind the van and then stayed there, bawling, until Carter called to me.

It was fully light when I walked back around the van. The gaping wound in my sister's chest was already healing. Her ribs rose and fell with gentle breathing. Her skin was just as pale as Sebastian's had been when I'd first seen him. She looked like she'd been carved from wax. But she breathed. Her heart beat. She was alive or something like it.

Carter and Sebastian stood over her. Facing off about something.

"You need to leave," Sebastian said when he saw me. The dreamy, drugged quality of his voice was gone.

"We're not leaving her here with you," I said automatically. "I know how you feel about making new vampires. It's repugnant. You despise her already. If you think—"

"Let me clarify. You must leave. All of you. She'll wake soon and when she does, she'll need to eat—"

I swallowed my disgust and said, "Then I'll feed her."

"No, she'd devour you." Sebastian pinned me with a stare. "Of course, you, my dear, would simply regenerate as a vampire and then our problems would be double. We know you carry the gene. But Carter and McKenna she would simply murder. None of you want that. Besides, there are plenty of fresh Ticks here. They are not tasty, but they will nourish her."

I shuddered. Had there been anything in my gut at all, I would have emptied it again. As it was, I merely felt my knees go weak. Still I protested. "I can't leave her alone with you."

"And yet you must. Do not fear, my natural repulsion for her will not kick in for five or six moons. I'll have time to train her. Perhaps in that time she can learn to feed judiciously. If that is the case, I'll come and find you."

I wanted to protest, but could find no words. For the first time, I felt the full impact of what I'd done. My sister was now a monster. I had saved her life and destroyed her all at once. It was entirely possible that I would never even be able to see her again.

Carter wrapped his arm around my shoulder and pulled me against his chest. He seemed to know exactly what I was thinking, even though I could never understand it myself.

I don't even remember climbing into the van, only that sitting on the bench beside me was Mel's pink backpack. Inside were the last vestiges of the human she'd been. The jacket I'd done so much to procure. Her stuffed squirrel. The last piece of Dubble Bubble from Uncle Rodney's. Her Slinky.

Before Carter could start the engine, I threw open the door and ran back to Sebastian. He stood over Mel's body, his expression distant. He looked up as I approached. I clutched the bag to my chest for only a second before I pushed it into his hands.

I couldn't stay to watch his response. I needed Mel to have this last remnant of her life. I needed her to have the things that had made her Mel.

Other than that, I don't remember leaving my sister in the care of a monster. Leaving her to wake as a newly formed vampire, all alone, without me. With only Sebastian to offer an explanation of what I'd done. In our entire existence, we'd never been apart for longer than two weeks. Now we faced at least six months apart. And more than time and distance would separate us from now on. We had been identical all our lives, until the moment I'd had her turned into a vampire.

I don't know if I was in shock or if I slept. At some point, I blinked and sat up, finding myself in the passenger seat of the van. I stretched and looked around. Carter drove. McKenna sat in the far back on the bench she'd once shared with Joe. Still and quiet. Shell-shocked and broken. She looked like I felt. Crushed by despair.

Carter looked over at me when I woke, but he didn't speak. He seemed to know that I had no words left inside me. Nothing left but grief and pain. For a long time, he simply drove. We all seemed to need the silence. The time to mourn the members of our party who were no longer with us. It seemed impossible that it had been only a few days since we'd left the Farm. Less than a week since Carter had come back into my life. He now seemed like he was a part of me. Like an arm or a leg. Something I could function without if I absolutely had to, but I sure as hell didn't want to have to try.

Just as the sky started to darken in the east, the highway turned away the setting sun and the Detroit skyline rose out of the darkness around us. Canada was literally right around the corner. Without Mel, getting there no longer seemed so important.

I must have sighed or made some other noise to give me away, because Carter turned and looked at me for the first time in hours.

"We're almost there."

"Yeah. I know." I glanced to the back of the van and saw that McKenna had fallen asleep, her head propped up on the hoodie Joe'd left in the van. Her nose all but buried in the last thing she'd ever have that smelled like the guy she'd loved. I suddenly realized I had nothing of my sister. Nothing except my memories and the face we shared.

To distract myself from that thought, I shifted in my seat and looked at him. "So after Canada, what then?"

I was amazed at how calm my voice sounded. Only a trace of huskiness betrayed the way I'd cried for hours.

Carter glanced at me. "I'm staying with you in Canada." His hands tightened on the steering wheel. "If you'll let me."

I was surprised. Not by his offer so much as my reaction to it. I would have thought I'd be too shell-shocked to feel anything. Instead, his words felt like a punch to a bone-deep bruise. "That's not what I want."

Canada had always been about keeping Mel safe. That fantasy was dead to me now.

His jaw tightened and he gave the steering wheel a little twist. "Then I'll get you and McKenna settled. Somewhere safe. Then I'll head back to base camp."

"Why don't *we* get her settled someplace safe and then head back to base camp together?"

His head whipped around and he stared at me. "You don't mean that."

I hadn't intended to say it. Hadn't really thought it through, but I did mean it. "Yeah. I do."

"Lil, you said it yourself. You're not an *abductura*."

"I know. But neither are you. You don't have any special gift, but you've been fighting this war. Hell, you've been leading the rebellion yourself and all you've had is the sheer dogged determination not to let them beat down humanity. If you can fight in this war, then so can I."

"But it's not what you want."

I gritted my teeth, swallowing back my grief. No, it wasn't what I wanted. I wanted my sister back. I wanted her safe and by my side. I'd been so ready to die to keep her safe, it never occurred to me that she'd be ready to do the same for me.

"No," I finally said. "It might not be what I wanted, but this is my fight now. I did so many things to keep Mel safe, and none of it did any good. I ran from the fight, but the fight chased me down and then beat me into the ground. I'm not running anymore."

We rode in silence for a few more minutes. It took me that long to realize he might misinterpret my words. "Carter, about me going with you . . . that's not about us." He shot me a glance and suddenly I felt like I couldn't breathe. "I mean, I don't expect . . ."

"Don't expect what?" he prodded.

"What you thought you felt for me—" I shrugged. "I mean, I'm not an *abductura*. I didn't do that. I mean, I didn't make you feel that."

"I know."

"But that doesn't mean it was real, either. I guess Mel knew how much I"—I cringed, saying this aloud—"crushed on you and she must have really wanted that for me." I could feel my cheeks burning and was thankful that the early morning light shining through the window was weak. I was surprised I could feel any embarrassment over my grief. Maybe it was best I was having this conversation now. I doubted I could even say these things aloud if I wasn't numb with pain. "With Mel gone and not even an *abductura* anymore, I don't expect—"

"Hey. It's okay," he said softly. He placed his hand on my knee and I looked over at him. "You just lost your sister. I don't expect anything, either."

"Okay."

Then a moment later, he added, "But just so you know, I also don't expect what I'm feeling to change."

"But Mel—"

"I wasn't anywhere near Mel for two years and I still wanted you. What I feel for you isn't going to go away."

"You don't know that."

"Yeah, I do." He gave my knee a squeeze. "Don't worry. I can wait. I got all the time in the world."

I knew that tone of voice from him. He wasn't going to back down. I was too tired to argue with him and too beaten to shove aside that last little bit of hope, so I didn't say anything.

As the Detroit skyline got closer and closer, I thought about my mother and her no-nonsense view of the world. She hadn't been the kind of woman who believed monsters were real. Or superheroes, for that matter. She had believed there was a logical, scientific explanation for everything. She'd been wrong about all of that. But she'd also been right about one thing. You fight for what you believe in. You fight for what's right, even when it's hard. Even when you want to give up. Fighting for what was right, no matter the odds, was heroic enough. You didn't need a superpower to do the right thing. You only needed the will to get it done.

I glanced over at Carter. And you needed friends to fight by your side. Whatever else Carter was—whatever else he thought he felt for me—he was a friend. He'd been there for me when I hadn't even known I needed him. I had no one else, but at least I still had him.

EPILOGUE

MEL

If life was music, this is silence.

I don't know what it is, but it's not life.

It's anguish. Bones regrowing too quickly. The popping of ribs snapping back into place. Fire burning through my chest. The bubbling, caustic heat of acid poured into a fresh wound.

A hunger gnawing through my brain. All my cells stretched, squashed, and realigned. Like a hand has reached inside of me and pulled out my stomach. My heart. My soul.

This is not my choice and it is as silent as a grave without dirt or coffin. It is as still as bones. The world itself must have vanished to make a hole in the music this deep and wide.

It must be death.

But then I open my eyes. The silence presses heavily against my eardrums. The world is not gone. The music is.

And Lily.

As Lily goes, so goes the steady drumbeat of my heart. I will have to learn to live without the beating or learn to hear my own. Without everyone's music in my ears, maybe I, too, will have a sound.

This place is a quiet as vast as space. Empty but not void. There is a stillness that is almost peace. Almost like black velvet. The beauty's in what's not.

Time crawls in the silence. Tick Tock. Tick Tock. Tick Tock. Tock. Tock. Tock.